"The difference between reading anything by Jeane Heimberger Candido and something produced by an academic "professional" historian is the same difference you have between a tale told by a combat infantryman, and the same tale told by a finance officer. When Candido writes, there is an immediate intimacy with the minutia. It is writing done through thorough, meticulous research, knowledge of the characters and topic, and the passion for the story. In other words— she isn't boring. Here's to her and those like her. Since the passing of Barbara Tuchman, there are darn few left."

— *Howard J. Popowski, Camp Chase Fifes & Drums,*
Former Sergeant 5th Kentucky (Louisville Legion)
The Mudsills

"Feel the one hundred plus degree temperature inside a Union ironclad on one of the inland waters. Know the feeling inside a smoke-filled casemate amid the crash of 12-14 inch shells bouncing off the sides. Ms. Candido's in-depth research takes you there for an exceedingly accurate look at life in the brown water navy."

— *Jerry E. Rinker, Collector Civil War Navy*

"Once again Jeane Heimberger Candido has taken good historical facts and woven a fascinating story with it. Her eye for detail and ability to bring the characters to life provides one with a wonderful experience. A first-rate book indeed."

— *Rick Musselman, Education Supervisor/Historian,*
Carriage Hill Living History Farm: Dayton, Ohio

Shepherd's Song

Jeane Heimberger Candido

Windstorm Creative
Bremerton * Port Orchard * Seattle * Tahuya

Shepherd's Song: A Novel of the Civil War
copyright 2001 by Jeane Heimberger Candido
published by Windstorm Creative Ltd.

ISBN 1-59092-113-5
First edition March 2004
9 8 7 6 5 4 3 2

Cover design by CKAD of Blue Artisans
Cover art by L. DeKern Lang
Maps by Jeane Heimberger Candido

All rights reserved, including the right to reproduce this book or portions thereof in any form whatsoever, except in the case of short excerpts for use in reviews of the book. Printed in the United States of America. For information about film or other subsidiary rights, please contact Windstorm's legal and contracts department, attention Mari Garcia at mgarcia@windstormcreative.com.

Windstorm Creative is a multiple division, international organization involved in publishing books in all genres, including electronic publications; producing games, videos and music as well as producing theatre, film and visual arts events.

This is a work of fiction. Any resemblance to persons living or dead is purely coincidental.

Library of Congress data on file.

Windstorm Creative
Post Office Box 28
Port Orchard, WA 98366
shepherds@windstormcreative.com
www.windstormcreative.com

This book is lovingly dedicated to
Walter Heimberger, Jr.
my father

Acknowledgments

"Words are not enough to do them praise" is the inscription I sign in all the copies of my first book, *The Redemption of Corporal Nolan Giles*. No one, even the eloquent and concise Abraham Lincoln, could frame in words the stamina and the resolution of three million American soldiers who followed their flags into the Union and Confederacy between 1861 and 1865.

But in the research and writing of *Shepherd's Song* I have found these words have an application on a different level to all of those who gave so generously of their resources and talents to make my second book possible. These people include those at the Columbus Metropolitan Library's main reference desk and the Upper Arlington Library's, plus the people, operations, and satellites that support their efforts. I cannot thank enough the librarians and staff of the Ohio Historical Society. Of special note are Ann Sindelar, Barbara Billings, Kelly Falcone, and George Cooper of the Western Reserve Archives, who were constant in their assistance, advice, efficiency, and, when I needed it, sense of humor.

Elizabeth H. Joyner, Supervisory Museum Curator, National Park Service, Vicksburg Military Park, supplied me with plans and specifications for the Eads' class ironclads in record time. Marty Schroll, licensed park guide at Vicksburg, threw away time and schedules for a tour that amounted to a campaign of its own. My thanks also to Robert Ferguson, Tribal Historian, Choctaw Museum of the Southern Indian, Philadelphia, Mississippi, and to the staff who were of such great assistance when I visited there. I appreciate the patience and cooperation of my co-workers and my fellows of the Columbus Barracks Civil War Round Table — James Baugess, Robert Feilds and John Young — who lent me volumes from their personal libraries for as long as I needed them. And who said chivalry is dead? Frank Unum, a friend and fishing guide, who, with my husband, jumped into a boat to retrieve pages of notes that were blown upon the waters of the Elizabeth River.

My thanks also to Windstorm Creative, its staff and editors, especially the support of my publisher Jennifer DiMarco, editor Cris DiMarco, and Natalie Brown who gave me every freedom to take risks and write the book I envisioned. To Anne Pici, college classmate and now composition instructor at the University of Dayton, who faced bravely the work of preparing the manuscript for publication. These women are warriors in their own right.

And there are so many who gave not just the solid reference but the intangibles of oral tradition and story telling. I am blessed to have had the friendship of Ronald Goodwin, who shared so much of the life and culture of his beloved Mississippi, and Civil War naval historian Jerry Rinker, who gave so unreservedly of his knowledge gathered over a lifetime.

The members of the Fourth Ohio, Company E, the Given Guards of Wooster, especially Rick Musselman of the Carriage Hill Living History Farm in Dayton, and Chris Smith, re-enactors who are among the most precise historians in the field. The Fourth Ohio are, moreover, some of the most protective friends a writer can ask for. My gratitude as well goes to the recruits of the many living-history regiments, both Union and Confederate, who, in the spirit of scholarship and goodwill, talked at length about their own personal "journeys" to become, body and soul, those old crusaders they interpret. I am similarly indebted to the veterans of World War II, Korea, Vietnam, and the Persian Gulf who were supportive of my first book and who on terms of strict anonymity, shared their own combat experiences, insights, fears, and even nightmares.

Howard Popowski, reputed historian, re-enactor, writer, as well as military musician, gets my deep thanks for not only access to his library, but also for his lessons in drill and in shooting black powder and ball. By virtue of his dog-faced experience as an ordnance sergeant in Vietnam, he inspired some of the color and off-color hues to my characters. His hot-line reference service, when confronted with those little land mines of facts and dates, cannot be underestimated.

I thank my mother Clara Heimberger Foutz and my stepfather Richard Foutz, for their unfailing support. To my children, Anne and Robert, with their firmly-fixed left brains, I am grateful for their encouragement and guarded vigilance that I always find my way back to the twentieth century.

My constant thanks goes to my husband Richard, who I can never thank enough, for his love, support, and for his patience over those long miles of battlefields infested with infectious plants, insects, and reptiles. He has never complained that his living space has been crowded by the books, periodicals, military manuals, notes, maps, pictures, and other research materials that mounted like Roman columns against the walls and corners. As a former army lieutenant in Vietnam, he too gave insight into the mind and heart of the soldier. Walking those roads again could not have been an easy journey.

And my final thanks is to my father to whom this book is dedicated, the late Walter Heimberger, Jr. He took the hand of a little child and stepped through the looking glass. He beckoned me not only toward his memories of the Fifth Air Corps in World War II, but also toward all the backward vistas of the past in American literature and history. This was his legacy to me. A man who had only an eighth-grade formal education was so well read and lived to be rich beyond any degree a university could measure.

—JHC

"Forward!"*

Perhaps the novelist understands better than the military historian, the essence of the Civil War was—and is—the mudsill; the soldier at the bottom. The military historian clinically analyzes wars by armies, corps, divisions, and brigades; by campaigns set in the east and west, north and south, and midways between; by generals, colonels, and captains. This novelist, however, walks with privates, corporals, sergeants and second-lieutenants—the men who carry the muskets, march, eat and sleep on the ground, march, fight, and march some more. These soldiers see the war from bottom up and not from top down, each a small cog not in just one wheel but in a system of wheels that turn the huge engine they call the army. In historical narrative the mudsills are referred to in the collective, such as Company C, Fourth Regiment of Ohio Volunteers, Kimball's Brigade, French's Division, Couch's Corps, Army of the Potomac. For it all the mudsill is still an individual, and one by one, each fights his own war with sickness, heatstroke and freezing picket duty. If he is fortunate to occupy that little swatch of battlefield where death is all *around* but not *on* him, he can live to be promoted—to the top if his luck holds. He then draws chevrons or shoulderstraps, better rations, higher pay, and moves up ranks to a job opening vacated by a comrade who was not so lucky.

By the spring of 1863, the Camelot the South had fabricated was in twilight. Grant was at the door of Vicksburg. Corporal Brenton Christie found intrigue on the Mississippi River in the Army of the Tennessee, a galaxy away in mind and spirit from the Army of the Potomac. It was this new frontier of the war in which Christie stood, swayed, and sunk on shifting sands; his horizons and purposes were no longer as crystal as they were in 1861. Here he found men—officers and enlisted—to his liking. Regardless of rank, from general down to private, they were all ingrained with that mudsill spirit. They were resourceful, resolute, earthy, self-sufficient, barely refined frontiersmen with the common sense, steadfastness, and humor typified by Abraham Lincoln, Ulysses Grant, and William T. Sherman. Early on they threw away the tactics of Napoleon and Wellington to fight a war of their own invention, a war of mettle and bluff against an enemy who was their measure. They used infantry, cavalry, engineers, intelligence, marines, and navy in ways that had never been tried before. They braved torrential rivers, swamps, and disease to fight a foe that came at them in many forms—conscripted regulars, state militia, civilian farmers, and slave patrols. Grant's Army of the Tennessee always kept going, in every season, *against* the enemy, never *away*, to push him down the spine of the country, then east, state by state across the southland, into Robert E. Lee's back door.

Brenton Christie is a boy made a man by the war. He is a serious soldier—not above a scheme or joke. He is not a hero, but he is heroic. He is not a saint or a devil, but he finds himself against his will at times in both camps. Unlike the figures of history, Brent Christie is not spoken of in the past tense, because he is a character in a novel; he perennially lives. He is not a unit of time, a measure or pawn of military historians, statisticians, and analysts. He is real with a fictional name, not unlike the soldier who fought at Borodino, Meuse-Argonne, Remagen Bridge, the Yalu River, the Congo, DaNang, Kuwait, and a thousand brushfires in between. He is lonely, hungry, homesick, tired, and filthy, but he seizes his weapon on the first command for one more charge.

Shepherd's Song was meticulously researched from personal accounts, regimentals, newspapers, letters, memoirs, diaries, military reports, to let the old veterans tell their stories for themselves. In gaining perspective about the inner life of the Mississippi family, I drew on volumes of folklore, oral tradition, letters, and books of nineteenth-century etiquette, instead of narrative histories. But I must thank particularly Catherine Clinton and Drew Gilpin Faust for their books on plantation and southern culture and then John R. Swanton and R. S. Cotterill for their research on Mississippi Choctaw culture. For the Grierson's Raid, D. Alexander Brown's *Grierson's Raid* put me on the right research track.

I have tried to draw fictional and historical figures as honestly as possible, and it has been my intention to make them breathe, to bring the reader into their inner circle around the campfire and on the march. In so doing, however, I have come to dispute some long-held traditions and beliefs of historians and have had to express the contrary when I thought it honest to do so.

Since the armies were enormous and confusing even to the soldier who lived within them, I have borrowed and adapted from the military history procedure's "Order of Battle" to list an

"Order of Character." You will find it in the back of the book. The historical and fictional characters are listed according to their rank and place in the army and civilian life. All characters listed in regular type are real, while fictional characters are in italics. This "Order of Character" is limited to the references in the book only; the armies were far more extensive and complex than I have listed here. Still I hope I have provided a means to present who is who and what is what more clearly.

—JHC

*I have taken the liberty of changing the regulation "Foreword" commonly used as the explanatory introduction to "Forward!" I think it better suits historical fiction of a military nature and is less ponderous.

Introduction

The timpani of far-away thunder echoes the long roll, the drum calling the old knights in Confederate butternut and the Union blue. Leadened hearts answer to the power of the song, the memories of dead comrades, and the stories of the battles. But their regiments are ghosts and their battlefields are grown over with corn and wheat, built over with mercantiles and houses. The world is well on its new course, too busy for reminiscences, for singing the old songs, and for listening to old yarns of long-dead causes.

And so the old soldier snaps his fingers and only his dog pulls to attention. With a cane to steady the quivering knees, with his fife in his pocket and his pipe in the brim of his hat, the veteran climbs the back hills to his exile where the sheep low. He brings his reed to his lips and with stuttering breath pipes "Home Sweet Home," "Peas on a Trencher," "Reveille," "Rally Around the Flag" for himself — and then "Dixie" for Johnny Reb.

Old phantoms in blue sack and brogans rise out of the mist of dead campfires and cannon exhaust and trudge down the hillsides to sit beside him and sing the old ballads of Vicksburg, Chancellorsville, Rich Mountain, Antietam, Gettysburg, and Appomattox. They remember how the shepherds mustered in great flocks to lead a dark people into the light, a country into a new union, and a blind people into a new age. The grand reunion meets again as long as one of them lives.

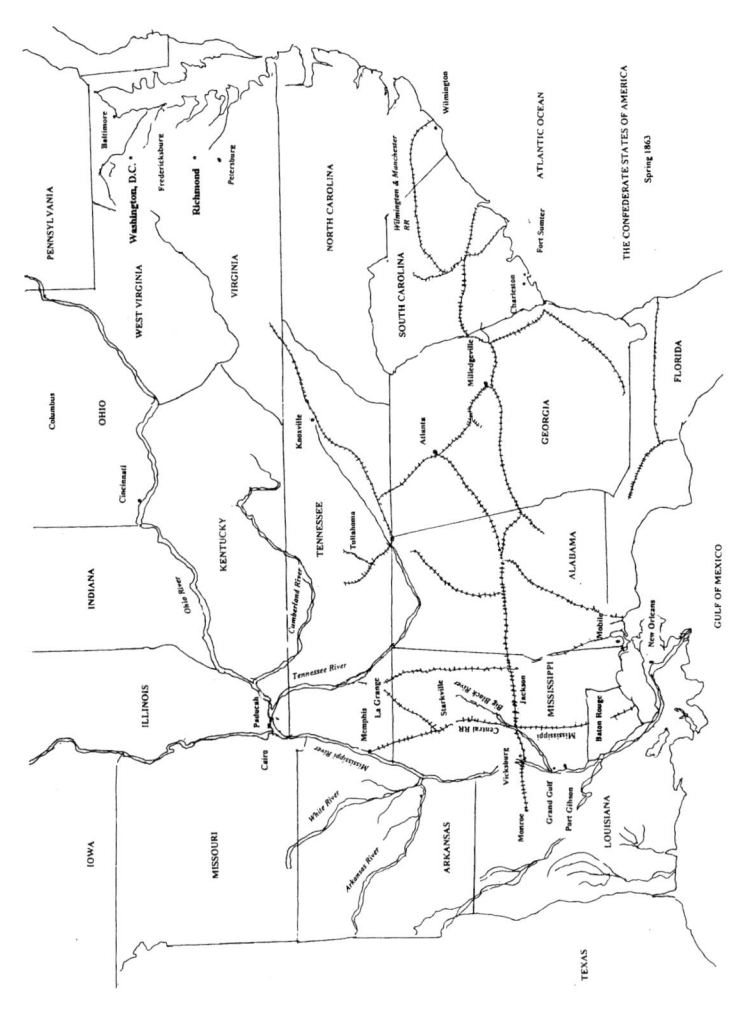

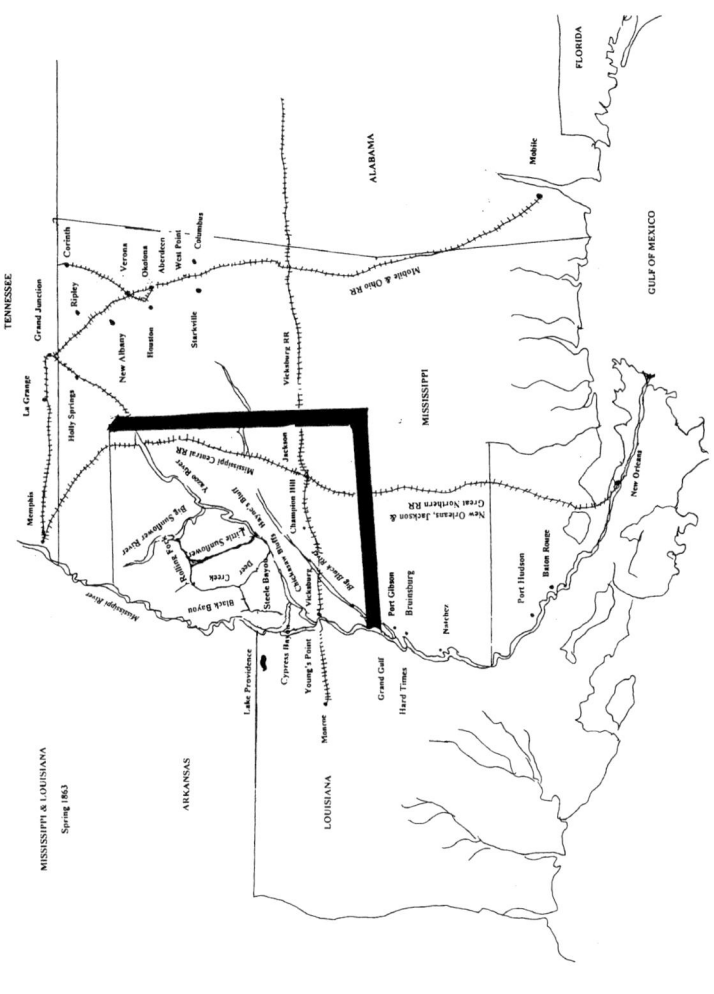

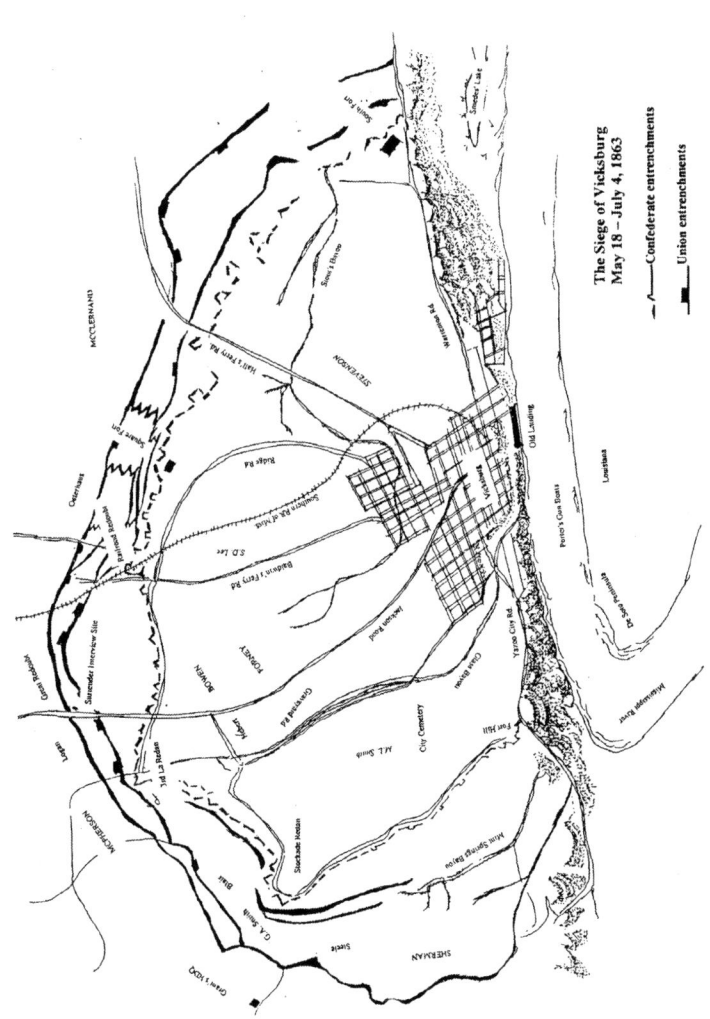

Shepherd's Song

Jeane Heimberger Candido

On Sang the Requiem of the Army of the Potomac
Mid December, 1862

Major General Ambrose Burnside, commander of the Army of the Potomac, huddled deep inside layers of Union blue wool. Even with all the fireplaces in the Phillips' mansion roaring to a hell-high pitch, his bones ached and he could not sleep for the shakes. Ague, he wanted to believe, but ague came and went with some relief in between. Bare-bone cold went down to his fingertips and paralyzed his mind with grief and disquiet. On the expanse of mahogany table in front of him lay a tray with a decanter half filled with very good brandy, and beside it, the field maps of Fredericksburg and Falmouth. These still bore his notes and orders on the bloody campaign past. Generals Hancock and Reynolds had been right—they did not win. Lee's Army of Northern Virginia still held the high ground, and on this side of the Rappahannock his own army clung to Stafford Heights, just as it did before the death of twenty thousand men.

Taking a page from Lee's strategy book, Burnside had tried to do what the Virginian had done so often and so brilliantly: hit the enemy simultaneously from two flanks, get behind him, and crush him in a vise. At Groveton and on the Peninsula Lee had played the plan to perfection. But the plan had not worked out that way when Burnside adopted it. He had never gotten behind Lee's lines. Lee had guarded his flanks with impassable barriers, the Massaponax Creek on Jackson's right and the canal and the river on Longstreet's left. Confederate cavalry insulated them beyond approach.

Burnside had been in the job less than a month when he sent his army against the Confederates strung out on Marye's Heights and Prospect Hill. Blue tides of humanity rose and ebbed, and in the end, they had been annihilated by converging fire. A squirrel could not have survived in the open that day. The exhaust from the cannon and rifles had eclipsed the sun and plunged the afternoon into premature night, hiding the casualties under rolling pillows of smoke.

From the first charge, field reports were all of death and disaster. By the hour they came in, adding to the "horrible arithmetic" as Lincoln called it. Whole towns in New England would have no men coming home that Christmas or any thereafter.

At dusk his generals persuaded Burnside to break the battle off, and he relented. Finally, he had asked for mercy, but Lee would not agree to a cease-fire to bury the dead and relieve the wounded from the field. So Union men lay in the December frost under a shroud of sulfur haze. After dark the Confederates, threadbare themselves, stole out from their lines to strip then leave the Union casualties to freeze and die slowly by minutes and by hours. When there was nothing more to steal, Johnny, maddened with euphoria over his day's victory, leveled his musket into the darkness. He set his sights and fired on the cries of the desperately wounded lying abandoned in the darkness. If the sobs did not abate with the first shot, the Rebel adjusted his aim and fired again. Sooner or later he got the silence he wanted. Then he reloaded and cocked his ear for another target.

Burnside had lost his reason over it, ordered another charge that he would lead personally. But his officers talked him out of it. For all his fire before the battle, Hancock was calm now. Unbidden, he had helped himself to Burnside's brandy but put the glass down untouched—he would do his drinking and his grieving in private. General Darius Couch, Burnside's second in command, was not so temperate. He slammed his resignation onto his commander's desk and left. Reynolds, ever the gentleman, just stared Burnside down. He too would not serve under a man who could not distinguish strategy from suicide.

Couch had been right. Hancock had been right. And he himself had been right. Burnside had tried to tell Lincoln that he was not the man to lead an army. This command took a soothsayer with a bit of the poker player. He had no talent for either. If ordered, he could hold a line until the angels blew, but coordination and tactics that worked so well on paper and in his mind reversed themselves in bloody practice.

Beyond where the star-shine blurred with the campfires on the northern slope was Lee. Rage tore within Burnside to wipe him off the earth. The wails of men nearly dead on the field and the dying in the hospitals rang in Burnside's brain. Hancock used to tell him of the banshee, the Irish angel of death who came for the soul of the damned. She shimmered in the night like these

Satanic Northern Lights, and she wailed on the wind so eerily that it drove a man mad. "Beware of the banshee," Hancock had said a long time ago. "She will never forget your name and will come again and again to mourn as often as she must until she is satisfied."

With the morning, the dancing lights flickered out. There were still disagreements about their omen. "The gods of war taking up the brave dead into Olympus," mystics said. The chaplains saw it another way: The display was a burning bush in the night sky. Burnside believed them all.

Colonel Parke moved noiselessly across the carpeted floor with a stack of newspapers. Burnside had to face them, "What does the country say, Colonel? Will they hang me or just let me resign?"

Parke rolled the papers up and threw them into the fiery mouth of the cavernous fireplace. "Sir, the reporters are not kind. General Meagher..."

Burnside groaned, "What does General Meagher say?"

The aide summoned his courage. "He says that you used the Irish as cannon fodder, that you wasted them on a suicidal charge up the hill as if they were of no more worth than back-alley dogs."

The general with the gentle blue eyes, who took reversals and disappointments as regular as his morning coffee, understood that this too was his lot. "What else?"

"Sir?"

"Tell me, Colonel Parke, what else they are saying."

"In Cincinnati, you have been hanged in effigy. Others say you were drunk, some said you suffer dementia, and others..." Parke's baritone hummed on, but Burnside lost track of it in the staccato of the crackling fire and the shouts of the soldiers playing out on the frozen meadow.

Dull opal moons hung in a long, irregular orbit around the barren hulk of a burned out chandelier. These grime-streaked lanterns scorched oil to smoke rather than light. The smudge coalesced in a black shroud over the dead and wounded laid out on the floors of the battlefield hospital. Desperate souls chanted a low music of weeping and delirium. Now and then shrieks of pain and howls of cold shock choked the song, but not for long. The hymn would be taken up again somewhere else in moans for water and morphine.

In a dark alcove a soldier whispered for his sweetheart, in a corner one called for a chaplain, and another, stretched over a surgeon's table, counted his sins, as drop after drop of anesthetic fell over the gauze that covered his face. Finally, he whispered a last Act of Contrition for only God to hear then exhaled an "Amen." So sang the requiem of the Army of the Potomac.

In the next rooms, the battered of Kimball's Brigade lay swaddled in nests of lice-infested blankets and tattered quilts too thin to warm the body or the soul. In these ranks were the butchered men of the Fourth Ohio, who had been given the right of the line. These Buckeyes had led the great blue charge up Marye's Heights and had stood in the full face of fire, only to pay the grim price for it. Their lines now reformed here in zigzags and oblique angles over the elegant floors of the Chatham House. Thomas Warner of C Company trembled as wind-thrashed wheat, his powder-blackened fingers dammed against the seeping gash in his hip. The blue parched lips of Archibald Dice of Company E were still now. But Captain Pritchard prayed while Dice's blood flowed across the floor to baptize Jamie Ferguson, Captain of Company I. The libation did not exorcise the demons that rampaged in a convulsion of thunder and smoke deep within the captain's unconscious.

"Rally behind the colors, men! Rally behind Corporal Torrence! Hold them, George! Hold them fast!" Beyond his morphine-induced twilight, Ferguson recoiled from the helix of the last canister that ripped apart the sky. His hands flew to his scorched eyes and his body stiffened.

"To the colors, men! Rally around the colors!" Corporal Brent Christie's feeble order was loud enough to rock the tenuous calm. Half-dead men threw off their blankets and struggled to their feet. Medical cadets, nurses, and surgeons wrestled one and then another to lay back but the corporal shouted only louder, "Here come the Irish! Hear that cursing? That's Hancock's anthem! Hold tight! We are not lost! Lay down, let them come over you!"

The Angel of Death cut through this bedlam, her veils unfurling in a wake over bodies nearly drained of their souls. As she passed, a few reached for her hand, but the rest shrunk back.

"Pick up the dead. Do not leave your brothers to the enemy!" screamed a phantom soldier from somewhere in the dark.

The ward was in near mutiny. The specter went straight to the young corporal fighting against two burly attendants. The cadets drew back but kept a firm hold on him. The angel's long spiny fingers brushed the boy's forehead and enfolded his face in her palms. At her touch his shouts stuttered, faded to whispers, and melted at last to a guttural croak. With the last caress, he fell back exhausted into his blankets. She paused to see if he stirred again, but he was nearly dead. Still, she waited. Her fingers hovered only inches from the tattered forage cap, the sorry treasure still clenched in his hands. She would take it and secure it under his pillow. Her touch stirred no more turbulence than a candle flicker, but the corpse bounded out of his blankets to seize the thief by the throat. He pressed his thumb against her windpipe as he had the trigger of a musket. His wide, vacant eyes ricocheted from face to face, bounding off the walls, oblivious to the murder he was about to commit. The angel — all of flesh and bone — froze in his grasp.

"Sister, do not move! Don't even swallow." Her Samaritan ordered. In his haste he sidestepped a raft of wounded, then over a few more, to come to her rescue. With infinite gentleness that belied his huge hands and powerful arms, he pried the soldier's fingers away one by one.

"Thank you, Mister Whitman, that was most careless of me." The nun straightened her wimple and smoothed the mud-splattered skirt of her habit. As if midnight strangulations were as regular as matins, sister then moved off to the next duty without another word.

Whitman's assurances were as soothing as salve, and the corporal warmed to lucidity. Cadets were ready with restraints, but Whitman waved them away. No need, he would stay awhile.

"Good thing you picked on Sister Louise, Corporal, and not her over there." The merest crease of a smile separated a drift of his gray whiskers. The tiny woman he pointed to was administering broth to a cadaverous soldier, and the gesture made her look peaceable enough. "Why, Miss Barton would have boxed your ears and hung you in the closet like one of her schoolboys.

Now, what's all this fuss over a battered tam-o-shatter?"

The wounded soldier stuffed the forage cap under his head and turned to the wall. Whitman settled down on the floor for some one-to-one, a critical medicine in short supply in the overcrowded battlefield hospitals. "You slept through supper again. That will not do. You must eat your share and take your punishment right along with the rest of us. No shirkers." The big nurse ran his rough fingers over the soldier's bandaged ribs. "The stroganoff was dry and the noodles paste. Steak from Delmonico's himself tomorrow though. Or was that tack, sauerkraut, and green pork I saw delivered by the barrel, compliments of Quartermaster Meigs? I get the two confused — their cuisines are so very similar."

Whitman's fingers came away wet. So the incision had ripped again, a grim defeat for the surgeons and Sister Louise, who had labored over the boy all last night again. Whitman doubted that the wiry little corporal had a thimbleful of blood trickling through his whole body, but still he was ready to fight. He had come here by the long route, hacked out of the ice where he had collapsed near the canal, Lieutenant Brophy still on his back. Both men had hemorrhaged into the freezing slush. A blessing to be sure, for the cold and ice stinted the bleeding that would in warmer weather have quickly drained them dry. It would be a miracle if either of them lived still.

But the boy held on. Whitman had been warned about these Westerners by his brother George, an officer in a New York regiment. These bummers were a grizzled bunch of veterans who did not die easily. In camp they were polite when they had to be but always conversed with the fewest words possible to outsiders, mute and raw otherwise. They were a law unto themselves, men who never boasted, but they were almost legend. When their battle flags snapped and rippled to their full length, the names and places painted in the stripes spelled a history of fighting and victory not known by any other brigade in the Army of the Potomac. These men never talked about it, but their pride showed in the fighting and made them bigger than their size when the shooting started.

This one called Christie turned back to Whitman. The soldier bit deep into his lip to stifle another attack of the shakes.

There was business on his mind that he clearly had decided to take up with this nurse an unworthy passivist as he was.

"I want you to take care of some errand for me, sir."

"Whatever you like."

"Mister Whitman, I want you to find Brian Quinn's body and send it home to his mother. I want him bathed, embalmed carefully, dressed with a new uniform and covered in a flag with the '4th Regt. O.V.U.S.A.' painted in gold on the fourth red stripe down. Put him in a decent casket. Bribe the quartermaster but stay away from the maggot sutlers—they will charge your eyes right out of your head for a pair of socks and then give you mittens. I'll give you the money for it. It's in here." Christie surrendered the precious cap that had nearly cost the nun her life minutes ago.

Whitman was certain the soldier's mind was gone. There was nothing in the ragged bummer crowned with cheap brass for such obsessive protection of it, but the nurse took it to appease him.

The corporal then pulled Whitman closer to keep their words between them only. "Turn it inside out...there's a false lining in the crown. Rip it open, please. My sewing is not so fine that you can't find where."

Whitman pried his knife under a gap in the seam and sliced away the threads. The lozenge of white muslin came away and with it a wad of Union script that had been secreted there.

"The Rebs might steal my coat and my pants, but they wouldn't want my hat. So I hid it there." Christie shivered again, then went on through clenched teeth. "Take it and when you have seen to Quinn, use the rest to help Nolan. Corporal Nolan Giles, Company C—he's around here somewhere. If he's dead, see to him in the same way as Quinn, but if he lives it's probably not by much, so make sure he gets an officer's berth on the train home."

"There's a lot of money here," Whitman counted it, then slipped the wad into his pocket.

"Sister has better poker players back at the convent than this blasted army of eastern swells, sorry cases all of them. Anything left over, see what you can do for George Torrence and the rest of the men of the Fourth. But use it up for them. Make sure they are treated well."

Blood blossomed across the soldier's shirt. Whitman

pressed a towel to the stain, but Christie, a fatalist, pushed it away. "Give it up, today or tomorrow—one day, give or take."

"Then what about your own casket, Christie, my boy? Not to be indelicate, but by your own admission your needs might be just as precious in that department as your friends. Grim as it is to say so, as long as we are settling your last will and testament, you should be seeing to yourself, if the truth must be faced."

Christie covered the wound with his blanket. "My father's funeral left my mother half dead. I think I shall save her mine and be buried here to salt the sacred Virginia soil for eternity. It is my last revenge." Whitman said no more but decided to put back a few leaves of script so that Christie would not be shortchanged by his own charity when the need came. The big nurse returned the cap, and the Buckeye caressed it, then settled back satisfied. "I want you to write Brian's mother something appropriate, befitting a hero. He died brave but lived braver. General Meagher will help you with what to say. Consult him."

"General Meagher?" The mention of the commander of the famed Irish Brigade was a revelation.

"General Meagher and Quinn were something like family, don't know how, but it was so and we all respected it. And tell Missis Quinn about Nolan Giles—he was like a son to her—she will want to know and make arrangements. But don't tell her too much of the mess here. That would do her no good. God knows what poison the papers have spread already."

Christie's eyes fluttered against pain and fatigue. In a few seconds he had control again. "Ever hear the expression 'see the elephant'?"

"Yes, I think so. I think it means to go into battle for the first time." Whitman beckoned the surgeon passing among the cots. The doctor saw the blood soaking through the blanket and moved away to ready his table.

"Yea, that's pretty close. But it isn't like that. It's not an elephant—it's a pride of panthers wailing and roaring as they come down on you without mercy, tearing you apart. It's fair. We would do the same. That's why there isn't much of our regiment left. We went up that hill with only two hundred ninety-seven officers and men—that's almost three companies out of the ten we started at. Now, we have even less. Almost eight hundred men down since last year. Some will come back from sick camp and the hospitals but that's still a lot of dead, wounded, sick, and missing—all gone up, down and sideways since West Virginia in sixty-one." He shuddered from more than cold. His phrases were breaking up into fragments strung together by stutters and dry swallows.

For a man whose business was words, Whitman was short of them now, but he wanted to answer something that would send this soul off in peace. But God and civilized men never foresaw suffering as this. Irish and Germans, New Yorkers and Pennsylvanians, comrades from Wisconsin, Michigan, Indiana, Maine, Delaware, and everywhere in between—their youth, that should have taken years to spend, was seeping out of them with every lurch of the minute hand.

"You furnish your parts toward eternity, Great or small, you furnish your parts toward the soul."

"What was that?" Christie eyed the nurse suspiciously. "That sounded like a prayer. I will have none of that."

"Nothing like it at all, just some words from a long time ago. And as far as you are concerned, an *Ave Maria* or two wouldn't hurt your prospects, son."

"Father Corby has had his chance at my soul and so has Father Dillon—two acts of absolution in one day, and I probably still have sins left over to keep me out of their so-called heaven. So if *they* don't have enough sacrament, *you* can save your breath."

"You don't believe in heaven or hell?"

"Oh, yea. I believe all right. I've been to both places more than once. Heaven and hell are near neighborhoods, you see?"

"No, I am not sure I do."

In an instant the corporal was far away. "Have you ever seen the Shenandoah in the spring? Oh, you must, you really must. God's garden it was, until the artillery moves up and the battle lines are dressed against Stonewall Jackson looming on the brow of the next hill. Then it's hell by the buckets full. Heaven or hell is not where you go. It's where you are, being in the circumstances you're in. You don't have to die first to go to either place—it will come find you." Then Christie changed the subject. "Would you write a poem about us?"

"I might at that," the nurse whispered. "Perhaps more

than one."

The hope comforted him. "The people might not forget us if you do. Forgetting, that would be a sacrilege—good men lost in body and mind. What for? What for? For whose sake...what for!"

The young corporal had worn himself out and slipped off finally. Whitman kept to his post for some minutes, waiting for Christie's soul to stay or leave, and then to know what to finally do with the last of the trust. Christie wavered between the two alternatives, finding sanctuary instead in a place midway in the morphine delirium and a campfire of long ago.

"Here's to General Burnside and his fondness for cheap death! I will be joining you soon, Jamie. Keep the campfire burning."

"Easy now. Rest easy. Let it go for awhile." The poet laid a hand over the soldier's blistered lips and they stilled.

It was just before dawn when Whitman escaped the wards to flush out his lungs with a wash of fresh air. But the night was unseasonably heavy and tepid, promising rain instead of another snow. At least the chloride of lime, spread like drifts of snow on the mountains of waste, would hold back the miasmal fetor for a couple of hours. They all could breathe a bit until it melted. Feathers of steam rose from the last dumping of amputated arms and legs. The slop from the cook pots overflowed the refuse trenches to wash down the hill to the Rappahannock. The grounds were pocked with ever deepening butchering pits and festering sinks, dug too close to camp for civilized men to tolerate. If it got really cold they would all freeze and there would be relief. But if the weather lived up to its promise, they would wreak, calling down a plague of flies and rats tomorrow.

Tradition had it that the boy George Washington had played in this rose garden and that Robert E. Lee had courted that great Virginian's adopted great granddaughter here. But neither would recognize it now or these beautiful hills stripped of the trees and scarred with whole cities of tents and shebangs as an army settled in for the winter. Already men were calling Fredericksburg their Valley Forge.

Whitman sucked on his empty pipe and dreamed of Cuban burley and warm, white bread. Back in New York friends would be gathering in the coffee shop to conjure up syllogisms about the sanctity of black freedom, the rights of the Union to win it and beatify the country again. They fashioned their logic out of clear vision and minds untroubled by the fear of death and untainted by cannon powder and spent blood. Then they would go to sleep under clean sheets and down quilts, smug with Christian benevolence. Whitman knew that it would be a long time before he would take his place among them again. These men here had taken him prisoner. He had found work that needed doing.

The ooze froze around his instep, forcing him back up on the ledge. He took another deep empty breath from his pipe before slipping it into his pocket. His peace was over. Commotion bobbed beyond the constellation of smoky campfires. Two Union pickets grunted the counter sign, passed the last checkpoint, and stumbled through the garden gate with a casualty cantilevered between them. Whitman turned back to alert the surgeons of incoming business. He held the door and the two half carried, half dragged their burden toward the inside table. Until the surgeons came, Whitman made the wounded man as comfortable as he could. He pulled back the waves of blue wool of the great coat. Already a stain was lengthening over the front of a shell jacket of oatmeal and brown. This casualty was not Union.

The Rebel swayed and bobbed, only the rough handling of his captors keeping him from keeling over onto the floor in a faint. He recovered himself with more embarrassment than any brave man had reason of. He straightened abruptly, the more determined to muster his faculties and make these Yankees understand that he had come over of his own free will. Without so much as the amenities of name, rank, or regiment, the prisoner demanded in a thick Georgia accent, "I wish to see the new color sergeant of the Twenty-Eighth Massachusetts."

"Directly. Let's see to that wound first, soldier." But the Rebel pushed Whitman away roughly.

"Now, that ain't polite," the Union picket growled. "Got shot trying to swim the river. I gave him my coat or the fool would have froze to death. Either he is stupider than a government clerk or he's got conversion. Thought you'd keep him alive enough so we can figure out which then shoot him at our leisure."

The second picket gave the Confederate the advantage of

slightly more brains. "Don't be ignorant, Boomer. He wouldn't have hailed us if he was going to invade us. He just would have come over with a few thousand uninvited friends, heralded by some of Alexander's cannon fire."

"What's your name, Sergeant?" Whitman asked as he pressed a wad of lint into the wound.

"Michael Sullivan of Cobb's Brigade. I'd like to talk to someone from the Twenty-Eighth. As I said already, I've got somethin' to deliver. Then I got to be gettin' back—my watch will be over and the lieutenant will be unhappy to find I'm gone."

"You don't think he knows that already, with all the fuss of shots and fishing you out on the Union side? You obviously have no respect for officers." Whitman probed again.

"Some I do, some I don't. About the Twenty-Eighth again..."

"Well, it shouldn't be too hard, Sergeant, since you boys played into them to the tune of about one out of two. There should be a few left right here lying about, but whether or not they would be up to talking to you I can't say."

An officer with a single star embroidered on black velvet shoulder straps stepped into the crescent of lamplight. "I heard from the picket you were asking for me. Is there something I can do?"

"Are you himself?" Sullivan measured the general up and down but with more awe than intimidation. Thomas Francis Meagher, Meagher of the Sword, was a symbol of pride to Irishmen on either side and here he stood having come at an enemy sergeant's bidding. The Rebel cursed the fates. Sorry fortune that the Confederacy's revolution was not to the liking of the Hibernian zealot.

"I guess you might be him at that." It was all Sullivan said as he reached inside his tunic.

The general's aide grabbed the Rebel's hand.

The pickets were insulted. "Don't be daft. You don't think we would bring him up here without cleaning him of his weapons, do you?"

Sullivan drew out a swath of rolled-up silk and passed it to the general, careful to keep his own blood from staining it further. As Meagher accepted it, the silk spilled over his hands and cascaded into an emerald wing faced with embroidered gold. The iridescent threads of the harp and the sunburst ensign caught the oily light and the flag was transfixed. Meagher drew the regimental colors up and fairly caressed them. It was some minutes before he remembered himself, "Sergeant, I thank you and speaking for them, the Twenty-Eighth thanks you."

The sentiment embarrassed the prisoner and he shrugged it away. "I couldn't just let somebody gobble them up. Your boys fought well, they surely did. I saw the color bearer's face as he went down—held the staff so tight, I thought he would take it to heaven with him. After dark I went out and took them for safe keepin'. I hope you will see they get home, General."

"I surely will. Yes, I surely will." Meagher whispered then recovered himself. "You have earned the good will and esteem of the brigade, Sergeant. You are welcome to stay with us, if you wish, past differences forgotten."

"No, sir, I wish to return to my own regiment."

"Not until we get that bleeding stopped and you change into some dry clothes, although the fashion may not be to your liking." Doctor Reynolds barked, as he forced his way through the circle and took command. "You could catch the fever before morning and end up dying in a Yankee bed with Miss Barton whispering sweet nothings in your ear. Then, what would your mother and the neighbors think?"

Meagher whispered something to his aide. The young officer saluted and evaporated into the night. The Rebel, his steel melted once his mission was completed, huddled deeper into the great coat to still the shakes that rattled him violently. Meagher reached inside his pocket. He unscrewed the lid then passed the flask to his guest, "Mother's milk."

The Confederate took a whiff, nodded in admiration of such fine quality, and took a long swallow. They said nothing more to each other. The only intrusion into the exclusive club was the commander's aide returning with his report: "Sir, General Hancock said that the matter should be settled between Irishmen. Divisional headquarters would make no official record of the incident."

Meagher smiled. "Patch him up, doctor." Then turning to his subordinate, "When the surgeon says he is ready to go, see to the safe return of our guest—unless you change your mind, Sergeant."

"I have unfinished work to do," the Rebel was not embarrassed at what he meant. Nor was the meaning lost on his host. "I'll be returning by your leave."

"As you will."

From the shadows, Brent Christie had watched it all. He hated Confederates in a pack—they had brought all this on them all, and they were an unrelenting enemy. Two days ago this man had shown no quarter, blasting away from his position in the rifle pits, with his mates three deep. They mowed down the blue regiments like winter wheat. And now this same enemy was some errant knight returning the colors of the men he had annihilated. This war was crazy.

The Rebel struggled as the white gauze cone was pressed over his mouth and the surgeon lay out his tools. Whitman collected lanterns from about the room and put them together at the table for the work ahead.

"How you feeling, Corporal?" A steward was leaning over Christie.

"Like I did when I smoked my first cigar."

"We're short of water, how about some brandy? There's a cellar full of good Secesh stuff down there. Won't stop all the pain, but we can give you enough so you don't care." The steward slipped a hand behind Christie's back to ease him toward the cup he offered. Only then did the steward see the emergency. He cursed. "You're bleedin' again, soldier. You just might be the doc's next customer. I feel sorry for you—all his knives are dull and he sure is cranky!"

What passed after that night were not days, for Christie they were illusions of faces and dreams that blurred like those Northern Lights. Terrible nightmares floated on tides of ether and chloroform. Lights bore him up and then flickered out, and he was adrift in the deep, endless voids that kept pushing him down into suffocating sleep again and again. He had no sense of being alive or dead, of who he was, of even existing. He was impotent, disembodied and drifting from hand to hand, from place to place. Everyone had some work to do on him. When they left, he was held captive in darkness and in a vice of excruciating pain.

II
The Shadow of Death
Christmas 1862

Gus was strong enough to carry a mule from Fredericksburg to Washington. That morning the big Dutchman had gathered Christie up like a sack of wheat to "re-file" him to another ward. But the bearer had only gone a few steps when the surgeon on some urgent business summoned him. He set his burden down by the front door.

"Warten, Corporal. Wait!" The nurse said and was gone.

Ward chiefs had been sorting men out and moving them into different wings according to the nature of their wounds and the care they would require. Doctor Letterman, the medical director of the army, ordered the fortunate to be loaded on ambulances and ferried down to Colonel Haupt's trains for the general hospitals in Alexandria. Those who could soon return to their regiments and those with no hope of surviving the trip were kept behind. The wounded were not actually told of this procedure, but it did not take long for them to catch on. By a process of elimination, as men went and he stayed, Christie saw his future—that he had none.

Now Christie turned to the sunlight and the grizzly chaos outside. The formal gardens were a ruin of ambulances, body boxes, and debris. Quartermaster barrels and crates filled with sauerkraut, onions, and flour rose like barricades; the empties were broken for kindling and heaped against the rose wall. As caskets were in short supply, blanket-shrouded corpses rested on pallets, balanced between barrels above the swamp oozing beneath. Wounded men lounged by the door until they could be dispatched. Without stop the trains ran back and forth to Washington, their quartermaster supplies and forage to the camp and their freight of wounded back. God must have had the assistance of angels such as Herman Haupt with his magnificent talent for organization and efficiency. How else could He have created the universe in just six days without having to wait for parts?

Gus worked the same way on a much smaller scale. A convalescent himself, Gus drew on unlimited supplies of spirits, tobacco, and morphine. Its ready quantity and quality he did not explain, and no wise man asked. These he supplied to the hardest-suffering patients in his ward. Gus's honorable services were free; he did not milk a man of his keepsakes, and he tended to his comforting ministrations before the victim had lost all dignity to the pain that ravaged him. When the provost prowled the wards for shirkers, the giant Dutchman and his medicines evaporated. The sisters crossed their fingers behind their backs and pleaded ignorance of any soldier the military police were seeking. When the coast was again clear, Gus materialized in another corner, the baggy pockets of his leather apron full of dusty bottles of pain killers, imported brandy, marmalade, and loaves of soft bread still warm from the oven.

That morning Gus had set in the middle of the ward an emaciated juniper planted more or less upright in a hardtack crate. In a great show, he had fastened candles to the branches, cascaded a long bandage over its three limp, yellow branches and hung squares of hardtack. "Tannenbaum!" he exclaimed proudly. It could have been "Eureka," "Voila," "Abracadabra," or "Lazarus, arise!" but there was not enough magic in the total of those words together to raise up the over-burdened sprig bent under the weight of all that ornamentation.

"Deutsch!" Christie hissed, careful to use the correct word the Teutonic Knights of the Ninth Ohio had taught him. "Who knows what lights their lanterns!"

But Gus's head bobbed up and down, anticipating the spectacle he planned for them that evening. In hums and ahhs, he labored to set their anticipation afire, but his English could not carry the load, so what came was not quite English and not at all German: "Ve vill licht machen, singen 'Tannenbaum' and 'Stella Nacht' und trinken hot schnaps and grog frum olt Rezept. Ja!"

"Was?" That was one-half of the total German vocabulary Christie knew outside of the expletives and profanity he needed to get along with the old Niners.

"Das Rezept..." Gus's hand rotated circles in front of his ample stomach, but he got only blank stares. "Kochen...uh...uh...

Rezept, you sprechen?" Nobody moved. Futile. Still he resolved this English would not defeat him. Slowly Gus let the letters line up like a parade of ducks before his eyes, then croaked them out one at a time, "K-o-o-o-k-que!"

Christie nodded. "Cook—recipe! I get it!"

But that did not carry near enough of a footnote for the next man, who leaned on an elbow and hissed, "I got the-lighting-the-candles part, that's near enough to my Scots—but what we gonna sing?"

Christie shrugged. "For some Rhine-water liquor, I'll sing anything he wants." His buddy bowed to sound reasoning, and Gus exited before he could be tested any further.

But the jubilation was not to be—at least not in all its luminescent entirety. Miss Barton found out about the plan and raised a fuss. It was not the schnapps she objected to. Hospital chests were full of it, in fact she would help Gus dispense it to patients so liberally as to keep the worst in a perpetual stupor till New Years. But lighted candles on a pine tree? The crazy Dutchman would burn down the hospital.

"Wake up, Corporal, and unbutton your shirt." A man in a surgeon's duster peered into Christie's eyes grim with intent. Beside him, Sister Louise stood mute as the doctor pulled back the blankets. "Come on, soldier, I don't have all day."

"Merry Christmas. Where's my turkey?" Christie sneered, turned his back, and pulled his blanket over his head. The holy day had dawned over the ward like unbreathable air. He, like his fellow patients, had borne the hours by being unconscious until rations were dealt.

"Merry Christmas. Depends upon your point of view, I guess. I want to listen to your lungs." With nothing else in the form of apologies or explanations, the doctor ripped off the soldier's blanket and pulled up his shirt.

The nun did not abide rudeness in her wards, not from raw veterans and not from surgeons. Even still, her words were calm. "This is Doctor Bellows, Corporal. He's come to help out here."

"What regiment are you with, Doctor?" Christie had never seen him on the battlefields before.

"I am with no regiment." Having said that Bellows went right to his purpose. He pressed the large funnel of a cold stethoscope into Christie's tender skin. The patient recoiled but Bellows held him fast.

A contract surgeon! Rumors of him—and doctors like him—ran like the black plague up and down the wards. They were not army, but civilian doctors with contracts from the Surgeon General to minister during periods of high crisis. They were paid more than the military doctors and had no loyalties to their patients, as did the regimental surgeons who came from back home.

Bellows leaned closer and the Buckeye caught the unmistakable trace of whiskey on his breath. Fingers hammered like fists against tender stitches.

Christie jerked away, "What's the matter, doctor, can't you find my heart?"

"One more word of insolence and I will report you to your commanding officer."

"Go ahead, it's General Nathan Kimball. He's in one of these wards somewhere."

Bellows pulled away and twisted Christie's head left and right. "I will have cooperation from you, Corporal...or..."

"Or what? You gonna put me into the army, make me drill, send me into battle?"

Bellows thumped Christie hard enough on the back to send him reeling. He whipped the blanket off, pulled the shirt apart, prodded and pushed the stethoscope deeper into Christie's ribs. "Breathe, soldier! Real hard. Now hold it! Hold it! Come on, you got more air in you than that—you had enough stuff to curse me to hell a second ago. Go ahead! Curse! Swear! Just breathe deeply when you do it! Again!"

It was an order Christie could take to. He wheezed and coughed a few prime expletives, favorites of General Hancock's.

The surgeon let them sail by and pushed against Christie's abdomen like an accordion. "Very good! Now say, 'Sam Hill!' It's more efficient. The little agitator has some purposes if in name only! In and out! Sam Hill! Sam Hill! Again! Again!" Finally Bellows let Christie drop back into his cot. The surgeon turned to the nun all but ignoring the rage burning through her cheeks.

"Sister, I think I want to go back in there and find that ball. Prepare this man for surgery."

"Surgeon Morrison said that this soldier should be allowed to... That he was..."

"What sister is trying to tell you is that this is the Valley of Death. We are all hopeless, but we do like to keep God waiting as long as we can."

Discretion was not at work here, Bellows snapped. "I gave you instructions, sister. See to it." The surgeon's face was a storm, but nuns were not intimidated by mortals and she held her place.

Christie saw the plan. Doctor Bellows here was either going to save him or hurry up his exit with a little experimental dissecting like he was some laboratory dog.

"Soldier, I will pray," the nun promised.

"You do that, sister." For the first time the corporal gave serious consideration to that recourse himself. Maybe even deserting. How far could he get, half-naked in the cold, and walking across Virginia?

In an hour the surgical stewards came for the New Yorker lying closest to the door. The boy never came back. Where he went no one would say. Then the stewards came with their folded litters for another and then another. Pairs of eyes from every bed watched them go by. Men who had cheated death more than once held their breath until the carriers passed the foot of their cots. Christie gauged his time on earth to be another two hours. He was short by ten minutes.

The stewards loomed over him like Gulliver. The biggest smiled broadly through gaping teeth, "Thy kingdom come!"

"What is the meaning of this? Where are you taking this man?" Doctor Morrison boomed from the foot of Christie's bed.

"Surgery," the attendants chorused meekly.

"On whose orders?"

"Doctor Bellows, sir."

The Fourth's regimental surgeon looked down at Christie. "You all right, son?"

"I'm still here."

"And there you will stay!" Dark eyes glared the buzzards back. Old Bones swayed from leg to leg, a cadaver needing burying if ever there was one. "I'll decide if the soldier needs surgery or not. Now get out of here. Where's this Bellows! Contract surgeons—nothing but blasted butchers! Experimenting on my boys! I'll have none of it. I'll have the man shot."

Davey Mahoney held to the shadows, letting the surgeon and the good nun pass well out of sight before he made his move. The corporal of the Eighth Ohio, Company B, slipped his bummer up his sleeve, then hitched the contraband upright between his belt and armpit. Then he gave it a reassuring squeeze into his belt to keep it from sliding. He stepped behind a hulking steward and about-faced one two down the ward, passing between rows of pallets until he found the one he wanted. Only when he got his old friend in his sights did he stretch an ungainly smile across his face.

"There now, Christie, me lad, so this is what has become of you?" Davey said as he collapsed like a telescope between two cots.

"Nolan, where's he?" Christie set upon his friend for news.

"He's around here somewhere. The captain said he lost a leg. Bad off, but holding. Surgeon won't let us see him. Said he's out of his mind with fever and grief. *You* could find him, I bet!"

"He'll make it, no worry. He's the only one of us who will go to perdition on his own terms. Did you see the way he anchored down the front and wouldn't give way? What about Quinn? Did they find his body?"

"Yes, he's on his way home."

Christie lay back satisfied. "Just us left, Davey. Just us. All the good times behind us. The easterners will outnumber us without respect now. And with your regiment and mine acting like the Hatfield and McCoys, the feud isn't getting any better..."

"Won't matter between us, we won't let it." But Mahoney knew the hard feeling would make them draw up allegiances eventually. Regimental loyalties grew thicker than religion.

Mahoney fidgeted on the floor, the contraband stabbing into his ribs. He was overburdened with news, but it all seemed wrong, more grief amid so much grief, yet somehow out of place here, and so long ago to be of no importance. Jaw paralysis. It was Christie who broke the silence first.

"Remember when the New York boys came in?"

Mahoney rolled his head back to enjoy the first sugar coated memory in a long time. "Weren't they a sight! They had as much knowledge of chopping wood as a gorilla does about crocheting."

The story was threadbare from retelling but it was the best Christie could conjure then to lighten his friend's load. A regiment of New Yorkers, as green as the timber they were to clear, were issued axes and went at the Virginia pine woods if not much in the way of ability, at least with a lot of steam. The Ohio boys, with a distinguished record in "fuel procurement," dating back to Camp Jackson, pulled up some ground and decided to watch awhile. The Zouaves swung and hacked, but their axes bounced off the green, frozen pine like rubber. Now seeing that they had gathered an audience, the Knickerbockers put their shoulders into it anew, so not to be regarded lazy by the prairie boys. The greenies swung in wide arcs narrowly whacking away precious body extremities to the man right or left of them. By and by some Wisconsin lumberjacks from the Iron Brigade bent down beside the Gibraltar boys also to watch. After a few agonizing moments, a Wisconsin sergeant suggested what had become all too obvious. "Well, boys, we better get in there and help those greenhorns before someone loses an arm and they won't be any good to us when the time comes."

Mahoney smiled what once was—full regiments of good comrades on the battle line and around the fire. The memory made his business all the more urgent. He flattened low and only when he was sure they were not being watched did he extract the amber bottle and slide it under Christie's pillow. "Fortification, when prayer just isn't enough," he whispered. "And I know how much you resort to prayer when it's cold."

"I'm insulted. I have been known to use the Lord's name often and widely." Christie pressed and molded the pillow over the bottle until he realized what gift had been given him on this day of all days. "Dearly beloved, we are gathered here to partake of the broth of God's harvest..."

"God? More like devil fire!" Mahoney winked. "Be careful! It's been in the battery wagon and froze twice. Ladled this sample right out of the core, so it's got to be about as potent as some of General Hunt's canister. Take care of it, lad, it's the last of the lot."

Christie leaned up on his elbow. "What? The supply get blown up by the Confederates again?"

Mahoney shook his head. "Naw, worse. Temperance. One of the Christian Sanitation ladies, with a nose like a coonhound, caught a smell of it. Anyhow, she made such a fuss about it with the provost. He tried to put her off. But before we could do anything about it, she got an ax and attacked the wagon. The lads were so upset, they wanted to sell her to the Johnnies for cigars. It was pitiful."

"Damnation to hell—isn't a man got nothing that is sacred?"

"Take care of it, boy, it's vintage."

"Corporal, are you in pain?" There was no mistaking the anguish on the wounded soldier's face. The nun was worried and pressed a palm to his cheeks. Christie pushed the bottle deeper under his head in case she too had a keening nose. "And you, soldier," she turned to Mahoney, "You look peaked."

"Me, ma'am? No, ma'am!" Mahoney scuffled to his feet. He was a head taller than the nun, but stooped four inches under her steel gaze. The sisters had the same effect from generals down to scullery privates.

"I think you had better leave for now, soldier. The corporal needs his rest," sister whispered.

"Yes, ma'am. Right away." Mahoney moved toward the door but just as he was about through it, sister caught his arm.

"Come back later. Bring a friend or two. He needs you. He needs all of you. He has not much time."

Mahoney looked back, and nodded he would. But he never did.

When he found Nolan, Christie thought he was too late. His comrade was nearly shrouded in bandages and sheets, and lay as still as stone. Nothing in all the world had terrified Christie like this. He forced himself on unsteady legs closer to the cot, but he could not take up the hand tethered in bindings. Either from the warmth of another body so near or the labored breath across his face, Nolan turned, "Quinn?"

Christie flinched, then steeled himself for what he must do. "Hey, boy. Take it easy. It's me, I'm here." Nolan did not recognize the voice immediately. An eye opened slowly, he studied the figure, finally all the parts came together, but it was not the face he wanted, and turned back.

Christie stepped closer. "Look at you, lad." Christie squeezed out a rag floating in a basin of murky water. He sponged away the sweat from Nolan's forehead. "It's over, Nolan, it's over. You're safe. Didn't you hear us calling you to fall back? You were hell bent on your own war to be settled there and for all time."

"Where's Quinn!"

The rag was rung nearly dry from the hard twist he just gave it and Christie soaked it again. So it was to be his punishment to tell the news. "Your pard won't be joining you, Nolan. He's dead. You were calling him in your sleep just now. He might come, but not in the way you want. Now, don't fuss. Nothing more can hurt him. He's safe in the hands of the Almighty. I bet Quinn's already having a reunion with his father and the other Sons of the Emerald Isle, and there's Jamie to look out after him. He's in good company."

Nolan pulled against his restraints, and tried to raise himself up. There was something he wanted to tell Christie, but the torment was so great he yelped like a wounded animal.

Christie damned himself. He carried it all inside, he just could not get any feelings out. Men were not bred to this—this was women's work or chaplains'. Nolan's hands flailed against their wrappings, rocking the cot until it would buckle. Christie grabbed one and then the other and held them down. "Look, he died quick and brave. There was nothing you could have done. You can take some comfort in that. And you are going home and doing it with the biggest part of your body that you enlisted with. Count your blessings. But you got to get better, boy. You got to."

"What for!" Nolan pitched back, and pulled himself up into a ball.

"Oh no, you don't." Christie ripped the gum blanket away from the gaping window. "Look! Daylight, Nolan! You aren't going to hide from it. Smell that—it's air, fresh air. It's freedom from this damned place and this damned war. Yeah, freedom! Fill your lungs with it. Don't turn away from me! You aren't dying neither. I've had a stomach full of friends' dying. You are the only one left. You're not taking the easy way out." Christie turned Nolan's face and pressed it down so that he could not move. Then he whispered into his ear. "You hear me, Nolan! Too many top-hat abolitionists and soothsaying editors want to forget about us, cause they think we were cowards. Not good enough for their high and mighty cause. We can't let the Rebels have the last laugh! And by damned, we are not going to let the people think we are trash. We aren't going to just slink away with our tails between our legs. All we got are the bits and pieces of good men to go back and tell them the truth. You aren't much, boy, half a body and half a mind, but you are all we got, and you are going to do it. You owe it to us, all of them, and you owe it to Quinn. You going to let them call Quinn a coward?"

Christie slipped Mahoney's bottle of Cannon Shot under Nolan's pillow. His tone was calmer tinged with the old mischief. "Take this—it's the family jewels. Toast the boys when you get back home...one by one, and then in companies, and then the whole regiment till you can see them clear and clean again. And don't forget yours truly. They say I'm dying soon as well. When I go, I don't want to see you riding my coattails into perdition."

Sister Louise's mind kept accurate time: her patient had been gone for three-quarters of an hour. As the moments ticked, she calculated the cost to his depleted body. Just when her patience had run out and now determined to have Whitman drag Christie back for his own good, he staggered in. He got as far as the arch and slumped against the molding. She had to nail her feet to the floor to keep from rushing to him. Just as Christie was about to fall on his face, Gus sided up as casually as if the two skulkers had met outside an off-limits tavern. The German lifted the limp, ashen body under his arm, and the two lurched the ten paces to Christie's cot.

His neighbor leaned up on an elbow just as Christie pulled the blanket over his face. "Doctor Bellows came through here lookin' for you. The grim reaper was unhappy that one of his souls might have escaped to the eternal without his help. When he found out you just wandered off, he really blew steam. I am glad I am not you."

Just at supper, Bellows strode up. "You know why I'm here?"

"To get another scalp for your belt, I suppose." Christie shoved his plate under his cot.

"A legitimate opinion considering the calumny spread around here. Perhaps I deserve it. Sister Louise has informed me that I need some work on my manners. She may be right. Never argue with a nun, soldier—they rank you and the retribution is painful. They can't kill you, but they can sure make you wish you were dead." Bellows pulled up a stool, settled down, and a measure of the ramrod went out of him. "Doctor Morrison has given me permission to talk to you about what I want to do. Sister says I should have done it first and stopped acting like a...well anyway, that's my problem." Bellows massaged his temples. "God, how I hate this place! I never saw so much blood. It's not even like saving men from dying, it's more like trying to bring them back from the dead once they got one foot in the grave. Anyway, that's my problem too. Where you from, soldier?"

"Delaware." Christie was watching him closely.

"The coast?"

"No. It's just a smudge on the map in central Ohio. And you?" Christie asked but didn't much care where the doctor came from, only that he take his business back there if he wasn't up to real war.

"Chicago...Bridgeport...Southside. You got any family back in Delaware?"

"Just a mother."

"Her pride and joy, I expect."

"Hardly."

"Well, we got that in common. My mother had marked me for the devil before I was even out of short pants. And I can't say she didn't have cause, but there was more where I came from and she wouldn't miss me. I'm the second down, tenth up out of seven brothers and four sisters. Raised in a part of town called Hardscrabble near St. Bridget's, not that you should know of it. Back there we get a lot of gunshots, bar fights, waterfront set-tos. You name it. We got it fifty ways before church on Sunday. A doctor learns a lot of medicine, and learns it before the professors can mull it over at their conferences and decide to put the procedures and methods in the textbooks. It was in one of those wards with a knife in my arm, that Sister found me. She thought I could be saved—or she wanted to save St. Bridget's from me. Anyway, she got one of the high rollers to finance two years for me in Budapest at Doctor Semmelweis's clinic. It might have been on the other side of the moon. But it was my salvation. Never loved anything or anyone so much. He is about one hundred years ahead of his time, and the medical boards will make him pay for it with his sanity I'm afraid. Anyway, he taught me something more of chest wounds and about cleanliness, which we could use high doses of around here. It wouldn't kill a doctor to wash his hands and his equipment once in awhile but you can't convince them of it. All this brings me to you, who will profit from my purgatory, if you so decide."

Christie was not sure he wanted to be the lamb in Bellow's redemption or a specimen to advance his career. But given time and place, there was nothing he could do but listen.

"I heard something in your chest yesterday, Corporal. More like, I didn't hear something. You didn't whistle when you breathed and not when you coughed. I think I heard where that shell isn't, so maybe through a process of elimination I can guess where it is."

"And you want to cut me and go searching through my insides based on that?"

"Yeah, that's about it." Bellows pressed two fingers lightly below and to the left of Christie's sternum. "There. Something in there is plugging up the air, probably pushing up against the lungs from on top, just under the skin, near as I can tell. It could be a clot of blood, it could be bone and tissue, or it could be the ball. I'm betting on that. That ball took a joy ride inside your rib cage a good four inches but I think it stopped there. That's why we can't get the bleeding to stop. You aren't bleeding from the hole, but up a ways. Only trouble is, your heart is a near neighbor. It's a miracle you are alive, but you are alive and that tells me plenty."

Bellows moved his finger only a fraction to the right from the place he had been pressing. "But it's a brag and a prayer that I can get it out so that you can live to tell about my genius. I was going to make that decision for you, but Sister said it's your decision to make. Guess she's right. So you've got to make it. But you've got to make it right now. There isn't time for candles and novenas. That lead is giving off poison and you're probably bleeding in there every time you cough. So you'll hemorrhage or you will rot from the inside out—and soon."

That was where it stood. Christie had only one more question: "If you don't operate what then?"

"You'll die. You're already turning yellow. We'll pack you up tomorrow and send you home to die in your own bed if you want." Bellows whispered. "I'll make Haupt take you."

"And if you do operate?"

"You may die tonight. It's just one trump card I'm dealing you and it isn't a high one even at that. I had more bluster yesterday."

"Doc? You a poker player?"

"Naw, I smoke cigars, swear, am bad tempered, drink, rarely attend church, and there isn't enough in an official version of the 'Act of Contrition' to cover all these faults, let alone the incidentals, so I stay away from cards. It's my one virtue. The only way God knows me by name at all is because my mother and Sister Louise pray for me all the time. So, if you think God and I are on a first-name basis and He favors me because of any family resemblance, you better think again. I'd say get another opinion, and the Surgeon General down to the cadets will bet I am going to put you in a coffin for no reason except for some research and a bad paper for the medical society."

"Then maybe we go for broke."

"You for it then?"

"Do it. And do it right away before we both lose our nerve. And make it good, or I won't pay."

III
A Collision of Comets
March 14, 1863

Frankenstein was more civilized company than the human freight; the convalescents, raw recruits, government bureaucrats, contractors, and scalpers packed around him on the steamer deck. He and the monster had gone off to war together, and the monster was, in fact, the last friend left from those earliest days. The novel that Christie now set against the wind was creased, bald, curled, and as precious as a deck of marked cards. When it rode, it rested high in his knapsack within easy reach, unlike another book he always carried—the *Four Gospels,* which languished deep in the bottom.

The novel had been a gift from his father for Christie's thirteenth birthday and suited him much better than the Testament, which had also been a gift. The Scripture however had been from his mother, and, as with all things, she had purpose in giving it. It was her last effort at striking the flames of conscience in her unruly son. Without so much as a word for his safety and good fortune, she pressed it into his hands as he left with his company on the train. But the book had not seen the light of day since Christie had prayed over the grave of his messmate back at Harrison's Landing. In the end he had not even opened it—finding deeper words in his own heart. When the revival fever hit the army last autumn, he had tried to barter the Bible for a pair of wool socks from a New Yorker. Even newly baptized and crisp with conversion, the Irishman from Brooklyn turned the bargain down. But he offered an instead—half a confiscated ham and the socks for the *Frankenstein.*

On the flyleaf of Mary Shelley's novel, his father had inscribed, "*Beasts and sinners make better saints and counselors than confessors and clerics.*" As in all things, his father was right. Every time Christie read it, the story spoke a different message, not the least of which was never to underestimate even the most delicate of ladies. They secrete monsters and demonic vengeances in the elegant and cultured rooms of their imaginations.

Shelley's monster still rampaged unleashed. Last night, a dinner of beef paste pie had boiled up a nightmare. The beast, conjured from the arms, legs, and minds of men with threadbare ideals, ravaged the land again, but it had taken on a new name—"Potomac." Abused and tortured too long, the monster took its wrath on the town of Fredericksburg, leaving it in ashes. Henry Ward Beecher and William Lloyd Garrison surged at the head of the bloodthirsty mobs to demand the head of the beast Burnside and its master scientist, Abraham Lincoln.

Christie had jerked out of his sleep in a cold sweat, not fully understanding the terror that cut straight to his heart. He believed in visions and he knew the dream portended something of his own fate—rancid meat pies notwithstanding. He waited for morning topside, huddled in the crevices between the crates and barrels of freight. But the night never lifted beyond the steel gray fog that sweated out an unrelenting drizzle. His slicker leaked like a sieve above and beneath, his skin was a feast for vermin. His incisions burned. He was hungry. The muscles in his calves were knots. He longed to unwrap himself and stretch, but the trees were flowering a spring crop of Rebel sharpshooters. A ball had pricked the bib of his bummer about an hour ago. And then his legs were dangerously close to inconveniencing three homicidal Prussian sergeants and an Irish lieutenant waging to the death a game of "Old Sledge."

Beyond the gunwales the brown, soupy Mississippi churned and foamed with logs, fence rails, and dead animals. Even a chicken coop and a broken dray swirled and churned over reefs, boils, and sawyers toward the Gulf. "Too thick to drink and too thin to plow," so the locals said. The famous river had been something of a disappointment, nothing to inspire songs and poems that he could see. What four-part harmony he heard was sung by foul-mouthed Jack Tars steering a deep-channel course against upstream traffic.

There were even some disagreements posed as to what river they actually rode. Western men argued the Mississippi was only a stream that flowed into the Missouri at St. Louis, and so the Missouri was the river of renown. Residents further south said the Mississippi was a short timber river that flowed into the Arkansas at Fort Hindman, making what flowed to Louisiana actually the Arkansas. This river was bigger than the old Miss and even bigger than the Amazon. Christie posed a new heresy founded on his perception as a life-long Buckeye. It was not the Arkansas, the Missouri, or any other but the extension of the Ohio River that they rode. It was Union water that flowed through Southern veins. Trailing all the way back to Pittsburg, the Ohio accumulated through its tributaries of the Cumberland and the Tennessee to be a force that did not stop at Cairo, Illinois, but elbowed south to flow all the way to New Orleans, making it the Grandfather of Waters. Any right-thinking mind that could read a map could see the river suffered from a clear-cut case of mistaken identity.

Christie had been making that very case an hour ago—and holding four tens—when the three Prussians and the lunatic Celtic lieutenant from Iowa threatened to throw him overboard and his heresy with him. Christie folded his cards to let the lunatic take the pot with two pair. So now under an oilcloth Christie huddled with *Frankenstein*. Nothing like the tale of a mad scientist, a rampaging monster, and bloodthirsty mobs to calm a soldier's nerves.

Even still he was not alone. The mournful stares of the gothic saints haunted him. These skeletons of grand old plantation houses swayed in rhythm with the breezes that pitched and pulled at rotting foundations. As he passed, the souls of esteemed dead generations gaped through dead-blank windows and mocked the invaders with muted curses. And they were not to be denied, by those who came too close.

At Greenwood the boat had come port around. There not twenty yards off, the long shapeless body of a runaway twisted from a rope hung from an upper gallery of a great house. Listing and near to collapse, the dead weight would all but pull it over into the bracken, cane and back wash. A milestone, the point of no return, here the black flag flies—no prisoners taken, no quarter given.

Guerrillas and slave patrols prowled the backlands. Not to be intimidated by the armies of either side, were the savage pirates, murderers, and swindlers ravaging in craven packs from Cave-in-Rock, Illinois, to Lake Pontchartrain, Louisiana. The captain boarded the windows of his steamer and ran with two crews day and night to keep a course well away from the banks. Passengers without inside berths, Christie among them, kept low amid gaps in the freight from breakfast to supper.

Christie should have been at home and not on this blasted boat at all. His thirty medical days were ticking away, and by next month he would be back in Virginia with no leave at all. He had barely limped off the convalescent train when his mother had put him on another going the opposite way. As recording secretary of the Delaware Comfort and Aid Society and correspondent of the Mount Vernon Ladies' Aid Societies, she had nominated him—and the motion had passed unanimously without his vote—that he escort their relief supplies to Louisiana and the home boys serving in the Ninety-Sixth Ohio. He had been shanghaied by due process with no appeal. And she was a woman with ulterior motives. War ravaged the country, but it had given the Widow Christie peace. It had been two years since Sheriff Powell had brought her son home from one of his wild nights and she was not willing to revisit those days even on a short-term lease. And there was something else...

Last night, Christie had found a letter his mother had written to his father's old colleague, a Mount Vernon lawyer, George Washington Morgan, the Ninety-Sixth's old colonel and now one of Sherman's black-sheep commanders. In it she had blatantly solicited a commission for Christie on Morgan's staff where her son could be of some service, stay out of trouble, gain promotion, and finally be of some credit to his father's memory. Apparently his mother had her own ideas about her son's future... that he should have one outside of jail. If war be the rising industry recruiting and promoting young men of promise, then war it was. Christie had demonstrated no talents for any other calling except carpentry, which put to despair her dream of a sacred vocation consecrating the heavenly host as a Dominican father. She was absolutely right, but he would get his own promotions on his own merit, and he threw the letter overboard. The Fourth was his family and his home now, and back with the Fourth he would go when this business was over.

It was nearly noon when the transport slammed into the pilings at Young's Point, the last safe harbor before the inhospitable Confederate stronghold at Vicksburg. The wharf wobbled and swayed, bobbing half-submerged by the freshet sweeping down Milliken's Bend. The cotton port was the temporary layover of a tightly knit conglomeration of mostly western regiments recruited from Wisconsin to Ohio, from California to Georgia, called the Army of the Tennessee.

"Come on, Corporal, time to go. Buck! Hank! Help the corporal with his Christmas shopping there." The dock foreman sneered at the puny human material Secretary Stanton was sending down to fight the Secesh. "Army just don't make them like they used to. Back in forty-six under 'Rough and Ready' well, we were a saltier breed, could fight Mexicans all day and carouse with 'sonorities' all night."

"Yea, Max, you could lift the world and spin it on your forefinger." The roustabout jabbed the third finger of his left hand at his buddy and with his other shoved a crate into Christie's back to bump him toward the gangplank faster than the boy was moving. If Christie's legs were under him, they were not yet perpendicular when Max gave him the shove starboard and he stumbled into a piling. Max spit the ragged tatters of a cigar into the wind. The tobacco shattered like shrapnel to rain plugs on Christie's newly issued uniform.

That day like all days, the disposition of First Sergeant Cyrus Boyd was cranky. He had awakened that way back in Keokuk, Iowa, October 24, 1861, to find himself elected first sergeant of Company G of the Fifteenth over his objections. He was in no way humbled for the honor and confided in his diary many nights since his desire to shed the curse onto someone else. Yesterday he had been detached from his company posted with General McPherson to ride down from Lake Providence on this fool's errand about a requisition, one in a sea of reports and requisitions that routinely went to the man in the moon when they should have gone to the god of Mars. And the boys would be coming down directly, so he needed to find some suitable real estate for them to bivouac.

The irony was that the last couple of weeks had turned into a fine vacation. General Grant had sent them up on another of his canal excavations. But McPherson, an excellent engineer and not a man to wear himself out on boondoggles, made more agreeable use of the time while not entirely disobeying orders. He had given his men something of a furlough, while he and a few handpicked officers "surveyed" the lake by moonlight in a craft equipped with a regimental band and several cases of confiscated champagne. While the commander penciled on his maps, the Seventeenth Corps camped, fished, hunted game, and had a fine time of it. Boyd had been forced to leave the first real vacation in a year to straighten out this mess, and he wanted nothing less than a head of a bureaucrat on a pike.

The sergeant was chewing on a breakfast of an unlit cigar when the looks of a shipboard scuffle had caught his attention. A member of the infantry seemed to be getting the worst of it. He was ready if need be to call in reinforcements from several nearby regiments who would enjoy breaking up the tedium of drill, fighting, and canal digging with a good brawl against river rats.

Boyd pushed through the melee and took charge.

"Up straight, soldier!"

Christie tilted his head an inch to the starboard, then pried open one eye only a bare red slit to see who it was who came to his rescue several seconds too late. Then he estimated where Max had fallen and was satisfied that the stevedore was under rather than over him—so the soldier must have carried the point.

"Can you hear me, Corporal? You need help?" Boyd pulled the newcomer to his feet and about-faced him toward the plank.

In his good time. Christie motioned Boyd to hoist a barrel and he picked up the remaining crate from the deck. "No, had trouble finding the exit is all, Sergeant..."

"Boyd."

"Brent Christie, Fourth Buckeye." The newcomer moved with his load slowly through the quagmire. "Never thought I would need sea legs to walk on land."

The sergeant spit. "Aye, the river and the blackguards and pirates who run it have had the best of a lot of us one way or another. Stay away from these roustabouts—a thieving, lying bunch of pagans they are." Boyd kept a watchful eye on the bad one only now picking himself up off the deck. "No Fourth Ohio down here, boyo. One, Two, and Three serving with Rosecrans in Tennessee. Aren't you supposed to be with Joe Hooker out east? You're lost bad."

"Sent down here just to deliver this bounty for the Ninety-Sixth. Then I'll be good riddance."

"Can't be too soon for you. You eastern soldier boys are too soft to last long down here with all your clear-weather fightin' on village green battlefields against paper collar Virginia generals."

"Wordy on first acquaintance, aren't you? And not the least bit respectful." Christie reinforced the caution with a weak finger jabbed into Boyd's stomach, "Sergeant, even with all deference due your rank, if there's anything left of me when I finally stop sinking, I'm going to punch you in the nose." He put the crate down on a stump and steadied himself. "You boys were still in Sunday school when we were fighting Johnnies in West Virginia. And I will bet you a Hooker, a Burnside, and a Pope and raise you one McClellan to get Rosecrans back. Then you will see what the Army of the Potomac can do."

Boyd sank back on his heels. The corporal had him there and he was sorry for the insult. Boyd had been one of Rosy's boys himself at Corinth last spring. Nothing wrong with old Rosy—take him back anytime over this Grant. With Rosy, the army would be doing some hard shooting again and not digging canals. Blast Grant anyway!

Christie studied this new port in the war, not liking it at all. Out on the river the tar-covered ironclads were rain-slicked to a patent-leather sheen. There the huge mud turtles wallowed amid the transports, barges, and tugs that puttered like a nuisance of water beetles around them. To his left a shanty town of shebangs, tents, and warehouses floated on a layer of scum, and somewhere in all that chaos was the Ninety-Sixth.

"Just point me in the right direction." Christie was eager to detach himself from Boyd and get on to business, "Got to see this load gets safely to its destination and I can be on my way home."

Boyd cursed the inconvenience the soldier presented. "This is a pretty big place. That eye of yours is puffing up like a mushroom, be closed shut by morning. You can't stay here on the landing; that's for sure. I don't suppose you made reservations at some de-luxe hotel?"

"I assume, like Providence, the army will provide for its pilgrims. The Sanitation Commission should have an empty cot for a night."

Boyd shrugged. Perhaps he owed the veteran at least a night of hospitality. The sergeant trudged toward a knot of men taking inventory of the recently unloaded quartermaster barrels. Christie was about to call Boyd back, not wanting him to undertake any courtesies to which he had not consented. But Boyd was his own authority, and with a finger pointed to Christie's crates and then another jabbed toward the camps beyond, he put his point across. The men nodded and got things expedited.

"It's all taken care of. Now come with me." Boyd motioned Christie up the bank.

"What's taken care of?" Even as the words were hardly out of his mouth, rough men pushed Christie out of the way to tend to the cargo he rested on.

"Corporal, you are one stripe short and you are still arguing with me. Your presents are going up to my tent for safekeeping till we can find out where the Ninety-Sixth has settled in. I told the boys there—provost most of them, but it's not supposed to show—that I had inside information that you was one of Alan Pinkerton's agents sent down here to see who was responsible for our stuff ending up on the black market. All infractions would be forwarded to the head pitbull for a proper chewing out. They were grateful for the intelligence. So your mother's marmalade will be getting priority treatment, even if General Sherman's drawers end up on Bragg's backside. And it will keep those river rats from coming after you for round two. Now let's test those sea legs."

With Boyd on his blind side, Christie sagged a little starboard, but all in all they were finally making good progress slugging through the shallow swamp which passed for real estate in the Louisiana tradition. They had not gone far when unceremoniously interrupted.

"Sergeant Boyd!"

Boyd froze. "As I was sayin' about pitbulls," Boyd snapped his heels in mock respect, "Lieutenant Canfield!" Boyd saluted and pivoted in the direction of the bark.

No taller than a roadside marker, an officer postured under a two-story Hardee hat with a brim wider than a Manchester umbrella.

"You two in a fight, Sergeant?"

"No, sir, he's just sick, sir, with a mosquito infestation."

The officer's face twisted disdainfully. "One of yours?"

"No, sir, belongs to Joe Hooker. Just here on special assignment, sir!"

"See to him then!" Already Canfield had wasted too much in the way of good manners and valuable time on subordinates for no good purpose. "Sergeant, I've been waiting for you. Do you think I have all day to fix your mistakes? Your last requisition was on an outdated form. Go to the Ordnance HDQ, get a new Class 1, and make it out properly. I hope you have your numbers with you. Your ordnance sergeant failed to list the inventory from last quarter. Therefore, your 'total accounted for' is light. Do so or your unit will be going into their next battle with empty rifles. We do not guess. Proper procedures, Sergeant. Army wheels are greased by procedures into a well-oiled machine!"

"Yes, sir. Presently, sir."

"Now, Sergeant." The officer turned on his heels.

"Damned!" Boyd snorted. The shepherd turned to his near-blind lamb. "It's a mile up the road and then my tent is half that in the other direction. No good reason for you to go out of your way. Wait on this bench. But don't go off on your own and get lost, and don't talk to anyone, and you don't know anything if anyone decides to talk to you, especially reporters. Politics among commanders is very delicate down here, and provost is very skittish about spies."

This would be no problem as Christie had survived so far by these same universal commandments, and so dropped down on a long expanse of warped pine nailed over two tree stumps. The sergeant went in one direction and in another the lieutenant, stiff legged and hip deep in boots as high as stovepipes. The subaltern had set his sights already on a new victim and was bearing down on him like a monitor.

Young's Point was an anthill of activity. The army was consistent, or by its presence made all things consistent. Louisiana was no different from Alexandria, Harrison's Landing, or Yorktown—muddy, controlled chaos, new troops arriving to replace wounded and sick leaving. It was a bustling city populated by officers in shoulder straps, non-coms in chevrons and clean-sleeved privates. But unlike the camps of the Army of the Potomac, he noticed immediately here high echelon officers with stars and eagles on their blouses moved without the retinue of staff which was as pre-requisite to eastern generals as tails on a kite. At first sight Christie saw the mutual respect, an easy come-and-go between officers and soldiers. A subordinate passed his superior with barely a salute, more often a neighborly "Hello, General!" or "Evenin', Colonel," a knuckle tapping the brim of his cap. The officer would consider himself saluted and reply with a nod or a puff of exhaust from his cigar.

Feeling was creeping slowly into his feet now and Christie eased himself up. But Boyd had been right about the eye—his vision would be in total eclipse in another hour. A long convalescence had made his reflexes slow; he had countered the stevedore's right in time but not the left. Still he had held his own. Max would be walking with a decided stoop and cursing Christie's memory with a squeak in his voice. The prodigal soldier tramped in narrow circles that Boyd had estimated were safely outside the dimensions of trouble.

Trouble, however, had a chart, timetable and compass of its own; it was well on schedule and right on course. In fact, it was only one hundred yards away, swathed to its chin in a Saxon blue greatcoat. The force was suffering the exile of his usual domain for a foreman's table in a damp cotton warehouse. He raised a page against the oil lamp and squinted. He had some of the finest commanders in the army, all with the worst penmanship. Once he ciphered it, what it reported was as grim. The army was hemorrhaging.

    An aide closed the door against the chill and stepped silently to the three-legged table. The commander did not look up, but tapped the morning report impatiently. "Can we return any of these men to duty?"

    The aide shook his head. "Doubt it, sir. In fact, I'd say those numbers are optimistic."

    The superior was getting answers not to his liking. He sensed there was more bad news coming. "Well, speak up, John?"

    The adjutant took a deep breath. For a couple of weeks now his boss had been acting like a tailor with too little material to make a coat for a very portly man. Like the tailor, he had a job to do, but with half the fabric he needed to do it. No matter how he tugged and pulled to bring seams together, there was always a gap somewhere. Still his boss would hear the truth. "Yes, Sam, in fact I'd estimate that another twenty percent couldn't make a march five miles, and another ten should be in the hospital right now, but they won't go."

    Two inches of spent tobacco was tapped into a saucer. The aide was glad to see the ash cool, but the cigar, suspended between the owner's fore and index finger, was a bare quarter of an inch above a stack of papers. Moreover, the two of them stood in the center of five hundred hogshead of Secesh cotton consigned to finance an intelligence network that Colonel Grenville Dodge had knitted together. It would do no good to see it go up in flames.

The aide eased the saucer under his boss's blunt.

"I dare say, John, when a soldier has a choice of facing the brigade surgeon or the Confederates, it's some testimony to the savagery of the surgeon and the efficiency of the enemy that he'll take the Confederates every time. Typhoid, diarrhea, small pox, black water fevers of every kind and description are killing by the company. I dare say the river is taking them faster than the enemy."

The commander did not like the arithmetic. He needed men. Nathaniel Banks, another commander with the same manpower problems, was slogging his way up from New Orleans to Baton Rouge and clamoring to be reinforced. He could use Bank's help here, or rather, his corps. Technically Banks outranked him, if he came he would take over. That would not do at all. But the men! He needed the men!

Already this opera suffered from too many prima donnas. There was General John McClernand. Like Banks, he was once a Democrat from congress, and another of the president's cronies. He had recruited his own army from his home state of Illinois and thereabouts. He called it the Army of the Mississippi, when it was in fact only a corps with the unlucky number of XIII. But while McClernand tarried back home getting married, Sherman had stolen those troops right off the wharf for an assault at Chickasaw Bluffs just north of Vicksburg. The whole battle had been a dismal failure. Now McClernand was telling every reporter with a sharp pencil and a finger on the telegraph key that he was going to show these lame duck commanders from West Point how it was done.

Although his troops had built a good reputation, McClernand was universally hated. However, President Lincoln was determined to keep McClernand on the Mississippi and out of Washington. On the river the little pasha would be working toward Lincoln's war instead of speaking against it in the halls of Congress. Every victory of McClernand's would be a vote in Lincoln's favor. This commander would have admired the president's genius if McClernand were Hooker's problem and not his.

The general needed a plan. More precisely, he had the plans; he just needed the men and the Mississippi to give him one break. Across the river was Vicksburg. On a sunny day, he could see that brand new courthouse with the blue and white flag just taunting him to come and get it. The city crested on a two-hundred-foot ridge overlooking a hairpin bend in the river. Twenty-two siege guns were expertly sighted there and tended by men who used them with the practiced skill of squirrel rifles. They had menaced Admiral Farragut's navy last year and evaporated any infantry sent against it. Nothing went up or down the river without being baptized by fire. Every plan to go around them, behind them, or through them was fought back. So the commander set his men to digging canals to bypass them, but the river was stubborn. If the Father of Waters were going to change its route as it had often done on a whim, it would choose its own direction and its own good time and would not be hurried to convenience the Union Army.

"Sir, these wires?"

"They'll keep, John. Washington isn't going anywhere despite your curses."

The aide rested the communiqués on the table. "Sir, Admiral Porter is waiting for you on the *Black Hawk*."

The commander pulled out his pocket watch. Porter would be pacing the quarterdeck, and he wasn't even late yet. He liked to please Porter; the admiral was one of the few men who didn't want his job. He folded up his notes and slipped them into a breast pocket, straightened his coat, and rubbed the blur from his eyes. The left lid drooped slightly and gave the head a slightly cocked effect, as if he were only half-listening. But this slow-talking officer was not to be shortchanged and never under-rated.

The general set his slouch hat down over his sandy hair and bent the brim forward to keep his cigar dry. Flanked by a couple of aides, and with his hands clenched behind his back, he moved through the heavy port traffic, his mind more on his troubles than on his direction. A fresh idea had been taking shape in the back of his brain and he would need Porter's help. Also his plan needed an infantry commander and he could think of only one man: "Cump." Red bristle-topped, with a temper to match, but he had the mettle and the git. "Lieutenant, invite General Sherman for mess."

The party forced a wedge through the crosscurrents of

men, carts, and horses. Cumbersome wagons and bed-enclosed "trucks" veered left or right, phalanxes of troops without a command guided left or right to let him pass without a zig or a zag. "Trouble" was now unrestrained and well on course.

Christie pulled himself deeper into his slicker and yanked the lip of his bummer down to hide the eye that was now blind and pulsating. The lifting and placing of his feet took all his concentration, the ooze sucked his shoes into puddles that overflowed his instep and would not let go without extreme effort. And so, from different points, two veterans who knew better than to be looking down when the rule of survival is to be looking up, moved onward. When the two comets collided, Corporal Brenton Christie's orbit was changed forever.

"What the hell hit me!" Christie back flopped into the cold, Louisiana slime, while his victim flailed in suspended animation beyond the pull of gravity. He ricocheted off the corporal, then off his lieutenant, finally going down headfirst and feet up. As he flailed hither and yon his prized hat pitched and yawed on the breeze, beyond rescue, then only to be ground under by the wheels of a commissary wagon. Officers leaned to help but slipped and slid as if they danced on ice. Twenty-gauge profanity whizzed like cannon shells from every man who saw what happened— some in awe, others in anger, and many among the lower ranks in dire sympathy of the corporal's certain fate.

"Damn! You should be looking where you are going." An officer sputtered as he hoisted Christie to his feet with enough jerk to snap his head from his spine. The newcomer was about-faced into the chest of a large, red-faced officer with eagles on his shoulders. "You clumsy jack ass. Don't you have the sense to watch where you are going?"

"Me? I wasn't *going* anywhere, *sir*. I was just standing here, *sir*, when this blind, dumb elephant plowed into me. Yell at *him, sir!*"

Only then did the truth toll in Christie's ears like a carillon of bells. "Sir, are you all right? General Grant, are you hurt? General Grant, do you want a litter?" The urgent refrain of "General Grant!" from twenty different mouths telegraphed bad news to Christie's dizzy brain.

John Rawlins, Galena lawyer and Grant's guardian angel,

was vexed and wise men trembled. Enraged to absolute speechlessness Rawlins pushed Christie into the custody of a lieutenant to see to his commander. The commander was alive and coherent, unhurt it would seem; yet he looked like a mortal casualty of battle. His coat and pantaloons were awash in red clay.

Then for no reason anyone could decipher, Rawlins smiled and the universe and all its forces relaxed. Rawlins kept this minor triumph under barely restrained good cheer. Bless the little bugger, what was the soldier's name? I'll buy him a drink at the first discreet opportunity. Yes, the coat was a mess now, but it was a mess before—muddy, tattered, coffee and tobacco stained, not to mention the cigar burns. After it dried it would be fit only as a mule blanket.

When the general wasn't looking, the coat would simply vanish like the pathetic slouch hat he had brought into the war. Rawlins would write Julia for an officer's coat and she would be only too glad to have one tailored and sent to her husband. Rawlins made an additional note to include a request for another hat. Grant was petting this old limp felt like a dead cat.

"Sir?" Christie braced himself for what ever came.

"I don't think there are any mortal wounds, right, Corporal?" Grant's tone was calm in spite of the chaos from which he had just retrieved himself. "The ground is like a sponge. Oh, that is a bad eye—I am sorry."

"Pardon me, sir. The eye is a trophy from another...uh... accident, sir. As for this, I should have been watching where I was going." Not a word was true, but in catastrophes involving two-star generals— apologies, unlike rivers, always flow uphill.

Grant was having no success reshaping the drenched hat.

"Sorry about the that, sir." Christie nodded. "I will buy you another one." The words were out of his mouth before he could call them back. With what? He had his boat ticket and enough money for another meat pie—corporals did not ride first class.

Grant jerked. Something curious in the circumstances here, as if he had lived them before. He focused more closely on the contrite face of the very young soldier. It ignited a recollection, barely a flicker in the mind that forgot nothing, especially a kindness. He eyed the young man closer. "Corporal, I am beginning to remember the face, but not the name."

"Brenton Christie, sir." He braced to attention. "Company C, Fourth, OVI. I will be glad to pay for the hat, sir, as I said."

Thankfully the general did not seem to hear that. Instead he said, "You're a bit far from home."

"I guess we can all say that, sir."

Grant smiled. "I guess we can at that."

"General, Admiral Porter is waiting." The general's conscience whispered into his ear.

"Yes, Mister Rawlins, presently. I wish to talk to Mister Christie here. We are old sparring partners, met back in Columbus. Do you remember?"

"Yes, sir, kind of *you* to recall." Christie was in awe. Generals were like elephants!

To Rawlins, Grant reminisced. "I was trying to get a commission from General McClellan in Columbus. Never had the opportunity to even get to meet the man, but Mister Christie and his friends were accepted readily enough even without references. Speaks well of General McClellan's respect for quality. So you had better temper your impatience, Mister Rawlins—his date of service ranks ours." Grant nodded and turned to go. He had taken a few steps and turned back to an aide, "Oh, Lieutenant, you see to getting the corporal cleaned up with a new coat. I don't want him going back home dirty and complaining about our manners."

The officer nodded. "Yes, sir."

Grant prodded his adjutant. "Step lively, Mister Rawlins. Admiral Porter is expecting us.

IV
Up the Yazoo

Admiral Porter *was* already pacing the quarterdeck of his flagship. Not like Grant to be late when the war was ticking down. Porter was by nature an impatient man and ready to be done with the hornets' nests at Vicksburg, Port Gibson, and Baton Rouge and to get the Mississippi open to Union traffic. Unlike many career naval officers, he had no friends back in Washington except for Lincoln, who had raised him two grades and given him precisely that job. Now the president was being told that he had made a mistake, Porter needed hard victories to keep Lincoln's confidence. He and Grant had that in common.

Porter was striding the hurricane deck of the *Black Hawk* as if it were the front porch of his plantation home. A deck was all the real home he knew—he had been at sea since the age of ten. His father had served in the U.S. Navy in the War of 1812, his brother was Commodore William Porter, another brother was Captain "Dirty Dick" Porter, and his adopted brother was David Farragut, at work against the Confederate forces in Louisiana not many miles down river. Only his cousin, General Fits John Porter, a corps commander and a favorite of McClellan, had chosen a profession on land. Even in a family of steel-nerved old tars, this Porter was something of a black sheep.

At that moment David Porter's mind was on General Martin Luther Smith and the Confederate siege guns that guarded the Mississippi. Everything coming down on the river and everything riding the rails between Monroe, Louisiana, and the eastern Confederacy had to pass through Vicksburg. Cotton, horses, grazing beef, corn, and wheat—all keeping the Confederate pulse beating—moved up, down and sideways along these two important arteries of river and railroad that intersected at Vicksburg. Lincoln said that we must have that key in our pocket and he was right.

Porter slapped the rain off his cap. When he was excited with some new plan, as he now was, he fidgeted and twitched with static electricity. His voice was sharp and a tad high for such an imposing man who might have been mistaken for a deacon with his long beard and stern eyes. All this had set his crews to buzzing as to what the Old Guard was up to.

Grant boarded the flagship without fanfare and extended a hand. Porter stifled his shock. The general had never been a fashion plate, but Grant must have spent the morning with a spade working on one of his own canals. Porter straightened his countenance and went straight to the matter, motioning Grant to a cabin. With Rawlins hovering about, he could not offer Grant a drink, but a steward poured coffee as black as oil. They took their places around a table spread with maps.

"Look here, Sam, I think Mother Nature has finally given us an ace—a couple of them in fact." The embers of Porter's huge cigar highlighted a spider web of channels hinged to the main river. "Vicksburg is here. And here is the Yazoo River forming a 'V' where it connects to the Mississippi, with Haynes' Bluff on the eastern ridge. That, Sam, is our door of opportunity."

Grant had stared at these points on his own map so long and so often he knew them like the lines of his own hand. "Go on, Admiral. If you see opportunity in that quagmire of alligators, sloughs, snakes, and Confederates you have my respect and my full attention."

"Sam, there is more water there than the map indicates. In fact, the valley there is practically all under water."

Grant smiled. "Yes, I have heard rumors to that effect. The men are convinced that God forgot to separate the land and water here. You seem to think that is good news."

Porter nodded absently—infantry humor had always been a mystery to him. As he talked, his cigar trolled a line a quarter inch above the map, heading upstream along the first and closest waterway to the Mississippi marked as Cypress Bayou. The cigar proceeded northerly, still up Steele Bayou, then jabbed eastward a few inches following a channel called Black Bayou, that connected Steele Bayou with a larger channel called Deer Creek. The cigar angled again north along this Deer Creek line, away from Vicksburg, which was absolute south." Grant waited for Porter to make his point.

"As you see here, there is another eastern connector at Rolling Fork that dead-ends into the Sunflower River." Porter smiled triumphantly, but Grant still had not seen the purpose of all this steaming up and down. "The Sunflower is clear sailing south to the Yazoo, landing us here, midway between Vicksburg to the south and Yazoo City to the northeast. That puts us well behind those hornets' nests at Chickasaw Bayou and Haynes' Bluff, which should make your General Sherman very happy. In effect, we are prime to hit one and then the other from behind, where the Confederates least expect it." Porter tapped his ring on the table for emphasis. "In our case, the shortest distance between two points is not a straight line—we must go north to get south. Interesting proposition, wouldn't you say?"

Now Grant understood how Queen Isabella felt when another old salt preached the way to China was west. Still, it had possibilities. "How long will it take?"

"Four days tops, I'd say—going against the current most of the way will take longer to be sure, but it is probable. The Sunflower River flows south into the Yazoo down river at a point safe from Fort Pemberton, where the Confederates have a stopper in the works. If we have infantry support, I think we can make this ruse work and be in Vicksburg by the back door."

This was a grand leap of faith for Grant. But he knew that Porter would not underestimate the Confederates, who were not shy, stupid, or slow. The population of Mississippi cannot be deaf, dumb, and blind; several ironclads smoking past their front gardens would raise some curiosity. They would certainly set their commanders onto it immediately. Porter knew if he got his boats stuck up there, there would be hell to pay if they met firepower—or torpedoes. The ironclad *Cairo* was at the bottom of the Yazoo thanks to one already. But if Porter was willing to risk it, the idea was better than anything Grant had right now.

Porter kept on. "Lieutenant MacLeod Murphy, who skippers the *Carondelet,* has already surveyed a good section of this enterprise and is very optimistic."

"You say the route has been explored already?"

"Sufficient enough."

The two commanders puffed on their cigars, oblivious to the stores of gunpowder a few yards away. Grant studied the plan again then looked up uneasily. "How sufficient?"

"Enough to make me think that we can celebrate Easter dining on rabbit in the Grand Hotel."

Grant was still not convinced as to the fine points, even though he very much wanted to be. He would not want to march infantry through that morass of choked swamp and high water without assurances that there was enough land so they would not get separated from the boats.

Porter then played his ace: "Would the general care for an upstream cruise to see for himself?"

"Yes, the general most definitely would."

The little tug *Alert* back-watered out of the slip and came about into the spring current. Rawlins lit a cigar of his own. Grant was not pleased and showed it. The aide avoided his commander's scowl, but the first inhale detonated a coughing spasm that doubled him over. Grant glowered again. If drink were his poison, Rawlins' was cigars. But no amount of chastening had kept his friend from smoking them in profusion. Then and there Rawlins was the only man of his staff he trusted implicitly. The general offered his cup, but Rawlins shook his head. Grant pushed it at him and Rawlins took it.

Porter turned discreetly to Mac Murphy. "Your flask, please."

A jigger "warmed" Rawlins' coffee, but he did not raise it to his lips. Grant growled, "Drink it, John, drink it down. That's an order. Then go below and get out of this rain. I am not going anywhere."

Porter moved ahead out of the exhaust and Grant followed. There the fragrance of lilacs and magnolias wafted over the acrid fumes. Ashore the arbors were serenity itself except for the high flood marks left on the tallest oaks — water rose here at a furious rate. Porter signaled to the pilot for a hard turn into the state of Mississippi, and Grant stepped back as the bow parted a curtain of reeds and scrub. The landsman took the sounding, "Quarter less three!"

Grant brightened. He remembered Porter telling him that there is nothing a sailor hated more than a lee shore and no sea room. But this was more than twice what was needed. He allowed himself the luxury of hope. "Still, I don't remember this creek on the map."

Porter smiled triumphantly. "It's an old cotton road — the whole area is under water to a span of about four hundred miles or more."

"Can you count it will hold?"

"Don't matter — with this rain and the dikes you blew upriver, water still flows down hill and as long as it does, the creeks and bayous will overflow like rain barrels. So pray for more rain, Sam. This time it's on our side."

The *Alert* kept her speed and with every knot the implausible looked more possible. If Porter did not know the exact content of Grant's thoughts, he could guess pretty close. With a little luck they both might just be able to keep their commissions long enough to draw a decent pension. After a few more minutes of easy go, Grant nodded. He had seen enough and Porter ordered the tug to swing around.

Once on land, Grant went straight to his office. Sherman was already waiting for him. The Buckeye's face was phosphorus with anticipation. Rumors were on the wind and he saluted his commander impatiently. Grant extended his hand. "General Sherman, I think I have a gift for you."

The sapling cot stretched between four rough-hewn posts but held Christie's weight securely, only two inches above the rivulets of water and mud flowing beneath. The business with the Ninety-Sixth had gone efficiently, thanks to Boyd. So the corporal could indulge in that rare luxury—sleeping in. His cap and haversack dangled from prongs of a stripped branch planted at his head like a tombstone. A roll made of his pants and coat supported his head. Since he was not required at reveille, he was enjoying Boyd's hospitality a few minutes more until the transport left. Here the army still used the Sibley and big-walled tents, which repelled the elements better than the smaller tent-halves used in the east. Boyd had extended this hospitality to the rest of the company sergeants, who had come down late last evening.

Boyd and Company G had been proper hosts. The entire Fifteenth Iowa was unique even by western standards. They were hard-bitten men; a foreigner would judge them without humor. In fact, the estimation was unfair, for they had a great fondness for the joke, especially when it was played out against the one man they hated more than the Confederates, their commander Colonel Hugh T. Reid. And they had gone about that very business last night. Christie had been rudely shaken awake sometime after midnight. Inches from his nose, Boyd crooked a finger for him to follow but not to make a sound. A few brave stars twinkled through rifts in the clouds; otherwise the night was white foam. Out of the river mist prowled demons on a mission. Their faces were charcoal-blackened and anonymous, instead of rifles they carried brickbats.

"What the..." Christie startled awake.

"Just watch," Boyd whispered. "The show is about to start." About thirty men surrounded the cottage, keeping just out of sight of the sentries. "That's where Hugh T. sleeps. The war can be an inconvenience if you can't make friends."

For a few long seconds the inevitable hung heavy in the air. Thirty arms windmilled—faster and faster they churned. A sergeant wailed like a hound, and on his signal every man let his weapon fly. Brickbats smacked against the clapboard siding of the headquarters, exploding like volley fire. As soon as the missiles were airborne, the saboteurs retreated back into the tent city. There was nothing but empty when the window sash flew up and a moon-faced man leaned perilously over the sill. He screamed obscenities and shook his fist at the empty night. "Sentries! Catch those assassins and bring them to me!"

Squads with bayonets on their rifles took off to all four points of the compass. One villain who had hesitated too long caught their attention in particular.

Boyd grunted, "That's Sergeant Gray, a little slow in the head, but makes up for it by being fast on his feet."

Christie had never seen such speed or such cunning at dodging and weaving through and around tents and campfires. Gray charged through one tent and back out the other side evaporating into yet another, as cohorts found some pretext to obstruct the way of the pursuing guards. Men who pretended to be asleep tripped the sentries and cursed their bad manners when the guards fell over haversacks or knocked over rifles.

Reid mooed at his posse and pounded his fists against the sill. "Move! For damn sake! Move!"

The ending was told by the sad report of a "Curplosh!" Men groaned and waited. A deathly silence lay over the camp.

Reid thundered from his window. "Did you catch him? Bring him to me! I will have him shot! Shot! Do you all hear me, brigands and pirates, all of you!"

A private sashayed up behind Boyd with good news, "Gray fell into a hole of cook slop and stayed under till the guards passed. Then he took sanctuary down with the First Kansas. When the sentries came through he was snoring in a bedroll like a bear. Safe, but he smells a fright!"

The watch with long faces and slower steps reported the news to their commander.

"You let him get away? You let all of them get away? You call yourselves soldiers!" Reid leaned so far he nearly tipped out of the window, so enraged he was. "They could have carried me away in my nightshirt, right out the back door, and sold me to the Confederates for stogie butts! I want heads on a plate by reveille!"

Boyd made a mental note. "Two fine inspirations those are. Yes, indeed, I must share those with the boys."

"How long has this been going on?" Christie was barely in control of himself.

Boyd was not making any apologies. "Since the day the rooster was elected. This outfit has had the worst damned command, full of thieves and scoundrels. The first batch were all arrested before we even left Iowa. Reid's no scoundrel—he's too stupid and lazy. To his advantage, they promoted him. You hear 'all's fair in love and war'? Where there is no love lost, what's left? As the Good Book says, 'Vengeance is mine sayeth the Lord,' well *we* are His instruments! And it is divine!"

"One day you will be caught!"

Boyd rolled his eyes. "And do what with me? Demote me to private, so I don't have to make reports, lists of duty, sick leave, tend to the million duties of this shabby outfit, baby officers, my sergeant major, my company captain? Send me home? Threaten me some more!"

So far there had been no repercussions of the incident with Grant, and Christie wanted to be out of sight and out of mind before anyone thought to make more of the matter. It wouldn't look good on his record among the rest of his misdemeanors that he got into trouble out West on such short acquaintance. He had barely closed his one good eye for forty more winks, when a sergeant accompanied by two unpleasant looking privates stalked in, splashing up the housekeeping. A brogan the size of a river barge kicked the leg of the cot, nearly upending the sleeper into the rill. There were entirely too many sergeants in the army for any man's comfort.

"You might be Brenton Christie?"

"I am Corporal Christie."

The sergeant nodded. "You are wanted at headquarters."

"Me? What for?" The pass, the boat ticket home, and two weeks left on his medical furlough would all be trash if this took longer than an hour. "I don't know anybody here. Look, Sergeant..." Christie pulled pieces of script he had won in last night's poker game and handed them over. "This is all I have—I'll eat coal till I get home. You can just say you couldn't find me, and in less than an hour you'll be right."

The sergeant was insulted, either by the pitiful bribe or the affront to his code of honor. "Can't be doin' that, boyo. I am not privy to the purposes of the high command, I am just their little Gabriel sent to fetch you into the presence. Maybe they are digging another canal, and you ain't had that honor, I bet."

Perhaps Reid had seen the face of the stranger and reported him as mastermind of last night's assault. Perhaps one of them sold him out to save his own hide. Perhaps... It was a long walk to judgment for a man with a guilty conscience.

They stopped at the wharf, there a sergeant nodded to an officer who turned up the gangplank to report to the same officer who had fairly eaten Christie alive yesterday. Colonel Rawlins motioned the corporal aboard and preceded him through the door of the little cabin.

"General, we got him before he left." Rawlins reported.

Without looking up, Grant motioned the bewildered captive inside. All this hurry then went into slow gear. Christie was forgotten while Grant went back to his maps and finished his dispatches. Outside, the transport's whistle blared. Christie rooted his feet to the floor to keep from pacing. The general remained huddled behind his barricade of papers, unhurried. His concentration was total—his pen stopped only when the other hand sorted through one pile and then another for some facts or figures he required. Then it went back to work, oblivious to the pages of correspondence flying like autumn leaves to the floor. Christie picked them up, smoothed them out, and secured them under the saucer the general used as an ashtray. He pressed the little plate down, and waited.

Christie had misjudged, the rumpled papers buckled, tipping the dish about ten degrees. Yet the cigar held. Still, it wasn't enough of a distraction to bring the general to cases. The transport whistle sounded a final all-aboard, and through the porthole Christie saw the heavy smoke of the boat's impatient engines.

Grant reached for his cigar, drew on it, and replaced it automatically. Without the dead weight of the tobacco the saucer bobbed, tipped a fraction more, and when the stogie was replaced, rolled—first over the edge, then it kept rolling over the desk until dammed by a stack of morning reports and orders. While no one watched, the smoldering tip blackened away the corners, until a yellow lip flared. Then the laws of physics took over.

Grant snapped his gauntlets against the flame bringing Christie up smart. "For heaven's sake, Corporal, you are getting to be an inconvenience." The general was clearly agitated enough for some twelve-pounder expletives, but the language remained virgin. "You are going to burn my headquarters down around my ears."

"Sir, sorry, sir." With no gauntlets of his own, Christie beat at the flames with a rag from the general's desk. The two extinguished the blaze but not before half the paper trail of the war was ashes.

The commander examined a sliver incinerated right up to the letterhead. "Now, what could that have been?"

"Sir, if I may?" Christie stuttered. The ink smudge in the corner distinguished it as one of those he had retrieved from the floor. "It was a letter to General Sherman, sir."

"Which one?" Grant's eyebrow went up in a perfect question mark. "I had a few."

Christie swallowed hard, not sure how his "peculiarity" might be received. "I think it began..." Christie stuttered, "'Headquarters Department of the Tennessee; Before Vicksburg, March 16, 1863. General: You will proceed as early as practicable up Steele's Bayou and through Black Bayou to Deer Creek and thence with the gunboats...'"

"How did you know that?" Grant's face was opaque. It was hard for Christie to gauge what Grant was thinking.

"I saw it when I picked up the dispatch, sir. It had fallen on the floor."

"Those orders had to be three, four paragraphs. How much can you recite?"

"I only caught sight of the first paragraph, sir. I wasn't snooping or nothing. It's just an ability of memory, good for card-playing." Christie bit his tongue; the general did not approve of gambling. Yes, he was making a fine name of himself with the high-ups.

Grant leveled the corporal in his sights, "All right, I won't have you shot for spying or gaming. Now what did the rest of it say?"

Christie closed his eyes better to read the communiqué still laid out clearly in his mind. "Uh... 'and thence with the gunboats now there by any route they may take to get into the Yazoo River, for the purpose of determining the feasibility of getting an army through that route to the east bank of that river, and at a point from which they can set advantageously against Vicksburg...' That's about all I saw, sir"

"That's enough, Corporal. I remember the rest well enough to rewrite it."

"Thank you, sir. As I said, I wasn't..."

"Snooping or nothing. I remember." Grant had heard of such minds that could fix what they saw whole and entire and then recant it as if the printed page were in front of them. Scouts and spies had such talents — reliable ones — yes reliable ones, these were in short supply. Grant picked up his cigar and set it between his teeth to give himself time to consider how to handle this wonderful gift that had dropped into his lap — much too good for the likes of Joe Hooker. Originally, he had called the corporal in to carry some dispatches to Memphis and Cairo on his way home, but now they lay somewhere on his desk or had burned up. But they no longer mattered, since Rawlins had copies.

"At ease, Corporal, we are all friends here." Grant took the Kossuth hat from Christie. It was the "rag" the soldier had used to slap out the flames. Before it had been dried and brittle with clay; now it was also burned and withered. He fingered it as pretext to what came next, "Corporal."

"Yes, sir, I guess I can't get out of this one. I owe you a hat."

"My thoughts exactly, Corporal. Generals are not rich — not this one at least. Do you have, say, seven dollars on you?"

Christie gasped. "Seven dollars? No, sir! That's two weeks' pay and a little more if you buy it from the sutler."

"Yes, Corporal. We are in agreement. I calculate about two weeks. And I am of a mind to collect."

Christie was sure he would not like the path the commander was tracking. A scheme was forming behind those blue eyes, to make them twinkle like jacket brass. Christie counted his minutes. Outside the transport whistle was blowing all ahead full, so he had now quite literally missed the boat.

"Your regiment is back in winter camp in Falmouth, so they won't miss you until spring. Well, there has been no winter vacation out here—never has. We are not a bear that goes into hibernation with the snow. Can't afford it with the likes of Forrest, Van Dorn, and Bowen out there. We have a different kind of enemy here and he keeps us hard at it year round."

Grant's voice was as respectful as if he were talking to a man of equal rank about old friends. "Corporal, I need you here. You have talents aside from soldiering that could be very valuable. I especially need veterans on my staff—men of energy whom I can trust. Now if you are homesick for mud and bad food, I can fix you up with everything that will make you feel at home on the Mississippi." Grant flipped the lid on a humidor. "I hear you were wounded. I think I can give you some easy duty and time to heal."

Christie took the cigar offered and, with courtesies over, Grant got down to cases. "Corporal, my men have been fighting for inches, digging canals and slogging their way down this blasted river for an entire year. For every mile, we have paid the grim reaper in sickness, battle, and fatigue, not to mention casualties. As you just read, I am sending a division up the river with General Sherman, and I can't spare a man from my staff. I need a scout on board with Admiral Porter as a liaison from my headquarters—an infantry soldier who is able to see and understand what is happening around him from that point of view. I want you to study the interior as you go, find evidence of troop movements, numbers, old camps, any activity on the water and in the backcountry. How much cavalry, militia, and resistance are being organized of slaves by planters? Are the Confederates hoarding? Have they supply depots and stores secreted in barns and silos? What's the temperature of the people?

"I need you to scout out any prime points of advantage we can use as telegraph outposts when we finally take the ground... and we will take it. But you will see what the navy may not notice because it is too busy about its own business. It will take General Sherman a couple of days to organize his division and his transports and rendezvous with the navy. When he does, you report to him."

It was a tall order for one hat and the general was not through.

"I am very worried about Joe Johnston and Sterling Price. Van Dorn came within a hair's breath of capturing my wife last winter at Holly Springs. That could have been embarrassing. General Forrest in particular can be an unpleasant rascal, and I have not heard of him in several days. That makes me uncomfortable. He is lurking out there and plans mischief. I can't afford any more surprise visits. When the need presses, it presses hard and in a galloping hurry. Colonel Dodge is hard pressed with other duties, and his intelligence network is overworked and spread thin. I need eyes to keep me informed, and General Sherman as well. I hear from the ranks that you are quite at home on ships."

Christie's head bobbed. "You have been grievously misinformed, General." There was nothing wrong with Grant's intelligence.

"Well," Grant suppressed a smile, "I have the feeling that you won't let me down—in light of the fact you owe the price of two hats, and I am asking for the restitution of only one. You are an honorable fellow, so you will feel that I have given you the advantage on the bargain and hasten to volunteer. There also could be laurels, for you just might be in the vanguard that punches into Vicksburg. It'll get your name in the papers. Well, then maybe not, General Sherman will shoot the reporters first and the Confederates second." Grant was reputed to be at least tolerant of reporters, but Sherman's animosity bordered on the cannibalistic. Those were the terms. "Two weeks and we'll call the tab square, Corporal Christie. I'll handle things with Washington so that provost doesn't go looking for you with a noose."

Grant was cunning. It all sounded like a compliment, but it was the purest form of appropriation. The general said he could not spare a man, but since Christie was not *his* man...well, if anything happened to him up the Yazoo and he did not come back, Grant's rolls would show no deficit—business as usual. Christie knew as well there were probably some complicated hidden whys and wherefores that went unexplained in these orders and would turn up later. They might take time in revealing themselves, and would come just as the general said—when the situation presses hard. But Christie had no choice.

"At your service, General."

Grant nodded. "You begin at once. Porter leaves in an hour." Grant shouted to the door of the next cabin, "Mister Rawlins!" The adjutant entered, and as if by Divine Providence—but in effect the walls were thin—he carried the orders and transfer all ready for signature.

Grant's pen paused in midair. He crossed out a word here and there. "Let's give this man some rank or Porter will have him stoking fires." So Grant wrote Second Lieutenant instead of Corporal. "There, that will give him a front row seat to all proceedings, and he will be important enough to be in easy reach should he be needed." Grant turned to Christie, "Now, Lieutenant, get down to the quartermaster for some shoulder straps and whatever else you need so that you will look the part and not embarrass us in front of the navy. How about a sash and sword? You can have mine."

Christie winced.

Grant shrugged. "Okay, we'll pass on the sash and sword. But get a good revolver. I saw some alligators in those bayous yesterday as big as cypress logs."

Christie swallowed. Liaison? To Admiral Porter! What would the Fourth say? The Buckeye was stunned. Rawlins was beckoning to the door, the newly minted officer dream walked behind him. Rawlins was enjoying the effect immensely, "Well, Lieutenant, you can't say we aren't the land of opportunity. In less than twenty-four hours you dump a two-star general in the mud and are promoted two grades, with a raise to boot. Most men would have done the honor for free and willingly suffered thirty days in the stockade. How do you feel?"

"I'll reserve judgment, sir. As for the raise, it could be a thousand dollars—I'll see little of it. Our sergeant major saw early on that giving me money was like giving whiskey to Indians. Except for a few cents to keep body and soul together, he arranged for my pay to be sent to my mother. So you had better put that bonus in escrow. If anything happens to me, you will be trying to get the hat money from my mother—even General Grant doesn't have enough rank for that."

Rawlins filed the knowledge for later. "Here, Lieutenant. A bonus. My compliments." Several cigars were inserted into Christie's hand.

The brand new swallowtail followed at a respectful distance behind his commander, Major General U.S. Grant, who had come up to see the admiral off. They were piped aboard an ironclad, one of several lounging in the river. This one was the *Cincinnati*. The admiral was jovial and Grant affected some of the same manner, but Christie could tell it was forced. The two gathered in close conference with another officer about half the admiral's age, who Christie learned was the captain of the *Cincinnati* and Porter's nephew, Lieutenant Bache. In some minutes another officer, Lieutenant McLeod Murphy, captain of the *Carondelet*, stepped into the inner circle. All bowed heads over what commanders never had too many of — maps, this one Porter was spreading out on the fife rail. Christie moved away to find a vantagepoint where he would be inconspicuously conspicuous.

Men with lines in their hands were impatient to be in motion. The *Louisville,* Murphy's *Carondelet,* the *Mound City,* and the *Pittsburg* idled their engines until the commanders dotted the last "i's" and crossed the final "t's." Their colors rippled at the bottom of the mast, ready to salute the *Cincinnati*, now Porter's flagship, when she came about to assume her place ahead. Then they would up colors and steam up river, along with four tugs and two little mortar boats, and if all went well, to make naval history.

Christie climbed the stairs that separated the first and second fore cannon ports and walked to the left of the colors to the rail of the top deck, which the men were calling "the spar." He felt out of place in this new country. In the infantry, regiments were made up of men from one state and companies mostly from a particular county. Here men spoke in a hundred different accents from many different regions. They were stockier than the foot soldiers, but not the least bit slower.

Mates and Masters Mates barked orders he did not understand. The navy was a breed with a language and a method of its own that he would have to turn an ear to. Officers were in every kind of jacket in the way of a uniform that appeared convenient. Some wore round regulation pillbox caps with visors, others the cooler straw boaters with wide brims. Sailors, or "bluejackets" Christie heard them called, were not wearing jackets, but blue, yoked, jumper blouses with square back collars. Some were beautifully stitched across the breast, while others were plain. Trousers were of a dark color of duck or cotton; only he wore the heavy, pale blue, wool pants. Many sailors were barefooted and bareheaded, while others sported a pancake brimless hat.

Aft was the wheelhouse, the housing that enclosed the paddle wheel. To his left towered the double chimneys, perhaps twenty feet above, dwarfing the color staff. Two-thirds of the deck aft was tented in awning.

"They make a fine pair, your commander and mine, don't you think? Pride and Prejudice. Don't stand near the slaughter pen. Bad luck!" There was the extended hand of an officer about Christie's stature but perhaps ten years older. "Acting Lieutenant Richard Hall, acting assistant surgeon, acting at your service."

"Corporal Christie, at yours." He had nothing to answer, not sure exactly what Hall meant by his estimation.

"Corporal? A little humble aren't you, Lieutenant?"

It was a lapse with a long story behind it, but Christie tossed it off. "Promotions don't last, not for me anyway."

Hall nodded quizzically. He had a pleasant but unreadable face. His manner was reserved, yet he was the only man who had offered any sort of welcome. Sailors, Christie assumed, were like infantry companies, keeping to their own family. "I have been asked by Mister Pearce, our Master's Mate, to extend our hospitality, see you don't fall overboard, get shot, or get suckered into a poker game with the gunners. As soon as your commander disembarks we can begin the short tour of the *Cincinnati*."

Grant was folding his maps and Rawlins was leading the way to the rail and the tug waiting along side. Christie met him at the gunwales.

"Mister Christie, I hope you are optimistic—that will add to your popularity around here. If all goes well, our next meeting will be in Vicksburg. Let us hope our fortunes are turning. Good luck."

"Sir." Christie stiffened into a perfect palm-forward salute that would have impressed the old Fourth. Grant nodded and turned to go back to headquarters, there to hustle Sherman and his division that would follow. Bluejackets and officers regarded them in a by-the-way fashion, more than a few with a sideways glare and a curled-lip grimace—Grant's spy was staying. Christie was left in the custody of Assistant-Surgeon Hall, and he was beckoning. "You have a fine ship."

"Boat, Mister Christie. Ships ply the seas; boats steam the river. Ever been on an ironclad before?"

Christie shook his head. Nothing about being closed up below decks even for a little while appealed to an open-air warrior. But Hall was under full steam toward the ladder. Christie could only follow.

"These things look big from the bank, but they are quite small—a hundred seventy-five feet by fifty-one feet. There are nearly two hundred of us all doing a job, so we try extra hard not to get in each other's way. A man doesn't have many secrets living that close."

The warning had been passed, and having done that, Hall motioned him inside. The casemate was low and dank. "This is the gundeck, for obvious reasons." With the ports closed, a few lanterns burned a low flame, a compromise between caution and light. The effect was thirteen naval cannon in bass relief against whitewashed walls and deck. Eight thirty-two pounders and bigger were set four at port and four at starboard. Two forty-two-pounders and an eight-inch, sixty-four pounder army rifle rode fore, and a thirty-two-pounder and a thirty-pounder Parrott aft. This firepower made a soldier humble. These were siege guns—one of them could deal a deathblow to a medium-sized warship. The boat was a floating fort.

Hall continued unaffected by Christie's dismay. "Crew sleeps here among the cannon in the winter, topside when it's nice and they can bear the mosquitoes. Officers' quarters are aft. My office is in the medicine room starboard. You can bunk with me if you like in one of the convalescent racks. Captain's quarters is behind the paddlewheel, but if you ever have need of him, he's usually up by the pilot house."

Even at relief from battle stations it was hard to hear what Hall was saying. Every ping, whine, and knock of the engines reverberated inside Christie's temples. "I bet it is noisy when the guns are working and you are under full steam."

Hall nodded. "God in all his thunder. But the cannon are seldom all firing at one time—usually one side or another, fore or aft." Hall's shouts only added to the din. "You learn to filter out the machinery noise until you can go a little deaf. The headaches will kill you in the beginning. That's because the oak shell is covered by two and a half inches of iron. With enemy shells bouncing off the casemate, you feel like you're inside the bells of Notre Dame on Sunday. The galley is amid ships here," Hall led the way through the hatch. "And this...this is the fireroom. This is where the dragon is caged."

In the next step Christie descended into hell. Blistering sulfuric steam slapped him in the face, the air was heavy with oil and soot, and it seared into his lungs as he breathed. He wondered how anyone could work down in these dens without air. The engineer fixed him with a queer look, but said nothing and kept to his work, ranging never too far from the speaking tube connecting him to the pilot house and the captain.

At heart of it all was the phalanx of five giant boilers, nearly twenty-five feet long, convulsing the water to steam—the heartbeat of the great engines. Aft, the sheer power of the pistons and shafts was humbling. The steel glistened with grease and steam vapor; one mechanic did nothing but wipe them down and oil the joints to keep the long pistons pumping. These spidery legs turned the wheels pushing the beast through the water. Coal heavers, bare to the waist and covered in black sweat, fed the mouths of giant furnaces without stop. Was it the shadows or the dirt, but . . . ?

"Yes, Contraband," Hall was matter of fact. "They escape from the plantations and come right up to the wharf begging for jobs, usually bribing their way aboard with food and booty. There is always a shortage of strong backs and we take on as many runaways as we can, pay them regular. In the summer it gets twice as hot in here as an August day in hell, and it takes a lot of coal to move us even at a snail's pace, especially against the current. Field hands are used to the heat and work and hold to with no complaint. If we ever need some punch, our engineer has been known to throw a bottle of oil or even a tub of lard in the fire and tie down the safety valves. It could blow us to kingdom come, but when we had to get by the Confederate shells at Island No.10, it was good chemistry to know. We don't talk about it much with outsiders, so discretion will be appreciated. The coal is kept in holds down below, along with the stores and ordnance, I might add. You get religion riding one of these boats, knowing that this much fire is only a few feet away from powder and shell."

Hall could have stopped there, but the navy was never good at humility. "We are a different breed than the white-shirt, salt-water boys with their rigging and masts. We have a different job to do on the rivers, which run too shallow for ocean-sailing ships. We draft six—seven feet tops—compared to the seafarers' sixteen to nineteen. We can load up with artillery, ordnance, and coal and still steam on heavy dew, get in close to the shore to pound hell out whatever is close by. Lieutenant, taken as a sum we are the next best thing to a man of war. Multiply us by four, we can make a mighty big impression." Hall's sermon in a nutshell: Love me, love my boat.

"Impressive!" was all Christie said. The compliment didn't do the boat justice to Hall's mind. But in truth Christie had never seen anything that deserved respect and fear as all this.

"We have our Achilles heel for sure." Hall put in, "There's no iron plating on the port. These boilers are all above the water line. If they are hit and they rip, there will be no river rushing in to cool down the steam. Last June the *Mound City* was fighting it out with the Confederates outside Fort St. Charles up on the White River. She took a thirty-pounder rifle shot through the casemate. It came in through the rear and just forward of the armor. It killed eight men working the gun and the charge kept going, blowing the steam drums. The steam exploded into the gun deck above, cooking the men alive. Those on top or near a port jumped overboard. Rebels fired down on them before they hit the water. Then the boat drifted under the Confederate battery firing from the bluff. Rebs just kept hammering until the *Conestoga* could get a line on her and pull her out. The able-bodied tried to lay down some cover while the wounded were fished out of the water, but there was little we could do."

Hall's tone thinned to the barest whisper, "Eighty-two died outright when the casemate filled with steam, forty-three died in the water, twenty-five were so badly wounded that they were nearly as good as dead. I lost a friend Harry Browne and Captain Kilty. Better men never plied this river." Hall forgot himself in these memories, and when he recovered he was more determined that Christie understand the navy had held its own against the elephant. "The *Cincinnati* is a survivor! Rebs have tried to sink her more than once, blowing holes in her from all sides. But she still floats."

"How long you been aboard?"

"Last January, a year. We've done our share of the war with your General Grant. Fort Henry, Donelson, New Orleans, Island No. 10, and a hundred other little islands and elbows in this river that don't even have names. That was before the admiral up there; we were under Foote then. The *Cincinnati* is slow and a bit clumsy, like dancing with your fat Aunt Betty, but you love her when you see what she can do and how she will take care of you when the going is bad. You get to feel every part of her." Hall drew himself up taller by three inches. "It's my recruitment speech. We even have our own baseball team."

"The Fourth has a pretty fair one back in Virginia."

"What rules you play by?"

Without so much as a backward glance, Christie quipped, "*The Articles of War* — except when we play the Irish, then we hoist the black flag."

The day had now dulled under a tarnished copper sun, and Hall was taking his leave. "We'll see you at mess. We tell time and take orders by the bells and the fife. You will catch on to them soon enough."

The spar was cool and Christie was relieved that the flotilla was already well up the Yazoo. The banks were a theater of actors moving off stage — farmers were driving hogs and cattle into the glens for safety. From horseback, locals watched the progress of the black iron turtles, ready to pass the intelligence on to commanders who would do something about it. As the *Cincinnati* coursed, civilization thinned to a row of empty farms hidden behind barricades of reeds, high grass, and scrub.

At the rail, Porter loomed like a soot-grimed statue. To his eye he held a spyglass and he was scanning slowly up and down the bank. Not finding what he was looking for, he passed the glass up and back again. "It has grown up in the very short time since," he said to no one in particular. Somewhere around here Cypress Bayou forked north from the Yazoo. But the confluence that had been so obvious when the expedition had been scouted was now giving the admiral and the crew some anxious moments. Extra eyes lined the lower gunwales, to which Christie added his own.

"All things are in the sight of Providence," a bluejacket mused. Christie had no personal experience with divine revelation. But God must speak to commanders. Porter's glass still scanned the banks patiently, minutely, repeatedly—and then it paused.

"There, Mister Bache, ninety degrees to the starboard!" Porter erupted triumphantly.

Christie would take the admiral's word on it, he saw only a solid palisade of reeds and cane ahead. The lead tug heard the bells and came about to drive a wedge through the vegetation where the admiral pointed. The lumbering *Cincinnati* followed. Christie braced against the rail. The growth rolled beneath with barely a hiss but it was not so accommodating above. Branches burdened low with Spanish moss clawed against the stacks. A half-dozen crows pitched, swirled, and dove out of the way, squawking epithets on the black-skinned amphibians migrating into their domain. Clouds of gnats, mosquitoes, and bees mushroomed from the backsides of broad leaves. Bluejackets slapped them away. At first chance they would soak themselves down in cider vinegar, inciting a general stench that offended none but Christie. The *Louisville* closed in tight astern, and the rest of the flotilla followed the Old Guard like three blind mice plus two.

It was a portal not only of distance but also of time. The vaulted ceiling of live oak, cottonwoods, cypress, and sycamores clustered so densely the day lowed in perpetual evening. Their interlaced branches secluded a world of unbounded vastness where the water and land pushed and yielded creating pools, islands, and sandbars. Stretches of spiny marsh floated like carpets over channels and large ponds of open, black water. It was a netherworld with no compass, unbroken except for occasional blades of sun slicing through rifts above. There the water glowed to iridescence, bleaching the blossoms and vines that draped the titan trees like holiday bunting. Cypress knees spiked through the sandbar like stalactites. Bloodroot glowed and early lilacs wafted their thick perfume.

The pilot veered a zigzag course in and among the cypress and sycamores. Soundmen counted their knots and sang out, "A quarter less three." Then he dropped the weight over for another reading. That was fifteen feet of water for easy going. An alligator as long as a monitor slid off a rotted log. Not intimidated by ironclads or cannon, the prehistoric beast sashayed with barely a wake toward a raft of water lilies. "There goes one of Sherman's spies!" The watch smirked.

Christie turned to the surgeon, "What's he about?"

Right then, Hall's role of goodwill ambassador got thorny. "No offense, it's just a little joke at the infantry's expense."

Christie would not be put off. "If we are paying the freight, I think we should be let in on it."

With nowhere to go Hall could only surrender. "It is rumored when Sherman was up digging the Duckport canal, an alligator got hold of one of his soldiers. The beast was determined to drag the wretched man to his nest, shovel and all. The soldier called out for his general to save him. Sherman caught hold of the lizard's tail, swung him about, and yanked on the soldier's leg. But the alligator held fast. With no gun and no knife, the general took his cigar—a fine, expensive brand—and plunged it down between the alligator's jaws. The lizard let go of the soldier and sashayed away, puffing like a steamship. Next day, the alligator came back with another soldier in its mouth. The precedent having been set, Sherman exchanged him for another cigar. So, the alligator struck up a bargain with the general that he would leave his diggers alone and even do some scouting—for payment in good cigars. Truth, so help me!"

Hall's face was as serene as an elder who had just read the Sunday gospel. The war ticked down as the infantry and the navy battled eye-to-eye. It was Christie who broke, "My friend, you ever repeat that story around a regiment of good infantry and they will chase you back on this cheese box, weld its windows and doors shut and set it afire."

"That's hatches and ports, not windows and doors!" Hall corrected.

"Semantics will not slow them down. You will be rats in a Chinese rocket."

A couple of bluejackets were hissing like teakettles, but Christie could only take it in stride and wait his chance to score.

But revenge did not weigh heavily on his mind long. Here the war seemed like a hallucination. God was in His heaven, birds chorused from perches, the trees were in bloom, magnolias and lilacs clustered against shade trees, and verbena trailed along the mossy islands. Miles of such delights passed by the bow. Then more miles. Porter did not worry; even Hall did not seem to be worried.

But Christie was growing more impatient with every blissful minute they glided on without infantry. Lurking in this botanical wonderland could be local wildlife of a most unpleasant predatory nature—armed with Enfields. The vision of five thousand little rifles marching along side, each carried by a blue foot soldier, would give him some peace of mind. If there were some solid earth on which to march.

A boat could not get up and chase enemy over land. If attacked, boats even with big guns could not retreat and choose cover and set up behind a high ridge. They had to take it where they stood. Christie did not like riverboats—in the words of the navy, not enough lee room to maneuver for a foot soldier.

Hours passed. Christie was running out of deck to pace. Time stood still. He looked larboard and starboard; there was no sign of Sherman. Sherman was not a handsome man, but right then any sign of his grizzled scowl would have been a beatific vision. Christie almost prayed.

For the past several minutes Porter had been cursing a map that sliced Mississippi up in four- by six-inch squares. He saved a fair measure for the pilot. Deer Creek was not where it was supposed to be. The admiral's maps, Christie had seen, were not as good as Grant's. Porter's were drawn on conjecture and some old sailor's faulty memory. But the pilot had bartered a bonus against boasts that he knew the route intuitively that he could take the navy to the Sunflower without a zig or a zag. However, the pilot was not quite so sure now.

Porter was not pleased. The pilot ignored the admiral's insolence; he was an independent river man, a civilian, a deity in his own realm. The two were not getting on well, and the pilot locked Porter out of the wheelhouse, speaking to him only through the window. It was a grudge Porter would never forget.

But this was the here and now. Porter turned from map to pilot and back again. The map showed the creek to be right here but it wasn't. The pilot's memory showed it to be right over there, but it wasn't. Porter demanded that the pilot produce Deer Creek or suffer the consequences—those he did not state in any detail, but every man understood them to be awful in the extreme. Their actual expression Porter would remember for his reports as temperate. But for Rawlins, Christie recounted them to be a veritable aria of blasphemy at the pilot, at the map, and at the Mississippi in general. Both the vigor and poetry struck the Galena lawyer dumb with respectful awe.

On his own the admiral put numbers to paper, rate times time, estimating they had traveled far enough. But direction was hard to point. He drew a bearing on his charts and then studied the terrain. After some cross-referencing, he pointed to a stand of high reeds and vines that closed up what he estimated to be the entrance to Black Bayou. Bluejackets stripped down, then eased themselves over the side and with scythes and saws worked to cut back the primeval jungle blocking the way. When they were done the admiral was proved right again.

"This is where fact leaves off and theory begins," Christie assumed and resumed his pacing. The boat was growing smaller with each lap around the spar. The bluejackets called Black Bayou a "channel"; Christie called it a "ditch." In fact it was no wider than a canal with obstacles spiking up everywhere, with banks giving the boat barely two feet to spare. The navy took a page from cavalry tactics: when you can't go around or over, the only other direction is through. The *Cincinnati* split through cart bridges and sheered away docks from their banks. Red River boats and rafts were crushed between the gunwales of the great dreadnoughts and the creek banks.

One after another the barriers were challenged and vanquished, until a line of bald cypress stood in the right of way. Centuries had given them bulk and made them stubborn. Porter gave the order to take them out by brute force. If asked, Christie would have counseled for caution, less bravado, and perhaps a snag boat. But Porter had not brought any of the three along.

"Full steam ahead!"

At the rate of three knots, nine hundred tons of iron and oak bore down on the first specimen. The boat knocked and reverberated. The paddles pushed the bow into the old titan, but not a branch shuddered. The engines surged, the relief valve wailed, the engineer upped steam, the paddles churned but the tree held.

"Back water and come at her twenty degrees to the right oblique!" Porter roared to the pilot.

The *Cincinnati* did so. Christie braced at the rail as she came on; three inches of bark were carved away. But otherwise she ricocheted to the left. Porter would not be defeated. He came again from the left, with no success except for a knick or two.

"At this rate you can cut her away three inches at a go, bringing her down in about six months." Christie thought his observation was at least as funny as the Sherman joke, but Hall and his mates were stoic.

The ironclad lined up on her again. The paddles windmilled and the gears hammered.

"All ahead full!"

In the end, Porter's will be done. The shallow roots tore away from the mud bottom, and the old tree smashed into the water to a chorus of huzzahs.

The process then became routine. Trees tumbled and were pulled one after another as the *Cincinnati* bore its way into the vitals of the Confederacy.

"You are such a puritan! Do you ever smile!" An officer asked as he handed Christie a cup.

Hall slapped his guest on the back. "Mister Christie, this is Henry Booby, acting master's mate. He really commands the ship or thinks he does and he takes all slights personal. You might as well get the entire roster. The guy over there, watching all this arm wrestling with the trees with no enthusiasm, that's Stevens, the ship's carpenter. He has to repair the damage if the tree wins. He's become a master at patching her up, but doesn't like the practice."

On hearing his name, Stevens nodded. "Aye. That's enough destruction for one day. We'll be dropping anchor here for the night, and let's pray for caution and open channels tomorrow. The admiral contends about four more miles tomorrow and we'll be in Deer Creek. If so, we will be celebrating St. Patrick's Day with General Sherman. I hope he is preparing a suitable reception."

Booby clanged his cup against Christie's, "Drink up—cuts the soot off the throat! And chew on this. We call it junk, I think you call it salthorse."

A rose by any other name was still quartermaster-issue bacon fat and it slid down Christie's throat like soap. Then the circle received Master's Mate Pearce, "When we get the boat secured, the cook will send up some mess. I smell dandyfunk."

"That would be a welcome addition to this," Christie sneered at the last in his hand.

"Even got some raisins to put in it, Lieutenant." An innocent illuminated by almond eyes pulled a small jar from under his shirt for Christie's inspection. "I am Henri, no last name, just Henri. See—real raisins."

The lid was festooned in the same calico as the shirt that overflowed the child like a choir robe. Christie examined both the shirt and the jar more closely. "Wait! Those are my mother's raisins! She sent them down with the ladies' aid supplies. You raided my mother's crates? I feel sorry for you! Wait until the Ninety-Sixth hears about this, Shiloh will be a footnote compared to real bloodshed!" Christie reached for the cabin boy. He ducked between Pearce and Hall as they pressed the Buckeye back.

"Now, Mister Christie. You down-home boys must learn to share. Your mother wouldn't want you to go off to dinner with the navy and not bring something for the host."

Christie relented. "You know, she wouldn't give me so much as a spoonful to test. The boy did me a service at that. But how did he outsmart the provost?"

Pearce had finally a subject to sweeten his disposition. "Found him stowed away in our stores out of Memphis. Made him ship's boy, since there were no other takers. His mother was a…" It wasn't that Pearce had a problem with the word "whore," but he had come to love the boy and respect his sheer genius for survival. "Well, Henri here is the fruits of her profession. When the Confederates surrendered, she took off with the army. Uh, I don't know why this is so hard to explain, Lieutenant, except that Henri is entitled to more respect than the circumstances of his birth would seem. Knows the river from Cairo to New Orleans won't say how he knows it but he does for sure. And he can cook, which makes him twenty-four-karat."

"Thank you, sir." Henri bowed, then pressed into Christie's hands a bowl of rattlesnake soup.

"Henri, how old are you?" Christie tried to sound offhanded. But that reflex to escape crossed the boy's eyes again.

"Eleven!" he snapped.

"If I were to ask the Creator how old you were, what would *He* say?"

Perhaps it was that one orphan knows another but Henri instinctively drew closer to Christie at the feel of his hand lightly set upon his shoulder.

"If He remembered me at all—I doubt if He does—I guess He would put me at about nine. Now, excuse me, sir, I got chores."

Pearce pitched the contents of his cup overboard. "Excuse me, gentlemen. I have to put the boat to bed. Mister Booby, will you see to setting out the guard? Enjoy your repast, Mister Christie. Now you are going to find out that you have booked a first-class passage. We eat better than you timber wolves in the infantry."

The night purred with the low talk of men who worked as close as body and soul all day, yet found news to discuss at night.

"I wonder if Jenny had our baby by now. If it's a boy, I will name him Abraham, but if it's a girl, I think Elizabeth—after her mother."

Another bent close to a cousin unfolding the last letter that tethered them to home. "Maybe, Mom beat the fever, but with her heart—well, what does Aunt Haddy say again?"

Up and down the line, like fire sparks piercing the evening breeze:

"I've heard nothing from Tim since Fredericksburg. You ain't got a newspaper do you, Cobb?"

"Anyone hear about a late frost in Ripley?"

"The Sunday school is having a fair to buy Bibles for us."

"Who stole chapter six out of *Madame Bovary*? Hawke, was that you?"

From the *Carondelet* a mouth organ hummed the little Shaker jig "Simple Gifts." The spirit infected a few singers and the song wafted through the dull smoky gloom. Christie tried to shake the effects away. Nolan and Quinn had sung it around the campfires. Rather Quinn had sung it in his rich tenor. Nolan was tone deaf but loved it just the same. Christie felt a haunting. Old friends breathed over his shoulder. He pulled himself up the ladder to the spar and crossed the casemate for a square foot of solitude in the press of men. He found it and settled down by the wheelhouse. But he was not alone long.

"Want a little game, Lieutenant?" It was Henri working a deck of cards through his fingers.

"Henri, why don't you take your business down to the *Pittsburg*. They got some new infantry on crew. They should be ripe. Take Mister Chance, in case you need him."

The cards disappeared into the cabin boy's pocket.

"You let Henri play cards with soldiers?" Christie shook his head at Hall's negligence of the boy's upbringing.

Hall despaired that all infantry could be so naive. "Henri, cut Mister Christie four aces. Just four, mind, and of different suits, to make it look honest."

The cards closed up between his little palms, shuffled, and fanned. He snapped them shut, and shuffled again. ("Never trust river men they are all liars and pagans.") Without taking his eyes off the Buckeye's face, Henri flicked out four aces.

Christie was impressed but not convinced. "Card tricks are one thing, poker another."

"Henri, deal Mister Christie a good hand — not a winning one — just enough to give him hope."

The boy offered the lieutenant the deck. Christie inspected it in the lantern light: Except for wear, no suspicious creases or cracks. Christie cut them once, and for good measure cut them again, then passed them back. Henri sliced the deck in two, shuffled them together without so much as a hiss, and kneaded them back into his palm. In a blur he dealt two piles of five.

Christie took up his hand. It had potential — three, four, seven of hearts and the six and eight of clubs. "Take two," he said and discarded his black cards. He was rewarded with two more hearts and laid them out. "Flush."

"Full house, tens over." Henri grinned.

"Henri, now deal Mister Christie what he needed to fill

that straight."

If he still believed in miracles, Christie would swear on a stack of Bibles that the boy thumbed a five and six of hearts right off the top.

"There you are, Lieutenant, a straight flush, if you had had only a bribe for the dealer."

"Where'd you learn to play like that?" Christie gave his cards back to Henri, and he slapped them in the deck.

"Natchez-Under-The-Hill—there was a boat my mother worked on." Unused to being confessed, the story came in whispered tones and deep breaths. "I used to watch while I blackened men's boots for two bits and a drink from their glass. I learned real good. One gentleman came to see my mother a lot and he was nice to me, let me ride sometimes in the saddle with him on this fine big bay. He taught me some, but he died, caught between two queens, my mother and some lady who shot him dead when he wasn't lookin'."

Henri shook a chill away and his voice was now matter of fact. "Mister Hall, Mister Chance and me will go visit the *Pittsburg* now." Christie watched Henri go, leaping from ship to ship, stern to bow, greeting his mates as he passed.

"He doesn't take advantage—cheats enough to just get by, so nobody minds." Hall turned back to his duties as host, or his duties to gather information on Grant's plans. "Now, it's not good for man to be alone." Hall waved a flask and two cups. The perfume of whiskey wafted under the Buckeye's nose.

"That's why God invented women, not officers."

Hall pivoted to go, but Christie caught him by the arm. "I apologize for that. I surely do."

"A man's mind can be crowded enough without company," Hall whispered. "I'll leave you to your thoughts, if you like."

"No! Even dead, they are unsavory company."

"They sound like my kind of people. I would be honored if you would introduce me." Heavy-soled shoes scuffed against the hard oak deck, then Hall went quiet waiting for Christie to take his own good time.

"I was thinking on West Virginia. God, things were clearer then. We knew it all better than the generals and were offended they never asked our opinion. Now we know twice as much and are only half as cocky. I had three mates, as different we were as the seasons and as inseparable. As far as the army was concerned, we made a bad stew—got into trouble regularly. Captain Crawford thought he would break us up and put us in separate companies, but our sergeant major took a personal hand in our rehabilitation and thought keeping us together would be easier than keeping an eye on us piecemeal. So our redemption became his personal mission. Quite an honor, if you can get by the inconvenience."

"Are they waiting for you back in Virginia?"

Christie swallowed a dry lump. "Jamie died at Harrison's Landing last summer. Even when he died, something of him stayed with us all the time. Then Quinn died at Fredericksburg. Nolan, if he isn't dead yet, is in a hospital in Alexandria without a leg. I feel like a widow. But you don't stop talking to them, bringing them with you even if they are gone. They got a vested interest in the outcome of this war. Once a member always a member."

"We heard about Fredericksburg. You guys from Ohio were first up I read."

"Yeah, we were. But I don't like to think on it, because it fills up your whole mind with rage and makes you crazy for too long. When I have a choice, I like to go back in my mind to the early days. Those times were golden."

Hall encouraged him to go there. "Western Virginia—what was that like?"

"A lot like here—cold, muddy and wet—but we cleared out the Confederates and gave the Union the good half of Virginia. After we fought all spring and all summer, the good fellows in the war department had us build Fort Pemberton up in the Maryland hills to hibernate for the winter—keeping us a safe distance from Washington or Washington a safe distance from us. When we got it snug, the army moved us again."

Christie's ghosts were turning to flesh, "Never saw so much snow! It started almost before the leaves changed. Holed up like bears in Romney nearly went crazy with boredom. Fights broke out over nothing just to let off steam and get some exercise. One night somebody from "C" broke a tooth in a brawl over a card game with some of the Seventh West Virginia boys out of Grafton. Boy, can those Irish cheat—better than us! Anyway, it wasn't the first, not the last, and this fight wasn't the worst.

"But I guess the high-ups had had enough, Sergeant Major Chase remanded all the cards and dice until tempers cooled. Told us to do something with our minds beside sin. He was a fine one to talk. That man could command four aces out of a new deck faster than God could make the lame walk. He and Henri would have made a fine pair."

With the conditions explained, Christie got down to cases, "Well, the next night one of the Seventh had made up a new deck—with two extra aces that he kept in reserve up a sleeve—and then we went at it again, just dealing justice. Then the sergeant major went at *us* again. But just us four, as if we were the cause. Not true, we were the finish, and the evidence was all slander! He sat us all down and threw a book at Nolan and told him to read it to the assembled. And to see that he did—Nolan could sometimes be an authority unto himself, even before he got stripes—Sergeant Chase eased down behind him like his guardian angel. Nolan found the start and proceeded with the dramatis personae of *Romeo and Juliet*. A tragedy.

"Doctor, was it ever! Nolan was smart, but he didn't have much formal education. With the first page, we knew this was going to be painful. What he read wasn't English to our understanding, but there was enough English in there to let you know it was supposed to be English and not Russian or Hindi. It was terrible! Nolan twisted and turned around the corners of couplets and ricocheted off the pentameter. The boy had no rhythm at all. I asked Sergeant Chase to let me read it, but Chase just shook his head and motioned for Nolan to continue. See, the sergeant was Ulster Irish, and I think he had it in for us real Irish of the emerald color but couldn't do anything about it under the military code. So he just sat back with this half-moon smile on his face, taking out three centuries of revenge with compounded interest. Sometimes he would make Nolan stop and reread a passage two or three times, just to watch us shudder. We got to detest Nolan as the instrument of our punishment. So we shunned him, which hurt him, we could tell."

The coffee wasn't hot anymore, but the whiskey was

taking over. A blessing upon the head of the naval surgeon who understood the pain of the soul and its medicines.

Christie's voice hummed, as if he were more there than here, "Night after night for a week Chase called us together and reread the charges, then Nolan was again ordered to continue with the 'Mont-é-gues' and the 'Capit-ú-lates'. We went through it about four times, but *Romeo and Juliet* finally came to an end — everyone dead, which was a satisfaction and a fulfillment of our curses all along. Chase gave us back our cards and warned that the captain had a copy of *The Complete Works of Shakespeare* in his quarters — it could be a long winter if we weren't reformed."

Hall smiled. "Four saints, I bet. The army's version of the rack, cruel and effective, even if flogging were more benevolent."

"Well three-quarters of us *were* ready to be reformed if only for a little while, and put the hard time behind us, but not the Scot. Jamie got the idea that maybe the torture wasn't Nolan's fault at all — maybe the fault was that the play had to be acted to be appreciated. So he made his mind up that we should all 'see the elephant' so to speak — put on the play for the company. And his mind would not be changed. He was sure that the snow and the boredom would make the men appreciate something else besides card cheating, but we would disarm them just in case. It was us or what the colonels had planned — drill, lectures on *The Customs of the Soldier*, and there was some talk about a preacher and a revival. Are you still awake?"

"Go on." Right then, Hall was sympathizing with Sir William and wondered whether he himself would have approved of such a plan to turn his tragedy into comedy. But the army will have its way.

Christie was oblivious to such abstractions and continued, "Well, the officers wouldn't give us permission — afraid of a brawl. Nolan said it was because they didn't think we were smart enough to put on Shakespeare. True or not, that only made us more determined. Since it was his idea we made Jamie play Juliet. He was the only one without a real beard yet. He struggled but we dressed him in a gunnysack and topped him with a wig of hemp braids down his shoulders. Oh, was he ugly! He'd lean down from the ladder and swoon into Nolan's face, 'Romeo, O Romeo, where for art thou, Romeo?'

"Hell-bent as he was, Nolan still had his limits. He told us we were crazy if we thought he was kissing that face! Well our little troupe rehearsed with spirit and spirits of the liquid kind, and the day came. Most of the regiment showed up for the performance—goes to show how desperate they were. We set out pickets to keep an eye for officers, then raised the curtain. Well, the boys were enjoying it all pretty well, although they were laughing and jeering so hard that they were rolling on the floor and crying. Then one of the Capulets using his musket as a pike in the street scuffle—dropped it. It went off like thunder! A ball snapped 'Tybalt' in the leg, and he rolled up tight screaming the worst profanity Shakespeare never dreamed of. We all beat out of there, leaving him to his profane soliloquy. He was in costume when the officers arrived, so they deduced what we had been up to. He was taken off moaning and whining, even though the ball barely grazed him. The lieutenant found the script and questioned him about it. The man crossed two fingers and howled like a hound at the moon. No more was said."

IV
The Sky Is Falling

Other ghosts were afoot in the night. An unbidden spirit came to seduce and then leave one of them hollow and craving. Iridescent as a flame, she knelt to caress his forehead then stroked down his cheek and finally lingered over his lips. She pressed so near he could kiss her. "Julia."

Hall stirred. Christie must be reliving the play in his dream. Hall shrugged and turned back to sleep.

"Julia" Christie called the name again. Unrequited desire stirred him awake, and her flame extinguished into the darkness. Christie called her back but she was gone.

What Christie would not give for a good old-fashioned forced march right now to stretch out his legs and clear the phantoms from his mind. He shook himself out and stepped over the other sleepers.

Pearce had just rotated the "dog" watch and was pouring himself another cup from the two-gallon pot hanging from the ladder. "Drink up—it's fresh. It'll be first light soon."

"Where is everybody?"

"Admiral gave the word for the gunners to sleep below and be at the ready. I think the easy sailing is done. We are going on faith in the Old Man from here out."

"When we started tearing away trees, docks, and boats, I thought we were exploring virgin territory. You concerned?"

"Yeah, I'm concerned." Pearce kept his voice low, but he had already decided to trust Grant's spy whose motives may be good or ill. But Christie had more experience with skirmishes and bush attacks than he did. "Last night I took a few men ahead. The banks are rising, the water line dropping, and the channel is narrowing. Getting these boats over to Deer Creek is going to be a tight fit. If we get wedged in up there, there's going to be hell to pay. And there's something else. Do you feel it?"

"Oh, yes, I feel it—too quiet out there. It's spring, and there's no plowing, no livestock grazing, not even a farm hound! Where did everybody go?"

Pearce shrugged. "Porter's not one to molest the citizenry, so they have nothing to fear from us. But they have gone to ground—for only one reason I can think of—they don't want to be in the cross fire. So my feeling is something is coming. But that is between us, not for *general* consumption, if you get my drift."

"I get your drift."

The master's mate was moving away, but Christie added, "Mister Pearce, I'm not just another pretty face. I'm used to working for my pay. I'm here if you need me."

"I'll keep it in mind."

Sherman could walk on water—or so it seemed. He had come up by tug ahead of his first detachments still being loaded on transports. The other two-thirds of his division was tramping by the long route—straight east from Eagle's Bend. As the last of Porter's flotilla was winding into Deer Creek, word came ahead to the *Cincinnati* that the general was at Hill's Plantation at the confluence of Deer Creek and Black Bayou. Porter doubled back, and when he saw the redheaded Buckeye waving from the bank, he hailed the general like a long lost son. Porter's elation was dulled only by the disappointment that, so far, Sherman was without a command at his back, especially those precious pioneers who could chop away a clear pass for his boats.

The admiral was a pillar of dark smoke beside Sherman's red flame. He shook Porter's hand heartily, "Nothing better in this war than a good pair of feet, Admiral. My pioneers and Mister Smith's Eighth Missouri boys are nearly up and the division is close behind. But we need something to walk on. Land, Admiral. Have you seen any?"

In truth Porter had not seen much of it, not in long stretches to suit infantry. The Deer Creek road, which was nothing more than a meandering farm path running along the upper bank, was washed out in sections, overgrown and broken with run-off in others.

"Unforgiving country this, but it is beautiful, General."

"I've seen it before. You remember, Admiral, I lived in the South before the war. I know every inch of this land we are tending to. It floods at a drop and dries up in an afternoon. It's a beautiful place—when it's peaceful. But when it's not, there is enough of men, insects, and two- and four-legged carnivores to make it damned unpleasant."

"You are still upset about the sharpshooters."

Sherman's jaw set tightly behind a brush of brass-colored whiskers. "Damned ungrateful! Some would have us make this war into a crusade to free the blacks. But there they were, rimming the lip of Chickasaw Bluffs and firing down on us like fish in a barrel—right on the eve of Emancipation. I would have Mister Garrison and his *Liberator* brigade of fire-breathing abolitionists to have seen them. That would have been stuff for an editorial I would like to read."

"You got the worst of a bad bargain, and that's the truth of it. No way to ring in the New Year, but we will even the score before it rings out. You remember what I said."

There was nothing about that travesty on Chickasaw Bluffs that Sherman would ever forget, "'We'll have Vicksburg yet, before we die,' I think you said. But, my dear Admiral, that can be a long time in coming. I plan to live a long life, and have done with this business by whatever means, with a lot of years left over."

Dispositions warmed with succeeding glasses of whiskey. After dinner the two commanders engaged in a contest of reminiscences and tall stories for the enjoyment of their officers.

Christie could not find in the animated Buckeye the gargoyle or the madman that the newspapers made of him. He was sharp-eyed, and even in a relaxed setting, shrewd and careful with his words. And there was no pretense or rank here. Sherman sprinkled his company with officers of every grade and unabashedly told stories out of school about fellow commanders.

"That Rosy is a fine general, but don't ever get him on the subject of soap. Then he becomes an engineer—and you know how boring they are. He is an expert on the subject and will hold you to the campfire for hours on hours on every chemical formula on the subject. He doesn't sleep, so he doesn't care how long it takes to explain all the whys and wherefores until you nod off. He is laudanum in shoulder straps."

The two commanders recounted each his part in the Battle of Fort Hindman on the Arkansas, but Porter took first laurels. "Hauled the cannon upside the hurricane deck, then wheeled the *Black Hawk* right along side their walls. When they saw the guns bearing down on their heads, the Rebels changed their mind about holding out till kingdom come."

"Or they thought it was coming a lot sooner than prophesied." Sherman raised a toast to the navy. It had been his infantry Porter supported. "Whiskey Smith said the Confederates weren't about to surrender in a dog's year. The Rebel captain was apoplectic—as red as his hair."

"Angry indeed, General, but I would be intimidated more if he were as red as your hair!" Porter jibed behind his upturned glass.

It was late when the party broke up. Christie was turning below, but Sherman caught his eye. "If you will excuse me, Admiral, I think you have one of our prodigals and I have need of him for a few minutes."

The two Buckeyes moved to the privacy of the bank. Sherman tipped an unlit cigar between his teeth—no reason to light up a two-star target for a Rebel sharpshooter. After surveying the jungle for some minutes, Sherman broke the silence. "What have you to tell me?"

"It's very quiet out there, sir, very quiet. I am pretty much shackled to the decks here. Not that I can't reconnoiter and catch up downstream—the boats aren't moving that fast. But the admiral likes to keep all his hands accounted for."

Sherman's patience was fraying around the edges. "I don't like this little expedition, not one bit. But I will be the happiest man if the admiral proves me wrong. My son Willy says that the only difference between 'blunder' and 'plunder' is the direction of the lead figure. He'll make a fine soldier some day with a mind like that.

"If Porter gets himself trapped up in the backwater Jeff Davis will have himself some fancy gunboats if there is no time to blow them up. I don't know whether I can even march a squad through this swamp, let alone a division and keep it intact. This ditch is too narrow for transports. I've got men strung out all the way back to the Mississippi. It's no better country where you're going, I can tell you. You up there and us down here coming up piecemeal. If this goes to hell, Lieutenant, the reporters will be feasting on my bones in the front pages. Well, that's not your problem."

Christie begged to differ. "With all due respect, sir, if we come to grief, it will be very much my problem. I will be in the bag with Admiral Porter, if you please, and as you said, you will be back here."

Deer Creek wound ten miles of snake tails. With less than a foot on each side, the *Cincinnati* inched upstream, tearing away everything in its path. Pearce greased the bulwarks to slide. If the banks were closing in, they were also rising over. Mister Ribbitt, the gunnery officer, did not like it. If trouble came, his starboard and port cannon could not be sighted high enough to clear a shell over the banks. Somebody joked that every man should relieve himself over the side and spit to bring up the water level. And there was the growing tension of men who feel like waiting targets. Bales of cotton were confiscated from the banks and piled along the gunwales for cover against sniper fire.

"Mister Hall, I hope you tars are a strong lot." Christie jabbed at the air ahead, "We may just have to get out and push or even hoist these *boats* on our shoulders and portage them." Words closer to prophesy than humor; it had taken torturous hours to maneuver barely a quarter mile. The ironclads behind were jammed stem to stern, twisted and turning in the elbows and bends of the stream to every conceivable direction on the compass. Lieutenant Murphy was beginning to show signs of the strain. He had come up to the *Cincinnati* to confer with Porter and see what God had wrought for them.

If there were not a Testament passage warning commanders that it was easier for a war ship to pass through an eye of a needle than through the savage wilds of the Confederacy, there should have been. The old music of low bowing branches scraping paint from the exhaust funnels brought eyes up skyward. As the boats went further, the jungle grasped them tighter to keep them back. Balanced on hogsheads of cotton, bluejackets, with axes and cutlasses in hand, tore and hacked at a thousand boughs that reached down from the sky. Even as the crew released a grill from the grasp of one vine, another branch intertwined its leafy tentacle into a railing. Then a frond slithered around a cable, or a bough pulled at the chimney, or a dead spike knifed through the awning.

Unholy noises of saws, chains, and chisels rasped deep within the engine hold and they rang through the backlands mixing eerily with the croak of bullfrogs, the cries of panthers, and the siren of birds. With the slightest twitch, mosquitoes, gnats, and no-see-ems exploded from under broad leaves and vine-choked branches, churning into a black cloud going straight for blood. Crewmen could only endure—they had not hands enough to slap them away, so busy they were against the forces that literally threatened to pull their boat apart.

Below the water line, men worked to free the gears and cogs strangled in weeds. Still a third squad labored upstream pulling stumps and debris out of their path. The *Cincinnati* could not "ahead" enough steam to break free, hit them hard, and take them out by force. Gears screamed and engines hammered, men cursed harder, and officers barked orders. For it all, hours ticked and the *Cincinnati* curled no wake. If the boat made free of one snair it drifted into another. With each foot into the primeval forest the *Cincinnati* took another wound. To the left, a railing cracked away. Then the flagpole snapped in two, and a bluejacket fastened the colors to the railing. Crewmen shimmied up the chimney with knives and cutlasses to be ready against what closed down on them next. It was then that it all came to crisis. The grill braced between the two, twenty-foot funnels hooked itself into a branch.

The ironclad floated on beneath. The stacks tilted. Strong shoulders pressed to set them aright.

Every bluejacket who heard the whine of metal never forgot what came next. When it was over men argued if Porter had ordered a full stop the outcome would have been different. But eight hundred tons, even in slow motion, does not stop even on an admiral's order, so it was academic — a tug of war the boat could not win. Men could only ride it out — watch, wait, and then get out of the way.

The vine whipped taut. Bluejackets three deep put more muscle to the stacks and heaved. Christie added his to those pulling at the supporting cables. It was not enough. The great chimneys angled astern. Men pushed harder. Rivets popped, fissures split crossways, then the grill snapped away and rocked back and forth in the branches. High and alone the chimneys swayed like ten pins.

"She's breaking! Clear away!"

In a clap of thunder the first snapped mid-length, and collapsed to the deck. As men scrambled the second came crashing through the skylight into the guns below. Shards of iron, glass, and wood flew like deadly shrapnel. The spar disappeared in a mushroom cloud of creosote and ash. In anticlimax, the grill came last pulling down half the forest ceiling and all that had called the jungle lofts home. The decks were in pandemonium! Sailors jumped and danced around muskrats, mice, squirrels and raccoons — and not too few snakes and lizards. Crew came at them with every kind of weapon, from pikes and cutlasses to brooms and shovels.

"Clear the decks!" shouted Henry Booby shielding his head with a barrel lid and swishing a mop after a muskrat. "The damned sky is falling!"

Hall dove for the hatch. "I'd better get my kit — one of these guys is going to lose a finger or two pretty soon."

"Don't forget your snakebite medicine." Booby shouted as he swept a reptile off the spar and took aim for another.

Men ran at cross-purposes, scooping up rodents before they could get into the commissary supplies and gunpowder. Wee beasties scampered one direction and then darted another, men in pursuit. A posse circled a specimen riding piggyback on a hapless victim.

"Get this beast off me!" Christie ordered as he slammed his back against the ladder and rubbed it up and down.

"The lieutenant has got a friend!"

"It's a little brother—can't you see the family resemblance?"

"Yeah, they both look like Grant."

Porter was shouting orders, Captain Bache was shouting other orders, to these Christie shouted some of his own through clenched teeth, "Stop jeering like crows! Get the beast! He's tearing me to ribbons!"

Finally, Booby, his hands now in heavy coal gloves, unhinged the terrified coon and held it aloft. "You want him, Lieutenant. He's your take first."

"No, Mister Booby," Christie wiped his bloody laceration with his shirt. "He's yours—my gift."

The officer bounced him by the tail. "Weighs five pounds, I bet. Henri could make him delectable." The animal was given over to the little cabin boy. "Henri, since it was an officer who caught him in a manner of speaking, seems only right it should go in the officer's pot, so Mister Christie can partake."

"Yes, sir." Henri saluted and was below.

Like manna from heaven, bluejackets brushed into gunnysacks some prime ingredients for stews and chowders for the days to come. The officers shouted for order, but chaos abounded. In a world to himself, the pilot snug in his octagonal house reinforced by an armor of roping, puffed on his pipe and pressed steady fingers to the wheel, guiding the boat toward its next crisis. With barely an inch or two of pull, he dodged and weaved around obstructions with as little as a foot of lee on either side. It had taken John Eads and his shipbuilders a hundred days to build these behemoths, but the jungle would have them wreckage in a day.

As first in line, the *Cincinnati* bore the brunt of the assault. But she left some to share. The pilot of the *Pittsburg* drifted wide and before he could correct himself ran dead on a rotted hulk of trunk cantilevered over the bank. The boat slammed against the trunk and snapped it clean through. Men congratulated themselves on their good luck—no catastrophe except for some termites and dust. True enough at first glance. It was the second glance that told different.

It was a small one but a panther just the same. Numb with shock, it got to its feet slowly, shook itself, and finding no kin it recognized as friendly, reared back. Trapped against the bulwarks of cotton and the stupefied bluejackets, the cat screamed. Those crewmen with the heartiest survival instincts and best reflexes leaped to upper and lower decks while the rest made for the hatches and slammed them shut.

From the safe vantage of the *Cincinnati's* deck, Christie and the crew dropped their brooms and pikes to watch somebody else pay their dues. Yes, their brothers fought valiantly — every instinct to abandon ship. Lieutenant Hoel, a deliberate and soft-spoken man when his authority was not challenged by predatory wildlife, bellowed orders from the safety of the pilothouse. "Clear that animal away! Back to your stations!" However, it was the consensus just then that the cat outranked the captain and it held the full attention of all hands — in particular, the one trapped against the casemate. The animal's next move would dictate his.

The cat slapped a paw against the river man's leg, slashing a shallow bloody trail across his shin. A buddy from the safe vantage of the spar stabbed a broom into the animal's face. Instead of cowering, the cat reared and snarled. Indeed, they were a remarkable set of well-developed incisors for a cat that age.

Master's Mate Henry Booby put in his two bits. "Come on, Meyers, my money is on you — I've seen you go after stevedores twice that size! Two out of three falls!"

Hoel bellowed through his horn, "Stand up to him, lad! He's only a cub. Don't let him smell fear! He'll hunt men for the rest of his life."

A crewman with a coal shovel climbed atop the wall of cotton. "Yep, he's just a little 'un."

Another came on the flank with a pike. He poked and waved. The captain boomed, "Move those bails off, man! Let him see the bank! Don't cut off his escape or he will attack!"

It was the first good idea so far. Bluejackets obeyed, but guardedly. Once the bank opened to full view, the cat turned his elegantly chiseled face to see that he was not being played false. It reared back and wailed.

"He's going to attack!" Veterans of bar fights from Cincinnati to Natchez backed away to cut the odds of being a double entrée.

"Where's the watch?" Hoel shouted.

"Right here, sir." A crewman answered up at the same time raising the musket to his eye. He set the near sights for the head and waited for the order to fire. Men up and down the flotilla booed and howled.

"What you doing up there, Chance?" The unlucky bluejacket named Meyers was counting his minutes.

"Watching. It's one against one. Even odds so far." Everyone except Meyers thought that funny.

"Stand back, Meyers, just a little. Give him room."

"I'm back so far, my atoms are merged into the casemate!"

From a safe distance a voice boomed up from the *Carondelet*, "You're bigger than he is! Wrestle him to the decks with a good ole Steel Town hug!"

Meyers spit a profanity and shouted for the watch to fire.

"Now, that wouldn't be fair. He's not armed and he might be Union." The watch clucked in mock seriousness and lowered his rifle an inch.

"Chance, you fire!" Meyers demanded.

The watch set his cheek against the rifle again. The cat settled on it haunches, yawned, then spied right and left to see if the way was still unopposed. Men opened it wider. Not yet hungry and having tired of the game, the beast bounded in one graceful leap to the gunwale, and in another, up the bank. Chance let the hammer relax. Meyers collapsed in relief. The crew hailed the animal back: "You old Rebel, you forgot your dinner!"

"Looked like old Jeff Davis to me!"

Meyers rasped, "Jeff Davis ain't comin' around where there is fightin' to be done!"

Men went back to their duties. Then Christie beckoned the Master's Mate aside. "A word if you please." The Buckeye was grim as he led the way astern. "How do you interpret all this?"

"Things go to hell at a furious rate!" Booby whistled, but he was still optimistic. "But our luck is holding."

"This is your estimation of luck!"

Booby was undisturbed. "I hear the general sent up a

courier. Sherman shouldn't be more than a day behind us. The rest of the army is marching over from Muddy Bayou. The whole division should be at Hill's Plantation by tonight and on the road tomorrow latest. We haven't made much progress, so they should catch up soon enough."

Soon enough, huh. It wouldn't be too soon for Christie.

V
"Going to Hell at Railroad Speed"

The coon stew suffered from too much pepper. More precisely, the officers eating the coon stew suffered from too much pepper.

"Cooks on the Mississippi aren't satisfied unless the food burns like lye—Henri is a student of that school, I'm afraid. No malicious intent on his part." Booby swallowed twice, but the meat still stuck to the roof of his mouth.

"Are you sure?" In spite of the cool breezes Christie was wearing a second skin of sweat. Pearce doused the inner flames with coffee. Hall tapped the meat with his fork as if it were a hand grenade.

"What's that smell?" Henri's head bobbed out of the hatch.

"I can't smell anything I can barely breathe." The Buckeye's falsetto would be cooled by a ration from the water drum. But his mouth burned even hotter after two cupfuls. Henry Booby passed some bread.

Henri sniffed the air. "Fire!"

"My sentiments exactly. It's like eating hot coals." Christie speared a vegetable so heavily breaded he could only recognize it as a relative of an immature cabbage.

The watch searched the woods. "Forest fire, I think, but can't find it, sir!"

"Peace and quiet are such a premium on this boat." Christie put his plate down to add another pair of eyes to those searching the bank.

But it was Booby who acted on what his senses read out plain and clear. "Sound the drums!" The mate shouted, "Close the cannon ports and hatches. I'm not taking chances."

Bluejackets tore through the boat looking for smoke. Brave men went straight to the ammunition and ordnance holds, but all was safe there. Buckets were filled and stacked while crewmen hosed down the decks. It was the forewatch who spotted it first bearing down from the front.

They were under attack! Cotton—bales of it—had been set afire and then rolled down the banks into the channel. Now it floated like small torpedoes on the current, churning fumes and acrid smoke.

"Sir, it's coming at us!" the watch shouted to his captain.

"All ahead stop!" Bache bellowed. "Get the grappling hooks and pikes! Get them out of the away before they set us afire!"

Men moved at the double quick along the snub-nosed bow. Those with the best vision posted themselves at the spar to guide the pilot and keep the boat from running aground in the smoke. Sharpshooters raised the sights on their muskets and waited for attack from the banks. Others anchored gumblankets over the skylight and wet it down to keep embers out of the gundecks and ordnance below. A second bucket brigade nearly trampled the first, bathing down the spar and the pilothouse.

The Confederacy seemed to have set afire the entire harvest. Spring breezes, which had been so refreshing an hour ago, now rolled the smoke up over the decks. Men wetted bandannas and towels and tied them over their faces, but still the heat was unbearable. Near blind and breathless, bluejackets made efficient work with their hooks and pikes, passing the frothing bales from one man to the other and finally around the sides. As one gave way from heat and exhaustion, another crewman took his place. Porter ordered those who were not absolutely needed on the decks to go below.

Henri passed in a blur, too eager to do his share. But Christie pulled him away, "Oh no you don't. Your job is to help Doctor Hall below." Henri hesitated. The lieutenant had no rank over him as far as he knew. The question was not up for debate, Christie barked, "Now!" And Henri disappeared through the hatch.

Crewmen worked beyond endurance. Many were now smoke blind, others were bent in spasms of coughing and choking, all were nearly incapacitated, yet still would not give up. Christie dipped a rag into a pail, wrung it out, and pressed it to the face of a sailor who was near faint. The man grasped the towel and screamed in relief as the cool water extinguished the fire in his eyes.

"Let me take over." Christie whispered.

The man pulled away. "Be fine, just a minute."

But Christie eased him back against the casemate until someone could take him below. It was relentless work. Christie heaved and pushed bales left and right. It was like rowing a tub sideways. He ran his tongue over blistered lips, but the juices had been boiled right out of him. The pike twisted blisters into his hand until he could hardly hold it. One bale and then the next, push, heave. He could not turn them over fast enough. He talked away the pain to take the next bale, but the energy was not there. His pike snagged and the cotton nearly pulled him overboard, in time the next man took it and pushed it off.

"Let go, mate, we can take over." But Christie did not hear. The fatigue embarrassed him; he would redeem himself with the next one. It came on.

"Pull away, Lieutenant." When Christie still refused, water—buckets of it—washed down over his head. He sputtered as hands took hold of him to lift him out and others clasped around the pike.

"God, man, you are on fire!" Booby rolled him in a blanket.

Christie could not believe it, but his sleeves were singed to the shoulders and his hair was ash. From a fire bucket Henri drew a tin of water. Christie doused the sparks in his lungs, and breathed deeply. But there was no air fit to breathe.

"Need a bloodhound to get through this mess!" Bache coughed. "Turn the hoses on the crew, keep them soaked down! Watch—keep a sharp eye for any man on fire."

The ironclad was a frying pan. Men coughed and staggered, but danger to the ordnance and powder allowed no let-up. Porter stood detached from it all. He just shook his head. He could not figure it. "Cotton—it's the only currency the South has left. They've got to be pretty desperate to burn it."

But Christie saw something else. Burning cotton, that's the

last resort of civilians. Cavalry or infantry would have come at them with muskets and cannon. So he figured the enterprise still had time.

As suddenly as the danger had come, it evaporated. The *Cincinnati* rounded the next bend and broke into crystal daylight. With the last smoldering bale drifting back toward the *Pittsburg,* men scoured the banks suspiciously, and turned their chins up channel for the next danger. No man had enough energy for a cheer or a decent expletive; that would come in the retelling at reunions years ahead. For now they massaged knotted muscles, coughed, and when the officers were looking the other way, passed a flask to fortify themselves for the clean up work ahead.

Christie said to no one in particular but Pearce was the closest, "They have got to be writing us up in Vicksburg papers by now. The admiral knows that the fired cotton was a quick fix to slow us down while reinforcements come up. I don't know what—militia, cavalry, maybe even the slave patrol—but I would bet a month's pay there is a lot of activity going on somewhere on our account."

Pearce had been thinking the same thing. "If *we* even get to the Sunflower River, the Confederates can be on the other side with something like the *Arkansas*. For that matter, a damned armada could be steaming up Rolling Fork right now! They could sink any boat and wedge us in here. The rest would be dammed up in the creek. And there is something else..."

Christie did not have to be told. "Torpedoes—like the ones that took the *Cairo* to the bottom. The Confederates could be laying mines over there six deep, with infantry just waiting in the bushes with the trip wires."

"You learn fast for a soldier whose brains are in his feet."

Pearce's arrows went wide of their mark. Christie had suffered nightmares even during the day of steam rams and monitors coming at them. And they would come reinforced on the banks by cavalry and irate farmers with squirrel rifles and pitchforks. He confided as much.

Hall had caught the last of these dire predictions. "What damage could farmers do?" he scoffed.

"I think King Louis and Marie Antoinette asked the same question, and let's not forget those soft-spoken Boston farmers at

Breed's Hill." In Christie's mind, anything that maimed was to be treated with respect, especially if its owner harbored homicidal intentions. "I have been in this war long enough to learn one lesson: never underestimate the talents of the Confederates. Do you think we could convince Porter to hold up this expedition long enough to take a squad ashore? I sure would like to see what is out there. We have been running blind way too long to my thinking."

Pearce agreed but for his own reasons. "Aye, your point is well taken. And I heard tell the coal is low, so we can lay in some wood. Live oak and white pine won't give us enough heat by itself, but it will make the coal go farther."

Porter's bravado was surface deep to buoy the members of the crew green enough to believe it. But the eyes behind the field glasses were red, circled and creased from more than smoke and soot. He too understood with every hour and every mile he was moving his chess pieces further away from Sherman's pawns toward checkmate one way or the other.

"Over there, sir!"

Men—two...five...perhaps ten of them—stepped out of the tangle to line up along the bank, so close the crew could read their faces and they theirs. Not soldiers with muskets but field hands with hoes there at the brink when their curiosity overwhelmed their caution.

"Break out the muskets and maintain a second watch." Pearce ordered.

But Bache added caution, "Do it slowly and with good order, Mister Pearce. I don't want to arouse any alarm from these men."

"Yes, sir, right away." Pearce did as he was told, but "alarm"? That was raised when the gunships rounded the last bend. In two years, roving infantry and cavalry had become pretty routine for these people, but nothing like this had steamed through their country before. These peculiar iron turtles with their wrecked stacks and broken rails, and with Lincoln soldiers riding on their backs, the war would be changing now! Not a word or a wave was exchanged on either side as the boats steamed by, but who would suppose they would keep such a spectacle to themselves?

The yeoman watched them come on placidly. He sucked his cob pipe and set the loose floorboards under his rocker clacking a steady tempo. He was of unaccountable age, inscrutable image, and esteemed the invasion as no more ominous than oncoming storm clouds. He was, however, a remarkable man, made so, because he was white, the first white man the crew had seen so far. Remarkable enough for the admiral to order a full stop.

"Mister Pearce, this is a curious race back in these shallows. He is half bulldog, half bloodhound." The admiral hailed the landlubber. "You there—what is your business?"

The Southerner rallied his faculties, pulled his angular, spiny torso up, and sauntered down toward the bank one leg at a time. He was in no great hurry—he had only his own schedule to keep and not the Union navy's. As he came on, he came sharper into focus. His face was weatherworn and leathery. The eyes were sunken in overlapping folds; pouches sagged about his cheeks and mouth affecting a perpetual frown and on the whole face a distemper. There was an edge to his bark—a beast untamed and under loose control.

"Overseer of this here plantation," he answered back. The farmer had no questions of Porter in return, seeming to know all he needed to know by what his eyes told him.

The impertinence of these naval men may not have struck the farmer as odd, but it did Christie. "With how-di-dos like that, do you think they will invite us in for dinner?"

Hall forced a frown. "Men have walked the plank for less." The lee between the boat and the bank was not two feet and the draft barely six. "You may not drown, but the leeches will suck you dry."

Porter called again, "I suppose you are Union, of course, if it suits you?"

The overseer removed his pipe to give the question the answer it deserved. "No, by God, I'm not, and never will be." He set his legs apart and stiffened his spine. "As to the others—my neighbors—well I know nothing about them. Find out yourself. But I'm for Jeff Davis, first, last, and all the time." With that, the overseer turned and walked toward his porch and his family, who had come out of the cabin. A black woman in a long, shapeless, dress levered a baby at her hip, with two more clustered at her legs. The overseer dismissed them, a flotilla of gunboats at his back door, as nothing more than ill-mannered company. "If you do not want any more of me?" And he kept going. From the state of the man's rough clothes, he had already put in a full day, and with his work done he was past ready for supper, which the admiral would delay no longer.

"Doctor Darwin would have found him a curious specimen, I think," Hall offered.

"And a terrifying one to ponder." Christie was not so detached. "There for the grace of God, go I." Did the backcountry breed such men from the cradle to be wild? Or was he ruined? How long did it take for a civilized man to live back here before he turned so untamed that no amount of civilizing could turn him back? A lesson for men at war—soldiers too long separated from civilization, marching in great packs across wild country preying upon other packs of men to deal savagery. A war waged too long... how long is that? Could he become a brute such as that? Could they all? Christie shuddered. "Not Darwin, Mister Hall, but Missis Shelley's monster."

Porter had more questions, but the farmer did not reply. "You can not have any more of me for I am not a talkative man at any time."

Porter smiled under his beard. "No, I want nothing more with you, but I am going to steam into that bridge of yours across the stream and knock it down. Is it strongly built?"

The man did not protest. "You may knock it down and be damned. It don't belong to me."

Porter shrugged and called the man back again. "Your voice says you to be a Yankee by birth are you not?"

This last footnote must not be misunderstood for he half turned to answer, "Yes, damn it, I am. But that's no reason I should like the institution. I cut it off long ago." The exchange was over.

Porter turned to Bache. "Go ahead fast."

The low bridge was not even a dare. The bluejackets stepped back; the nose plowed into the frame and tore it away from its moorings. It was a small victory, hardly deserving of the reaction it got. But men had been tethered too tightly for too long.

They let go, down the line they cheered loud and long. Christie cheered along with them, but only because Porter was watching him. If he could, Christie would save his raves until he could wash them down with confiscated champagne from a Vicksburg cellar.

Porter waved back to the overseer, who had again taken to his rocker. "You need General Sherman to teach you manners, you heretic." And to the business at hand, "There will not be much daylight left, Mister Bache. Let's tie up."

Bad speed—barely a half mile that day with all the convolutions and distractions. With such Pearce must have carried his point with the admiral about the need of a surveillance party. While the boat was being secured, a knot of men with muskets was gathering on the deck, Captain Murphy in their center.

If Porter had not seen fit to invite Grant's lieutenant, Christie was not going to stand on ceremony. This was army work. Christie reminded Captain Bache he was here, "Request permission to go along."

"You have no authority here, Lieutenant."

"I know that, sir, but I do have experience. General Grant wanted me to give any assistance I could. Can Mister Murphy shake out a skirmish line? Does he know what evidence of cavalry or infantry to look for?"

"All right. Mister Murphy, I'd be pleased if you take Mister Christie with you. Take his advice if you think it strategic."

Murphy nodded dutifully if not enthusiastically and motioned his patrol to follow him up the bank. Christie drew his revolver, primed it, but restrained himself from taking the point. Instead Murphy motioned him to his side. "You said something back there about a skirmish line?"

"I think it advisable."

"So do I. If you will."

Christie motioned a bluejacket to the center, shook out men forming two lines and a reserve—in principle—small though it was. Then Christie gave them their first lesson in infantry reconnaissance even as they moved across fallow fields.

"No reason to rush. It's getting dark so take your time. The center watches everything in his front, the flanks to the right and left. Move to the outside no wider than your peripheral vision. Study everything all the way through and beyond. The key is not to move too quickly that you can't take it all in and not focus on anything to the detriment of something else. But don't underestimate the importance of even the smallest thing. Look out for any glimmer or shine, a change in the shadows, a flutter in the trees, wilted branches used for cover, the sing of metal against metal, a flush of birds or retreat of squirrels. Anything suspicious, see it and flag a halt—better be safe than sorry. If there is fire, close in a circle back on Mister Murphy and fall to the ground. But don't take your eyes off the alarm. Watch where the smoke comes from, and be able to report it exactly to Mister Murphy."

The line moved, but Christie restrained Murphy from moving to the front. "Officers lead from the center and slightly behind. It isn't cowardice. If anybody starts shooting, your men will need to find you, you don't have to find them." Murphy was not convinced all this was necessary, but he had gotten what he had asked for.

Civilization had come to this part of Mississippi in small doses—farms were widely spaced and small. The cabins were raised on stilts and consisted of two wings combined by a dogtrot between, no porch or fencing except for a pen. No frills or fuss. The houses were dark and empty. Bluejackets were surprised by that.

"You know these are ripe for the taking."

"I don't know why they leave them. The general order is not to molest a family, they have a better chance of keeping all if they were here."

The squad followed the creek, slowly fanning inland until they came to a large house anchoring a farm that had obviously been profitable. The paint was still unblemished and the shutters hanging on all hinges were closed and trimmed. Christie motioned men to check the rear, and he waited until they were in place. Upcoming, they surveyed it well—no inhabitants or livestock, not even a farm dog. Murphy motioned the left to search the cabin and smokehouse. Christie accompanied the right to the barn.

Dank and dark as a cavern, except for the well-trodden ground and scatterings of manure, it could have been built yesterday. It was hollow, devoid of even a spike of hay, straw, or a cup of oats or corn. With nothing to report, the self-appointed leader motioned the men out almost immediately. "Shall we join

Mister Murphy?"

But Christie lagged. Men eager for the safety of their boat rolled their eyes skyward and shuffled their feet by the door. "Sir!" It was not a question but a hurry-up.

But Christie would not be hurried. The wee voice of his old sergeant major warned that their work was not half done: "The small things, man. The answer is always in the details."

"Gentlemen, let's light these lanterns please." Behind Christie's back, men exchanged cross-eyed looks. Christie set a match to the wick to signal the rest to do likewise. Lucifers snapped and the barn was bathed in a tallow glow. Anything "too" one way or another was so with a reason worth deciphering. "Again, please, and don't forget the corners." His tone of command amazed even him—bizarre how a pair of shoulder straps reformed a man's attitude. To make the lieutenant happy, the squad made a show of examining every nook and cranny in minute detail, but they found more "empty." Finally, the self-proclaimed leader announced. "*Nothing*, sir. Ready, sir."

"Presently." Christie descended the loft. Instead of joining the rest at the door, he brought the lantern to ground level and duck-walked from wall to wall. He rubbed his fingers into the earth floor. Then the lieutenant swept the lantern over it all one last time. As they filed out, Christie picked up something he thought worth keeping.

Murphy was waiting impatiently for them at the gate. "Neat as a pin. Not a matchstick, a smear of butter, piece of cloth, a dram of milk, honey, nothing. This place is ready for sale."

The detail who examined the smokehouse reported nothing. For his squad, the anonymous bluejacket spoke up for the barn survey. "Likewise, nothing."

"Not exactly," Christie interjected.

Eyebrows arched, throats groaned—only Murphy wanted to hear more. "Something of interest?"

"That 'nothing' you dismiss so quickly is itself an ominous intelligence. A family abandoning its farm, especially in a hurry, may clean the house of blankets and valuables and even the larder, but would it clean a barn so bare?"

Murphy's impatience now had an edge. "Your point, Lieutenant Christie."

Christie held his temper. He remembered what it meant to be Grant's man. "The point is, Mister Murphy, somebody has been here, hungry enough and with enough hungry horses to clean that barn to the bare walls and to the bare ground. And about the bare ground—there were tracks of horseshoes, lots of them. The floor was still damp and those tracks were deep, so they probably stood there awhile, probably overnight."

"Farm animals do that?" the squad leader put in as his mates stifled smiles.

"Cows are never shod. No, horses occupied that barn awhile or couldn't you smell the difference in the manure? What we saw was the droppings of horses. No, I make it out to be cavalry."

"What makes you suspect it cavalry, and very hungry at that?" Murphy was warming to Christie's survey.

"There would have been plenty of evidence of an infantry camp—the fields would have been fouled. But as we came up I saw them untilled and clean of dead campfires. The officers would have camped in the house. But you said it was neat as a pin. Infantry officers are rarely so fastidious in their housekeeping. Which also makes me think it's cavalry—maybe state guard, careful about a neighbor's holdings."

"Continue, Mister Christie." Murphy was growing to respect the soldier and his tone advised others to do the same.

"A small squad out in the middle of nowhere wouldn't sleep in the open with all this rain if they didn't have to. And they wouldn't leave their horses in a barn and sleep in the house—too far from their mounts if taken by surprise. No, they slept in the loft, with their horses underneath. Wise—horses are too dear. Mounts are being raided by other Confederates. Horses are not like uniforms—lose one, you can't just stitch up another."

Christie took a breath, and gave them the sum, "No, it was a small squad of cavalry, so damned poor that they wouldn't leave so much as a crumb. Probably ate out of their haversacks, built a small fire just enough to brew what they are using for coffee nowadays and then covered it over. Yes, they were very careful about not leaving a trace. That's *very* good cavalry."

"You got all that from an empty barn, Mister Christie?" Murphy took in his surroundings with new eyes.

"Well, there was one more thing." Christie opened his palm in the glow of the lantern. "A chip of hardtack. Probably raided from Union supply wagons. So I'm guessing they might be Van Dorn's men, Forrest's men, Featherston, or some other cut from the same cloth. If the Confederates have hardtack, they got it from us. They don't manufacture it as a rule. I don't know about you, Mister Murphy, but that makes me very nervous. I'd like to know which way they came and which way they went."

"All right, let's go find some tracks and then back to the boats—if you agree, Mister Christie."

"I'd only add on the double quick."

The bad news was read in the tracks. Christie estimated several horses; some tracks were deep—mounts carrying two men. They headed north, parallel to the creek and upstream of Porter's ironclads.

Armed with this intelligence, they went to find Porter. The squad had just passed through their pickets as the sky was fading out. Murphy turned straight to the spar, but it seemed he had a second thought, paused, and turned to the Buckeye. Christie was lagging, still scraping his shoes on the plank under the baleful eyes of bluejackets who were sensitive about mud tracked on holystoned decks. "You will join me, Lieutenant?"

As they entered Porter's cabin, the bells of each boat rang six nearly in unison from deck to deck. The end of the third watch. The bells had grown as familiar to Christie as the chimes of the old grandfather clock back home. Twelve hours were divided into four watches: noon, four, eight, and then midnight. The bells sounded each hour. Two bells the first hour, four the second, six the third, and finally eight, with one bell marking the half-hour. Four bells at nine o'clock—"douse goes the glem" lights out in steerage.

The fourth day into the expedition, the veneer of adventure had worn down to the bare wood. The terrain was more of the same—a jungle of tupelo gum, live oaks, and sycamore choked by scrub and cane. Rarely was it broken and only by short expanses of vacant farms and empty cotton fields. The short reconnaissance had only made the boat smaller. The signs were clear—Christie could do nothing about changing direction, hurrying up, slowing down, turning back, or even making the fleet less conspicuous. How could he make five gunboats inconspicuous?

The prodigal paced the spar back and forth until it drove the crew to distraction. As Grant said, when the need strikes it strikes hard and in a galloping hurry—not at all the catastrophe Christie wanted to face in an open boat with the banks above the cannon sights. If the flotilla made four miles that day, a high expectation considering the zigzag channel and the obstructions, Christie paced twenty. If prayers moved men, Sherman's division should be coming around the bend on angels' wings.

The crew bore the strain no better, every hour weighed like three. Each man went about his duties with one eye trained on the banks for Sherman, if their luck was good, and for Confederate cavalry if it went bad. To let off steam, Porter ordered drill for all hands. Christie saw that every man took his turn at the big cannon, small arms, and later fire drill. All hands not involved with the business of the ship were piped to their places. While the gun crews went through the numbers below, atop Pearce drilled the defense teams to resist boarding. On command they thrust and parried pikes, arms waved and tossed phantom hand grenades, cutlasses gleamed as they cut wide bloody swatches in the sunshine—the *Cincinnati* was the better of its phantom enemy.

"I hope the Confederates can't see this. I'd be embarrassed." Christie whispered.

At last, the day flickered out. It was then that men wrestled with their private demons, tension burned like a low-grade fever. Not far off, a sailor with the cloth for a new jumper and a threaded needle sat down beside his mate's lantern to hear a letter read for perhaps the fourteenth time. A man back on the *Mound City* broke out his harmonica to play "Home Sweet Home." The music was a lullaby to the infantry, and Christie soaked it in even if it wasn't played very well. But a sailor rasped up from the *Pittsburg,* "Don't you know something a little more lively?"

"No!" the musician bellowed back. "That's all I know."

Hall bristled. "Must be infantry—a bluejacket knows you don't play 'Home Sweet Home' on a boat. It's bad luck."

The player had not gotten two bars up when the report of something like a hiccup—that is, something small—went into the drink followed by something like a large hiccup—that is, something large—going into the drink. Judge and jury had spoken. Pearce leaned over the fife rail and summed up: "Now that's not a reflection of his talent, lads, which you estimate lowly, or his blasphemy of our high traditions, which he probably transgressed in benign ignorance. We should be a little quiet, show some vigilance and keep low not to excite the locals to our presence any more than necessary. Douse the lanterns, men, and except for the watch, all rest easy. Tomorrow may make a test of us." Men accepted it, but not for one moment did they believe it.

Christie climbed the ladder and resumed his constitutional up and down the casemate past the extra watch. Hall and Pearce were also topside studying the nothingness and what could be lurking out there. As he reversed stride, Christie also paused. He could barely make out the watch on the bank. Did restless butternut scouts pace in their lairs, their worn boots deepening trenches into the mud? Were they filling the chambers of their navy colts with cartridges? Were men with muskets lounging in the rocks and tall grass upstream waiting for the gunboats to come up? Where? When? Now? If not how soon?

Christie was embarrassed at the pounding of his heart. Sherman! You could have marched by way of Mexico and still been here yesterday, unless you met the enemy. Then the enemy would be between us. If...if...then Christie squared his shoulders. No, Sherman was no faint-hearted McClellan who allowed anything or anyone keep him from an appointment. Christie resumed his pacing.

"You're going to wear the deck out that way, Lieutenant." Bache was leaning against the pilothouse. He poured off some of his coffee into a second cup. "Maybe this will settle your nerves."

Out of respect Christie took the coffee but he did not want his nerves settled. No, he wanted them on edge. Then Hall joined them, saluted his captain, but said nothing. Christie went back to study the nothingness. He strained harder, watched with every faculty. When it came, he doubted he had seen it at all, it was so subtle—nothing or nearly nothing. Was it there? He refocused on it, compared it against everything it could be to make sure he wasn't fooled.

"Damn!" The lieutenant went off like a pistol shot. "Look

there!"

"Where? What do you see?" Hall spun around, as the watch turned rifles to the direction.

Christie jabbed into the darkness. "No, a light! There it is again!"

"Maybe a doe watering its fawn. Even alligator eyes glow at night. Could be anything." Even though, Pearce was giving the alarm due respect.

The pilot pointed his head out the window in the same direction at the same time Christie shouted, "There!"

A flicker in the darkness, very little brighter than its competition of fireflies, tracked eastward and disappeared. Another followed, and then another in a loose necklace of lights. A fourth came at double the distance of the third. They almost gave it up, but there was a fifth and no more. Slow enough for men on foot rather than on horse, but going fore—moving to their front. Were there lights also moving aft that they could not see? The flotilla was being intercepted, or were they being surrounded? Christie stood rooted to the oak deck. What he would not give for the old Fourth right here, with muskets and full cartridge boxes. Christie wanted to move, to be about some enterprise to head them off. Instead, he was stuck on this tub—yes, by your leave, Mister Hall—armed to its teeth, but a wallowing, stuck-in-the-mud dinosaur.

Time pressed down on them as they waited for what came. Christie paced and no one stood in his way as he circled the spar, his eyes always over his shoulder. In an hour, perhaps less, the truth told. The bark of farm dogs? No, too rhythmic, more like the ticking of a mantle clock. Christie was well acquainted with the crack axes make. "Somebody is chopping down trees!"

"Sherman's pioneers!" Hall breathed.

"Possible!" Christie listened. "But I think it is coming from ahead!"

"Confederates damming up the channel." Hall moaned.

Christie pitched the dregs of his cup into the creek. "That's my guess."

A bluejacket poked his head over the ladder. "Lieutenant, you are wanted at the bow."

Porter and Bache had not been waiting idle. Bluejackets

were loading cables and tackles into a tug. Murphy stepped to, "I have asked for your attendance personally. We are going to investigate the mischief the Confederates have dealt us."

Christie nodded, "I would feel more at home with a musket." One was handed down to him.

Ensign Boss sparked the engine and the *Ivy* eased up the creek by the light of bow lanterns.

"Watch there! Easy ahead" Boss cut the engines to let her glide on Murphy's order. The golden aureole spread wider over the bow. It was worse than a dam. The trees as they fell—from one side of the bank and then another—interlocked into a barricade. Field hands scurried like river rats over the top and up the banks.

"Gunner, pepper the shore! Get those Confederates out of there before they drop another tree. Keep your guns on the banks and fire on anything that moves." The howitzer swung around, its rapid shot pinged and thudded into the bank.

Murphy cursed. "There's our real enemy, gentlemen!" The choppers had been very efficient in a very short time. "Ease into her, Mister Boss. Slow now." The officer turned the bow head on to nudge the nearest tree without wrecking the bow. The screws churned up water and mud, Boss throttled down, the engines gave all they had, but nothing budged.

"That's enough, Ensign. Let's not wedge them any tighter." The little boat came at it from the right and left, but there were no easy solutions that night. Murphy sighed, "We will have to lift them out, gentlemen. Lieutenant Christie, if you will take charge of our defenses. And I will trouble you to find a stout tree and secure the tackle and lines for leverage."

"As you wish." The howitzer was an attractive weapon for his purposes; Christie regarded it with new respect. "Does that thing come loose?"

"Yes, with a little effort."

"Well then, may I borrow it and place it on the bank where it could be of better use?"

Murphy nodded that it should be done, then turned to his meager crew, "Volunteers for the shore!"

"We'll go!" It was the old barn detail. They slapped Christie a sloppy salute, "The lieutenant is used to ordering us around," the self-appointed leader snapped his heels in mock respect.

Blushes would be unseemly but the night was dark enough to hide Christie's crimson cheeks. This landlubber was beginning to share Grant's respect for this mud-water navy who could turn themselves into pretty fair infantry if need be.

How many of these pickets had he walked in nearly two years? Yet he never got used to them. They were always a heart attack waiting to happen. The first had been back in western Virginia with Jamie. They almost shot Colonel Andrews' horse when it burst out of the scrub without first returning the password. By some fortune they had held their fire and caught the beast instead of turning it into ration meat. The men had been praised for cool heads at assembly the next day.

Behind Christie the navy worked with all deliberate speed. The block and tackle jerked and scraped as trees, as big as masts, were roped and harnessed, and pulled out of the creek.

VI
Checkmate

Porter was an old sea dog who would not give up his bone. With warnings enough for any sensible man, the admiral instead set his course ahead. In the pre-dawn hours, without bells, whistles, or drums and with only stem and stern lanterns, tars felt their way upstream. Mister Lincoln's expeditionary flotilla, valued at over a half million dollars, plowed tea-colored water toward Rolling Fork. Porter, guiding on a star that only he imagined, believed the last challenge to his grand plan was behind him. If he were the only one who believed it, that was enough.

Christie was not a praying man, but he was a betting one. He would wager nothing on the sanity of the commander cameoed against the dawn. But he would put all his worldly wealth, less the price of Grant's hat, on the chances that ambush was less than a few hours away. He put more estimation in hoof tracks than lucky stars. If Sherman weren't close up, this brand-new lieutenant would be soon eating boiled pea vines and sweet potato tea at Pearl Bridge Prison. The bow of the *Louisville* rode six feet astern, and like a parade of elephants, they moved toward the inevitable. "Well at least we won't get lost!"

The breaching sun streaked the clouds like heather foretelling a clear warm day. Sailors kept to the routine as silent as undertakers. As they went the business of pulling the barriers from the channel went on, and Christie watched the banks reach higher over the spar and close tighter to the sides. When the bends jackknifed by ninety degrees and the ironclads needed five more to come around, men fastened her nose to pulleys and lines hitched to the oaks and pulled her around by brute strength. By sunup the lead tug, riding higher than the ironclads, pulled ahead and around to scout the next bend. She had barely lapsed out of sight when her whistle squealed.

"What now!" Christie moaned.

What Porter saw through his spyglass all but levitated him. Christie thought he would take flight. "Bless me, God! There!"

Deer Creek all but dead-ended to the starboard. The near-stagnant channel pooled and seethed through a sieve of reeds and grasses, but the signs were there. Any man could see it. A mile, maybe half, and to the east—the Sunflower River. When the boat had come fully around, every crewman saw it too.

Porter shook both fists into the air. "Rolling Fork! Yes! Mister Bache, do you see it! We made it! We have won, I tell you! We have won! That is the Little Sunflower just ahead, and the big one is beyond the bend! There—you can hear the boats on the big river." Porter shouted down from the quarterdeck. "Cheer, Mister Christie! I order it!"

"Well, sir, I have it ready."

"You're a Presbyterian, Mister Christie, you always want your miracles under your hat before you believe." Porter leaned over the rail and fairly willed the doubting Thomas to sail his cap into the air.

"That's true sir. Another Presbyterian by the name of Stonewall Jackson taught me way back never to count my miracles before they hatch. If he had a brother, he'd be right up there waiting for us with guns and a brigade of infantry."

The *Cincinnati* swung starboard. This last about was going to be a corset squeeze between two sheer ridges covered in scrub. Atop were two Indian mounds cutting off clear sight of the rest of the channel and the tug ahead. That little voice with the Ulster brogue was shouting loud and clear in Christie's brain: "You can bet your virginity on ambush, boyo, any soldier worth his salt can see it!"

Perhaps Porter had little voices too; he did temper his engines. To his credit, a double ring of sharpshooters were ordered up. But he feared ambush less than he dreaded delay, and a slick of broadleaf willows and reeds lulled innocently on the placid surface dead ahead predicting just that.

"What's that? Guide?" Porter pointed to the new menace just ahead.

A plantation runaway squinted in the direction the admiral pointed, then shook his head. It was an inconvenience nothing more. Porter's finger throbbed again, but the guide was optimism itself. "Sir, it ain't nothing but willers. They cut 'em and let 'em there till they need 'em. Your ships can butt right through 'em easy 'nough."

"That so, huh!" Porter turned back to the pilothouse to get a second opinion, but the pilot was stoic, barely acknowledging the admiral's presence.

No, the admiral had only the guide and his own best instincts. Porter scoured the skyline. Would ahead be so much different than what they had already braved behind? Fifty-fifty, either the Confederates were or were not there. So close—by Almighty Providence, they were so close he could smell it. He needed ten or fifteen minutes to get the *Cincinnati* through this last breach, and then she could protect the rest as they came through. And if they made it, the Sunflower gave him room to maneuver enough to run two maybe three abreast to blast anything in any numbers the Confederates threw at them coming either way... anything he knew of. The tug's whistle squealed again. A decision: go forward...back...victory...humiliation.

"Ring all ahead full!" Gears and shafts heaved the paddles through sheer mud. The gunboat lurched, then steadied herself into a slow, easy glide. Christie rested his fingers over the pistol strapped at his side.

The guide would have been right and they would have "butt through them easy enough" if the boat had been a deep-wedged sea-ship. But the shallow-draft, flat-bottomed hull plowed *over* the raft of weeds, sucking them up into the gears and the tumbling paddles. The willows, with a tensile strength of wharf lines, wound over, under, and through the machinery like yarn on a weasel. Deep below, five boilers whooshed steam into two engines, and relief valves screamed when it had no place to go. The stokers heaved, the engineer threw oil on the flames, the furnaces thundered, but even the best faggoted wrought-iron rod could not budge. The dragon clamored and died. The *Cincinnati* was dead in the water, clogging up the channel like a cork in a bottle. The rest of the flotilla drifted into the stern helter-skelter, wedging into a logjam.

"Damnation!" was all Pearce whispered. "We are in it now!"

Although Christie felt God had little to do with it, Pearce's sentiments expressed his feelings exactly.

Porter took hold of the guide, shook him, and demanded he be put in irons if some could be found. Pearce was the next target of the admiral's rage. "Break out the axes! I will be bound this will not defeat us! We are going to have at it again."

The housing was already off the paddle wheel and men poured, lemming-like, down into the works. Pearce followed. When he bobbed up again, the diagnosis was bad: "This is the worse bind yet. It will take us two weeks to clean that mess. No less."

"Is there no end to it?" Porter slapped the rail. His answer came by immediate reply. Artillery rocketed over the decks. Men went for cover and pulled the hatches over. Porter reached for his bullhorn. "Misster Murrrphy, with meee!"

The long-suffering lieutenant, whose dream this whole expedition had been, raised an arm against the lead hail and clamored up over the decks to the flagship. He found Porter by the pilothouse in the wide open, shouting orders above the din. A crewman was forcing a sheet of boilerplate on his commander against the shrapnel. So the man would get under, the admiral reluctantly took it but let it hang limp from his arm. In his other hand he held his spyglass for stalking the direction of the attack.

"They are coming at us, Mister Murphy, from both banks! Take a company of men, get up on that high ground there, and drive those men out. Draw muskets and take a howitzer." He passed the glass to his junior. "There! Establish your position there! That summit just down and this side."

Murphy nodded and began to siphon off a team of sailors who would make good marines.

"Request permission to go ahead with the landing party," Christie shouted above the din.

At first the admiral seemed not to hear, but finally he leveled a steely gaze on Grant's man, who had prophesied this catastrophe, and therefore, had brought it down upon them. "No, I think I will have need of your other talents very shortly. And for God's sakes, get down! The enemy is shooting at us, can't you see?"

"Sir, with all respect, might I make the same suggestion for yourself," Christie pulled the admiral down just as shrapnel exploded a gash in the hemp-armor of the wheelhouse.

"Infernal inconvenience! The Sunflower is just over there. I can smell it. Mister Murphy came only yards of being right. He deserves to see this through."

"Yes, sir."

"All right. Get down there and keep the men under cover."

But the crew had already evaporated, except for the sharpshooters, who had taken position behind the cotton trenchworks. Hall was tending to the first of the wounded. Murphy was moving his squad of bluejackets off in the *Thistle,* giving orders in high Celtic humor. If profanity were canister, the channel would be cleared directly. The gunnery officers were cursing—all they needed was a high foot or two and they could fire the fore guns diagonal and support Murphy's advance.

Hall ripped open a package of lint. On the floor a delirious sailor pressed his filthy bandanna to his forehead and mumbled profanities one after another. Hall motioned for a bandage and Christie handed it to him. "Speaking of Sherman, did you see him back there?"

The soldier shook his head. "But he isn't too far back he can't hear. He'll be coming up directly..." if the Confederates haven't swung around and cut him off. Christie didn't say it, but he thought it.

"Go below and keep that clean." Hall ordered and the wounded man staggered out. Hall turned to the next and went to work calmly, methodically encircling the bloody wrist with layers of linen. He split the end, and tied it off. "If you get close to clean water, Marks, keep that wet."

At that a crewman broke in to summon the surgeon. "It's Henri and he's hurt bad."

"Where?" Hall and Christie asked as one.

"On deck—he got pinned behind the bow."

Hall made for the hatch, but Christie pushed him out of the way. "Look, Florence Nightingale, you're gonna have to keep your petticoats down or you'll get your head blown off." Christie shoved Hall below. "I will find Henri. You are more important than I am. Now stay low."

At risk of exposing themselves and too busy with Confederate riflemen in the trees to rescue the cabin boy, the sharpshooters could only point to where they last saw him. Christie inched that way, keeping low behind the bulwark of cotton. He called, but there was no answer. A few yards ahead blood, the color of molasses, trailed from a wedge in the bales. Christie pulled himself by his arms through a tight space around the shooters, between the cotton and the gunwales. There he found Henri wedged tight into a ball. His shoe overflowed with blood and twisted away from his leg at a ghastly angle.

"Henri, you all right?"

"Go away." Henri pressed back tight against the gunwales but could not keep his body from vibrating in spasms. The last minutes of life were seeping out of him.

Christie pulled a tuft of raw cotton and pressed it against the ankle. Henri bit through his lower lip but he did not cry out. In respect, Christie would not see the tears streaming down the boy's cheeks. "Well, you aren't hurt so bad," Christie lied. "What say we just stay here a minute, get our breath?"

In seconds blood oozed through Christie's fingers. He released it. As the compress came away, sweet sticky purple streamed into Christie's face. He pressed another and it reddened almost to the touch. This time Henri screamed and kicked but Christie did not let go.

"Easy, boy—just going to get this stopped. You're making a mess here." Christie worked the lace out of the boy's shoe. Rotten thread broke off in his hand, but enough came to tie around the tiny ankle. Christie frisked his blouse for something to lever. No options—he ripped the cover of his blessed *Frankenstein*. He rolled it into a handle, set it in the loop and slowly twisted the tourniquet tight. Henri shivered, then fainted. The leg would have to come off.

Hall was not without a plan of his own. He left his patients and squeezed through the crowded passage. He found the gunnery lieutenant. In seconds the rear ports opened. The maw of a cannon poked through and boomed empty smoke, scaring the crew of the *Pittsburg* to death. The Rebel snipers swung their barrels that way, but the shells ricocheted off boilerplate. In those precious seconds Christie pushed Henri through the nearest gun port.

Henry Booby was there. "I've got him."

"Watch the leg!"

The mate's huge hands encircled the child, all but enveloping him in the safety of his muscled body, and he sped him to the medicine room.

Too big to squeeze through the port, Christie made for the hatch where Pearce was waiting. "Porter is blaspheming your name through the engine horn. He's in the pilothouse and wants you up there. Go down through the boiler room and up the shaft."

When he finally bobbed topside, Christie banged his head on Porter's iron shield still swinging from his arm. The pilothouse was crowded with sharpshooters firing through the windows, the captain, his aides, and the pilot. As spare as he was, there was no room for him, and Christie curled up to wait the commander's attention.

Porter was tending to several emergencies at once. One ear was cocked to Lieutenant Murphy's courier making a report on the firing ahead. While he talked, Porter was writing furiously into his order book and shouting directions to Bache. "As soon as it's dark, we can unship the rudders and let the current back us out of range. I hope that puts us a little closer in Sherman's direction. But I am not going to skedaddle when I am four hundred yards from the Sunflower River! I did not come this far to turn tail and run at one more Confederate inconvenience!"

"Sir!" the courier wedged through Porter's constant stream of instructions. "Mister Murphy says it's Ferguson's sharpshooters and Featherston's Mississippians in front of us, with Alabamians in close support. He heard them shout names in the lull of the firing. Lord knows who else is coming up, but it is getting mighty hot up there. Lieutenant Murphy is pressed and asks for support. If we can sweep 'em now, before the reinforcements come up, he says we can make the river. We can see the funnels from the steamers running the Sunflower. We can do it, sir. Murphy said it's within reach."

"Send my compliments to Lieutenant Murphy and tell him to hold on, I am seeing to his request." So such sentiments would not be entirely empty, Porter ordered the mortar boats to train their guns on the Confederates. He finished up his writing and finally turned to Christie. "Lieutenant, we are going to hell at railroad speed. Read this and make sure you got it down."

Christie read:

> "GENERAL SHERMAN: We are within one mile and a half of Rolling Fork, having undergone an immensity of labor. Had the way been as good as represented to me I should have been in Yazoo City by this time; but we have been delayed by obstructions which I did not mind much, and the little willows, which grows thick that we stuck fast hundreds of times."
>
> And then Porter got down to cases: I beg that you will shove up troops to us at once I am holding the mouth of Rolling Fork against troops, which have attacked our two hundred men. We have only two pieces of artillery they have six, and two hundred men. It takes all my men to defend the position I have taken. I think the distance is only fourteen miles by land. I shall look for these reinforcements. I send you a dispatch from Captain Murphy. *Please send on troops.*
>
> I think a large force will be used to block us up here. We must have every soldier to hold the country or they will do it. Our difficulties increase.

The time was now. Christie read it again, closed his eyes to see if it ran in front of him. He did not believe it though. Porter had five gunboats with two hundred men each that was a regiment. More than enough for a good try, if each man could carry a gun and shoot straight. And they were not entirely unsupported; there were a couple of mortar boats and some tugs with howitzers. If the big ironclads could back out and find just a few yards of open space, they could use the starboard guns. In the Shenandoah, Captain Mason had held off Stonewall Jackson with less. Christie would have made the point but Porter was not taking suggestions just now.

"Got it?" Porter hoped, but was far from satisfied. Grant's man had better live up to his reputation—he could be their last chance.

"Got it, sir!"

Porter then gave the message to the Negro guide who had advised that the "willers weren't nothin'."

Then Porter turned back to Christie. "I want you to go with Tub. Sherman should be somewhere between here and Hill's Plantation at Deer Creek. If anything happens to one of you, no stopping to help the other. Keep going. Do you hear?" Christie nodded and Tub did the same. "Then get ready. You will go after dark."

Christie dropped down the hatch. He found Hall in the galley patching up the last of the wounded. Men were all below now. "Come night, another man and I are going over the side and back down stream to hustle up General Sherman."

Hall nodded. "How are we coming with the wheel? You hear anything up there?"

"Nothing on that score. Doubt if they are working on it. Too dangerous out there." Christie leaned back into the gunwales to wait. It was a fool's errand—he would rather be reinforcing Murphy or doing something about those men in the trees than groping his way through Mississippi jungles in the dark. At least Porter had been paying attention about the needs for skirmishing talent, that land duty was the army's responsibility. Still, Christie was glad to be getting off this boat, rather than just sit, wait, hope, and mark the hours, seconds at a time.

Shells whined overhead punctuated with the staccato of

musket balls pinging against the iron.

Featherston's name was not strange. Boyd had talked about him. He led a brigade—three regiments at least with cavalry as scout. If there are only two hundred up there as Murphy claimed, where were the rest? Had General Stephen Lee sent them to cut off Sherman? No matter how Christie calculated it, the gunboats ended up marooned. But Porter would never let the Confederates have them. He would order them blown up. There was enough ordnance and powder to make an explosion heard all the way to Washington. Secretary of the Navy Wells would eat Porter alive when he hears it!

With the dark, the word was given for general blackout. Just as soon, an immense, black hand wrestled Christie awake. "Time to go, Lieutenant," Christie had not met many black men, but their reputation had not been kind—they were wild-eyed and stupid. Tub was calm, deliberate, with a sure gaze that hinted no fear. Tub's danger was as great as his own, if they were captured. But he was ready. "We got to go now, sir."

Christie followed Tub over the side. They splashed between the gunboats and the banks.

"Get that Sherman up here!" a bluejacket rasped from a porthole.

"Good luck, leadfoot."

"We'll be prayin' for ya."

Past the last boat, Tub charged up the bank, pulling Christie after him and the two were into the brush. Tub wove in and out, leaves as broad and sharp as sabers slashed and scraped as they went. It was hard keeping up with the fleet-footed field hand as he bounded through the night following no course but his own compass. When they had outstripped any enemy that might be on them, Tub made for the road to pick up his pace. But surgery and months of convalescence made Christie's legs heavy, and his lungs had shrunken into dry leather bags.

"Don't wait for me. You know the admiral's orders!" With one hand Christie motioned the field hand on and with the other massaged the old incision that weakened him.

"Easy, Lieutenant, we gonna make it in plenty of time." Tub slowed up alongside his comrade, measured his pace, and adjusted his own to it. "How does that feel?"

Christie's heart eased into the regular four-four beat of the old double-quick. "Yes," he admitted, "that's better."

"I told 'em I didn't need no guardian angel. Sailor boys be too soft...and clumsy!" Tub caught the soldier to keep him from falling. "Better odds, what dat means. If you be a planter boy, I'd leave ya. I still might, if I hea da hounds." Tub said no more. It would be every man for himself. Devil take the hindmost.

Suddenly Tub cut away from the road onto a deer path. He was homing on instinct, a steeplechase, straight across country. Christie's legs were getting back their old ginger; the Fourth infantry was making a fine show. He set his sights on Tub's white shirt bobbing ahead like a ghost.

"Shout out, Lieutenant, if ya lose me."

The ground was rutted and treacherous, river stones turned and slid under his shoes. And there was something else. Christie skidded but did not catch himself before the plop detonated like a torpedo. Manure! The stench was gagging and small consolation that they were now safe against hounds that preyed on runaways and not cows.

The long miles through the unbroken night were bought at a price. The lead in Christie's legs weighed harder to pull, he soaked with sweat, and his reserves were draining fast. He could not coax his body—the old power was just not there. Tub sensed rather than saw the interval widen. The lieutenant limped and wobbled. When he could go no more, Christie collapsed and vomited.

"You still sick, Lieutenant." Tub pulled him up. "We slow down awhile."

"Not we, just me." Christie wiped a sleeve across his face. "You got to go on. That's an order."

Tub shook his head. "No, Tub don't listen ta officers unless it pleases 'em. I'm a free man now." The slave pulled him up. "You be alligator bait by mornin', the ants eat you alive, or the Johnny cavalry git you. No good how you figure it. Git up, Lieutenant!"

Christie pushed him away. "If the Johnny cavalry captures me they will throw me in the stockade. You, you will be hanging from a tree."

"No, you not be so lucky as you think. I hear they shoot

you. You help a slave runaway." Big muscled arms wrapped around Christie's mid-section and heaved him to his feet. Then Tub spun him around in the direction of the road, and pushed. Christie catapulted forward. "Every time you stop, you git another, so git." Christie got. "You Lincun soldiers are a bony lot. We got fed better down on the plantation. Listen, we got about five miles ta go. I reckon on making it by as near after midnight as I can." The big Negro pushed him again. "Don't ya fall, or I'll run over ya."

Christie pushed every distraction, every fear, out of his mind to strip the task down to its simplest sequence—one foot and then another, one and then another. On that rotation he put his entire concentration. When he got into a steady rhythm, the thud... thud...thud anesthetized his mind against the pain searing across his back. He let his thoughts travel anywhere they wished—nothing was off limits.

The Shenandoah, the spring they marched up the valley looking for Jackson. The apple blossoms that blew like snow in their faces. The Lurray caverns with the luminous pools of mineral water. The houses of fieldstone framed by climbing roses. The long arbors where lovers could walk and tease, perfect for seducing that first kiss. How long has it been since he felt the warmth of a woman's lips against his, her waist between his hands, the press of her body?

Julie! Her scented chestnut hair, the pearls in her ears, the lace and silk around her luminescent shoulders...a balm to his pain...hypnotic morphine. What was unpleasant burned away, leaving only a cameo of Julie, the image that had visited yesterday morning. She was mirth and mischief without restraint, with only a trace of powder on her cheeks and no other adornment to distract from her sapphire eyes. The flames of the Yule log glistened and shimmered against the garnet silk of her Christmas gown. He had pledged his love to her—she was barely fourteen, he a year older. Hope was in full bloom then. His father was alive.

But when he died it all dissolved. When the affluent fall from grace, there is no quarter in society that will forgive or comfort them. The rich turn away from bad fortune as a contagious plague. They are embarrassed. The poor are disgusted that whole fortunes can be lost, when they themselves could never have it once.

Water swirled up to his chest, a bare distraction, so

tenaciously did he hold on to his visions. Sand and silt burned into the scars but he willed it away.

She was the wife of a man of position and society now, her father had seen to that. Probably a mother three times over. Had she kept the pearls he had given her that last Christmas and the silver scapular he had pressed into her hand the night before she married? Did she think of him?

"Who goes there? Advance, give the password, and be recognized!"

Tub pulled up fast. Union pickets or Confederate ambush Christie could not tell. The picket snapped again, "Give the password, and be recognized."

"I don't have the password, friend!" Christie barked.

"Union or Confederate?"

"Union, Fourth Ohio!" Reflex from a tired brain, that was all.

"Wrong answer, Reb—no Fourth Ohio down here!" The hammer snapped and locked. "That your brother?"

Christie fumbled to correct first impressions before they were shot on the grounds of gross stupidity. "I am Lieutenant Brenton Christie, transferred to General Grant's staff. I am a special courier from Admiral Porter with an urgent message for General Sherman."

"What's that name again?"

"Christie!"

"Stand easy."

The breeze cooled the hot flush radiating from his face. Christie tried to steady the pounding in his temples and slow the wheezing. Tub watched him curiously. The wait was interminable while the guard ran the name through his personal inventory of officers. Then pickets stepped out of the darkness with muskets drawn.

"Well, we called for the lieutenant and he will pass you up to General Sherman, but you better be who you say you are or you ain't going to get any older to impersonate anyone else anymore." The sergeant drew back, "What's all over your uniform, man, you stink!"

No one was in a happy mood that night. Tub pulled the dispatch out of the havoc in his hair. "How long ago did you last see the admiral?" Sherman asked evenly, not at all sure he hasn't being suckered by a Confederate spy. The only signal of the general's inner strain was the tip of his cigar that glowed under his nose.

"Sundown."

Sherman flipped the case on his pocket watch and held it up to the light. "It's three o'clock now, dawn in four more hours. Adjutant, wake up Colonel Smith; tell him he is moving out at first light. I will be coming up with Colonel Ewing as soon as he arrives."

"That might be too late, General!" Christie stepped into the glow of Sherman's festering cigar.

Sherman fixed the dilapidated lieutenant in his sights.

Christie gave Sherman a better grasp of the emergency written between the lines of Porter's S.O.S. "The admiral is up to his eyeballs in Confederates. His boats are snagged in reeds and dead in the water. The fleet is cut off. Lieutenant Murphy is making some defense of it, sir, but he's only got a few men, and the Confederates are three regiments thick at least—Featherston he thinks—no telling what's riding down on them now."

"My scouts tell me that it is only home guard."

"Your scouts are wrong, General. Dead wrong. It's a brigade with something like a Whitworth. I heard it."

Sherman regarded Christie for one long second. This was no green officer Grant sent up there—not likely to scare and make giants out of shadows. The general and his men had heard Porter's cannon around noon. Sherman turned to the field hand. "You, boy, can you lead us back in the dark?"

"Yes, genrul! Sore can!" Tub's head bobbed and his eyes bulged unnaturally.

"Adjutant, get Missouri and the Illinois men up and on their feet. They are moving out with Colonel Giles Smith. I will find Colonel Kilby Smith—he is supposed to be coming up with his men on the *Silver Wave*. Let's hope they have been hasty. We will follow as soon as I can get them shaken out and pointed in the right direction." Turning to Tub, "Get yourself some water and get ready. We'll be collecting here presently. And, Lieutenant, get yourself a clean uniform. Private, see to it."

Christie plunged his face into the trough to cool the fire in his cheeks. If Sherman gave him five more minutes he could strip down and soak, and he did not care if he poisoned every horse in the army doing it. His whole body was on fire—how he wanted a bath and to soak till he wrinkled. "What's this with the balloon eyeballs and 'sore can, genrul' stuff?"

Tub wrapped his dripping shirt over his head "I hear General Sherman don't like smart niggers—in fact, your General Sherman don't like niggers at all."

"So what if he don't?"

"It's just smart to give people what they want. They cooperate if they think they in charge."

Too soon Sherman arrived with his aide. He made no effort to hide his surprise that Christie was dressed and ready to go. "You're staying behind, Lieutenant."

"If it please the general."

"You are dead on your feet, man, and I remember you weren't in great shape to begin with." The adjutant pushed the lieutenant aside. Sherman had been in a terrible mood, thundering at the troops—rather thundering at the troops still strung out across Muddy Bayou, too far away yet to hear their commander cursing them. As it was, two regiments had trudged, swam, and slung grapevine bridges to get this far. Sherman knew it would have to do.

"I can hold my own." Christie insisted.

But Sherman thought otherwise. "Do as I say."

The Sixth Missouri and the Sixteenth Illinois settled down beside their brothers of the Eighth to boil up coffee. Before they got it fairly going, the drum thundered. Sergeants passed down the ranks with crates of candles. Colonel Smith bellowed, "It's dark out there, boys, so stick this in your gunbarrel. It'll keep the water out and give you a little light. Just don't set your hair on fire." Matches were struck and tapers lit.

On the order, the drummers set cadence, and a river of flickering lights filed onto the Deer Creek road. With Tub striding up front, leg for leg alongside Giles Smith, there was no one to know what Christie did and where he went. So he took a candle from a sergeant and blended in with the forward regiment, one more blue-clad soldier indistinguishable in the dark. He hoped that Murphy was still there on the Indian mounds.

A river of candles wound through the blackness. The

column was barely warmed to the march when dammed up behind a barricade of freshly hacked trees. Smith bristled. Christie moved out of the shadows. "Sir, get used to it. The locals have been playing these games with us all week."

The colonel barked at the nearest officer, "Take a party through those plantations and get their field hands down here. If they put them there, they can sure as hell take them out." As the officer moved off, the colonel pulled him back. "One more thing, Major, warn the good people of Deer Creek—if one of my men is shot up there, I will hold them personally responsible two to one, and I don't care who." Then the major regarded the officer standing there in clear violation of orders. "Well, Lieutenant, you just might save yourself a court martial by being of some use."

"Yes, sir."

The delays came in a string. The Deer Creek road was washed out, further up it was flooded. Tub and Christie had bypassed these hazards in the press for time. But with an army at his heels—and armies were like trains, they did not travel efficiently off the beaten track—Tub kept to the roads no matter what. With cartridge belts wrapped over musket barrels and pitched high over head, troops waded chest deep through runoffs. One small drummer boy was nearly swept into the creek if a burly ordnance sergeant had not caught him by the scruff of the neck. He handed over his weapon to a corporal and whipped the boy onto his shoulders, drum and all.

By mid-afternoon on Sunday Lieutenant McLeod Murphy was putting the last cartridge into his revolver joining the last three in the chamber. Just as he was running out of ammunition and hope, the Confederates received an infusion of new blood. The colors of the Fortieth Alabama marched up to fill in behind the Mississippians. By Murphy's estimation, there were about fifteen hundred Confederates in his front, lining the banks, and probably another battalion surrounding his boats. Murphy pushed his cap back on his head to rub the sulfur and dust out of his eyes. The howitzers were low of ammunition and the men were rationing every shell. An hour ago, the lieutenant had made his bargains with God and with every assault since he upped the wager. Right now he stood just short of monastic vows. The war had boiled down to this—death, capture, or a lifetime of honorable celibacy—hard choices for an Irishman to make.

So far God had not cast his lot with the Union men, and so far the Confederates needed no divine intercession. Murphy calculated his options and they came up zero. He could not go forward, and he could not go backward with the sharpshooters converging fire on the boats—that way was out as well.

"Sir, something going on in our rear!" A comrade rested his weary back against the hill to study the commotion swelling up behind. "It's the Rebs—I think they flanked us."

"Why don't I hear a yipe and a yell? Such a prize would let loose a proper Rebel yell just to rub it in!" A second chorus of throaty huzzahs shook the Mississippi forests. The bluejackets bobbed and weaved. Murphy pushed the sailor's head down—his curiosity had for a second gotten the better of his caution. A shell nicked a tree an inch from the man's ear.

"Well?" Murphy prompted. "What do you see?"

"There's red flickering through the trees. Can't tell the flags yet—all I can see is red but from this range the uniforms... well they are lookin' very gray, sir!"

Murphy despaired. "Stephen Lee's boys from Vicksburg." The bluejacket squinted harder. Again Murphy pushed him down. "Fool, jack-in-the-box, get your pumpkin blown off."

"Oh-o-o, sir!" The sailor let out a war whoop of his own. "Them aren't Rebs!" He slapped his captain on the back, "Sir, they are just dusty old Union infantry. Sherman's up, sir. That's our own candy-striped flag cutting through the trees. She is a pretty sight, sure!"

The news was too good to be true. The man was raving. Another volley whizzed over their heads. But the temptation was too great. Murphy twisted to see for himself. "I'll be...!"

By Giles Smith's pocket watch it was four o'clock—twelve hours of marching, swimming, climbing just to reach the gunboats—and the real work had only begun. In two years of war he had never seen such a mess. The ironclads were at loggerheads in tight and looked abandoned.

Musket and heavy cannon boomed out of the east. Smith went to work. "Lay out by file on the flank, Colonel, and clear those sharpshooters out of those trees!" Officers barked orders, echoed by other orders, and soldiers evaporated into the bush. Forward troops peeled off into a skirmish line, while the rest fanned out behind them to press the Rebels away from the boats.

It was slow, hard work. Rebel sharpshooters kept hot fire on the reinforcements until the blue line pressed. Then butternuts dropped from their perches. Those that could drew back to form a new line to renew the attack, but Smith's reinforcements made it almost an even match. The Rebels held fast. There was the prize of the gunboats to be had. Mississippi rifles fanned out to outflank Smith and cut off Sherman. The Confederates in one hard push opened up with everything on all sides, enfilading the boats as well as the troops. Porter opened up with his forward cannon, with a long fuse on the shell so not to endanger Murphy's beleaguered outpost.

When Smith found Porter on the *Cincinnati*, the admiral was clutching the general order to blow up his ships. His officers had been briefed and were making preparations to pour out the gunpowder and turn the cannon inward. But they had made slow work of it, still hopeful.

"With your help, we can still blast our way through, Colonel. All is not lost."

The army kept to its work. The enemy was falling back, but fighting every inch of the way. When they had room to breathe, Porter gave orders for work parties to break out under the protection of the skirmish line. The rudders were removed and the boats drifted down the river with the current. The first shall be last and the last first—which was good news for the *Louisville*. It had enjoyed the relative protection of being the last boat upriver through the tangle, furthest from the battle, and was blessed to be the first to back out.

Christie dropped down the hatch of the *Cincinnati* to find Hall. The progress through the passageways was slow, the handshakes and back slaps nearly upended him. The surgeon was working outside his medicine room. Christie stepped over men luminescent with sweat and blood. "How is Henri!" Hall looked up, held the Buckeye's gaze evenly then slowly shook his head. Then he went back to work.

Murphy and his men clamored aboard in an orderly

fashion, belying any concern at all. The lieutenant took his place in command of the *Carondelet* and without sleep or a hot meal in two days went to work. By Sunday the gunboats had fallen back six miles, skimming off the banks and clanging into each other like dice. The infantry kept apace, providing ample cover.

Sherman met up with them about twilight. He had been giving a fair account of himself as a foot soldier, legging well ahead of the Second Brigade along the crest of the banks. As he caught sight of Porter's beleaguered boats, Sherman ordered Colonel Rice to deploy his brigade into the swamps and surrounding fields as far as solid ground went and sweep all Confederates out of the area.

Colonel Kilby Smith of the Eighth Missouri bounced bareback on a confiscated plow horse, saluted heartily, unabashedly ecstatic at meeting his chief. He slid down and offered his mount to his superior. Sherman leaned closer to hear his subordinate's report, all but drowned out by a chorus of cheers from Porter's bluejackets popping out of the gun ports like gophers. Then Sherman leveraged himself onto the animal's back. With one hand on either side of the harness, he galloped up the narrow road to find the admiral. Behind him, more regimental flags floated over a long column of blue caps hustling up the bank. Behind that came Ewing's Brigade. If Featherston were in a fighting mood, Sherman would give him plenty.

The general found Porter still in the wheelhouse. "We can still have at it, if you are game. We can about face and punch through."

Porter shook his head. "My boats are wreckage. Pemberton can have the entire Confederate navy and army on the other side by now." The admiral looked east longingly. "No, I think we must call the plan quits." Sherman accepted the verdict, but obviously did not like it.

By the twenty-seventh, little less than two weeks after the expedition had cast off, the flotilla had completed the forty-four miles back home to the Mississippi. The dismal sight of the battered gunboats brought men to the banks. If the beleaguered crews were expecting compassion, they got instead, "Don't go bush whacking without infantry!" "Say, is that an alligator skin floating on your pole?" "You take him prisoner or just eat him there?"

Porter was not to be baited. He was lucky and he knew it. If the Confederates had used solid shot instead of exploding shells, if they had planted mines in the muddy creek beds, if they had attacked and boarded en masse, he would be writing his memoirs from a Confederate prison in Richmond.

Two days later the last two of Sherman's regiments dragged into camp from their long trek from Eagle's Bend. Coated in leeches and scum, they were in no mood for jeers and boasts from Missouri and Illinois troops on saving the river navy single-handedly.

Christie would remember it all not in a sequence of days, but from image to image, crisis to crisis. The vibrant palette that painted the backcountry of the bayous and all its wonders would be eternal in his memory. He loved it the way Sherman did. He had been infected by it, never having seen anywhere so exotic and so beautiful, but he never wanted to set foot on another boat again.

While the Jack Tars and the army toasted each other, Christie threaded through the campfires to his cot pitched not far from Sherman's headquarters. In his knapsack was writing paper that he had parlayed from Hall for the price of one of Rawlins' cigars. Then he took up his pencil.

The brute back on Deer Creek had brought him to this. That it was an omen—soldiers without anchors to home or a star to guide on would turn savage. There were rules about how letters should look and the course they took, and for a minute Christie anguished over how to start. In the end it was a luxury— he could say whatever he wished because it would never be read:

Young's Point, Louisiana
March 26 '63

Julie,

Do you ever hear me calling you? If it weren't for the sound of your name in only my mind, I think I would go mad at times. I just need to say it out loud, to know that there is somewhere else than where I am and that there is someone else other than filthy, chigger-bitten soldiers beside me and enemy in front of me.

I have no right to think of you, but I do and as my own. Your memory is an amulet, I would have no courage to fight without it. There are days you are with me so close I can feel your breath. And then you are gone and I can't find you at all.

Don't hide from me, Julie. I have no hold on your present or your future.

Those belong to your husband. But the past is ours. We did not steal it.

There can be nothing lustful in holding on to it. I am an empty man with a long way to go. That is all I want.

Brent

VIII
Oats in the Nosebags and Five Days' Rations
Mid April, 1863

The cannons and caissons of the hard-bitten Seventeenth Ohio Independent Battery sliced through the flooded road, the crews shouting for everything in front to get out of their way or be baptized in mud and scum.

Christie bestowed an Irish blessing on the heads of the gunners and slapped his bummer against his dripping blouse and pantaloons. In a quarter of an hour he was due at headquarters to settle his debt with the general, turn over the last of his reports. In forty-five minutes more he would be aboard the next transport up river, and by the end of the week be back home with the Fourth in Virginia.

"Taking Stanton's name in vain, Lieutenant?" Rawlins returned Christie's salute from the decks of the steamship *Magnolia*. "Now what would General Grant say if he heard you?"

"He'd say, 'Good effort, Mister Christie, but you are not yet the match of Major Wilson in vocabulary or Colonel Rawlins or General Sherman in vigor and fire'."

"You could not be spreading calumny that your superior officers partake of the devil's language?"

"And put the devil to shame doing it!"

Rawlins motioned Christie toward Grant's offices in the ladies' cabin. "The general is waiting for you." Christie turned to pitch his cigar into the river but the adjutant held him back. "The general wouldn't approve of a waste of fine tobacco. Take it with you."

Either it was the first of the morning or the last of the long night, but Grant was already puffing away like a smoldering volcano, exhaust rising from a heap of rumpled uniform. A stub of a pencil was clenched in his hard-blistered hands. He studied the map of the trans-Mississippi as if real troops, cannon, and horses tracked deep ruts through its gullies, bayous, and broadlands. The general put a blue pencil to the terrain and scratched an arc from La Grange, Tennessee, along the eastern rim of the state of Mississippi to the Southern railroad and then swept southwest to Port Gibson. He tracked another, this one beginning at Young's Landing, straight down the eastern bank of Louisiana to Hard Times, then crossing the Mississippi at Port Gibson. Both lines converged on Port Gibson, which Grant marked with an "X." He drew long on his cigar and surveyed his work again.

Grant was a puzzle. The rumors had been rife about him not only in the Army of the Tennessee but even as far east as the Shenandoah. He had been branded a drunk and a bumbler, but that did not fit the man there so confidently mapping the juggernaut of his next campaign. Where did this assurance come from? Grant had been a failure in every endeavor except the extremes of love and war. He had not been born into influence or wealth; even his own family had dismissed him as a no-account. He grew up without opportunity, money, praise, and the counsel to inspire such boldness and invention as he had displayed so far in this fight. Out of years of loneliness and setbacks he had cultivated a rough, honest intuition on his own. He trusted his own sense implicitly and formed his own judgment on what those senses told him. Grant was a majority of one. Christie sensed that Lincoln must be something like this. And Stonewall Jackson. Although he could not be sure, Grant and Jackson seemed alike in their daring and all-out-or-nothing wagers. All of them western men, quiet men who would not interrupt their inner voices with too much talking.

Oblivious to his audience, Grant finished his work. With his pencil poised at Port Gibson he made three more sweeping diagonals, tight and parallel, driving northeast to Mississippi's capital at Jackson, which he circled and slashed through with another "X." Finally, he cut a line straight west, finishing the box with Vicksburg nestled tight within its apex. Box it was.

The commander leaned back in his chair, took a long drag of the cigar, as if the smoke quenched the immediate thirst for the prize. Grant threw back the dregs in his coffee cup and winced.

"Fred? Is that you?"

"No, sir, it's Lieutenant Christie."

"I thought you were Fred. I promised his mother I would keep a better eye on him. I bet that boy is ponying up to Cadwalleder for a cigar. Smokes them behind the warehouse. Doesn't think I know." The general motioned him nearer, "Mister Christie, come here." Grant eased back so his junior could see the map's full length. "In Mexico when I was a lieutenant I thought I knew more about war than the generals. Now that I am a general, I can use some of the advice of you brash lieutenants."

It was a dose of humility that became the man. "I hope it's not your next canal project, sir. If it is, I can guarantee mutiny."

Grant's eyes flashed like Chinese rockets. "Wouldn't General McPherson and General Sherman have a hemorrhage?" Grant looked back to his charts again to assure himself that the work was still there. For a time he forgot the lieutenant to examine every line again, but he changed nothing.

Christie counted down the minutes of his commission by the length of ash building at the end of his cigar. He flicked the burnt tobacco in a spittoon, careful this time of the general's dispatches. Aside from the Steele Bayou expedition with Porter the staff work assigned him had been not unduly hazardous and his stitches had healed. At first he had been charged with redrawing Grant's maps according to what he had seen on Porter's aborted enterprise. In the last days he had been a courier, trusted to carry sensitive, verbal dispatches between Himself and his generals. The experience gave him an insight into this western breed of commander. Christie had found William Sherman efficient and straightforward, gruff but never vindictive if he trusted you. He was a man who wrestled with demons and harbored grudges, not to be trifled with or underestimated. McPherson was young, brilliant, affable, and tireless. McClernand was an egotist and opportunist, which made him dangerous to his troops and to his superiors.

Among the division commanders he liked General "Black Jack" Logan, an Illinois politician with natural talents for command. On his first mission to Logan's headquarters Christie had found the general sitting in front of his tent wearing only his big black Hardee hat, his boots, and his cigar. He was playing a fiddle, singing ribald songs and in no way thought his behavior or his uniform or lack of it spectacular or unmilitary.

These men would turn future sense to present tense, stab its boldest punches; by their rules and on their terms the war would be won—here in the West. Christie fought down every temptation to take the general up on the offer of a transfer and be a part of it.

"You ride a horse, Lieutenant?" Grant asked absently.

"Yes, sir." Christie's mouth went dry. The general had drawled that same nonchalance when he had put him on the decks of Porter's gunboats.

"Very well?"

Knowing of Grant's excellent reputation for horsemanship, Christie was unwilling to boast but he used to ride quite well. "Pretty fair, sir."

"Good enough to ride with cavalry?"

"Union cavalry? Sir! Definitely!"

Grant smiled. "It wasn't an insult, Lieutenant." He shuffled through a pile of dispatches. "Well, rest assured, you are going to head north, but I am giving you a vacation from the river for a few days which should be of some relief to you."

"Sir?" So that was why he asked if he could ride. Christie relaxed.

Grant proceeded with the easy tone he used with men of equal rank or at least equal intelligence. "Now listen carefully, Lieutenant, these are the instructions I want you to take to General Hurlbut in Memphis. I want General Sooy Smith from his base at La Grange, Tennessee, to make some demonstrations into northern Mississippi here—noisy, but not venture too far or commit himself too heavily and get in over his head. At the same time I want to set loose the hounds. General Hurlbut is to put Colonel Benjamin Grierson and his brigade of cavalry in motion as soon as possible. They are to ride along this line from La Grange east and then straight south, staying as close to the Mobile & Ohio Railroad as they can. I want them in the saddle certainly no later than the seventeenth. That's two days from now. He is to move and keep moving south and southwestern until he gets to Port Gibson." A tall order for one colonel and three half-sized cavalry regiments riding unsupported and hell bent through enemy territory. But there was work for them to do.

"Along this route he is to play havoc with the rail lines, to fire the supply depots, cut the telegraph wires, and whatever else he can find to torment the Confederates and keep their attentions in his direction. While he is at it, I want him to make sure that nothing in the way of cannon, rations, ammunition, and materiel gets west to General Bowen at Vicksburg or Grand Gulf. My scouts report that my old neighbor from St. Louis is turning Port Gibson into a fortress, a bloody inconvenience if I land my troops there. Admiral Porter will have a devil of a time driving Bowen off those cliffs. I want Grierson to raise such a ruckus that Pemberton, Stevenson, and Martin Smith think they are being invaded from the east while I am coming over from Louisiana to land there at the bottom of the Big Black River. I will not be able to fool Bowen long—he is too smart. But if I can fool the rest of them and they don't re-enforce him no matter how loud he screams, I will win the race."

Grant continued with the easy tone of a man who made his own miracles and expected others to make theirs in agreement. "Admiral Porter assures me that his swamp navy will have no trouble in running the Vicksburg guns and ferrying my men across the river once we get south. I will have landed all my troops to meet Grierson when he rides in. So timing is imperative—you must make that clear, Lieutenant. He must be there no later than the twenty-seventh. His cavalry will be helpful during my march to Jackson. He will have knowledge of the terrain since he would have just been over much of it so soon." Grant circled Vicksburg and obliterated it with another "X." "I intend to bag the fox through the back door."

Christie was riveted! Right in front of him were the plans for the greatest invasion ever to take place in American history—navy, cavalry, marines, three corps of infantry, a system of scouts and spies, and engineers. Grant would march through enemy territory with three corps, without supply lines, straight for the jugular. If the scheme worked, Grant would sever the vital arteries of the Mobile & Ohio, the Southern, and the Mississippi Central railroads. All reinforcements, communication, beef, cotton, and corn traveling along the north-south and east-west routes would be blocked in Mississippi, where all these courses intersected at Vicksburg. The rivers would be under the control of the navy all the way from Pittsburgh to Port Hudson—that nut Banks would soon crack if he were half as good as Grant. The plan was a bullet to the heart. The Confederacy would hemorrhage. Then Lincoln would have the key in his pocket. Christie could not take his eyes off the map, even though he could hear his commander giving him more instructions.

"I want you to convey to General Smith the urgency that Grierson keep the pressure up and make Pemberton fret." Grant leaned back and smiled. "That's like giving the fox permission to raid the hen house." Then Grant turned to Christie. "I want you to memorize these orders and convey them and these markings to General Hurlbut and to Colonel Grierson just as I have given them to you. But tell them no more about my plan except their part—walls have ears. Will you do that? There will be no written dispatches to fall into Forrest's hands, should you be captured. I am relying on you to recount them just as I have outlined them to you." Vicksburg, his career, the fate of the Army of the Tennessee, and perhaps the war, depended on Grant's invasion played to perfection and in secret.

"Yes, sir."

Satisfied, Grant turned to other business and Christie knew that he had been dismissed. But by way of reminding the general of their bargain, Christie cleared his throat and jammed his hand into his breast pocket for the seven dollars. "Sir?"

Grant looked at it absently, "What's that?"

"To replace your hat, sir."

Grant smiled sheepishly. "Oh yes, my hat. Well, Lieutenant, my wife made me a present of a fine hat and a new coat just recently for my birthday. So I am willing to forgo the debt for this last favor. If you have no questions, you should be moving out presently." Christie saluted, but Grant remembered one more bit of news for him yet. "Lieutenant, General Kimball will be reporting back to duty. Right now he is tending to some urgent military business for me in Arkansas, but I plan to bring him closer to the fold to help out with my plans here. I remember you were quite fond of him."

"Yes, sir."

"Perhaps you could work with him again. Think about it on your trip and report back to Colonel Rawlins if your plans change." With that, Grant turned back to his desk.

If Grant's business was urgent, General Hurlbut and his subordinate William Sooy Smith worked by slower clocks. Christie had been cooling his heels outside headquarters for a couple of hours after the first briefing. Hurlbut had listened attentively, but with not much enthusiasm. Then he had Christie wait until summoned. Christie was called in to brief the commander again and then ordered to ride on to central Tennessee to General Smith's headquarters. Smith was not at all excited about Grant's plan either, but then he was seldom excited about any of Grant's plans—they depended too much on boldness and individual initiative, which were hard to gauge and never to his liking. So Christie was ordered to wait again.

"Hurry up and wait! As if the world turned only when generals gave it permission." The young lieutenant was doing nothing but lounging outside headquarters and growing older by the hour when a bearded lanky officer, moving too swiftly to acknowledge salutes, bolted up the steps.

"Colonel Hatch, General Smith is expecting you," Smith's staff settled down again to go about their business, and Christie took his ease on the steps near a sergeant whose entire identity was concealed behind a froth of phosphorescent beard.

"Who is Colonel Hatch?"

"Commands the Second Iowa Cavalry." The sergeant took no pains to hide his disdain of the lieutenant's ignorance. "You haven't heard of them? Rides with Colonel Grierson!"

"Where *is* Colonel Grierson?" This went more to the heart of Christie's business.

The sergeant was not in the habit of advising strangers on the whereabouts of senior officers and grunted that the visitor had his quota of information for the day. Christie leaned back and waited, but not long. Presently the colonel of cavalry bounded down the steps.

"Lieutenant Christie, with me!"

The earth was spinning again. It stopped at Hatch's tent crowded with officers, some lounging on campstools, while others standing, but all listening eagerly, as Christie went through the script again. The colonel digested everything with a cool, logical head. His officers too liked very much what they had been asked to do. When Christie finished, Hatch nodded and sent Christie outside to wait some more.

The Buckeye took his ease on a crate in the April night. He would have been asleep if a grizzled sergeant had not rattled him awake. "Colonel Hatch said we are to issue you a decent horse and get you outfitted to come with us."

Christie bolted to his feet. "There has got to be some mistake."

But the sergeant didn't see how or where any mistake had been made on his part. It was all very straight forward to him. "Well, take it up with Colonel Hatch."

Christie did so, pushing aside a lieutenant and a sergeant guarding the flap.

"Well?" Hatch looked up from his field desk.

"I think there has been some mistake."

"That so?" The colonel stifled a yawn. With nearly two years in the saddle, Hatch was used to "mistakes" and was taking this one in stride.

"Sir, I am infantry."

"That so?"

"Assigned to the Fourth Ohio, Army of the Potomac."

"That so?" Hatch gave Christie the full attention of one eye, while the other returned to the report he was signing.

"Yes, sir. I am supposed to be on my way to Virginia in the morning to report for duty."

"That so?"

"That's so!" Defense rested.

Hatch left the grievance on the back burner while he finished his other paperwork. Then he barked instructions to the sergeant to get the regiments up and ready at first light. Recalling the impatient lieutenant, he added in a by-the-way fashion that convinced Christie that the colonel and all his minions were deaf in both ears. "Lieutenant Christie will be joining our little foray as a scout of General Grant's. Introduce him around so the men recognize him and don't shoot him by mistake. Oh, and get him a fast horse—that spavined piebald won't make it ten miles. And get him a carbine and a couple of revolvers."

"That's what I told him, but he had some fired-up idea he was going east," the sergeant said.

Hatch turned to Christie, whose brain was paralyzed in shock. "You should be proud, Lieutenant, you are going after big game. The Confederates down here are bigger and meaner bugs than what you are used to in Virginia. Isn't that so, Captain Forbes!"

Forbes had been lounging in the shadows, Christie only noticed him now. The captain did not extend a hand, and even slumped further in his chair. "Forbes, Captain, Company B, Seventh Illinois." Then he turned back to his colonel, "Sir, what is your last word on Colonel Grierson?"

"Due in tonight by train." Hatch sounded exasperated. "Damned time to take leave. If Colonel Grierson does not arrive in time, we are still ordered to move out at dawn. As soon as the officers are assembled, send them in. Sergeant, pass the word: oats in the nose bag and five days rations in haversacks—make them last ten. Double the ration for salt. Make sure each man has forty rounds. Oh, and see to our guest here."

Forbes rubbed the wedge of beard under his chin and eyed Christie. "Lieutenant, I don't know how you got into this outfit, but here you are and here you stay. We didn't know much about this enterprise until you told us, but what we do know is that you are ordered to come along. That came by telegraph signed by John Rawlins, Colonel. You can write a protest if you want. I will file it away in case somebody might find time to read it after the war. But for now, you had better get ready."

"Yes, sir." Defeated, Christie followed the sergeant out of the tent.

Even if Christie was in no mood to talk, the sergeant had plenty enough words for them both. "Lieutenant, things move pretty fast around here. Now for the army making a mistake, I never heard it admit to any. Take Colonel Grierson for instance—hardly the man you would put in the saddle. You know he used to teach music and choir singing? Got a fine voice around a campfire, but I wouldn't pay money... Never anything to recommend him to the cavalry by any stretch of the imagination, except if you count a few months with the Ohio militia. Did you know he was from Ohio? Home state of yours by the sound of your twang. So, to tell the tale, the colonel doesn't even like horses. Still don't. Got kicked in the jaw as a boy — nearly knocked him into eternity. Dented his face and blinded him for two months, I hear. So when he volunteered up he asked for any branch of the service except the cavalry. So what did the army give him but cavalry? Some official thought he would look good in a saddle. Done a fine job of it too, in any case. So, Lieutenant, my point of all this is it's a matter of give and take. They give you cavalry and you take it."

The sergeant pointed to a fly tent. "You had better get some dinner, we are heading out at first light."

"You take what you are given." So this was why Grant asked him if he could ride. He had been shanghaied...again.

His luck was all bad that night. The only officer at mess was the sawed-off lieutenant who had treated Boyd so badly back at Young's Landing. His coat was buttoned only at the neck, but the front fell in a wide gap over a stomach that had expanded since they had last met. The orderly set a plate of sweet potatoes, rice, beans, and biscuits before Christie. Canfield's mouth was too full to bark, but he tapped his fork on his dish and waved for a refill.

Between mouthfuls Canfield examined the newcomer closely, debating whether the visitor's influence with the on-highs merited a show of courtesy. "Don't I know you from somewhere?"

Christie shook his head. "I don't think that you do. I am new here."

Canfield turned back to his plate, scooped up another spoonful, and shoved it into his mouth. "I'm new here as well. Assigned this morning to Colonel Grierson's brigade. I've been emancipated from the quartermaster's desk and am bound for some real action! Cavalry is the only place for a real man!"

"Is that a fact!" Christie gave him full points for nerve. The swagger was a direct insult to the jaeger horn that gleamed atop Christie's forage cap.

"I'm attached to Colonel Grierson to advise him on the latest in tactics."

"I wasn't aware that Colonel Grierson was in need of any help in that area."

Canfield studied him with a cold eye. "Colonel Grierson is not regular army, does not have the benefit of academic credentials."

"Seems to be doing fine learning on the job!" Old habits of quick and easy rebuke itched and Christie's knuckles curled.

"Not good enough. Confederate cavalry has been making fools of us right along. When Van Dorn took Holly Springs and smashed Grant's supply lines, he nearly captured Missis Grant. And wouldn't that have been a mess?"

"I hear that Missis Grant is more than the match of any general on either side!"

"I was being serious!"

"So was I, Lieutenant. Uh, I don't think we have been properly introduced! Lieutenant Christie, your servant!"

"Canfield, Brighten Canfield! West Point. Class of '62."

"Class of '62. That so." Christie seemed to remember that Winfield Scott had siphoned off the best of '62 and graduated them in the summer class of '61 to put more officers in the field after Sumter. So if Canfield hadn't made the cut, he was not a bright shining star — more of a cold moon. Christie bit down on his fork to keep from laughing in the man's face. Just wait until the ranks put it together. "Lieutenant Not-So-Bright Canfield" a moniker that will follow him throughout the army like a rat's tail. Christie pierced a wedge of pork fat and it followed the way of the depleted rice and beans to soothe the roaring lions in his stomach. The sweet potatoes he left to congeal in an inch-deep pool of blackstrap molasses.

"Gonna eat those?"

Christie pushed them over and Canfield scooped them up.

The verbal duel was interrupted by a head peaking through the tent flap. "Colonel Grierson wants you at headquarters, sir." Canfield rose. "No, sir, Lieutenant Christie, sir." Canfield slumped back on the barrelhead and regarded Christie with that cold eye. Christie could not account for the exact reason, but he knew at that moment he had made an enemy.

The night air turned his breath to steam, and he was chilled through by the time he got to headquarters. Grierson's lieutenant handed Christie a cup. All the chiefs were present. Colonel Edward Prince led the Seventh Illini and Colonel Reuben Loomis, who had succeeded to command Grierson's old Sixth. But Grierson was every inch the heart and soul of it all. He was tall and imposing and held the respect of every man there. He had led them through the heart of enemy territory and out again.

He spread his map of Mississippi over the table. "Now let's see if that Confederate traitor was worth the fifty dollars I paid for this. Lieutenant, you have my attention." The price was worth it to Christie's estimation. This map showed the state in acute topographical detail—its pine woods, farmlands, rivers, and sloughs. Christie traced his finger as he relayed the orders for a seventh time. Grant had been right; Grierson did like the plan. When Christie finished, the colonel was smiling and his officers were smiling back.

By way of conclusion Forbes handed his commander the latest telegraph. "It says here that General Grant thinks the lieutenant can be useful in our upcoming enterprise. He thinks much of his talents of reconnaissance."

"It says where...sir?" Christie did not believe it for a moment.

Grierson smiled at the genuine shock bleaching the young officer's face. "You were unaware that you would be joining our little expedition?"

Christie bolted, "Excuse me, sir? The sergeant's news was the first I heard of it."

"Lieutenant, it says here as of the sixteenth of April you are a member of the staff of the First Brigade, First Cavalry, Sixteenth Army Corps of Major General Ulysses Grant's Department of the Tennessee, which should be good enough for any man. But I can assure you that if you stay with us we can keep you from getting shot at least by one of Hooker's firing squads, or by one of Robert Lee's sharpshooters. Of course, Van Dorn might mistake you for a jealous husband. But wouldn't it be a greater honor to be shot by him or a general such as Nathan Forrest rather than by a Virginian?" Grierson slapped Christie on the back. The colonel liked very much the mission dropped into his lap and the courier who brought it. "Cheer up, Lieutenant, I can use another Buckeye around this camp, and things promise to be exciting. I hope you can ride—we can't have you slowing us down."

"Yes, sir, I can ride."

Grierson was already up and pulling on his gauntlets. "Hatch!" The colonel looked up, "Edward, this is Lieutenant...uh," Grierson checked to his back.

"Christie."

"We've met."

"Good. General Grant has urged us to make good use of him. Since you two are of long acquaintance, I will assign him to you. He said that Lieutenant Christie would know what was expected."

Colonel Hatch suppressed a smile. "Is that a fact?" Hatch regarded the lonely lieutenant as he would any fish caught on his hook.

"Well, we will make him feel quite at home."

The flat vowels of New England sarcasm rankled. And he had better live up to expectations. Hatch seemed not the man who tolerated mistakes. The surly quartermaster sergeant was now formally introduced as Richard Surby, and he took Christie hostage to turn him out, if not in fact at least in appearance, as a lieutenant of cavalry. This Surby did with a vengeance.

Used to being light on his feet, Christie could barely walk now with the arsenal weighing him down. He was braced in itchy new cavalry pants with the reinforced seat, boots to his knee and a red flannel shirt under his sack coat. There was a saber swinging from one hip, but of a different design from the usual cavalry model. This was more of a bayonet that could be fitted onto the carbine with one hand. But Christie hated it; the saber was such a bloodthirsty weapon. Something in one of his father's book on the Samurai he had read as a boy: The sword was minted by its craftsman with a soul of its own separate from the warrior who wields it. Once it tastes blood, it thirsts to be satisfied repeatedly. Its victories and sins are its own. This saber looked new. Christie vowed never to use it.

A holster with a navy colt nudged into his ribs, and there was enough ammunition stored in his belt to blow him sky high should he be hit. From the waist down Christie looked cavalry; from the waist up he was still infantry. He wore the four-button coat with the blue shoulder straps and the bummer with the brass insignia. Surby dared, "You going to keep that, Lieutenant?"

"Damned straight, Sergeant!"

Sensitive of the low regard infantry beheld cavalry, Surby snapped, "You got complaints? You been wounded twice I hear, Lieutenant, any more good luck with the infantry and you're out of lives."

Christie ignored him.

The camp bustled like a hive around and apart from him. Troopers were cooking rations, repairing their gear, testing cinches, cleaning weapons, and loading cartridge belts. When it was all secure, they sat down to a few unregimented minutes to write the last letters home for awhile. Rumors surged and flowed, but no one knew exactly where they were going and how long it would last. But they could guess. "We are gong to rip a seam down the back side of the Confederacy and kick Jeff Davis in the butt!" One old veteran wrote to his wife, "P.S. Use the new seed for the south acres, the old corn will be rotten!"

Christie had posted himself near headquarters should he be needed. His pride smarted from being cast as another expendable by a general he did not think could tell a lie. Well, Grant never lied—he just did not serve up the whole truth on the first course if not entirely necessary. His prerogative. Christie was in the middle of whittling a stallion's head out of a chunk of kindling when Surby found him.

"Lieutenant Christie, would you come this way?"

"Sergeant, every time someone with three stripes starts the conversation with 'Will you come this way?' I know I have trouble. Why don't you just spit it out? I am prepared for anything, so do your worst."

"This way, sir?"

Christie shrugged. "All right, this way."

The two walked through the low-lying fog of campfire smoke, passed a camp street of mottled swamp grass and miles of tents. On the perimeter the horses were corralled. Standing alone from the line of mounts was a corporal holding the reins of a honey-chestnut bay. Even in the shimmer of reflected campfires Christie could see the animal was magnificent. He stood about sixteen hands, the intense, intelligent eyes studied the man as he came on—to appraise him as he was being appraised. From his withers to his flanks, he was compact, broad chested, and sturdy, his legs on veritable springs. They were straight and well planted. Christie circled him and the animal let himself be admired. The horse was outfitted in an officer's blanket and a McClellan saddle, with matching reins remarkable for the absence of a mouth bit. Instinctively, Christie was drawn straight to the noble face. He slipped off his gauntlet to let the animal get his scent and then slowly pressed his palm up the dish of his nose and brushed the forelock away from the blaze. "What happened to your tail, boy?"

"Sir?" The sergeant handed Christie a sliver of paper and flicked a match for him to read it. But the refugee from the Fourth Ohio pushed the paper away. "If that's a bill for the horse, Sergeant, you got the wrong man. I couldn't afford him if I lived three lifetimes. I will be riding old Rickets until the Confederates catch up with me. Just let me dream for a minute."

"Gunshot, Sir."

"Excuse me?"

"His name is Gunshot. Arrived this morning."

"Sounds ominous."

"The dispatch, sir, if you will read it, I think it will explain everything."

The sergeant snapped another match and Christie took the paper and held it near the flame.

Headquarters Army of the Tennessee

Lieutenant Christie:
Trust Gunshot to be a good pard on your expedition. Return him when you report to me.
U.S. Grant.

"I'll be..."

"Care to try him out, sir?"

Christie was lifted into the saddle. He grasped the reins reverently. It had been five years since his mother had sold Sabine, the last and best vestige of his old life. Grant's generosity humbled him. The animal pranced and circled. His impatience and spirit was a challenge not to be underestimated even by an accomplished rider. Surby stepped back, and Christie reined off so horse and man could get the measure of each other.

Spirited, yet highly disciplined, Gunshot tugged and twisted to find open space. Christie took a firm hold of the reins just below the ears and chirruped. The guards watched them head for the stream. Christie let him prance back and forth along the bank to get his bearings. Even with slack reins, the animal did not jump or even bend to drink without signal. After a couple of swift circles and counter circles, Christie set the animal's sights and hunched low behind the neck. Gunshot was not in any hurry, and Christie feared he would buck or shy. But as the bank sliced away, he catapulted over the water effortlessly. Christie returned the same way but added a second obstacle, a near fence, which Gunshot took one-two in an easy rhythm. Christie confessed that the rider was not worthy of the animal.

He pulled Gunshot up stock-still and wrapped the reins around the pummel. He rested his palms on his thighs, pressed his knees against the horse's flanks, and nudged his feet just behind the girth. The lightest touch and the animal was off. Christie pulled and the horse obeyed. With the press of a foot to the left, the horse's rump rotated left around a radius set by his forelegs, planted to the spot. Christie counter signaled and the horse stopped then counter-rotated right until commanded to stop. Standard cavalry maneuvers, but Gunshot did them as if he had been the paragon of the specifications.

A small crowd had gathered, more to admire the animal than the rider. So far Christie had not challenged himself for any amount of honest respect from the animal or his new comrades. But the risk must be dared if he were to ride with these men. With the brush of his heel into Gunshot's belly, they trotted along the stream where the banks were higher and the leap wider. Conscious that, at the very least, Surby was studying him, Christie forced himself to keep his hands on his thighs and the reins wrapped around the pummel. What he could not control was the pounding of his heart.

"If you dump me in the water, I will be the laughing stock of the whole camp. It's what I deserve, and I won't blame you at all. I've got gumption to ask on such short acquaintance, but I will be eternally grateful if you give me this one favor. It's up to you."

He stroked the animal's long graceful neck and then he straightened in the saddle. He locked his feet in the stirrups and pressed his knees into the ribs.

With a nudge Gunshot shifted his gait from a walk to a canter and, as if reading Christie's mind, he rolled into a full gallop. The few short yards of ground to the water's edge pounded beneath them. At the bank the horse took flight, piercing the wind like a shooting star. He cleared the chasm and landed his rider down as smoothly as a magic carpet. Gunshot shook his head at their private conspiracy. Now, what Christie's audience thought of him he did not care—he had won the respect of a better soldier than himself. It was all he could to keep from shouting to high heavens, "Did you see me, Father? Did you see that! I finally did it!"

General Grant had fine taste in horseflesh. If he gave you a job, he provided the best tools to do it. Christie slid down. Gunshot basked in appreciation. Precious nuggets of sugar Christie had palmed from the officer's mess were slipped under Gunshot's nose.

"That animal is not a pet, Lieutenant, not good to spoil him." Surby strode up. His gaze said it all—the animal was worth five of the lieutenant.

"Some have a right to be spoiled." Christie ran a hand down Gunshot's long neck.

"You might be right at that." Surby pulled out an apple and handed it to Christie.

"Why, you fraud!" Christie did not know what to make of this cynical sergeant who was at least ten years older and, in spite of the rank, still measured himself Christie's superior in every way. But time would tell.

"I just said it was bad practice to make a pet of your mount, I never said I didn't do it myself. For a fact, it's a privilege accorded only officers to bring fine animals into the service. The men get Hobson's choice. But we try and keep the same mounts—makes a horse more than government property. But to get an animal like this, God or a general must owe you big!"

If Surby were fishing for explanations, his bait came up empty. Christie pulled a brush from the saddlebags, but the corporal relieved him of the reins and promised to bed the animal down for the night.

The only disturbance in this perfect scene was the chill blowing through the corral. It unsettled the horses and unsettled him, this sense of foreboding Christie could not shrug off. He had breathed it before—the premonition that death hovered somewhere close. He shuddered without being cold.

"You won't be gettin' sick and not be goin' with us will you, Lieutenant?"

"Don't worry, Sergeant. I won't be missing the party. I've a score to settle." He smelled bacon and biscuits frying over campfires. More than the food, Christie longed for his own mess and comrades to warm the loneliness.

"If you got any letters you want sent, Lieutenant, better get them to the captain's tent by 'Boots and Saddles'. It will be your last chance until we come back. I hear we are going to ride south and play smash with the railroads!"

Christie moved off without so much as a word and Surby did not salute. Captain Hatch had watched it all from the safety of the shadows. With the Buckeye gone, he conferred with his sergeant. "Well, how's our boy doing?"

Surby spit. "Quality Hill brat—probably related to Grant's wife, like the rest of his no-account staff. Nobody learned to ride like that in the infantry. I'll wager he's after a medal at our expense, so he can run for Congress. Damned! Cursed with two blue-blood babies to wet nurse this trip."

"Well, there's a lot of ways to handle that." Hatch patted Gunshot enviously.

Outside Hatch's headquarters, Christie sat back on an ammunition crate to write Julia another of the letters that went no further than his haversack:

La Grange, Tennessee
Past midnight. April 17/'63

Julia,
The earth has tipped over and I have slid into a pile of horse s—t. If you want a little fun "join the cavalry" they say. Well, it does look to be a party soon!

When a general has you by the reins, a man has no more

determination in the placement of his own feet than a horse. Tomorrow my boots will be swinging from the stirrups in the combined company of Illini and Iowa plow feet. Charity has dried up among this lot and they are a cranky breed of wasps who act as if they have been insulted with the burden of toting along a cricket. But we shall see.

Is your hair still long around your shoulders or have you grown so society as to pile it up on your head? Do you still ride down along the river where we used to meet?

The daffodils should be thick along the bank there? I remember the lilacs and the dogwoods made a pretty bouquet. Those old places and dead promises are all that I hold to, even though they are dust.

Brent

VIII
Boots and Saddles

On Friday, April 17, 1863, Grant lit the fuse to his grand invasion. The black pitch was fading to gray as the long, blue column funneled through a sweaty haze that promised rain. The column of seventeen hundred men moved by twos down the narrow road, followed by a small battery of light artillery, a chaplain, and only a few forage and supply wagons driven by farriers and teamsters. In no particular hurry, they eased their mounts past the little college and the Seminary for Ladies and on down the street that channeled between two flanks of old houses rimmed by gape-toothed fences and wasted gardens. On the hill, public buildings now flew the yellow flags of hospitals, and these already swelled with wounded and sick. When the weather warmed and the fighting intensified, the rolling hillsides would be a snowdrift of white tents sheltering the overflow.

Grierson rode at the head of his column with Colonel Reuben Loomis. Keeping pace parallel on the western road was Colonel Edward Prince's Seventh Illinois, followed by Hatch's Second Iowa. Guiding on the right of his company, Captain Henry Forbes rode, his eyes already pinched and sunken to half crescents between a brush of brows and round, sun-weathered cheeks. Back in the column rode his nineteen-year-old brother, Stephen.

The brothers had had words this morning. Christie had come upon them unexpectedly. They took no efforts to be discreet—time was short and the point needed made. This country ahead was not new to Stephen; he had seen it before as a captive last year. On his way to a Confederate prison, Stephen Forbes had been nearly dismembered by an angry mob. His guards saved him at risk of their own lives. Stephen was risking his luck again. He had no will to be a hero, but he was bound to be a part of any mission his regiment fought.

The meeting had not ended well. Henry Forbes worried about his brother. Stephen had said it as a warning, not a threat, but he vowed he would never be taken prisoner again. It was as simple as that. As captain, Henry had some authority to keep Stephen in the back where he belonged. Since he was small, Stephen's place would be behind the big men riding big horses. But Stephen had the heart of a giant, and when the fighting burned, he would be in the front, slashing into the thick of it.

Grierson pulled out his mouth harp. Serenading itself with a chorus of "Rally Around the Flag Boys," the column floated on a cloud of red talcum kicked up from the road angling between the high hedgerows of tanglewood. The first morning rays had already set the deep pools of black water to steaming. By noon their poisons of slime and mosquitoes would make breathing generally unpleasant.

Only twice did Lieutenant Canfield come into view, once at the first break, the second at rations. At the fire he was going on at length about being the last nut to fall from a family tree blooming with military glory—four generations of collective experience was at the disposal of his superiors. With no appreciation for such blessed good fortune, officers moved away with their plates of beans and biscuits, forsaking their captain to Canfield. In no time, his good manners having cooled Forbes pleaded some urgent business with the colonel and evaporated into the countryside. Canfield trailed on his heels. Christie was leaning against a tree, scraping his plate, when Forbes strode by. Christie nodded and Forbes turned on him in such delight as to overwhelm him with solicitude, leaving Canfield to languish in the backwash.

"How are you taking the ride, Lieutenant?"

"Fine, sir." Christie sacked his brain for some topic in which to engage the captain because the captain seemed to want to be engaged. But being of short acquaintance, nothing came readily to the tip of his tongue.

"I think the easy ride will be behind us soon." Forbes nodded.

"I think so too, sir." Christie winced. *Now, genius, say something about the weather and the captain will know you are brainless.*

"If there is anything you need, the quartermaster will gladly fortify your rations. We are all friends here." Canfield inched closer. "Ahh! If you will excuse me, gentlemen, I think the colonel is seeking my attention." Then Forbes evaporated in a curtain of oaks.

Christie lazed against the tree and swirled his cup so the coffee would pick up the sugar in the bottom.

Canfield spit out the dregs of the rebuff. "I bet your butt is on fire!"

"Pardon?" Christie relaxed in the luxury of his status as Grant's man, giving him the prerogative to spurn pedigreed lieutenants.

"Soft butt cheeks not used to a hard saddle and a good day's ride." Canfield hissed.

"Well, in the infantry, we have a way of thinking that a fighting man survives on the strength of his brain, not his butt, and his body will follow."

Canfield reared and then let the insult go. "You aren't worth a good whopping. But stay out of my way." Canfield turned on his heels, but his stride wanted swagger to make the insult sting. Instead, he hobbled and jerked. His knees bowed and his butt swayed as if on sagging hinges.

Grierson's long blue ribbon of troopers glided under shaded roads leading in the direction of Ripley. When the column broke into the open, the sun thawed out the knots and ague of a damp winter, and before it could be unpleasantly warm they were cool again, riding through another orchard. Christie rolled in his saddle to the leisurely rhythm and was nearly asleep when Gunshot stopped dead. Ahead, voices—some heated, others beseeching—volleyed back and forth. Christie followed Hatch, who reined his horse in that direction. They soon found Colonel Prince engaged in a battle of words with a local who was keeping up a ready fire despite his meager number.

"Sir, the sergeant took my hat—a new one, sir."

The sombrero was balanced rudely over the ears of Surby's horse, and the sergeant had already drawn his knife to make the appropriate alterations for the ears. How new was up to debate, but it was probably of later vintage than the rest of the boy's suit. Three inches of tanned bare leg gaped between the frayed ends of his jeans and the high-topped shoes of warped leather. The pantaloons would be too short by half by the time he grew big enough to fill the slack in the butternut jacket. But he reposed like a lord in royal robes upon the seat of his mule cart.

Colonel Prince mustered some show of decorum, and for a moment Christie thought court was in session.

Surby pleaded a defense on the grounds of gross insubordination. "But, sir, he called us 'Yankees.'"

Prince scowled at the farmer. "Now, even though we are at war, boy, there is no cause to be insulting."

"You is Yankees. I can tell by you uniforms." The boy was not about to be connived out of what his eyes said to be true.

"No, my misguided lad," Surby said as he took up his knife again, "We are not 'Yankees,' we are *Westerners*, not to be confused with our eastern brothers, who fight only gentlemen planters and only in good weather and on clear fields." Surby shot a sideways glance at Christie. "And your hat, my man, will be the price of a hard lesson in ett-ee'-cut!"

Colonel Prince shook his head helplessly and reached for his wallet. He withdrew a two-dollar greenback and handed it over. The boy brightened, pleased that he had bested the sergeant with his own commander. A Yankee greenback would beat Confederate script even on its home soil. He nodded that the matter was resolved to his satisfaction, and Prince turned to net additional return on his investment.

"Any place we can get water around here?"

The driver surveyed a wide three-sixty. "Well, there is the Ellis Plantation and the Falkner Plantation."

Prince took note of the directions and decided the first to be more convenient. The driver pulled off the road until the column got by. Christie maintained his pace behind Colonel Prince as they leisurely rode up under the canopy of live oaks thirty miles later.

"Sir, over there!" At the same time Christie and Surby spied the grayclads scampering toward the woods.

"They are yours, gentlemen, be my guest." Prince urged them on.

Sergeant and lieutenant set out at a dead run. Gunshot, livened to the game of chase, pulling ahead in spite of Christie's grip on the reins. Protocol prescribed these prisoners belonged to Surby and the men of the expedition, but Gunshot bore down on the Confederates and headed them off short of the woods.

"Well, sir, I think we have cornered the gray foxes. Now to defang them." Surby motioned for their weapons to be taken.

Once relieved, their hands flew up, and the captives were herded back to Grierson, who was making himself at home in the ample rooms of the Ellis home. His hungry command was already emptying the silos, ransacking larders, smokehouses, and springhouses for dinner, and filling gunnysacks for later. In an hour, pullets were dressed and roasting, biscuits were baking, and coffee boiled up from the campfires on the grounds.

Forbes motioned a place for the newcomer under the willows. "Sit down, Christie, enjoy the bounty of the Confederacy. We eat free tonight." His invitation was gracious, but Forbes and his officers still held themselves aloof. The dinner passed in easy back and forth among men who had known each other from boyhood. Christie said little, and his discretion made his presence, if not agreeable, at least tolerable to his hosts.

Before he had been admitted to Grant's staff, Christie had never smoked. But Rawlins had spoiled him. Now he craved a cigar to cap this fine meal, but he had bartered them away for Gunshot's forage. Instead, he excused himself to walk the kinks and stiffness out of his legs. As he rounded the garden wall, he found Henry Forbes in quiet conversation with Stephen, who obviously did not like this second chapter of the lecture read out to him. Christie was backtracking not to interrupt, but Forbes, having caught sight of him, called him back.

"Lieutenant, I wish to introduce my brother." Christie extended a hand and the younger man took it cautiously.

The captain was backing off, "Well, Stephen, remember what I told you. Even with the stripes, no grand gestures. We do not need to test mother's friendship with the Almighty." With that, the older man moved away to tend to business.

The two strangers were quiet for some minutes. Christie was dry for something to say, not at all privy as to why Forbes initiated the introduction. "Everything blooms here...trees...bushes. This is beautiful country. I hope the weather holds."

The young trooper nodded, glad that there was something in which he was in agreement. "Perhaps it seems a bit strange to talk of such things as pleasant weather. Especially in the light that we came down here to kill our fellow man and carry distress to his families, to dislocate the country and destroy life wholesale. For my part, I don't hold to a grudge and have always tried to keep myself human, to remember homes like this one and the places where people have hearts and charge all this to the accounts of war and stern necessity."

Two years ago, Christie would have abused such talk. Now he tolerated it, even if vengeance for lost friends weighed heavily on his shoulders. But Stephen Forbes, for all he had been through, possessed a benevolence and innocence that Christie did not have and perhaps would never have. And for a minute he envied Stephen his gentle soul. For his part, Christie made no apologies watching the hen house raided, quilts and weavings tied behind saddles, and the blooded horses rounded up from the hollows where the family had hidden them. The war was sinking to its bottom level, but in his mind the South had asked for it when the first cannon shell exploded against the masonry walls of Sumter. Compared to any other invading army, any other time in history, the South was getting off easy. Stephen had saluted and excused himself before Christie even realized he was gone.

Somewhere in northeastern Mississippi
First day of the long ride

Julia,
The men talk of home...of the future...of the past...but never now. The war wouldn't be so hard if only I had someone to fight for, someone back home to pray for and to pray for me. And so I don't pray. I wonder if my mother still prays. When I was a boy she used to make an event of it every night in the living room with her prayer book and her beads.

I met a man who cooks worse than you, and it stands to reason the army made that his specialty. He conjures over the caldrons of the officer's mess like Macbeth's witches, and I dare say, with the same ingredients. His dumplings are as hard as grapeshot and his coffee – the color and taste of tobacco spit.

He is only slightly more agreeable than your mother, especially in the morning, and he's better looking now that I compare the two.

We have been raiding the larder of a Secesh. By the time the infantry comes up the pickens will be clean and all that will be left to spice their mess will be tree bark and swamp water.

My love to you on this gentle evening.
Brent

When the bugler called reveille, all but the boldest stars had faded into the cobalt blue sky. The regimental flags hung limp in the acrid after-glow of low simmering coals. Long-suffering troopers rolled up blankets and sorted their gear, then fed their mounts before they would breakfast themselves. Saddles that had been pillows were now slung over horsebacks to cushion a softer part of the trooper's anatomy than his brain box. Cinch straps were pulled snug, threaded through the ring, and secured as neat as the Windsor knot of an English lord's tie. With "Boots and Saddles" men stood at attention and waited shoulders even at the nose of their mounts for the day's orders and the command to start.

The three regiments readied to march, if not with snap and polish — although that could be mustered for show — at least with efficiency. Except at the far end of the garden, where Lieutenant Canfield, on his own authority, was dressing down a trooper for his equipment. Rage bristled behind the private's tight-lipped grimace.

Christie could not let it pass. "Lieutenant Canfield."

"Just a minute, sir." Canfield turned on the two-story private, who could have sent this peacock into eternity with one swipe.

"Now, if you please." Christie never gratified himself with saving Canfield's life that day, but most certainly he had.

Canfield was forced to dismiss the trooper to answer the call of a superior whom Canfield recognized only in terms of political expediency, not in quality. Although Christie wanted to verbally dissect Canfield into quarters, he restrained himself. "Lieutenant, I think courtesy will go a long way toward making us more welcome in this outfit."

"That is the least of my problems, sir!" Canfield seethed. "From my days at quartermaster, condition of equipment has been my main concern. The scabbard especially is battered and in disrepair."

Christie could not believe Canfield's stupidity. "Do you know why that scabbard is dented?"

"Bad discipline," sputtered Canfield.

"No, Lieutenant, so that it doesn't rattle. Less noise to awaken the sleeping dragon. This isn't parade ground cavalry. Where have you been?"

Had Canfield ever seen the elephant? How could he, having been until lately attached to headquarters by a short leash of papers and forms? Yes, that was it. This would be Canfield's first time out of the army's home offices. In fact he was the only one untested in these ranks. The dressing down was a fraud. Canfield was scared. No, he was more than that. He was a man who had not plumbed the depths of his own courage and must worry how shallow those waters went. This would be his first time in battle, and he would go in surrounded by veterans who had long memories. Canfield bore watching.

Disengaged from these workings of his brain, Christie's voice kept to the point. "Even if we could keep the brass shiny out here, we don't need mirrors showing the enemy where we are. You will learn the more subtle rules of getting along if you watch more and say less. I urge you to adopt that policy, Lieutenant." Christie turned on his heels and tramped through a curtain of willow fronds.

In the cool morning shadows, Surby had watched the confrontation over his breakfast of fresh eggs, sweet potatoes and coffee. Christie passed him without waiting for the salute that never came, and therefore did not see the smile cracking the sergeant's leathery face. "Morning, Lieutenant Christie. Fine morning for a ride."

"Sergeant."

The Second Iowa had wanted to lead the column, had requested to do so. In fact, they even knew where they were going, having visited the town the Christmas before. And so by rights they should have been kicking up dust instead of breathing it. But third in the hearts of their countrymen, so they were third in the brigade that eased cautiously the few miles into Ripley at just about eight o'clock.

There were few people on the streets. Those that lingered did not act surprised at the sight of Union cavalry coursing through their town as easy as a parade. Among the stoic was the druggist peering out his apothecary window. As he churned the poultice with his pestle, a widow in mourning weeds waited at the counter. She clucked her tongue at the long line of blue troopers filing down the main street like a train free of its tracks.

"Will you look at that! The war will be overflowing into our back yards if Mister Falkner doesn't get his rangers back home. Don't we have any home guard left to keep these Yankees from our doorsteps?" She brushed away the wisps of forelock of the baby who slept undisturbed deep in the soft down of blankets.

"Falkner is in Vicksburg, Missis Harmon. Colonel Smith ought to be here about someplace. Though not much he can do with some long-in-the-tooth militia and boys against Union regulars. Here we are— enough for two nights to smother the colic. Anything else?"

The widow bit her lip. Did she dare? How many of her mother-in-law's complaints were real, and how much was just grief? Even more, how she needed a night's sleep herself now if the baby could be quieted. So she asked if Doctor Bell had left a prescription for laudanum for Mother Harmon?

The reflection of the long Union line trailed unbroken across the wall mirror. The druggist checked his records. The prescription was long exhausted. Widow Harmon had been Jenny Farlow only two years ago—fresh, pert, and bold until she had married Jason Harmon, a man who seemed to shine in the very constellations of Mississippi politics. Then there was Shiloh. Now the blush and starch were out of her, what with him dead, his children, their child, his mother and the plantation on her hands. "One more," he lied. "I will make it up?"

"Yes, please."

"Be no more than a minute. Sit yourself down there. Mira has made some tea for me, but I have had little time to drink it. You help yourself while it is hot, and I will finish this up."

Jenny Harmon was grateful for both the chair and the tea.

That same afternoon, Grierson gathered his commanders to announce the first chapter of his scheme. The meeting had not gone well enough to suit Hatch. Now captains closed around him, Hatch relayed the bad news. "The Illini are creating a diversion, we are moving east toward the Mobile & Ohio, just beyond the town. Scare the bones out of the townsfolk. Make it look like we are hell bent to tear up the track."

"We going after the railroad?" Canfield was chomping at the bit.

Hatch shook his head. "Not really. Just make it look that way. It's well guarded. But we need to create some distraction to keep the home boys off their game. We are going only as far as the Molino Road to play fox in the hen house and to be within hailin' distance of the main body, should need come. Then we rendezvous with them tonight. Nothing to write home about, but stay alert."

The Molino Road cut a channel through a grove of lilacs that perfumed the air with a heavy sweetness. Nestled in boxes of white fences, small farms fought to grow wheat and corn from the rocky soil that had nurtured cotton before the war. Orchards of pear, peach, and plum had already budded, and since the spring had been wet and lately warm, nuggets had already formed in the heart of the blossoms. But the day would turn bleak. From the west thunderheads pulsated with lightning and growled with low rolling thunder. In anticipation, Gunshot roused and pranced.

Secreted by the wood line beyond the border of houses, Colonel J.F. Smith sat amid the three hundred and fifty men of his first Mississippi Regiment of State Troops. They watched the long Union column snake behind the swallowtail guidon. Smith remembered the Second Iowa from last winter—a big regiment, well armed and superbly outfitted. Now they came again, unmolested through the heart of his country. Smith's hands tightened around worn leather straps. He rode a swayback horse and fed his troops on meager stores dealt out in fractions by his Mississippi neighbors, while the Yankees were growing fat on what he was forbidden to breach. The double standard rankled.

"Shall we go after them, Colonel?"

"You want a scalp, do you, Billy?" Smith counted the enemy line and multiplied by four. About two-thirds strength since last time.

"We ought to do something—can't just let them ride through us easy like."

"You ever hear the one about the five-hundred-pound grizzly, Billy?"

"No, sir."

Smith had not taken his eyes off the column. "Where does a five-hundred-pound grizzly sleep?"

"Where's that, Colonel?"

"Anywhere he wants to. For the time being that there is a five-hundred-pound grizzly and we are going to let him be. But since you are hot to do something, how about you ride up to Chesterville and let the town know about this. You do that, boy. Don't get distracted by anything else—there and back." The lad saluted smartly and slapped the reins of his horse, but Smith caught the strap. "Take the back way, and tell them, while you're at it, that we will be keeping an eye on things. But I have a feeling that this regiment isn't stupid, not going to ride into enemy territory on a bluff. They have some support somewhere about. And just so you feel better, we will sting 'em if we get the chance." The young cavalier felt better with that.

Smith was true to his promise. From the safety of woodlots, barns, and outhouses his sharpshooters pitted Hatch's advance with sporadic fire. Squads braved the open, fired a volley into the column, and melted back into the countryside, daring the Iowans to give them chase. But Hatch did not lose his head, even with a few of his comrades dead and wounded on the ground. His men extracted their weapons and waited for the order to fire. Their colonel surveyed the horizon and the half dozen Rebel riders strung out on the edge of the orchard. "Return fire if you get a target. But we don't know how many are hiding just beyond those woods, and we aren't getting suckered into a trap. Keep the column moving."

Lieutenant Halfworth nodded in complete agreement. But Christie's every instinct was to go to ground, to put up cover, and get ready to return fire in earnest. The column presented a target as broad as a fence. Ball puckered the road just inches from Gunshot's right hoof. One nicked Christie's pummel, another hit a trooper just in front and he fell to the ground. Gunshot pranced and twisted toward the enemy, holding back was a furious effort. A second volley thudded into the dirt to the left, not close enough to present danger, but nevertheless where the animal could see it.

"Can't you control that horse, Lieutenant?" Canfield snickered.

"What is it, boy?" Like a compass needle the mount addressed every report, his nose to the front and his rump to the south of it. Christie purred, "Is that how you lost your tail, boy? A cannon shot to the rear? Would make *me* nervous. But we are getting no revenge today."

Grierson was just settling into camp below New Albany when Hatch rode in, hot, dusty, and out of sorts. Wounded were lifted down from saddles, hoisted out of ammunition wagons and the ambulance, while the able-bodied went to see if their Illini cousins had left them anything for supper.

If there was a storm collecting outside, there was another collecting inside the Sloan Plantation where Grierson was making himself at home. Long vowels and rolled consonants of Mississippi discontent were rising to a fearful pitch from the central hall. Gauntlets raised clouds of dust as they were slapped down on the French-imported table. Grierson relaxed his long frame into a tapestry chair. "What is it, Captain. Is there a problem?"

The plantation owner, a squat man with a monogrammed kerchief vibrating against his ruddy cheeks brushed by the adjutants. He was quivering with rage and insult down to his feet, which rocked from toe to heel as he stuttered his outrage. Sloan assaulted Grierson in tones of bare-knuckle condescension. "Why don't you cut my throat and be done with it! Cut it I say—I cannot stand by and watch you molest my land, my home, my women."

Grierson's cheeks ripened and tears glistened in the weather-dried creases of his eyes. "Women? Have we molested any women, Lieutenant?"

The commander could have turned right or left, and as luck would have it Christie was the officer Grierson enlisted for his charade. "No, sir. Saw some sorry-looking dogs as we came up. Been in the saddle some days, but I think we would still know the difference."

"There, you see, Master Sloan? Your sorry dogs are unmolested. Therefore, you can assume we would exert a greater restraint where your women were concerned, provided my men can tell the difference."

"I will have you know those are the finest hunting hounds in Mississippi!" Sloan hiccuped spasmodically. With Grierson reclining in the chair, the planter now had more or less the advantage of equal height and went at the commander face to face. "Cut my throat! I do not wish to see more. Put me out of my misery. Yankees in my grandfather's home, sitting in his chair, drinking his brandy..."

"Brandy?" The cry went up from parched throats. Grierson's entire officer corps channeled down the halls and through the house, bypassing silverplate and crystal in pursuit of liquid invigoration.

Sloan was boiling over. "My grandfather—he must be spinning in his grave! Cut my throat!"

The commander was warming to the bait. In his youth Grierson had written several operettas, but here a role in a delightful farce was just being handed to him. "Well, if you insist, Mister Sloan. Lieutenant, take Mister Sloan out and give him his wish. Make it far out back—I don't want his squealing to scare the horses."

"You mean slit his throat?" Christie tried to affect the same solemnity as his commander.

Grierson's finger slashed a line across his Adam's apple. "We don't want to seem inhospitable. You do have a knife, Lieutenant?"

Christie gauged the neck to be about the size of a ripe watermelon. "Sir, nothing that size."

Surby pulled his Bowie from its sheath. The steel flashed a razor-thin glare across Sloan's face. The master blanched and collapsed into the divan. The sergeant was enjoying the role and waited only for his cue, "Sir?"

Grierson looked up and nodded absently. "Yes, Sergeant, that should be efficient!" Christie nudged the master up to his feet, but he twisted free.

"Allow me, sir." Surby and a fellow sergeant took Sloan by his shoulders, raising him two inches off the varnished floors, to half drag and half carry the planter toward the rear. Sloan squawked in protest.

Beyond the circle of blue uniforms, a woman of miniature dimensions and a self-possessed manner forced her way into the melee. "Please put my husband down, sirs."

Grierson peered over his map. Standing as coolly in the middle of the enemy as if *he* had surrendered unconditionally to *her* authority stood Missis Sloan, with barely an eyelash aflutter. But Surby was not to be intimidated by any Southern woman, highborn or otherwise, and continued with his burden as ordered. She spoke quickly, "Colonel, my husband can be, well...quite melodramatic...he's French on his mother's side and rather excitable. His explosions should never be taken at face value."

Grierson rose on dead legs and smiled politely. "I will be most happy to accord you the life of your husband. You have nothing to fear—my men are all of the highest quality. I will discharge your husband into your custody. Now, if you will excuse me."

Missis Sloan ushered her apoplectic husband from the room before he would give the commander a change of heart.

With the affair settled, Grierson gave the orders for the next morning. That Christie figured in them at all surprised him. "Lieutenant Christie, I sent for you. I am ordering Major Love with the wounded and prisoners back to La Grange. That will leave Colonel Hatch a little light on his staff. With your fast horse that can sniff out Confederates, I think you can be of value as advance scout. You will be briefed more in detail later."

"Yes, sir." With that, all junior officers were then excused. Christie pivoted to leave.

Canfield blocked the door. The two exchanged silent dares, finally Canfield stepped back and Christie moved out into the rain.

IX
A Duel of Knights

Ohio-born Lieutenant Colonel Clark Barteau wore Confederate gray with two gold stars embroidered on either side of his throat. He led his Second Tennessee Cavalry southeastward down the Pontotoc-Okolona Turnpike, searching among the rain-swollen gullies for signs of Yankee horseshoes. Smith had sent him word that a regiment of Union cavalry was prowling nearby, going exactly where he was unsure, but when last seen were dangerously close to the Mobile & Ohio. Telegraph wires sizzled between Vicksburg and General Ruggles' headquarters in Columbus, but neither had yet decided on the direction and size of this new Yankee nuisance. The outsized estimate went as high as six thousand an entire division heading right for Houston, Mississippi. That dispatch was not yet cold when Ruggles received another from Captain Ingate, quartermaster at Okolona. Pemberton had forwarded it in a rush because Ingate's estimate of Yankee strength was two thousand strong, with five mounted howitzers traveling on the Houston Road.

Well, Barteau had been on the Houston Road and there was not a blue-coated invader for miles around. The troopers could be in retreat or leading him in merry circles. Barteau had been ordered to give chase with less than one-sixth the men, and he would give his best effort, size meaning nothing, if he found them. But first he must find which report was accurate, which direction these phantom Yankees were going, and what they meant to do. The Tennesseeans had been riding hard in the rain, finding nothing as the evidence disappeared in the washout. Now they smelled like wet sheep, were hungry, and out of coffee.

"Ingate is seeing phantoms again." Barteau had lost his enthusiasm for ghost chasing.

Grierson's whereabouts was festering ulcers not only with the enemy but also with his own superiors. He had gone into a rabbit hole and not come out. Back in La Grange, General Hurlbut, a glass of whiskey in his hand and a cigar grimly braced between yellowed teeth, paced back and forth, stopped and swayed from right to left foot. A dispatch from General Halleck lay on his desk.

The Chief of Staff was under the impression that Grierson should have cut the Mobile & Ohio Railroad near Tupelo and the Mississippi Central Railroad at Oxford. That notion had not been on Grant's map at all, but the great sheik in Washington was under this misguided impression because General Hurlbut had given him that misguided impression.

It was now Monday late and Hurlbut had not heard from Grierson since his column had ridden out last Friday. Halleck, a commander who liked to conduct the war from the relative ease of his armchair, wanted assurances to pass on to his boss, Secretary of War Stanton, that all his chess pieces were still on the board and moving with artful precision. Hurlbut took another drink. His staff traded glances behind his back. Such glances had been more frequent lately—since his promotion to corps command, the general had begun to drink heavily. Grant would not be pleased.

Fortified with false courage, Hurlbut dictated a message to Halleck: "Grierson will cut the railroad, if he lives, at or near Chunkey Bridge about Wednesday night or Thursday." Hurlbut poured himself another three fingers of whiskey and prayed that prophecy would become fact. Then he added a postscript. "No news here of any moment. Your obedient servant, S.A. Hurlbut."

From the window of his Vicksburg headquarters, Lieutenant General John Pemberton could see to the far side of Crawford Street and the Convent of Mercy. The once elegant garden was now full of litters filled with more sick than wounded—dysentery, measles, typhus, and ague. The stench of turpentine told that ague was taking its toll—men were bathed in it to break the fevers. If lightning struck the convent right now, it would go up in a fireball.

The pounding of hooves and the ambulances rolling on whining axles had been unceasing all night and now today. Sister Ignatius Sumner and her small army of nuns had been stacking the patients like cordwood under the fly tent until they could be gotten inside out of the rain. And they took all comers as if they believed that the brick walls of the school would swell to accommodate them all. The habit of Mother Superior was soaked and mud-spattered. Her white linen was soiled and limp, and her veil, which had faded from black to brown, repelled rain like a funnel down her back, but she kept to her work, making system out of chaos. Postulants walked behind her and did as best they could with water and broth. Medical supplies were now so short that they were saved for only the most serious cases, which they knew would be coming soon.

What drove such delicate women to such work, he could not understand. Bless them, these angels of Mercy. Their attention to the men was a godsend, and as conditions worsened—Pemberton now knew they would be hell very soon—the sisters stood as the only rearguard of medical solace for the population as well as for his troops.

"Have you heard anything?" Pemberton asked of whoever tread into his office.

"No, sir."

"I must know what the enemy is planning. Is it an invasion or a raid?"

The aide shook his head helplessly, and Pemberton bit his lip. "Take another message to General Ruggles in Columbus." Before the aide had pen in hand, his superior had dictated the dispatch. But he did not need it repeated, this one was not unlike the others: "I hear from several sources, but not your headquarters, that enemy is approaching Pontotoc. This is a mere raid, but should not be unmolested by you." Translated, "Get your butt in the saddle and stop the Yankees, or I'll find somebody who can."

Ruggles did not take the scolding well. He had dispatched Lieutenant Colonel James Cunningham with his Second Alabama Cavalry in the direction of these damnable Yankee invaders. They were to help Colonel Barteau in any way they could. Colonel Barteau could use help—in twenty-four hours he had ridden sixty-eight miles and had not yet spotted the first blue coat. The Yankees had evaporated.

In truth, the Second Iowa rode only a few miles from Barteau's regiment. With hoots and hollers Hatch's regiment was cutting a path through Houston, dashing down the streets making a show for the citizens. They turned off the main road and tore through a wheat field, churning up the soft loam and cutting a swath fifteen feet wide. If given the luxury of ripening, the grain would be baked into bread for the hungry troops fortifying

Vicksburg. Now it churned under the hoofs of on-rushing Union troopers. The Second enjoyed its role center stage while Grierson's column passed invisibly around the town. Wire operators dashed to their telegraph keys to notify the capital that a regiment of Union troopers was on the move. A regiment! That was all they reported because that was all that played in front of them.

The subject of all this wild speculation was keeping time to Grant's clock. Five days into the ride, Grierson was dead way between Oberdeen, just east of the Mobile & Ohio and Grenada on the fork of the Mississippi Central Railroad—ten hours ahead of Barteau. The two forces would finally rest on either side of Houston, but they were too exhausted to fight even if they knew of each other's existence. While Barteau's troops greased their kindling with hog fat to get it to light in the rain and readied a poor-man's dinner from their haversacks, Grierson's colonels were gathering around the table of the Kilgore Plantation. The captains lounged along the full length of the varnished hall, glad to be out of the weather. Soon Grierson would call them in. He had another snake to throw down the pants of the Confederacy. It was late when he finally spread the map flat across the table, picked up a porcelain coffee cup, sipped its contents, and smiled at his orderly. The orderly nodded knowingly and the meeting began.

"Gentlemen, we have been very fortunate, if not with the weather, at least with the Confederates. But they will not let us alone much longer. We must be more vigilant, and I have a plan in need of your full cooperation. Love's little train heading back north has created a wigwag of heads, but it will not distract the Confederates long and we will need another feint to confuse the enemy. This is what I intend to do. I will take two regiments on to Starkville, but I want the other one to jab General Ruggles make him anxious about his railroad." No one needed be told what regiment that would be. "Our goal is still Newton on the Vicksburg railroad, a hundred miles ride down into the throat of Mississippi. That is General Pemberton's main artery east and west, but if we can make him think we are after the one while we are after the other, perhaps we can make him dizzy and get both. It's a game of sleight of hand. Colonel Hatch, is this kind of game to your liking?"

Colonel Prince placed a congratulatory hand on Hatch's

shoulder.

Grierson went on, "Besides Lieutenant Christie, I am giving you Lieutenant Canfield to use as you need." Hatch scowled thanks for nothing. "This is what I want you to do." Grierson leaned over the map. "I want you to ride near West Point. Destroy the warehouses, depots, and telegraph wires. Then ride south, and keep it up. Get to Macon—Columbus if you can—and tear out that spur. The Second Iowa will earn its pay if you do half that. Then high tail it out of there. The enemy should be on you by then. While we're heading south, you entice the Confederates to follow you north through Okolona and do what damage you can if you get time. Don't try to join up with us. It's hell bent for you back to La Grange by the steeplechase route. By the way, if you would grant me the use of your assistant-surgeon, I would be much obliged."

Hatch nodded, "Doctor Yule will serve you well."

Out in the immense spread of lawn, dice cracked against a metal plate, cards shuffled to lucky chants, and under a willow chapel the chaplain with a few faithful in prayer began the "Sign of the Cross." Others finished up their hasty suppers and stretched out against the campfires.

"Reminds me of my bride's cooking." The nostalgic private fed the rubbery ham to a plantation dog promptly taking his prize to the edge of the garden hidden by withered cane.

"Yes, but I am sure she has compensating virtues, Matthew," his pard put in. A wink passed between the two, who missed such gentle luxuries. Both troopers sat back, watching the dirt fly beneath the animal's legs.

"She did at that, Jessie, that she did. I think I will have some of your medicine so I can sleep—my lumbago is tugging at me."

"Matthew, see that fool dog? I bet he has got a stash of bones in there. If I were a mind...even a Sesech dog shouldn't go unplundered."

"That's curious. Now that old winter ground should be a bit harder to make fly...unless..."

Jess gripped the dog, while Matthew scooped out the dirt, stacking the bones beside the anxious animal. "Well, well, what do we have here?" With his knife Matthew jimmied the catch on a metal box. In the darkness two men rejoiced in what a few minutes of enterprise could beget. They divided the treasure, then filled the empty box with the bones and returned it to the ground.

"If the bugler rattles that horn at three tomorrow morning, well, from then on Grierson will be waking his troops with a hog yell, that's all I got to say." The private reached for his carbine, unscrewed the buttplate, and dropped three rings and a locket into a niche. His partner secreted his take in the hollowed recess of his Bible.

Two officers dropped down the steps of the verandah, snapped their matches against the railing, and touched the tips of their cigars. Christie did not recognize their voices, but from their conversation he judged them to be of Prince's regiment.

"Looks like Grierson is getting rid of the deadwood."

"Horses and officers, for a fact. Can't fault him, though, they've held together so far, but the Iowa boys are not family. Did you see Hatch's eyes? Fired like meteors!"

"Well, this is as far as they are going. And Grierson will be well rid of the two greenhorns."

"Only one greenhorn by my count—he's a cudgel, with his rule books and inspections. Yesterday, got into it with Steele, no-account-for-stupid. Lucky he wasn't flattened. The other one has seen the elephant enough times to be welcome at my campfire any time. I'd give the family silver for that horse."

"A snoop just the same. It will be good to be riding with just home boys again."

The officers were interrupted by a third. "Mike, the colonel invites you to join him for a brandy, good-bye party for Hatch. Seen Lieutenant Christie? Colonel invites him along."

"Not seen him, nor expect to. Keeps to himself a lot."

On the gallery, Christie kicked his blanket out and dropped the saddle at the head. He was nearly asleep when another sergeant on another errand aroused him.

"Sir."

"What is it?" Christie hissed.

"Sir, it's Lieutenant Bellard. Thought you might be able to help."

"What's the matter with him? Sick?"

"No, sir, just feeling poorly. Thought maybe you might sit with him a spell. Death in his family, feeling grieved down deep. A couple of us are afraid he might bolt for home. Won't talk to me, but you bein' an officer of his grade..."

"Where?" The sergeant pointed to a lonely shadow hunched on the side stairs. "Doesn't he have friends around here?"

"Yeah, but doesn't want to be pitied. You being a stranger, he might open up to you."

Christie did not follow the reasoning but promised he would do what he could. He found the sufferer amid a few comrades. They thanked Christie for coming and then eased away to give the two some privacy. Bellard kept his face buried in his hands.

"Lieutenant, you all right?"

The head fell back and Bellard sighed deeply. "Sometimes the weight gets so heavy I feel like my shoulders are going to break."

"Want me to fetch the chaplain?"

"Had enough of the chaplain's damnable theology. He said Molly's not goin' to heaven—it wasn't a real marriage."

"Molly? Is she badly ill?"

"Not now. Dead, so the last letter said. Leaving me with three little ones. Molly—the most perfect mate a man ever had." The officer bowed his head so deep into his chest that Christie thought he would be sobbing soon.

"I'm deeply sorry. How long you been together?"

"Nearly fourteen years. No ceremony, no papers—she just came up to the cabin one day and moved in. Beautiful gal, no other ever came in-between."

Christie sat like a lump. "Did she go peacefully?"

"Thanks be to the Lord. Expired in my father's arms and that's a blessing...went in her sleep, so he wrote. She slept with him after I left—not like her to be selfish with her love. I didn't mind. I couldn't deny them. When I was home, she kept us both warm in the same bed on a cold winter's night. God, she could heat up and be affectionate! It was good she went that way—not alone. I wish I could be as strong." The trooper stiffened, but the grief was too much and he was near breaking loose.

In Christie's mind hearing about a man's private passions

was unseemly, but Lieutenant Bellard went on now that the dike had broken. "She was a vision. The most beautiful dark brown eyes, filled with more love than in a whole book of prayers. Never got fat and never lost a tooth—beautiful until the last day I hugged and kissed her good-bye. She just stood there watchin' me go and cryin'. Dad put an arm around her and they went into the house together. I am glad they found comfort in each other. That's the last sight I have and it will have to do." Christie laid a comforting hand on his arm, but Bellard pulled free.

"You will have the memories." Christie could have lived on without any more of those backcountry recollections, but Bellard felt he had found a soulmate.

"That I have. I'll never forget her walking at my side up by Willow Lake. She loved to go walking on the banks every night after supper. One night a storm surprised us—rained so hard it about blistered our faces. But she just looked up at me with those beautiful, trusting eyes. Nothing could hurt us as long as we were together. The rain glistened like a crown over her long chestnut hair and rolled over her hard, naked body. She pressed close to me, we two against the storm."

Christie cleared his throat, but Bellard was unstoppable now. "A gale tore through the hollow like it was going to take us away. She was nearly lifted off her feet, but not one bit of fear crossed her face. No, it was one of those times I knew she was something from heaven, a soulmate come hell or high water. But she didn't like thunder and lightning. When the sky lit up in a razor flash, Molly lit off. I couldn't keep up. I called and she called back, but I lost her in the glen. Then everything went quiet and dark as pitch. I thought she fell into the gorge. I screamed her name, but nothing. I was 'bout to go back and get help when I heard her callin'. It was the most miraculous thing—her voice chimin' over the ridge. I followed. There she was, standing in the middle of this light, like she was transfigured or something. On the edge she was, just standing there radiant in a heavenly light." Bellard was fully absorbed in his visions, bringing Christie further inside with every word.

"In her mouth she was carrying a thunderbolt. Yep, she had caught a thunderbolt in mid-air as quick and clean as if it was a possum. It was probably aimin' for the cabin like a meteor, and she caught it and saved my father and all. The thing sizzled and crackled in her teeth. She meant to bury it like a bone. But no, I made her haul it back to the cabin, and we put it in the lantern and it burned for six days and seven nights. If that doesn't show Divine preference, I don't know what does."

A chorus of snickers told the new boy he had been had. Bellard's face was awash in tears, he wiped them away and slapped Christie on the shoulder, "Well, thanks, Lieutenant. I am feeling much better after our little talk. I hear you are shoving out tomorrow, so we won't be seein' each other again. I won't forget your comfort tonight."

"Bellard?"

"Yes, Mister Christie?"

"Is there a Molly?"

"Yes, Lieutenant, to be sure—the best coon hunter in the county."

"Did she die?"

"Yes, sir, that part is true."

"Well, when you get home, I hope her pups are so excited that they warm your leg with sentiment. And your chaplain was wrong—she'll be going to heaven, but you won't."

"Sir, that is hardly Unitarian."

Surby waited in the darkness until the performance broke up. Christie recoiled as if the sergeant had come with some new mischief to inflict. But the noncom was innocent this time, "Sir, Colonel Blackburn would like to see you, sir, a meeting."

Business was well underway in the outbuilding formerly used as the plantation summer kitchen. Blackburn was in the center of perhaps two dozen Illini troopers. "Tomorrow the real work begins. I don't have to tell you that we are sticking out like a sore thumb down here. Sergeant Surby and I have decided to help our chances with an advance patrol of scouts. This is nothing new. What is new, gentlemen, they'll be wearing Confederate uniforms, or the nearest thing we can contrive."

The room was deathly quiet. Blackburn continued. "Surby will head this team of rangers in that he is more familiar with these environs from his civilian days on the railroad. But you have been especially chosen by your captains. I know what you are thinking—since when does the cavalry put you in front of the firing squad for superlative duty? And you are right. If you're caught you will most likely be shot or hanged as spies. And riding ahead on your own hook—your chances of capture are pretty good if you can't talk or shoot your way out of it. And you better keep an eye to the rear. You might even be mistaken by the more nearsighted of our own and be shot on general principle. But, gentlemen, you are the best we have. We will take only volunteers so if you get an attack of common sense and decline the honor, I will understand. It will not affect your record—you will be accorded the honor of continuing our ride and getting killed or captured in some other way. So, those who would like to leave may do so now."

Blackburn looked into the faces of each man. His gaze was returned measure for measure. No man moved.

Surby had known the outcome all the time, "Well, then I will be taking measurements and preferences over here—first come first served." The sergeant stepped beside a pile of dirty laundry scavenged from prisoners and plantation ragbags. The plan obviously had been in the works for some time.

As the first man stepped up, Surby sorted through for something that would fit—nearly. The trooper held up his new issue: a filthy muslin shirt with broken buttons and a pair of butternut pants stained at the knees. "If my mother ever knew I was wearing something like this—even into enemy territory—she would sob her heart out. "

Officer status did not garner Christie special outfitting: faded Levi's, long and ragged in the hems; and a bleached calico shirt topped by a vest of tea-colored brown silk—minus three buttons. There was the scent of mildew and stale bourbon about it. In Surby's hands were two huge shoes that could never have been worn by the same pair of feet. These he handed to Christie along with a pair of oversized socks. The Buckeye put them on, and the extra bulk of cotton leaked like a tongue through the smiles of open leather. The transformation was curious. The blue uniform had made him an expendable foreigner with the brigade but in the camouflage of the enemy he was a member of a brotherhood of elite scouts. War made no sense.

"I am sorry, Lieutenant, but that fancy cap of yours is

going to have to stay behind. Colonel Grierson will hold on to it, until you meet up again."

Christie caressed the tattered bummer with the Ohio brass then handed it to Surby.

Men were groaning and laughing like boys dressing up for Halloween. "You look handsome enough to take out my sister, Lieutenant." Surby added, "You know, sir, you are the only one out of the Iowa boys Colonel Blackburn chose, but Colonel Grierson almost let the surprise out of the bag yesterday. It's an honor."

"I will try to remember that when I am lined up in front of the firing squad."

But there was one more piece of unpleasantness on the sergeant's mind, and he began the subject by way of apology, "I beg your pardon, sir, but your mount..."

"Gunshot? What about him?" Christie did not like what was coming.

"Fine steed — too good for a butternut private."

"He goes where I go...by order of General Grant. Discussion finished." Surby's jaw set but Christie was not budging, although he did add by way of further explanation, "If you lose him, I will be in the army for two lifetimes paying the general back. The man exacts hard bargains."

"I understand, sir." Clearly, Surby didn't, but even sergeants come to realize that there is an end point where even flat foot officers can be pushed. Surby grunted — they think the infantry owns the war.

"Well, you men look like a regular outfit of shotgun guerrillas." Blackburn surveyed them approvingly. "You are as ugly as the enemy. That's why you are riding ahead so you don't give the brigade a bad name. To your advantage, you will be breathing clean air on a regular basis, as long as you breathe air. At 'Assembly' you will meet with me, except for you, Lieutenant Christie. You will report to Colonel Hatch for orders. And one more thing before you are dismissed, gentlemen." An orderly passed among them with a tray. When each man had a cup of something that smelled like cognac, Blackburn raised his in a toast. The rest followed. "Gentlemen, I give you the Butternut Guerrillas! May we all live a long life and toast our bravery, success, and good looks in many future reunions."

"The Butternut Guerrillas!" a throaty chorus answered.

"What you waiting for, Lieutenant? You're one of us." Surby clanked his against Christie's cup.

Christie nodded. "For better or worse a marriage it is, Sergeant. I will drink to that."

The Kilgore family thought they had been visited by the devil twice in one day when Barteau and his Tennessee contingent rode up the plantation drive. The Confederates were outfitted in Union ponchos captured from supply trains and were looking more Union than the newly outfitted Union scouts who had cantered out that morning.

"Your comrades have cleaned us out already." The mistress stood on the top step, her hands on her hips and something near satisfaction on her face.

"Our comrades?" Barteau winced. "How long ago?"

"Two hours, not much more. I heard talk about attacking the M & O."

The officer put his column in reverse. The day before he had marched and countermarched and only gotten straightened out too late. He had found Smith and his home guards, who had better information as to what rabbit hole the Yankees had disappeared into. In this country of narrow farm roads and cow paths canopied in tall oaks and sycamores, it was hard to believe that something as large as a cavalry regiment could be swallowed up without a trace. But it was true. Now he was tired of the cat-and-mouse game. If he could get in their rear and hammer them against the home guard protecting the railroad…

Now Barteau had the scent of blood and he put his troops into a gallop, reining the horses down the slippery roads without letup, following the tracks heading east toward West Point. Persistence paid. As they came over the crest, Barteau caught his first glimpse of the rear of Hatch's forces. The Confederate could not believe his luck! Hidden by fog and rain, he was able to close the distance without being detected. At one hundred yards he allowed his men the luxury of their Rebel yell. It was premature. The Union guard was electrified. They fragmented—the smartest tore across country and disappeared into the woods, the rest kept to the road in full sight of their pursuers.

"I think we have got them, Major." Barteau said.

"I hope so, sir, it's going to be a hell of a ride."

With rain slapping their faces, riders beat boot heels against flanks to close ground and keep the enemy from escaping. But the Iowans would not make it easy. They had the advantage of well-fed blooded stock and disappeared in the mist. The Confederates kept to the chase. By noon the rain had stopped and the sun had burned off the haze. The Yankees had disappeared, or very nearly. Rainwater pooled in the imprint of hoof prints following east.

Finally Barteau saw some confirmation of what he was looking for. At the wood line a lone horseman stood his mount, watching the Confederates come on. There was nothing remarkable about this hardscrabble soldier except the animal he rode—it was magnificent. But there was only him. Had the Yankees gone another way? Could he have been fooled by tracks from a squad of local militia or a slave patrol? Could that man be one of those? A horse like that said so. Barteau waved. The man waved back, then galloped into the trees. Barteau decided to follow—the man seemed unsociable for only a local who should be concerned about Yankees. When they had cleared the bend, the truth was told. Barteau had guessed right.

The scene was so innocent; Barteau doubted his own eyes. A handful of Yankees threaded through acres of bushes picking berries. So sure that they had eluded their pursuers and so attractive were the overflowing briars the Iowans had posted no lookouts.

Barteau nudged his mount forward. Critical seconds ticked away. Each gray trooper took stock of what clanged or rattled and wrapped it tighter. It was an unnecessary precaution. Lightning ignited a convulsion of thunder and the skies poured out. Behind an opaque curtain of rain the column came on, closing the distance to a quarter mile. Only thirty seconds more, no Rebel yell this time. Then somewhere a carbine cracked and the bullet spewed a geyser, just inches from Barteau's horse. A second took a man behind. The Yankees perked up like so many field rabbits and scrambled to their horses.

"Bugler! Sound the charge!" Barteau, at the head of his

command, swooped out of the mist to surround the stragglers before they knew what was upon them. The Confederates were grateful for the prize of Union-made firepower, and secured them under their ponchos. But Barteau was not happy. The sums were not tallying. Somewhere there were more—ahead tearing up the track or behind going for another prize. Had he been the one suckered? Would he be ambushed from behind? Something was very wrong.

Barteau studied the landscape. The road funneled between high-rail fence on one side and thick brush and live oaks on the other. Beyond was Palo Alto and the railroad. He guessed the main body had gone for the railroad. Was there still time? Could he surprise them and bottle them up in the town before they got to the depot?

Barteau turned to his provost now ushering Yankees to the rear. "Lieutenant? Did our fish tell us anything?"

"They are from Iowa."

Barteau scowled. "And what else?"

"Nothing else, sir. Where they are going and what they planned to do when they got there is still locked up inside them. They are a cantankerous lot."

"Well keep at it, Lieutenant. Maybe we can find out for sure what's going on here. "

"Yes, sir." The officer shook his head. "And they say *we* are a stubborn people. These won't budge and are as arrogant as savages..."

Barteau turned to his second. "Major Morton, I want you to take Smith and his home guard and four companies and guard this road on both sides. See where I mean?" The major did. "Good, I want you to hold your position there while we attack them from the rear and flush them out."

Smith and his regiment of farmers went into line alongside Morton's four companies to guard the opening of the mouse hole. Billy licked his lips, but he was the only one hungry for bloodshed. The rest were tense and quiet, pulling ancient revolvers out of oilcloth sacks and hoping that their powder would stay dry.

The rest of Barteau's regiment disappeared into the trees. But someone had seen him. Fire split from the tree lots. Barteau returned it, then with his column rushed toward the edge of the town and up to the local church. Union cavalry waited inside. Gun barrels butted out precious stain glass, and the two forces went at each other for over an hour.

"Captain, bring up that cannon! Mister Christie, swing around and scout the perimeter. I want no more surprises!"

Hatch berated himself for his predicament. He had ordered twenty-five to fall out and ride down into the woods to search for stock. Lieutenant Christie had been sent to scout. It was he who had signaled his commander with the first fire into the Gray column. At the same time he had alerted his comrades to skedaddle. But only a few had made it back to the lines. By then the Confederates were already bearing down on them. Lieutenant Christie's warning gave only a few seconds to form a defensive line. He lost the scroungers, but he saved the regiment.

A rider burst out of the thicket. Canfield raised his carbine and took aim at the Confederate bearing down on him. A trooper pushed the greenhorn to the ground.

"They are going to hit us front and rear. The front is already sealed off." Christie reported.

Hatch bellowed, "Captain Smith!"

"Here, sir!" the artillery officer shouted from his position.

"Put your cannons in the middle of the road, aim for dead center, and wait for my order. Company H and Company E, form a picket on either side until I can get another line bent around to guard our backsides."

Men moved as Hatch directed. Colt revolving rifles cocked, and full cylinders were packed with seven charges. Hatch had trained these two battalions as mounted infantry, and their ground-fighting proficiency was paying dividends just now. Soon, two lines were poised back to back and ready. Hatch blinked through a pungent cloud of sulfur. Good, God, was it teatime? He came unglued. One of his other squads was sipping buttermilk, compliments of a local mistress who had nothing less than fine crystal to put it in.

"Here they come!" Christie shouted. Barteau broke through the trees and charged in a flying wedge.

"All right, Mister Smith, I want you to take your time firing. Wait until you can get a dead aim, then fire at will! The rest of you, aim for the front! Those boys over there on the edge of the road near the woods, the ones just standing there—damn if I know what they are doing." Hatch pointed to Morton's unsuitables.

The regiment emptied their guns full into the face of the Mississippi home guard. Smith gauged the elevation of his gun even as Barteau rode at him. He snapped the lanyard and the cannons fired. The Confederate charge recoiled; men dropped and horses bucked. Barteau retreated to reform and reload.

Barteau charged, was fought back, and charged again. When he could not get close, he baited and suckered, but the Yankees stayed. He skirmished and fired for over two hours, this way and that, but they could not break Hatch's line. The Iowa commander had not been as careless as Barteau thought. The day was waning. Barteau was nearly out of time and very much out of patience.

In front, Smith and Morton were having a hard time keeping the cork in the bottle. Smith's locals had never held against such fire. Sergeant Hager pulled terrified men into a front line. But Union fire was relentless. With dead neighbors on either side, raw recruits soon had enough. One pushed himself up off the ground gauging what was worse—the Yankees in front or his sergeant behind. Hager raised his sword over his head and shouted in the minuteman's face to hold or go to hell. He threw the sergeant out of the way, and ran. Others followed—running for hell if it was safe from Yankees.

Soon the colonel's stand was nothing more than a good intention. He and his lieutenants were shouting obscenities by the mouthfuls to hold, but his men were taking to the woods. Billy stood up to fire the last chamber in his revolver at the enemy. Just as he turned for the rear, the ground exploded under him.

"We had them, Colonel. We could have bagged them all. It's a crying shame. All we gave them was a lively chase." Sergeant Hager cursed the empty ground he stood on. There was nothing for Morton to do but call a retreat. The dead and wounded were left where they fell. By a reverse of fortunes, the captive Iowans became the captors. They scrambled among the dazed Confederates retrieving weapons, some of which had not even been fired. They formed a forward line and took up the fight as Morton and Smith retreated.

Unaware that his plans were shambles, Barteau charged

again. With no threat to his front, Hatch turned his entire firepower into their faces. Barteau's men fell like mown wheat. He reformed to charge again. He wanted to hold the Yankees here. Lieutenant Colonel Cunningham had sent news that he was riding hard with his Second Alabama to give what help he could. Barteau could still bag them. He looked around him; his command had enough for one more charge. He gave the order.

In the end it accomplished nothing except more death. Barteau gave up. But then Cunningham never came. His advance scout had caught sight of Grierson's two regiments heading toward Sparta. Mistaking this to be Barteau's threat, they had set out after them. If Cunningham had turned right instead of left, Barteau would have had his reinforcements to snare Hatch's regiment.

Wednesday, April 22
Some place God forgot.

Julie,
Thinking of you refreshes my soul. You are a portrait in that green velvet dress you wore to the St. Patrick's cotillion back when Jamie MacGowan was romancing you. I don't think he ever forgave me for taking you away.

So many of the boys of the Olentangy Pirate Brigade are gone. Our secret society based on a life-long vow to never kiss a girl. I think George Torrence broke the rule first.

But Jamie broke it the most. He forgot all loyalties as soon as he got a girl in his sights.

George Torrence. He was a man before he was a boy. Never took him for any kind of hero but he was our heart and soul on Marye's Heights. Stood fast against all the fire around him, just whipping the colors like a tornado and screaming at us, "Up and at 'em! Steady by, boys! Give 'em hell."

He yelled until a cannon ripped open his head.

Lost nearly all the club at Fredericksburg. Tom Warner, next to Nolan, was the baby of the regiment. Somebody dragged him back from the field. You know better than I if he lived. He will make a splendid chaplain if he did. Had the hell scared out of him enough times.

Watt McCollough died before he could be commissioned so the family will never get the benefit of his promotion to lieutenant. Not barely twenty.

I am the only one left of our club, and except for my lapses with you, still faithful to its credo. Haven't kissed a girl in five years, seen none worth kissing in the last two.

But I think about it. For what I've been through, saving God's people from slavery and preserving the Union and all, I think God owes a couple. But only you, and that's against the rules I know. So I guess I have His duebill and the privilege of just thinking on the pleasure.

I love you still.
Brent.

"Lieutenant!" Hatch stood over him with an air of impatience. "I appreciate what you did for us today. But I am inclined to ask you for another favor. I need someone to go out beyond the pickets to find out what the Confederates are up to. They have been mighty quiet the last couple of hours. I think the home guard is gone — but the regulars — they worry me."

Christie finished the thought on his own: And since I am dispensable, I am your best candidate. But all Christie answered was, "Yes, sir."

"Report back to me as soon as you return."

Christie folded the letter, put it with the others in his saddlebag and left his belongings with the headquarters' guard. Then he saddled Gunshot to scout where the Mississippi militia had broken under the Union guns that afternoon.

The night was oppressive and black; the breeze made a drizzle of the rain water slicked on the leaves. The only light was an intermittent pulse of lightning. Christie cursed himself for forgetting his poncho. He had just turned about to scout the opposite direction when Gunshot shied. It was so unexpected for an animal who was unflinching in the face of fire. Christie chirruped, but Gunshot swung his neck and planted himself into the ground.

"See in the dark, can ya, boy!" Christie whispered. He slid down and pulled his revolver. He felt his way blindly, gently tugging at the reins for Gunshot to follow. The wind picked up, and then something slapped him in the face. Christie blessed the God that kept him from firing, bringing on a regiment to save him from a low-swinging branch.

He took a breath and started again. Gunshot balked and he pulled. Caught off balance between his forward step and Gunshot's backward tug, he tripped and went down on his back. Christie dropped the reins to get a firmer grasp on his pistol. Something had him by the leg and he kicked it away. It growled.

"Who goes there!" Christie aimed into the void. His fingers trembled against the trigger. He turned the barrel low and cocked the hammer.

"Help me!"

"Who goes there!" Christie demanded.

"I'm here."

Christie inched closer, his pistol in one hand, the other patting the ground ahead as he went. He concentrated harder; finally he found what had ensnared him. By the size, he was a mere boy. "Where did you come from?"

He was wet and smelled sweet of dried blood. Christie raised the head onto his knee. The boy's body stiffened and jerked with pain. He tried to answer but nothing came. So Christie leaned closer, the boy tried again, but the effort convulsed into choking spasms, with fresh blood splattering into Christie's face. Christie pulled his canteen around. The boy took it hungrily, only he gagged and vomited the water back up. He sunk back and began to shake. Christie hoisted him higher and set the spout to his lips again but the boy pushed it away. "Can't."

"What's your name?"

"Billy?"

"Where you from?"

"Houston."

"What you doing out here, Billy?"

"I was here with Captain Smith. Came out to fight Yankees." He opened his eyes wide enough to take in the whole world. For the flickers of lightning what he saw was Christie's ragged uniform. Billy sighed. "You ain't no Yankee, you a Reb? I thought you might of come to take me prisoner, but you came to get me. I knew Captain Smith wouldn't leave me to them. I knew it. And God would not let me die alone." Billy searched the face. "I don't know you, do I? But it don't matter. You stay with me, brother? I won't keep you long." Billy reached for Christie's hand.

He slid a piece of paper into it and curled his fingers around it tightly. "Take this home for me, will you, brother?"

Christie nodded. "Yeah, I'll take care of it."

"It's my will. Tell my family, I died brave. It'll mean somethin'."

"Sure." Christie pressed the face close to his chest. Before he knew what he was saying, he began the only words that could bridge the worlds between them.

"Our Father, who aren't in heaven. Hallowed be thy name..."

Billy gasped, "Thy kingdom come. Thy will be...Thy will be done...oh...oh my God it hurts! On earth...as...as...it is in heaven. Give us...this day..." He tightened his grasp on Christie's palm to draw enough life to finish their prayer. The paper crackled between.

Christie held fast, "…our daily bread and forgive us our trespasses as we forgive those who trespass against us."

Billy gasped, "As we forgive…" He gasped and the hold softened.

Christie finished the prayer as reverently as he had ever said it in his life. Then he pressed the boy's eyes shut and leaned to gather him up in his arms. There was plenty of night left to give this one Rebel a burial.

Lightning flushed the blackness to daylight. A carbine cocked. "Dirty Rebel. Come back, did you?"

Christie spun around. "No!"

But the hammer slammed and the barrel flared.

X
A Table in the Presence of my Enemies
Mid April, 1863

<u>GATES OF HEAVEN</u>
<u>NO SOLDIERS NEED APPLY</u>
No reprieves!   No alibis!
No Loitering!

By order of the Lord High, not one raw dogface snored under the shadows of the magnolias; nor by twos and threes tilted over cups of noxious soup; nor by four and five hunkered over a deck of cards; nor even by the dozen bobbed to the rhythm of profane camp ditties serenaded by the fountain's wistful arpeggios. It was a strictly by-the-Good-Book, Sunday, steam-pressed, civilians-only congregation praying under the magnolias, by twos and threes meditating by the willow, or by fours and fives singing their psalms by the grotto, or by the dozens recanting their sins in the rose garden.

"Bounty substitutes all of them," sneered the soldier at the gate. He rattled the bars.

One of the elect parted company with the congregation to see to the clamor. The soft blue eyes of the saint locked with his son's in holy torment. He shook his head, "I know you not." He turned, and walked away.

"Father! Let me through!"

A sixty-nine caliber wad of spit hissed by the bummer's ear. "Well, here you are at last, Mister Christie! Did you not hear me callin'? We have been waiting for you since Fredericksburg, at no small inconvenience to the Almighty and ourselves. Cook three-days rations, of loaves and fishes — we move out at dawn."

A full-moon grin twisted on either side of his ragged cigar. "Did you expect harps and hallelujahs for your schemes and capers? Your head resting in the lap of angels? There will be no heaven for you, no hell either, and you are fortunate for that, me boyo." Sergeant Major Solomon Chase checked the name on the roster. "You are among the unfortunates to have died before being mustered out, so it is an eternity you'll have on your feet in the army. And beyond that, certainly, there is the matter of General Grant's horse that you are accountable for. 'What be bound on earth be bound in heaven' — you will remember the small print in your enlistment." Chase raised a bony finger toward the assembly of ragged troops, "There to, lad, and there will be none of those smart aleck officer privileges. I know you for what you are, Mister Christie, a mudsill, marching at the bottom-end of a very long line. I'll be with you all the way, and our numbers will grow as we march. This war is not near won and we will be legion by its resolution. And there will be crusades beyond that, sure." Christie hammered the gates for rescue, but Chase held him by his shoulder, laughing like the yelp of a wounded hound. "Sound the bugles! All present and accounted for, Captain McMillan."

"Get away from me!" Christie thrashed. "I am dead and

done with you! My soul is my own now!"

"You see, he fights Satan for his immortal soul, poor lad! I told you he was a Christian, Rachel." Toweling the fever from his forehead calmed him, but only as long as the feminine ministrations stroked his face.

Her attendant was not so sure. "Miss Carolina, why would Satan feel a claim on that soul if they had not made bargains in life?"

The counsel for the defense did not answer. All she knew of him was that he had been brought to her father's surgery wounded, covered in blood, leeches, and mud, shivering like a willow. For three days he had boiled in the poisons of a fever that threatened to take him at any moment. He was a ragged remnant who would not die without a struggle. Rachel never let her mistress tend him alone and kept a small pistol in her apron pocket lest he rise out of his sheets to attack them both. When his torment was most violent she begged Mister Collin to sit. This last storm had been the worst but it had parted the clouds.

"There, our Confederate angel has landed at last?" His nurse dabbed again at his face. "You must be exhausted from your hard battle with the Yankees?"

"My what?" Bees buzzed in Christie's head, and his leg was on fire. He did not know where he was, but for the moment he was satisfied he was not in the eternal brigades or in a Confederate stockade.

"Yes, this Lieutenant Bright, or something you defame so violently—a murderer and a craven coward by your estimation. And there was a Sergeant Chase. I have come to hate him as well in your behalf." Smiles set aflame her oval face, finely sculpted porcelain framed by wings of raven hair caught in back and knotted at the nape of her neck. The luminescent brown eyes studied rather than merely glanced over him, their intelligence and humor marred only in left profile by the sag of the lid and jaw beneath. She was buttoned to the neck in severe mourning, unrelieved even by a slip of lace at the throat. For it, her face and manner was maternal rather than coy or even worse pitying—even though he reached for his leg.

"You are all here," she assured him. "The bullet passed clean through the thigh. You will heal very well if you rest. My father, Doctor Graham Bennett, has more patience than your battlefield surgeons and so he gave that leg a chance instead of... well, there is no need of discussion of that." He was then subjected to a flurry of pillow fluffing and coverlet smoothing, "There is a scrape where another bullet creased your scalp, but it is not very deep. So I think you will mend with such faculties and senses you had — and perhaps a few more for better vigilance the next time. You are in my father's surgery and can remain, unless you have family nearby? We can write your wife if you like."

"I have no wife."

That reply was clearly unexpected. "But you spoke of a Julie..." He turned sharply away and she knew she had misspoken. "No matter. You can rest here as long as you need." She did not babble self-consciously, but said only enough to help him get his bearings and assure safety in his confused mind. Then she quieted so he could rest.

Christie did not know how long he drifted between twilight and sleep. He was only dimly aware that the sun set and rose again, and that he was being fed and medicated. All these were signaled by the chimes of her voice wafting through his brain. The pain was not as intense as the wound at Fredericksburg, so he lay in warm, rose-water-scented muslin and nursed a voracious appetite. That he was wounded, and possibly dying in the confines of an enemy home beyond all rescue did not alarm him at the moment. Christie found it best to sleep or pretend sleep while the one called Rachel was there, and she was there most of the time. But he looked forward to the visits from the magnolia, the one with the large, compassionate eyes who had not yet told him her name — and who was now tending him with her bodyguard nowhere in sight.

"My father counted the scars in your chest. You have been carved up more times than a Christmas goose. And you are a mess of mosquitoes and chigger bites. Rachel put salve on them, but I am afraid you will be on fire for another day or two. For it all, you are a lucky fellow." She went back to her ritual of blanket smoothing.

"Oh yes, I feel very lucky." The dream still unnerved him. He had seen his judgment and been given reprieve for no reason he understood except perhaps the matter of General Grant's horse.

These accounts payable he kept to himself.

But his nurse understood none of this, only the lack of gratitude she saw and heard, and this she did not approve. In the tone women reserve for mischievous boys and drunken husbands, she brought him up short. "If you like, we can put you back in that ditch where Eban found you. It should not be too long before a panther or a Yankee regiment comes along. We have had an invasion of both of late, ravaging our hen houses and terrifying the innocent. The Yankees will probably bid the higher for you, though. You don't have enough meat on your bones to feed even a decent-sized cub. What's the quartermaster feeding you soldiers, riverweed? Lord knows, his wagons have skinned our larders clean. Can't see where our men get the benefit of it, though." When she was agitated as she was now, her words tripped over her tongue with a slight lisp. This embarrassed her more than him, and she quieted herself until she could regain control of them.

Rachel was not so benevolent. She had questions on her mind. Until Christie could come up with suitable answers, he pleaded amnesia. The ruse would not suffice long. From the knot of her mouth, the disdain on her sable face, and the glare of her over-large brown eyes, Rachel made the intruder understand she did not approve of this new infestation lying in her clean sheets — a very bad fish he was.

"Well, Miss Carolina, I suppose he will live?"

"Now, Rachel, be kind. He is feeling a bit raveled."

"Who is he and where does he come from? I want to know that right now."

"He has not been able to answer for himself. Yet, he's one of ours — that is all we need to know at the moment."

Rachel was not convinced by half. "No army cavalry around here I heard tell of — not ours at any rate. Just boys and old men of the militia shooting our cows and dogs in the dark. Real cavalry would be of some comfort with those Yankees tearing up and down our roads, turning out the best families. Hope he doesn't eat much. You a part of Van Dorn or Forrest's band?"

"Neither."

"Come to bag those Yankee devils tearing through our town?" Rachel would not have found any answer to please her and she shook her head. "Well, you too late — been through already, no help from you."

"Perhaps that is how he came to be wounded, Rachel. Eban did find him near West Point where there was fighting with the Yankees. Or maybe he was just waylaid on the road by the cavalry that tore through here—or by brigands. The roads are not safe for enemy or friend these days."

"What say you?" Rachel put the question squarely to the latest intruder in her well-ordered life.

"I was going to Vicksburg," Christie croaked. Rachel was ready with more questions, but his mind was befuddled, his mouth dry, and his tongue stiff—too great a disadvantage in a war of wits with these women.

"So you say! You don't talk like anybody from around here. You sound Yankee."

"Rachel, how can you tell? He has barely any voice at all. And keep in mind that General Clark and General Pemberton sound like Yankees."

"That's because they *are* Yankees."

"Well, they have Confederate hearts, converted and baptized in the Cause by the love of good women. Pemberton is our only hope of holding Vicksburg, and this soldier believes in him enough to risk death to join him there."

"Huh, a Yankee don't change his spots just because a woman is blind to them. Soldier, I be here close, you behave yourself." The point was well made: the wages of sin would be painful. Rachel turned toward other duties. "Miss Carolina, you got enough blankets on that boy to suffocate the breath right out of him. And you stay well back—can't tell what plagues he's got."

His nurse banished the warning away. "She is afraid you will steal my virtue."

"Miss Carolina, you watch your manner in front of strangers." Rachel turned from the door. She would abide no disrespect or dispute from black or white. "You certainly didn't learn talk like that from the sisters. Your father is not too sick to have words with you."

"Father had his chance to make a wife of me and the sisters a chance to make me a nun. Both failed. Now that I am an old spinster, I plan to live the life I wish and be as irascible as Aunt Suzanne."

"She died a spinster."

"And never regretted it for a moment."

Rachel shook her head and pulled her mistress toward the shadowy hall connecting the surgery to the rest of the house. Christie heard nothing of the rest of the exchange. He had pretended sleep, and soon he was.

"You wore him out, Rachel, with your accusations. And he is holding on to life by a mere prayer."

But the housekeeper looked back at the stranger and wished fervently that he had never been found. She fixed a gentle warning on her mistress, "Never mistake a ferret for a kitten—your hen house will be the poorer." Rachel turned on her heels, but said over her shoulder. "You had better lickety-split to the dinner table. Mister Collin has been into the port since three and he is in high agitation. Your father had dinner in his room. You may see if he ate it."

Carolina did so, but not before turning back. Her patient lay at peace with his demons for the first time in three days. In his sleep he was profane, and awake he was gruff and defiant. Yet his eyes were the color of the Erin flag, and once the dirt and blood had been washed away, he was handsome, with traces of innocence not yet hardened by the entire killing. Yes, he was well born, that she could tell, nearer Collin's age more than her own. There was nothing to fear from him. Rachel's suspicions did not trouble her at all.

In Vicksburg two years ago she had seen many like him marching past her convent window toward the wharves and the transports bound for Arkansas and Tennessee. Back then the war promised to be a summer of jousts and tournaments, and the boastful knights affecting white armor in their uniforms of gray and homespun.

"What a fine legion they are. They will be a saber stroke!" She had predicted, watching them address ranks from her classroom window on the top floor of the Mercy School on Crawford Street.

But Mother Superior Francis de Sales Browne had shaken her head and crossed herself. She was too old and had too much of the Puritan blood in her for such romance. "Pity these poor lambs. You will get a fine look at their Cause when it washes back in waves of sick and wounded. We can pray for righteous thunderbolts, but the Yankees don't have to. They forge it in foundaries, and it comes out in rifles, cannon, and ammunition by the trainloads. I grew up there and I have seen it. Yes, our soldiers will come back. But we will be singing requiems instead of anthems then."

"God will not let our Cause fail!"

Mother Superior had drawn herself up, "I think God is a parent who loves all His children, Cain and Abel. I think He will have cause to weep for both."

The battles of Elkhorn Tavern, Island No. 10, and Shiloh; Fort Hindman, New Orleans, and Memphis had proven Mother Superior's prophesy true. These same knights had come in a flood and were laid out on the floors of the little school in tatters and pools of their own waste. The school of the Sisters of Mercy had become a hospital to the rafters. The nuns had bathed and nursed them, blue and gray alike, and had prayed over the living and the dead.

Carolina had worked until she thought she would drop. She had stood by the bedside of any man as long as he needed her, ladling weak broth between his lips, changing his dressings, calming his fevers, chanting the beads. She had muffled their screams as the surgeon reached for his amputation saw. They had coughed blood in her face, vomited into her lap, bled on her habit. And when it all had defeated her, she had written the condolence letters and fought back the tears. "Sister, tell them that I died bravely and to keep Johnny at home or our name will die."

Carolina had fought the old barbaric methods of cannibalistic medicine doing what she could, seizing everything she had learned from her father—to the distraction of the doctors and the nuns. When she had taken it upon herself to wash down an entire ward in a solution of chloride of lime to stop the rampage of hospital gangrene, the surgeons would have had her boiled in it. These new-fangled European shenanigans proved no good in their eyes. That wounded legs and arms stopped turning black merited her methods not even a second consideration from the high gods of the Confederate Surgical Board. So she had washed still another ward to prove her point. Even Sister Sumner had despaired of ever teaching her obedience, even though the vows of poverty and chastity suited her very well. Carolina had stepped off the train just two days ahead of the ambulance carrying Collin home from Virginia.

She still walked with a silent cat-soft tread and would have passed invisibly down the back hall except for the rustle of her petticoats. Her father used to hear her way off, but he did not call out anymore, though the door was ajar and his paralysis had not affected his hearing. She tapped twice, but still he made no answer. She looked in. He reclined against a mound of blankets and pillows, enveloped in his book. He was communing with the dead and this séance, like the others, would not be interrupted.

"He is awake, father." Carolina called. But the surgeon made no sign that he heard or cared. "We are about to have dinner." Nothing. "Do you wish anything?" Nothing! "A cup of tea?" Nothing!

She waited, but not even a disordered glance did she get as he turned the page. For some reason beyond her comprehension, a childish riddle of Collin's jumped into her mind: "Does a tree falling in a woods make a noise?"

An empty decanter stood by Collin's untouched plate, another—this one full—was being upended into his glass. The plate of sweet potatoes and pork lay untouched by his fork. His face was flushed and strained, his hand vibrated even as he drank—and Collin had been drinking heavily. Still, his words, if venomous, were even and sensible.

"Rachel tells me that you have finally raised Lazarus from the dead! How soon will our gallant young knight be ready to resume the holy crusade?" He refilled his glass yet again, but not hers. Although he was younger by three years, his face had aged and grayed decades in the past two years.

"Not now, Collin, I am in no mood, and get out of father's chair. You are not head of this household yet!"

The bullet went straight to the heart. His honey-colored eyes bronzed with insult, but he did not get up. "I might as well be. Father is in exile. He did not even bother to dress today. Is he still upstairs reading his bible—the gospel according to Saint Lorin Bennett, Captain of Company C?"

"Don't be blasphemous!"

"Why not! It is one of my few luxuries now in this old mortuary."

"You are vile!" Tears welled in her eyes, but she willed them back.

The hardness softened around his jaw. Collin would have preferred some vase hurled at his head, or even a good curse, her forbearance was punishment of the worst sort. When he spoke next, his tone was calmer, "That mongrel trooper Eban found, I ask you again, is he going to live?"

"Yes, I think so."

"I am glad for your sake, but not for his. You have only postponed the inevitable. Nursing him must have taken your all—you look as if you have another of your headaches."

He was right, her temples throbbed. "I will not have you mock him. Have some respect in your soul for a fellow soldier of the Confederacy."

"Yes, the Confederacy—a men's league of corps turning to corpses. A Shakespearean turn, that. What a eulogy that would be over the graveyard of the Cause."

"Why must you do this?" She could not see him clearly, either for the twilight washing him away in a glare of copper or her fatigue. She massaged the tightness around her eyes.

"Why? You used to so enjoy our little dinner-table debates. But then we were of the same faith then. State's Rights, wasn't it? I forget, what rights were those? Our peculiar institution of 'servants,' I think we call it? The Yankees call it 'slavery.' Slaves or servants—a difference of opinion only. It was academic. We Bennetts have no slaves, nor do half the farms in the south. Rachel and Miles were freed when mother died, so into what loophole do they fall? How can the South be so rigid or the North be so sanctimonious? Cries of 'Free the Slaves' are emblazoned across newspapers sold on the same street corners that foreign women and children pass going from the slums to the black caverns they call mills and factories! When I was at Harvard I saw them, and those charnels run by the block in those fine abolitionist cities! But the radicals see with a blind eye these legions that work in these mills—and then point to the black souls needing freeing down here? What freedoms have they? Those immigrants and poor! Do they qualify for this emancipation of Mister Lincoln's? Heaven's sake, Louisiana and Mississippi have more free blacks fighting for our Cause than Boston has for theirs. How can we make them understand?" Collin drained his glass. "I wonder if one for one they were tallied, how our slavery would stack up with theirs?"

Collin sat back exhausted. "Yes, to answer your unasked question, Father Kessler and Uncle Nathaniel have been here. You were tending our foundling and I spared you. Kessler was bound to administer his Extreme Unction over him, and then the poor soldier would have had to die just to be polite. They never concern themselves about over-staying their welcome or if they *are* welcome in the first place. They put me in such a good mood... Uncle Nathaniel and his talk about free trade and European intervention. I am bound the man believes in Zeus, Apollo, and the lot."

"They mean well." Her attempts at forgiveness were flint and Collin exploded.

"Intervention is a pipe dream! By my faith, the English and French don't want our crops, even if we could get them through the blockade. The English have cotton rotting on their wharves already, and what with Indian cotton and Egyptian cotton...only ones who want it are the Yankees, and from what I hear, they are taking it by the shiploads without so much as a by-your-leave — along with our live oaks which they turn into ships to fight against us. We've got cotton by the warehouse full! What we don't set afire to keep out of their clutches, they confiscate and sell. It doesn't seem to matter to them that their cause is funded by the same black servitude as ours. A pleasant debate — resolved: Does the cause of the Union and emancipation baptize slave cotton and make it holy?"

"When the British come, they will turn the tide."

Her brother put down his cup with barely concealed amusement. "And why would they do that?"

"Who?"

"The British — why would they come to our aid?" She looked up suddenly, just as Collin bit down, and braced himself against another stab of pain. He threw back what was left in his glass and swallowed it down. She reached for the decanter, but even in a haze of alcohol and rage, he was quicker.

"As father says to come to the aid of gentlemen. You have

had enough, Collin."

"Don't be fooled by pretense, Carolina. The British were never gentlemen. What gave you that idea?"

"How can you say that? You remember Lord Dearing—such exquisite manners."

"Compliments, toasts, lace ruffles, and fine linen, only subtle weapons to further their ends in treachery, conquest, and duplicity—diplomacy just as deadly calculated as their cannon. Ask the Welsh, the Irish, the Scots, the Hindu? What will the British get in return for their investment in the Southern cause? Dry fields and cannibalized cities. No, their Labor Party will set fire to every Man of War before they allow it sail to the aid of our peculiar cause. I think it is the first time in Parliamentary history the Socialists and the Quakers have ever found a cause to agree on, and they are adamant that England will stay in England. Face it, my darling, the South is bankrupt and adrift in an open boat."

"This is not a court of law, Collin. You do not have to prosecute the entire South for your affliction. I still believe in my soul that England will come. There is the principle of..." She broke off but not in time. They had been brother and sister, of two bodies but of one mind, too long for him to miss her direction.

"Yes, Lorin would side with you in a heat about principle. I can remember him slamming his fists down on this very table: 'And we would not let the rabble insult us, by God!' Then he went off to fight that 'rabble' to make them take back their slurs. Dolled up in gray uniform, sash, and a saber. I was so impressed, I went too, but you did not sew my uniform. Mine was sewn in a Jackson prison. For all your rosaries, you got a corpse and a cripple. You should demand your money back." His face was flushed garnet and nearly delirious. "Do you think they buried him in that uniform, Carolina, and grandfather's sword, the one General Andy Jackson gave him? Where do you think that sword is? Up there in Maryland rusting in the grave, or is that silver hilt swinging at the hip of some Yankee officer? Does he pull it out over the campfire and say a prayer for the soul of the big Rebel who wore it, or perhaps for his widow, who pined to death for him?"

"You're drunk, Collin! And I am weary enough!" Her head dropped into her hands. He did not mean it, any of it, that she knew. It was the pain talking—pain made raw by grief and drink.

Collin shoved his plate away untouched. "I am heartily sick of sweet potatoes and rice. And, my sweet sister, there is not enough good stock left for a decent drunk. I am not yet so degenerate as to sink to the stuff Miles hides behind the back step." He pulled himself up unsteadily and bowed respectfully. The ball of the knee joint had not slipped into his wood stump, and he flinched as he worked it into the place. With what dignity he could muster he turned to his sister, slumped at the end of the table, and placed a hand over the soft weave of her chignon. She was almost asleep. He was relieved she was not crying. He bent and kissed her cheek and with difficulty straightened again. Then he withdrew a cigar from his breast pocket and scuffled out the gallery door, a big hound at his heels.

Outside, it was not the cool breezes that soothed him—it was the promise of something else. He returned the cigar to his vest and turned abruptly, taking extra time to pick up rather than drag the dull leg. When he was sure Carolina and Rachel had not followed, he opened the French doors and stepped inside. The further door had been left open to let the rooms breathe.

The last amber shadows were falling across the face of the sleeping patient so still he might be dead, but that was none of Collin's affair. He gently pulled the door closed between the consultation room and surgery and went to the wooden box on the desk. He withdrew the key and unlocked the apothecary cabinet. His prize stood on the top shelf. From the bottle he poured a few grains into a kerchief and replaced the bottle perfectly within its rim of dust. With the prize safely in his pocket, he closed the office door and escaped.

Somewhere down the long tunnel of a hallway, a clock beat like a metronome. It was well past noon when Christie finally awoke. How long he could disguise himself as a son of the south he did not know. The food was the first challenge—the smell of the burnt sorghum and sweet potatoes was nauseating. "Yams" his mother used to call them, even though they were not quite the same thing. They had always been a tug-of-war between them. She had been adamant he would eat them—at least the act of obedience would nourish his developing character. He had been as adamant that he would not, and she would scold him. "There will be a time when yams will be all you have to eat and you will be grateful."

Christie emptied the dish into the chamber pot. At least Grierson would be eating well. He must be halfway down the state, traveling lighter for having rid himself of at least one headquarter's snoop. But Half-wit would be right there at his elbow. Christie was so lost in thought, he did not know he had a visitor until the man spoke.

"Well, son, not hungry?" Christie guessed it was the good doctor who sat at the foot of his bed huddled in a chair. He must have brought it with him because there was none there before. He was feeble rather than old, but his regard was alert and critical. Nothing cordial passed between them, only a cool, clinical appraisal of the other. "We can get word to your people, let them know you are alive at least."

"Not necessary, sir." Christie stuttered.

"Oh yes, soldier, but it is. You men have no idea the litanies that storm heaven in your behalf. You have left an empty chair somewhere."

"Not in my case, sir, so I will not be troubling you on that score." In themselves the elder man's words were solicitous, but the tone was commanding. Christie saw that he wanted to be done with him, have him gone quickly to some other port in the storm. Christie wanted to be gone as quickly, but he could not alibi up a Southern family to take him. And he could not just walk out. He had tested the leg last night when he thought he heard someone just on the other side of the door. Thank goodness he had been wrong, because the leg would not support him to the hall let alone through the Mississippi wilds.

"Well, you rest, and when you feel like talking a little, my daughter will write a letter for you. She enjoys such good works of mercy."

The man turned chair and all. Christie swallowed down his shock and regretting his coldness, watched him wheel toward the door. "I thank you, sir. You have performed a miracle in saving my leg. The brigade surgeon would have sawed it off."

The doctor saw no compliment in that. "Good Lord, if this

war lasts, we will not have a whole man in all the South. Well, you rest. Carolina is a good nurse—should be, I taught her." The door closed and a key scraped in the lock.

Miss Carolina's patient was not about to die. Carolina would not have it, and Rachel would not have it—they did not cater to defeat in any form. The next morning Rachel came with a basin and a pitcher of water. There was soap and a razor on the tray. "When you are presentable I will bring you breakfast. Don't expect much, we don't got much."

"Thank you for asking. I feel so much better this morning," Christie called to her back. She turned on her heels and gave him that don't-give-me-that-tone grimace for which mothers and sergeants were so famous.

He framed himself in the mirror and took up the razor. He did not recognize who it was who looked back. He felt uneasy with the reflection—an old soul in a young body, or was it a young soul in an old body? A beard: to be or not to be? He was still deciding when Rachel made the decision for him. Even though she said nothing about the matter directly, it was clear from her knotted lip and her cocked eye that she expected the stubble to have been gone. That cinched it—it stayed. He trimmed and shaped it, and wiped his face with the towel. The toilet was done as far as he was concerned. Rachel growled, but Christie ignored her. The North could do a little rebelling of its own.

Now, he examined the dishes with false enthusiasm. "What is this?" If it weren't bread and water it was the closest thing to it.

"Boiled bread, rennet pudding, sweet potatoes. Good for your stomach. See that you eat all of it."

Rennet pudding—that's sheep intestines! She wanted him slicked up for this? He pressed the spoon down on a marble of hard dough. It crumbled. He tasted it cautiously. It was not dumplings and cream, but it was not hardtack either. Not a bad compromise, considering.

Routine descended into tedium. In the morning Rachel dusted and straightened him like a corpse in a coffin. At noon Carolina came with his lunch and a cup of apple tea—more of a honey-tasting amber syrup she swore had curative powers. What followed was sleep and suffocating nightmares.

Dinner was more rennet pudding, sweet potatoes, and the apple toddy. Rachel set the tray on the table, when she could not wrestle him awake. "You will drink it when you are hungry enough! Ungrateful little snipe—insult my cooking with your possum shenanigans. You never got better than my kitchen in those army stews. That you should put on attitude, I will make you sorry."

It took all his concentration to force himself awake, and could only when hunger overpowered the craving for sleep. But he could not eat much of whatever it was they gave him. Then he fell back, to drift in half-dreams till the twilight flickered out. But he did not rest; his mind was too agitated. Where was Grant? Where was Grierson by now?

The nights were barbarous. He could feel his condition turning for the worse. He twitched and vibrated in sweat, his tongue swelled until he thought he would choke on it. The shakes did not subside in the morning but rattled when every sense wanted sleep. He cursed them all. Even with the warm spring breezes, he begged for blankets. His heart raced. He wanted water only water. He refused to eat and even poured Carolina's elixirs into the chamber pot. There was no count of days until the ague cooled, two or three at least.

"Where did you get the name Carolina?" He had awakened to find her there sitting quietly by his bed. It was an innocent enough question, but it startled her somehow.

She snapped her book shut and slid it into the folds of her gown. "My mother...she came from South Carolina. My father used to tease her that when she married she became, by the Rule of Ruth, a Mississippian. But she got the last word when she named me for home. 'Now you will always have a little Carolina that you cannot change.' How prophetic—in more ways than she intended."

"Read to me from the New Testament, I've had enough fire and brimstone for one lifetime."

She cleared her throat. "I don't read aloud very well as you may have noticed."

"I would like about anything, or is it some scandalous book of psalms you have there?" He reached for the book but she pulled it away. "Come now—wouldn't you like my redemption added to your long list of good works? Let me find my favorite chapter. I can turn right to it." She did not budge. "Come on!" He reached out. Before he could make too much noise, she surrendered the book up. He turned back the rich gold-embossed cover. Camouflage! "Good heavens, woman! It's a wolf in a lamb's fleece!"

She reached for it. "I do not know what possessed me to give that to you!" She went for it again, but he slipped it under his blankets, where no lady could reach with good grace. "You must give it to me. If father found me with it he would be in a rage. I think it is against the law to have it."

"Some say that the Union President places the blame for the whole war on that book."

Carolina nodded. "I think I would have to agree with him. A war under false pretenses. Miss Stowe should have had more children to keep her busy—and we would all be living in peace. I would say that a planter would not be in business long if he treated his workers in such a manner, nor receive the respect of his neighbors either."

"You have servants?" his words were guarded.

"We have no unwilling servants. My father is a doctor. We have no crop to harvest, no grounds to preen. In spite of their Catholic traditions, my parents had strong Calvinistic attitudes that work was good for children's developing character, so what had to be done, we did it—any more and they hired Eban to do it."

"Rachel?"

"Rachel is our housekeeper, duly paid and respected as a freewoman—freer in her opinions and actions than any of us children were ever allowed to be. It is not widely known, but she can come and go as she pleases, and believe me, she has threatened to go more times than I can count."

Such invasions into family private matters were unmannerly, he knew. Asking them put her into a difficult position, but her rudeness in not answering would be a greater sin than his. And this enemy family intrigued him, it was not living up to the lurid reputation Greeley and Garrison had painted.

She pulled away a pillow so he could sleep again and with the other hand reached behind him in a futile attempt for the book.

In one motion he had his arms around her, and pinned her against his chest in a vise. He pressed one hand across her mouth firmly, and put his lips against her ear. "Forget the book—that secret is safe for now. Just answer this. What have you been putting in my food to make me sleep? Laudanum?"

Her face was white. He repeated the question, but she only shook her head.

"Your father then? Don't lie." She fought against him, but he held tighter.

"Let her go or I will shoot! And wouldn't that be the pity, for your leg is some of my best work." The LeMat was aimed straight for Christie's head. The surgeon would not need a good aim at that range; the shot would spray all over the room. But he wouldn't shoot, not with Carolina so close. But there was something in the man's eyes—Christie's hands dropped away and Carolina pulled herself up. She straightened her dress and looked back at her patient. Christie positioned himself over the book tellingly.

He held her captive and she knew it. "Father, no reason to over reach. It was not as it seemed."

The doctor reddened. "I am not a fool. Couldn't be one of Van Dorn's wolves, now could you?"

"Father, such an insult!" Carolina affected a calmness with such quickness that Christie thought she must have had much practice. "You have a mistaken impression. I had tripped over my petticoat in getting up. I fell against him. He was keeping me from dropping to the floor on my face. The floors are slick—I think some water was spilled."

Carolina could play her father well. Christie thought her excuse lame, but being the only one on the table at the moment, he supported it with a nod only.

The doctor lowered his weapon. "Yes, well." He was not completely convinced, but his daughter was collected and not at all alarmed. "I have sent word to Colonel Barteau that you are here. I am sure he will be glad to help you find your way to Vicksburg—or wherever you belong—as soon as you are well."

Barteau! An alarm went off in Christie's memory. He should know the name, needed to know it. His emergencies were mounting. "And why would this Colonel Barteau know about me?"

"Colonel Barteau commands the Second Tennessee regiment. I would think if you fought around here you would know each other."

Was it Barteau, Hatch had fought near the M & O? No one in the Second knew the Confederates by name. Was that it? Why was his brain whirling? "Why would the colonel know a mere corporal? There are so many and we come and go quickly." Christie hoped Bennett would provide the clue his brain needed to fetch up the memory of Clark Barteau. Yes, *Clark*, that was his name, he was sure. But how did he know that?

"If you are who you say, he would have knowledge of your command at least. We will soon find out. Until that time, you, my young friend, will be—how do you say—confined to quarters."

"Father, you can't keep him locked up in here until Colonel Barteau can make time to answer your summons."

"It shouldn't be too long. He is in Mississippi on the trail of these Yankee marauders. I have extended him the hospitality of our home. If he and his men are as hungry and frustrated as I think they are, and if our friend is not who he claims, Colonel Barteau would want to know whether or not he has a Yankee spy working against him. Now, Carolina, will you kindly leave while my patient and I have a little talk?"

"Father?"

"Now!"

She jumped, as if the revolver were leveled at her. After she had left, Bennett closed the door and rolled closer to the bed. "If you are Confederate, I am proud to have you in my home. You have obviously suffered in the service of our Cause. But if you are a spy, I will hang you higher than Haman."

"You could have killed me when you operated on me and you wouldn't have had to worry. What is one more soldier either way?"

The option had struck Bennett as unthinkable. "I guess you could see it that way. But when all I wanted was to be a doctor, I took an oath that all life was sacred. That was forty years ago, and now I believe that the lives of the blue troops are no more sacred than a roaming dog pack. They have killed one son, wounded another, and turned this state into an asylum of widows and orphans. But if...well...if you are a son of the South, I did right in repairing your leg and giving you sanctuary."

"And if I'm not? Colonel Barteau will hang me for you. Isn't there something in your precious doctor's oath that makes you responsible for my death secondarily?"

Something in what the soldier said made sense, for the pistol dipped in his hand, but then he righted it again. "You could help clear yourself."

"How?" Christie would keep his words few. Grief was a kind of insanity, not to be underestimated. He was not trained in this kind of warfare.

"Tell me your name. You have not even told us your name. Why not?"

"A simple enough request—it is Brent..."

"First or last?"

"Last. The first is James." Christie grabbed the name of his precious deceased comrade.

"Where are your people from?"

"St. Louis. I think I said that."

"Live there? What did your father do?"

"My father is dead, my mother's people come from St. Louis." This much was true. And there was enough of his mother's family still in St. Louis if anyone cared to check—but not too closely. They were of fire breathing abolitionist conviction.

"What was her people?"

"Mercantile."

"What else?"

"Nothing else—plain people." Christie arched an eyebrow but showed no other agitation. "I have nothing else to say. If Colonel Barteau or the provost has more questions, I will answer them as best I can. I am sorry to say that the results will be anticlimactic. For the past two years I have been guarding railroads, warehouses, and fat generals, their wives, and wagons of their baggage—except for some agitation I saw in Corinth, Arkansas, and in a few other places. But as for questions about my family, I would rather not talk about that, if you please. Nothing of importance as far as the country's security or yours, but personally quite painful." Christie relaxed against his pillows.

"What are you hiding?"

"Hiding? I am not hiding anything. My family is my business, and the disposition of its loyalties...well...those are not so easily explained...especially at gun point."

"At last, something I think I understand." He released the trigger and rested the weapon in his lap. St. Louis had been at war with itself even before Sumter. Their own General Bowen had lived there, had commanded its militia before the war. His first battle was in that city back in 1861, when that old guard split down the middle and fought against itself and against their own neighbors for possession of the arsenal. He had lost and had barely escaped with his men. Those loyal neighbors of Bowen's now were the First Missouri and they fought against their friends and neighbors marching with Grant.

It was like that all over. Families were literally torn apart. Portraits were turned to the wall; names were blotched out in family Bibles and never whispered again, even in prayer. Such wounds needed extreme delicacy, yet they tarnished a family name, never entirely to be rubbed clean in proper Southern society. Had the boy been forced to turn his back on his family to follow his conscience? Carolina had said he had been raving about owning his own soul. Bennett softened. "I am sorry. I cannot even estimate your grief. Do I have your word, you are a gentleman and a patriot?"

Christie restrained a smile. "You have my word—that I am true to the colors I have defended."

Bennett relented. "Then you are invited to my table as soon as you are able and can stay here until you are well enough to join your regiment."

"Thank you, sir."

Bennett did not offer Christie his hand as he took his leave. "You are a lucky man. I came very close to shooting you." The doctor opened the door, withdrew the key and put it in his pocket. "Rest, now."

XI
My Enemy, My Comrade

Liberation, even in small measures, makes a captive drunk, especially when washed down with very good bourbon. Collin Matthew Bennett poured a very good bourbon and not much else. He stood, as melancholy as a defendant, watching a hanging jury file into the box. As it was, they were his family and his confessor settling themselves around his table for supper. Impossible but true, Christie had to give him this, Collin was even more ill at ease than the Union convalescent taking his seat among them. There was an Aunt Mamie and Uncle Nathaniel Powers, a couple as perfectly matched as gargoyles over a cathedral door. Then there was the Right Reverend Father Francis Kessler in the robes of false humility. At the foot of the table was Carolina, glowing like sunrise on the blighted landscape.

She motioned Christie by her. "Please sit by me, James."

"You have a beautiful family," Christie lied by way of politeness' sake.

Collin glared at him from the head chair, and Christie's good intentions crashed to the floor in shards. This was indeed a family that hoarded its Southern charm, unfriendly, even by Yankee standards. Even with the windows open from floor to ceiling, the room was stifling. Heavy perfumes from the bud trees overpowered the aromas of fish, sweet potatoes, and molasses rising from the tureen in the center of the table.

"Father, if you will give the blessing." Carolina bowed her head and the rest followed.

Kessler nodded solemnly. "Dear Heavenly Father, we, your unholy and unworthy servants, lay prostrate before you and admit our unworthiness even for this menial repast. But we take it up as fortification to do Thy holy will. We pray for Thy eternal favor, Thy will be done."

"Amen." They chorused.

"Amen?" Christie smiled. If Rachel heard that solemn judgment of her cooking as "menial," life on earth would be very akin to hell without bail for even a priest. Christie's status being on the slimmest of terms with the lady as it was, whispered instead, "May we all rest in peace."

Collin finished his bourbon and refilled his glass with wine. Carolina sighed and assumed the duties of hostess. As for the host, it had taken Christie five minutes to dislike Collin Bennett, ten more to hate him intensely, and a full half-hour to take it all back — with interest.

Collin struck him as a shadow player, one of those self-sufficient men who had by the rule of entailment watched and learned much but said little, taking always a secondary role to the heir apparent. So he and his drink were company enough, and he made little polite conversation. He was obviously not feeling polite; he had been treed by a yelping hound. As the soup was passed, Nathaniel Powers bombarded him with the whys and wherefores regarding foreclosures and conditions, of dalliances and illegitimate issue newly arisen from a case long extinct in Collin's pre-war career. Then after several minutes of citing precedent for precedent Uncle Nathaniel realized he had been talking by himself and to himself, so he set on a new prey, "Are you a lawyer, Mister Brent?"

"No, but my father practiced. He never bragged about the profession though and used to say lawyers, not punishment, were created as a consequence of sin." The table went dumb — he now faced a hanging jury.

"Please explain." It was a bid from the old lawyer, spoken as solemn as a judgment of guilty.

"Yes, do," Collin had caught the scent of blood. "Your father sounds like quite a philosopher."

The room went stone silent. Christie was the subject of all expectations. The fugitive stumbled with "uhms" and "uhs" until he found the path he wanted to take. "With apologies up front to the book of Genesis: when Adam and Eve committed the sin that lost them their home and innocence for all progeny, God and Satan met at the gates of Eden to discuss the fate of mankind and how the case should be decided. It comes as no surprise they could not agree, each claiming rights for the souls of the wayward children. Was it Adam's sin or Eve's? (My father maintained that it was Adam's — that men always beg their weaknesses onto their wives.) Should they be tried separately or together? Punished separately or together? Do the children inherit the sin? After they had been quibbling for a century or two, they admitted the need for representatives to take over the case so they could tend to other work. Between them they created the species of lawyer, taking some qualities of good and evil from both. But neither God nor Satan was satisfied with the result, for there was not enough divine or demonic in the finished specimen to suit the other. But once a bureaucrat has been created, it cannot be taken back, and God let the breed evolve as it might, doing good or evil until He had the last word at judgment." Christie swallowed and continued. "The citation, he said, is somewhere in the footnotes of the Old Testament, and being a loyal son, I never disagreed with him." Christie thought he heard the faint cry of a mob carrying faggots and burning torches.

"And what are you!" Carolina's uncle studied him closely.

That was a question with many answers, but Christie dismissed them all as even more impertinent and suicidal. "Mister Powers, my father never pushed me into law. Since I had some skill with my hands, he hoped I might have become a surgeon. Instead, he died when I was young, and I became a carpenter."

"A tradesman," Missis Powers was not sure she approved of such at her table.

"A journeyman, madam...very proud of it I am."

"Bravo!" Collin saluted. "An honest laborer! We see so few in polite society!"

Missis Powers rebounded. "Your mother must be disappointed."

"Yes, ma'am." Christie was stung—not because she was wrong, but because she was right.

"Your mother must be worried about you." Carolina saw the same point, but differently.

"My mother's concerns are not with my welfare." If he had sounded unnecessarily brutal, he had not meant to. "She and my father had bred independence in me, and she assumes they had done it well enough not to stay awake nights worrying about me."

"You speak well—as if you have been to university?" Father Kessler took up the interrogation.

"I have had the good fortune of one year and part of another."

"May I ask where?" Collin studied him quizzically.

"Ohio Wesleyan, seems a long time ago. I was sixteen." Christie wanted to call it back—too much wine. His alias had been Missouri. He could only plane off the edges and make this blunder fit the round hole in the square puzzle that was his false identity.

"You were very young for university. I think you are not at all what you seem, James." Collin had thought his tone discreet, but his sister regarded her brother askance—there will be no more cross-examinations of disabled veterans at her dinner table.

"Where in particular is that, if I may ask?" Kessler was not bound by chastisement from backcountry spinsters. The parts were not adding up to an agreeable whole in his mind either.

"Delaware, Ohio. My father had people there, and I went to stay with them for awhile."

"It did not dilute your principles on secession, I pray." There was compassion on Carolina's face; he was confessing a great trial. "How did you stand up to those people?"

"Excuse me?" Christie smiled in spite of himself. "Delaware is not the edge of Sodom. The people I met there were civil, intelligent, and mannered. They did not eat soup with their fingers or sleep with their horses."

"I don't know, have you ever seen their children?" That such had come from Carolina's Christian mouth and not her brother's drunken one shocked Christie. His astonishment delighted her.

Christie rose to the defense of all Union men and women before good sense could stop him. "I feel that honest people of intelligence can disagree..." A lamp flickered in a private room and a lost memory, the recollection made the temperature all the more uncomfortable. The specter of a young student sitting at his mentor's table, as elegant as this one. The scholar was prefacing a well-turned dissent with those very words, "I feel honest people of intelligence can disagree..." Christie's father's owlish grin bid his student continue into the philosophical snare prepared for him, "Yes, Mister Barteau, they can, but is that your only defense?" Only with supreme effort could Christie keep himself composed as he groped for the point he had been about to make out of so many visions swirling in his head.

"Tell me, what do *you* feel?" Carolina filled his glass with wine and bid him drink it. The soldier looked as if he were going to faint.

Christie thought hard before he spoke. When he did, to his surprise, his voice was matter-of-fact. "I was going to say, with all due respect, I feel that a great mistake has been made when we underestimate the Christianity and the civility of those who disagree with us."

"How is that, sir? Is it a mistake to stand up for one's people and one's principles unequivocally?" It was no question, Kessler was making a cold accusation.

Grant's lieutenant did not know what to say, and so he spoke the truth. "You know when the fighting stops, there is an unspoken truce between the Rebels and the Yankees, and we stack rifles so they don't go off by accident. We meet between the lines to gather up our wounded and bury our dead. Sometimes we end up helping the enemy with his wounded and dead, and he with ours. Nothing is ever said in the way of thanks or of apologies. Then, if there is time, we play cards, trade tobacco for coffee, talk of home and the families we left behind. We don't waste good air and precious hours talking about the war and who was right or wrong."

"Indeed!" Kessler was unaware such fraternization was routine in the ranks, where he felt righteous hatred should be the rule.

"I remember," Christie continued undeterred, "a...a...Yank who talked about the vineyards he grew in Ohio. Those acres along the Erie were the proudest achievement of his life, not the stripes on his shoulder or the battles painted on his regimental flag. He talked about wine, sugar, casks, and all. How he worried that those grapes were not being tended well now that he was gone. He died next day. But in the time we were together, he never once said a word about principles. We all knew where he stood by the color of his uniform and the direction he aimed his rifle. I assume that the issues are as plain to all of us here, so why not discuss happier subjects and leave the war beyond the horizon for awhile, especially when the ladies are so lovely, the dinner so delicious, and the men...well...the men are..."

"Grouchy, sullen, and irreverent. Even if you are too polite to say so." Collin was pleased to see the smug priest bested. "I have breathed the same heresy, James. Principles are easy to carry when you have got two good legs and arms and your stomach is full. Yes, my feelings were quite the same—until Fredericksburg and I got in the way of Yankee shrapnel. Although I wasn't so fortunate as you to have had a doctor like my father. And now I am not sure what principles brought me that far. All I remember are my loyalties to my comrades that kept me there until I was hit."

"Barksdale's Mississippians," Christie returned.

"No, the Oktibbeha Rescue, if you please, recruited right here in Starkville." Collin raised a glass in salute to which Christie raised his own.

Now Christie knew where he was. Grierson had come through here while Hatch kept all eyes on him at West Point. How bad had it been for them here? Christie regarded his situation all the more delicate. He bid Collin continue. Better to suffer the effects of regimental pride—a plague that every soldier spreads. It did not take much prodding to set Collin off on the glory road.

"I think now the Oktibbeha Rescue is a part of the Forty-Eighth Infantry under General Powell Hill, a Virginian, for God's sake. Can you believe the insult of Mississippi being led by a Tidewater blueblood? There are far too many Virginians running things, if you ask me. Then we were with Featherston's Brigade, Anderson's Division, and General Longstreet's First Corps—no better general in the army than Old Pete Longstreet. And since there is such a hunger for principle and its effects at this table, perhaps, James, we can give our guests a taste of it, and when they see it is vinegar and wormwood, they will not crave it so heartily."

Collin turned to Father Kessler, who had made such a case of principles. "We were a part of the skirmish line just beside Cobb's Georgians. I was quartered just behind the Telegraph Road, a miserable little mule path that would have washed away except for the stonewall that saved it—and us—from annihilation. Behind it, Longstreet's soldiers were six deep and his batteries strung up the hill. The Yankees may have been beaten but they weren't giving anything away. Their General Hunt hammered the town into an inferno with his batteries—nearly got cooked alive with hot shot. Then they came at us in waves, straight at our faces. I never saw braver men anywhere...not anywhere. There is not a coward in their ranks."

"What is that, 'hot shot'?" Mamie Powers asked.

Carolina had not heard the question. For this was the first time Collin had ever talked about his life in the army—not even in letters—and Carolina nodded to James Brent for finally opening the door. Even in the torment of these visions, she had never seen Collin so calm.

"Solid shot heated nearly white hot. Then it's loaded into the bore of a cannon up against a wet rag to keep the powder from discharging before it's supposed to. It is what we mean when we say 'hellfire.' So hot, a building combusts as soon as it is hit. This General Hunt of theirs shelled us without ceasing, and the town was a caldron. We were stationed as sharpshooters in the farmhouses just out of town the night before. That morning the cannons started again. Some of my men got out. I could hear others who were trapped. They dropped out of the windows. Barksdale's skirmishers, who had been up by the river, were filtering back, so I knew the Yanks were coming. I gave the order for every man to follow them.

For a moment, Collin was lost in the memory. When he spoke, his voice was barely a whisper. "When the wind caught the smoke and blew it away, we could see the Yanks forming up on the road. There had to be a hundred thousand of them. I remember all those colors, flags everywhere." Collin was lost again in the enveloping smoke and fire. "We made it back and was the third line in the trench behind the wall. We went at each other for hours. Up they came without stop—division after division—in the open, men bare of cover. You had to give them due.

"The captain needed a courier—he was afraid the Yanks would break to our right. So he sent me to Longstreet's headquarters. I was on foot, in the open on the face of the hill when something stung my leg. That's all I remember. I couldn't move and the ground was just erupting all around me. Charlie Seuger came for me—he jumped right out of the artillery explosion, like some angel. He coughed and screamed like a hacking crow. So wound up, he didn't even know his hair was on fire. I told him to run for it. He just picked me up like a sack of meal. 'You may give orders like a lieutenant, but you bleed just like a private.' I can still remember his face, smudged and coal black as a witch's cat. He..."

Christie's wine glass shattered in his hand; the crack split the silence like a pistol-shot. Collin snapped into consciousness. He took his surroundings in slowly—at first surprised at where he was. Blood was dripping onto the table linen from cuts in Christie's fingers. Collin saw, but he was dumb and immobile.

"You are bleeding, Mister Brent!" Kessler pressed a napkin against his mouth and gagged. Mamie Powers winced and turned away. Carolina pressed Christie's hand into a linen napkin.

"I beg your pardon, ma'am. I am so clumsy." The pressure of Carolina's palm against his hand flustered him. "My manners have been in mothballs far too long. I grip everything as if it were a rifle."

"Your manners are gallant. Those glasses are too brittle, fired with not enough sand, I fear." Carolina examined the wound to make sure no more glass hid under the skin. "They are only scratches, thank God. We are having a difficult time getting you well, James."

Collin gaped wide-eyed. "I also apologize. You should have stopped me, Carolina, we have upset our guest."

Carolina tied off a clean napkin around Christie's palm. "Please drink, James. If it does not calm your nerves, it will calm mine."

The large blue hound was nosing at his master's boots, eager for reassurance that the catastrophe had not been his fault. Collin nuzzled the dog. "Fleas, boy? I know exactly how you feel. Had the same trouble. But don't let Carolina see you scratch—she will boil you up in a caldron of lye soap." Collin laughed to lighten the mood. Then he filled a fresh glass and handed it to Christie. As Christie rose to accept it, Collin also rose. And he remained on his feet after the glass was taken. Christie too remained standing waiting for what came next. Collin regarded Christie intently, then he raised his glass. "To flea-bitten comrades!"

Aunt Mamie was aghast, " Collin, you are so coarse!"

Christie was humbled by such a gracious gesture. Slowly he brought the glass to his host's to let them ring, "To comrades!" he whispered, "in the end."

But Collin misunderstood and replied, "Yes, to the end."

Missis Powers fanned herself as if on fire. The events

around the table confused her. She wanted assurances, gallant knights to the rescue, oaths of annihilation of the enemy, not this.

Her husband needed them as well. "Was there news of that wretched Yankee cavalry? Have the Palmers heard anything more—they have a son with Weatherall? He must be after them sure."

Neither Collin nor Christie replied. Assurances were not in over supply from convalescents and amputees.

"Well, I will not be cowered by rabble. No, I am prepared." The grand dame's powder puff cheeks were crimson. "Your Uncle Nathaniel would not leave me at the disadvantage of these rogues!" The two soldiers exchanged glances of barely suppressed smiles, while Mamie fussed into her reticule for proof.

Collin affected a solemnity that tugged at the corners of his mouth. "And how, pray tell, will you scare off a brigade or two of Union cavalry, my dear aunt?"

"You have some respect, Collin Bennett—we ladies are not entirely helpless." She withdrew a derringer, its barrel about the size of a very large thimble.

It was a remarkable fossil. Collin examined it more closely. "Yes, that is one fine cannon. That will paralyze the Yankee column for five minutes at best—with fits of laughter, if they have a sense of humor. Be careful—you will probably shoot a horse's ear off."

Christie swallowed twice yet he still minced his words, "M...m... ma'am, I wish we had had a bushel of those at our last battle." Tears streamed down his cheeks.

"This is no laughing matter, gentlemen!" Uncle Nathaniel took the weapon and passed it back to his wife. "The devils have cleaned out Doctor Kilgore's stores. No telling where they are now riding on our best stock. Do you believe it? They come down on you and then cut back like a cyclone. With half of our best men in Virginia and the rest in Tennessee, we are ripe for the picking."

"Not quite. I happen to know from intelligence that General Bowen and General Smith keep Grant guessing." Collin would not surrender just yet.

"A man fights best on his home country." Kessler had crossed the bounds, but he did not care. "We need our men at home, not in Virginia."

You pray for that and I will pray right beside you. Christie estimated if all the state troops in the Army of Northern Virginia were broken out and sent home to fight the devil at their own doors, Lee would be a lonely commander.

"They are fighting the enemy *before* he gets to the door, is their way of thinking. There is a lot of Mississippi blood wetting the fields of Maryland and Virginia, just as there is Missouri blood wetting the soil of Mississippi." Collin spoke for every soldier who challenged the politicians and civilians who did not think the army kept to their timetables to step up to the line. "I say, Good Father, why don't you enlist if you believe so much? We have an abundance of chaplains, but we are always short of rifleman. We will say our prayers back here dutifully and do our penance, and you can write us letters keeping us on our resolutions like Saint Paul did for the Corinthians. I promise to collect them—every one—and have them leather bound and published."

Kessler's face bleached white. Carolina choked. But Mamie Powers had plenty to say, and her cares were closer to home: "Our towns and farms are strung out too far to be of help to each other. We need every man to form a vigilance committee. We could all be dead in our beds without our neighbors being aware of it."

Now Christie *was* insulted. "There are no reports that the Yankees have put ladies and children at risk. At inconvenience, certainly, but they still sleep in their beds at night—even if it is with one less quilt." Now he understood why Grierson took no civilian prisoners. What would he do with a wagon train of them like Mamie Powers? And they were of so much better use buzzing up hysteria in their own neighborhoods.

"Sir, the Yankees are making war on women and children." In frustration, Missis Powers slammed her fan against the table. It was no more than a snap, but she had breached the limits of etiquette—a greater crime here and now than Yankee plundering. She bit her lip and turned to her husband. Nathaniel Powers registered nothing on the surface, but his disapproval was in the slow, deliberate motion of raising his wine to his lips. She raised hers and finished it down. "What I wouldn't give for a cup of tea again."

Christie tried to sound comforting, for the poor woman was clearly terrified. "Ma'am, it seems the Yankees are more intent upon smashing the railroads, telegraphs and the paraphernalia of war to bother ladies such as yourself."

"No one ever claimed the Yankees were gentlemen except you, James." Carolina dared.

Christie knew the course the war would take and they did as well, if they thought about it. Intentions begin honorably enough — to keep the confines of war between the armies and away from the people. But men die, battles are lost, war escalates. Angry men have sewn a wind and what does scripture predict? A whirlwind. The fury swells with every passing month. Determined generals will exert every means to win, and equally determined generals on the other side will exert every energy to the opposite. They will no longer be able to keep a rein on the bloodlust.

And it had started long before now. From the first, barbarous atrocities raged throughout the Appalachians. In Kentucky, eastern Tennessee, northern Georgia, and western North Carolina men were burning farms and savaging their neighbors on a whim and a whisper of disloyalty. Arkansas, Kansas, and Missouri raged in their own sectional infernos even before Sumter. War was not a duel between gentlemen, or a tournament between knights!

Christie's silence was telling Kessler volumes. As if he had been reading the soldier's mind, the priest said, "Soldiers must never forget that they are children of God."

It was a gauntlet that Christie would not take up. Instead, the waylaid Buckeye set his glass on the table carefully. He could not understand this passion for war by civilians. Collin had not even approached the subject. Nor had he, until prodded. Now it passed as dinner conversation. "Let's adjourn to other subjects. For the moment war is not on our door step."

"Before you do, it is about time women expressed some opinions." Carolina swung into the offensive, enjoying the joust of wills usually reserved for men.

"And what pray is your opinion?" Christie returned Carolina's smile for sweet smile.

"Oh my — and now, Mister Brent, you have certainly let yourself in for it." Collin then set well back in his chair to ward off the blast he knew was coming.

"And your reasons why I should not, dear brother?"

"Women should be seen and not heard. Children should be unseen and unheard."

"Well that would keep us both quiet, Collin."

"Sister, we are upsetting Aunt Mamie. She loves to talk of war, but does not abide bad manners at the table. War in principle, but not in practice."

"No, Collin. You shall not deflect me from what I was about to say. All right, I shall tell you plainly, which I must do so Collin can understand. There was nothing to keep the South from secession, nothing in the Constitution, for I have read it over—it is merely a gentleman's agreement. From the beginning, this nation has been an uneasy marriage of opposites. Do you not agree, James?"

"Yes, James, disagree at your own peril!" Collin dared. "You have one good leg and two good arms left—which would you like to sacrifice next?"

Christie picked up Collin's dare, then replied with his best milk-and-honey voice, "Miss Carolina, I am no lawyer, but this President Lincoln is, and he says the Constitution does not allow secession. President Davis is a lawyer, and he says it does. There is a Congress in Washington and one in Richmond full of lawyers, which accounts for a lot of opinions—all in disagreement—with little getting done. This is an inconvenience but not disastrous, as long as they are kept to their ivory halls with their law books. However, I am of the opinion, if a third of them could sew, a third could knit socks, and a third could cook, they would be of much better use to the army, and would carry the point. Things being as they are, since so many lawyers built this fire. I think Shakespeare is right: whether spoken from the mouths of fools or butchers, the advice goes, get rid of the lawyers."

"Here! Here!" Collin raised his glass in salute. "An excellent point! However, since few of us have talents for gainful employment elsewhere, we are less use than swayback barnyard mules."

"War is no laughing matter." The priest turned a steel eye on the two who were fast forming an alliance against him. Ideals were being mocked by those who should be carrying their banners.

"Father, quite the contrary." Collin then affected a breezy

tone. "I was in the war for a year and a half and found many things to laugh at. In fact, if I had not laughed from time to time I would have gone mad. James, I have heard of your Texas Ranger Thespians in the west. In the east we had our Stonewall Theater Brigade—not acceptable in polite society, but no one made the mistake of thinking *we* were polite society—not even Stonewall Jackson. I do think my favorite vignette was the one-act presentation entitled 'Medical Board.' You must have heard it."

"I admit I have not," Christie shook his head slowly.

Carolina covered her eyes. "Then you are blessed in the sight of God, James, because Collin has tortured every other unfortunate visitor with it."

The host launched into it before he could be stopped. "The curtain goes up and the surgeon is at his desk, playing solitaire and drinking brandy. A courier enters stage right with the news that there is a badly wounded soldier outside. 'Bring him in!' The surgeon finishes his whiskey and lays a gum blanket over his cards so his game will not be ruined. The bloody unfortunate is brought in and laid on the table. The surgeon chooses a saw and an ax from his medical trunk."

"My dear nephew, must we?" Mister Powers pleaded that this story was going nowhere appropriate for a lady's ears.

"Yes, bare with me, dear uncle, it is very funny."

"A minority opinion, dear uncle. Offer it up for the poor souls, and until this melodrama ends, we envy them," Carolina groaned.

Collin inhaled enough air to get to the end without giving segment for another interruption. "The surgeon stares down and shakes his head. 'I am sorry, soldier, that leg will have to come off.' The soldier, a true Calvinist, believes he has thus done his share and will then be entitled to go home after the operation. 'No,' the surgeon shakes his head. 'You can drive an ambulance when you get well.' Then the surgeon picks up the soldier's twisted arm and shakes his head. 'That too will have to come off.' The soldier asserts that then he would be useless to the army and so would be sent home. 'No, we will make you a cook when you get well.' The surgeon turns the boy's face to get a better look at the blood streaking from the temple. 'That head will have to come off.' 'Then sure I will be sent home,' the eager soldier begged. 'No, we will make you a general.'"

Nothing! Collin searched from one to the other of these sour Quakers, hoping that at least one appreciated brilliant farce when it was presented. Instead, embarrassment floated above them like swamp air. He had about given up hope, when at last, a report. A hiss swallowed but would not go down. Then the dam broke behind Christie's napkin, overflowing with a profusion of apologies to Carolina.

Collin accepted it as applause overdue. "There, you see? It took a real soldier to appreciate my story."

"It took a gentleman who has had enough breeding not to let his host suffer such humiliation as he deserves. After that, I think we are in need of something a little stronger than this 'lemonade' father thinks proper wine for ladies. Collin, I think you must make your specialty."

"Yes, do, Collin!" His aunt was already giddy.

"We will wait for you out on the gallery." Carolina motioned her guests toward the windows.

As they went Mamie Powers turned to her niece. "And how is your father, Carolina? I do hope he is recovering. We have not seen him at church. Will he come for the day of humiliation? He must set an example. Do you think we could look in on him for just a little while? Perhaps we can raise his spirits."

A cloud passed over Carolina's face but she recovered with a false smile. "He makes small strides daily. No, he keeps quite to himself and wishes not to inflict his grief on others."

"Such a brave soul." Missis Mamie crossed herself, "Lorin's death crippled him so, and then Laura's following so quickly with the baby and all. I do hope he will be getting out soon."

Collin's uncle followed the women out, but the priest waited behind.

"Join the ladies, Father, James will help me. We may have only two good legs between us, but at least we have four dedicated hands."

The priest eyed them both curiously—two schoolboys contemplating a conspiracy for which he would be the victim. Abruptly, he pushed the portieres aside and went out.

Collin exhaled deeply and the false cheer dissolved. "Yes,

Aunt Mamie, a day of humiliation—who would want to stay in bed and miss that?" He reached for two fresh glasses and a bottle from a secret alcove in the sideboard. "You are going to need this, James." He brushed aside Christie's reluctance and filled a glass for each of them. "To family dinners and hell! Sometimes the two seem very much the same."

Christie was impressed at Collin's capacity for liquor, but knew he could not hold his own and keep the camouflage going.

"Here, here, man! You will have to do better than that to live up to your frontier reputation! I thought you western troops could drink straight kerosene without flinching." Collin poured himself another. Perspiration broke over his forehead.

"Are you all right?" Christie asked quietly.

"Of course I am all right. These little soirées are most invigorating, don't you agree? Get the heart pumping the blood to the brain—yes, just like a hemorrhage, and you and I know how exciting those are." He would hold back no longer. "What do they know of the war? Where's the crème de menthe?" And then, loud enough to be heard in Louisiana, he yelled, "Carolina, the crème?"

His sister pushed aside draperies of faded brocade. "On the top shelf. For heaven's sake, Collin, a potato has better eyes than you."

"The Cause is as much theirs as it is yours...or mine, I guess." Christie did not believe it, but he thought it was what a southerner would say.

Collin turned on him, "Is it? They talk thunder and brimstone, but they cringe at the first scare of enemy!" Collin held his drink aloft. "Did you see Kessler recoil at the sight of your hand? A couple of drops of blood and he nearly fainted dead away. They want war, what would they do with it on their doorsteps? Except for Carolina, who has done her share, they have not seen the elephant, and he is a big, ugly monster when he is on the stampede. If this enemy could have been defeated with bluster, we could have won the war four times over by last Christmas and never left our porch. This enemy...I fear...we have underestimated him. This Grant, Rosecrans, and Sherman—there is something different about them. They are hungry lions. They have been inconvenienced by Van Dorn and Forrest, but they will come again—and keep coming by any route until we are all finally treed." Collin nodded at the circle of family outside, "Aunt Mamie is right, the devil is at the door. I fear for them—they will dream their visions of the Cause and never see the boot."

Collin raised his glass, but Christie pulled it down. "Do you think you should?"

"Drink? Yes, James, I think I should."

"No, be so hard on them. You and I had our hate and our boasts in the beginning, you remember? We burned them out in one battle after another. After awhile, you fight the man in the other uniform—but you don't hate him. I don't any more. The enemy is no different than I; I am convinced of that now. We fight for our union, he for his. And for our buddies—we don't want the dead to die for nothing. And so we go on. The people at home, all they can do is read about the slaughter in the papers. They must feel so helpless. It's a shame, this beautiful day ruined with the talk of war when it does no good, no good at all."

Collin may not have understood, but as a good host he accepted Christie's point and let his anger cool. "All right. Now let's see if I can remember how to make them something pastel and refreshing without using arsenic." There was a shuffle of crystal decanters. "I don't have any ice. Hell with the ice. They can drink it warm." He poured off the contents into four goblets and then he paused. "Do you hear it sometimes?"

"What?"

Collin's eyes were vacant as they were before, and he whispered not to be overheard, "In my sleep, I hear my brother. I can't get to him, and so I watch him die again out between the lines. I see it all over again. In the morning, before the world floods in, I forget, it never happened...no war...no death. I think I hear him talking to Carolina in the next room. I never realized how close father's voice was to my brother's. Then it all hits home, none of it is real. I have to live with it all over again."

Christie did not think he could put like feeling into words. "I hear the voices of my friends. You know they aren't there, but you hear them all the same. Maybe they are there. Maybe they don't go to eternity until what put them in the ground is resolved. But once they are in your dreams, it happens over and over, as if you are being given another chance to save them. But you can't."

Christie was haunted by other phantoms, "And there are

the drums, the long roll, and the cavalry bugles. It comes and goes, the music of war, off and on when thunder breaks or horses pass."

"And the blood rushes into your head and your heart pounds," Collin nodded.

"You hear them too?"

"Every morning—as if they were outside my window," Collin searched Christie's face for some assurance that they were both not mad. "Sometimes, all I want to do is turn it off, gag the voices, forget, get some peace."

In the hospital Christie had seen that same look on men who died when they should have lived. They had seen too much—or blamed themselves for deaths they were powerless to prevent. Nolan had been like that, refusing all forgiveness and compassion as being unworthy of it. The guilt was a poison that killed from the inside.

"You miss your regiment. Will you go back to them?" Christie asked.

"A one-legged lieutenant is no good in the infantry, and I can't cook. I am not there, and I am not altogether here either. It's a bad arrangement." He set four glasses of julep on a wooden tray, in another two he poured straight bourbon. "This will have to do. The silver has gone to the Cause. Carolina donated it in heaping boxfuls years ago. We can push the tray on the cart." Collin nudged the butler table with his walking stick and Christie gathered his crutches.

"Are you sure you want to give them that?" Christie whispered as they crossed the threshold. "There is enough alcohol in those drinks to blow up the house. You might kill your poor relatives—or the sweet-tempered Father Francis of Assisi—and then who would give you absolution?"

Collin grumbled, "You are so sheltered, James. Those old biddies could drink lye, belch flame, and sleep through the night like babies."

The two veterans straightened their masks to do their part in this charade of polite conversation. "Here we are. I have juleps for everyone except James. He wanted something stronger against the pain. I join him only to be polite." Collin chided.

Christie admired him: Collin turned lies into compliments as naturally as any other gentlemanly art.

"Does the leg bother you much?" With a drink in her hand and eager to make amends for her earlier outbursts, Missis Powers turned her sweetest smile on Christie.

"Not when I have such a beautiful lady to distract me." She blushed and lowered her eyes. Oh, wouldn't his mother be proud to hear he had put forth his best manners in the house of the enemy? Survival can make a man a bear or a lamb, a debate that would interest General Sherman very much.

The company had left just before the storm. Collin retreated to his room. Christie lingered on the gallery to watch the rain, too exhausted to escape for the moment. In two years of the army he had never known such luxury as this house and its bounty.

"You wish anything else, James?" Carolina produced her father's humidor and Christie accepted a cigar for later.

"No, go ahead, I insist. I never understood the idea that cigars were too strong for ladies, yet we must change diapers that would knock a crow off a manure wagon." She paused while Christie lit the tip. "You are scandalized that I have opinions and express them?"

The war had taught Christie something of ambushes, and this was a question no man could answer and live.

"Don't be embarrassed, James." She sat down, unbidden. "You see, disfigurements can be liberating...yes, I know. You are so gracious to pretend not to notice, or pretend it doesn't matter, and I pretend you don't see it. Thank you for that. But it is there and I have come to accept it. It could be you have seen so much of ugliness my face does not distract you. But it bothers others very much, and in a lady it is unforgivable. In their eyes the condition goes to the soul. My disfigurement put 'Paid' to my merits as a belle. So I gave up pretending, simpering, and glowing. Later I found my deformity had its privileges. If a lady shocks by her very appearance and knows that she is out of the running in the marriage derby, she can speak her own mind—and enjoy herself— for she has nothing to lose. It is quite liberating. Collin indulges me that. Don't you see?"

"You are withdrawing yourself prematurely sure."

"By my own choice, thank you. I had an offer a few

months before I went into the convent. I think my dowry had something to do with it. Mister Martin Wyatt, a widower with seven children by two wives both dead before they were thirty. His children were between two and fourteen as I remember—a couple of sets of twins in there somewhere. He asked for my hand, but it would have taken more than one hand to raise seven children and run his plantation. He was not a man who kept to his hearth fires very long at a stretch. When I confided that I had decided upon the convent instead of his name, he was insulted. It all worked out well in the end. My father bribed the good sisters with my dowry to take me. They took it, and in a suitable time I proved unsuitable. So they returned me, but kept the donation as suitable restitution for all the trouble I caused. Meanwhile, Mister Wyatt had married my friend Alexandra Conners instead. She had three more children in three years. Would have had a fourth, except Mister Wyatt went off to war."

Carolina reflected quietly and then concluded thoughtfully, "Should have been Sandy gone off to war. She could have used the peace and quiet." Carolina set very serious eyes on him, for she was confused by what calamity that set his face to contorting.

"If my heart were not already taken, I would marry you this minute, Miss Carolina, I surely would."

"Why, Mister Brent, I have the feeling that I might even accept. Wouldn't we make a pair!"

No one talked of days or dates as if they did not matter. Christie saw no newspapers. Perhaps Carolina or the doctor forbade them in a house already overwhelmed by tragedy. Collin left to where he never said, but he remained intent on being gone most of the time. He returned at odd hours, morose and unresponsive, if he returned at all. On those occasions when he did not, Christie would find him in the cloister garden the next morning wearing the same suit as the day before, offering no apologies for his personal neglect. And regardless of the time of day, Collin availed himself of the stores in the wine cabinet. Fortified, he would be up again to venture to another unknown destination or, on another whim, go no farther than the gallery and collapse in a chair.

If Collin found his relatives a nuisance, he did not find Christie so. He never sought out the convalescent in his room, but if Christie happened to be close by, the young Confederate would take his ease by him. They never again talked about the war in public or private. In fact, they talked little, and their friendship grew on that.

For Carolina, her confinement was as voluntary as it was monastic. Every evening she and Rachel retreated to her sewing room to spin and weave blankets for her beloved soldiers. The clackity-clack of the loom barked through the house as rhythmic as a locomotive. The good doctor kept to his bed, and there was no more talk of Colonel Barteau.

Christie calculated as best he could that the month was drawing to a close. The time was having its affect. He used only one crutch to support himself now, and he traveled around the grounds as often and as far as he wished and no one took him to account. For all their pacing around Carolina had come to call them both the carrousel cavalry.

In spite of the hospitality, the walls were closing in on him too. The pretense of the lies he fashioned made his moods black with apprehension and guilt. Now that no one pressured him on the whys and wheres of his counterfeit identity, he was afraid he would get careless, forget a detail, especially one he had conjured when he was delirious. And what evidence had he left behind? Christie had not seen his uniform at all. So where was the will Billy had given him, and what else had he left in the pockets? None of it had been on the table when he first woke up.

Now, he wore a fine suit of Collin's. But it did not fit this inner man. He was homesick for the blue uniform, the baggy, lice-infested blue uniform. And the colors—Christie ached to see the candy-striped flag instead of the Bonnie Blue that snapped and rippled from the front rail. He felt adrift in a foreign country. He missed his comrades—the no-nonsense Buckeyes who spoke English with a hard edge backed up with hard sense, not with the soft vowels and upsweep lilt of the airy South. And the army was moving without him. Had Grant landed at Port Gibson? Where was Grierson?

With the storm that afternoon, came an early night. Carolina and Rachel talked about the herbs for the kitchen as well as the doctor's apothecary that would need replanting if they washed out. Collin had evaporated after dinner, and with no male company, Christie retreated to his sanctum early.

Having traveled the route so often, he did not take a lamp, but leveraged himself over his crutch, down the back gallery and through the dark passage door from the consultation room to the surgery. He stopped on his way for only an instant, to sweep the way ahead. In five minutes his door was closed, in no more than ten all was darkness and quiet.

Only then could the intruder emerge. He rose from behind the desk and he too went straight to his work without light. The key was gone from the box! Extracting his pocketknife, he slid the blade down the seam between the doors and jimmied the lock. He palmed the bottles, feeling their shape and size until the right one was familiar in his hand. Just as he had it and was making his escape, the room flashed from dark to light. The cabinet door slammed against the wall, leaving the thief standing rigid and exposed in the lantern glow.

Christie held the lamp ahead as he hobbled closer. "You do not look well, friend." In truth, from shock and sickness, Collin vibrated so violently Christie thought he would fly apart.

"I can't sleep. The pain—sometimes I can't stand it." Collin steadied himself against the cabinet.

"Relax yourself." Christie took a step but the doctor's son backed away. Christie went no farther.

Collin ran a kerchief over his temples. "I will not let father accuse you of stealing his medicines, if it comes to that. You must believe that."

"I believe it." Bennett's accusations were not what troubled Christie at that moment.

"It is just...that...sometimes I think the surgeons took my leg with a hot knife and left it inside." Collin laced his fingers around the bottle so tightly that his knuckles strained white. He was so weak and unsteady he could not stand much longer. Christie eased him toward the chair, and Collin collapsed there. "I take only enough to get me through."

"What is it?"

"Morphine."

"How do you take it?"

"I slice a little of the skin back on my knee and drop in a grain or two."

"Your father doesn't know?"

"What? That pain has made his son a coward? That I steal regularly from his medical closet? Or that I am in such agony half the time, all I want to do is put a gun to my head? Well, the answer is no to all counts. If you would be so kind, I would prefer he not know. The doctor is as dead to the world as Lorin. May he rest in peace—both of them. And you will not tell Carolina! I don't need her hovering over me." Collin was bent nearly in half. His left hand clenched his right; still he was unable to control the trembling. Christie reached to take the bottle before he dropped it, but Collin drew back. "No."

Right now, Christie hated the whole war—Union and Confederate. So this was their Cause—and their fate in front of him.

"Say it—you're thinking it, so why not say it?" Christie shook his head, unable to translate what Collin interpreted from the expressions on his face. "You think I *am* a coward. Say it!"

"No!" Christie shook his head. "I would not call you a coward, and I will whip the man who does. What can I do? You know taking this stuff is nothing to be ashamed of. It's quite normal. Many soldiers, as well as gentlemen and ladies, take it as regularly as coffee for their pain and no one thinks the less of them."

"They do not have martyrs in their families." Collin pulled his coat around him. Even though it was warm, Christie set a blanket over his shoulders.

"So what will you do when this is gone?"

"I have thought of that. If I were any man at all, I would turn this supply over to the medical department. There are men at the front who could be redeemed from all manner of anguish with this. But here I hold on to it to feed my own demons."

Christie knelt beside Collin. "Just tell me what to do."

Collin surrendered the bottle. "Just put a pinch of it in my kerchief there...there...yes. It only takes a little." Christie did so, then tied the ends carefully, and handed it to Collin. He grasped it hungrily. Just having it in his possession gave him some comfort. Then Collin handed him his knife. Christie set it on the desk. "Put the bottle back in the cabinet. There is plenty enough left. Every time, I say this will be the last, I will have the courage next time. I hope soon I will find it." Collin then rose, and Christie leaned to steady him.

"No, no, two cripples—we will fall over each other and wake the dogs."

Christie laughed in spite of himself, and set Collin back into his chair. "You stay here and do what you have to do. I will leave you alone. Leave only when you have your strength back. But if you need me..."

"Yes, thank you." Surprise as well as gratitude was in his eyes.

Christie returned to his room, closed the door, and doused the lantern. He lay in the dark, but sleep did not come for a long time.

It was well past midnight when the suspense broke. At first, he thought Collin was in trouble. But the sharpshooter would have had the good manners to pound the door or fire a gun, not ring an infernal bell. Every rattle of the clapper sent electricity coursing up Christie's spine. He flew from his bed and lit his lamp. The house must be on fire! He held the light as tightly as he could in one hand while he worked his crutch with the other getting to the hall with all possible speed. But there was no flurry in the house—Miles was not racing for buckets, Rachel was not clutching fire grenades. The racket clanged again—from up the stairs. The invalid doctor, he must be in distress, either on fire or perhaps suffering from an attack of apoplexia.

Christie had a discipline that could hold him in a battle line against cannon and musket fire full in his face, but that infernal bell—his brain screamed for mercy. Christie set the lantern on the step, and all but upended himself in his haste up the stairs. Short of breath and dizzy, he swung himself inside the doctor's room.

"At last—someone! I was ringing for Miles but you will do. I am in great need of your assistance." Doctor Bennett was not choking, fevered, famished, or ablaze; in fact, he seemed alert and spry for an invalid and not the least bit sleepy in spite of the hour. On the night table his lamp glowed beside stacks of books and writing paper. Even though the night was warm, a low fire burned in the grate. Bennett huddled under a drift of blankets, and a cascade of pillows cradled his back. The potentate was on his throne and all was in its place, except for one small detail. There was no rolling chair. If he were paralyzed downstairs he must be paralyzed upstairs. Unless…

Bennett pointed impatiently to the mantle not five steps away from his bed.

"Would you be so kind as to retrieve my volume there — yes, that is it." Bennett cleared his throat impatiently. His hand still clasped the handle of the bell.

If he rang it, even one rattle, Christie knew he would lose all reason. "Yes," he rasped, "I will get it for you, sir."

"That's a good lad. That leg a little stiff yet? Well, walking on it will loosen it up for you. Yes, that's it."

The calf leather binding was cool and glove-soft in his hand; the book was gilt edged and its cover monogrammed LSB. Christie let it fall open. Every page was scripted in elegant calligraphy.

"Here now, that is a private matter." Bennett slapped the silk coverlets and they rippled on waves of air.

"Is it now?" The diary buckled in Christie's grasp. "Then it must be pretty valuable."

Bennett's arrogance hardened. "What are you talking about? Give it to me, if you please." Instead Christie leaned back on his crutch and held it fast. "Give me the book! It was my son's, and it is very precious to me."

"How precious is that?" Christie thought—to bring a convalescent out of his sick bed in dead of night to retrieve it for you? But not nearly precious enough for you to get it yourself? The simmering embers eased the cramp in his leg, so he rested near the mantle for a moment. The effects loosened the tension in his whole body. Slowly, Christie lifted the book to arm's length. Bennett did not disturb himself to meet him even part of the way. So the arm dropped back. "On reflection, a man's secrets should go to the grave with him. No one has the right to read his inner most thoughts, not even his father."

"Give me the book!"

"I have come all this way and would meet you halfway

more. What—two—perhaps three steps, not a great distance for you to exert for such a treasure as you esteem. You must come and get it yourself, that is, if I don't decide to do Captain Bennett a service and burn his diary to save his privacy. No man should have to suffer two judgments—here and in eternity."

"What!"

"If getting up is good for my limbs, it must be good for yours since yours are undamaged. So I say for the last time, come and get the book. But be quick about it—my arm grows unsteady." Christie heard the words, they were his, cold and angry.

"You are insolent and no gentleman." Bennett hissed.

Christie agreed. "Well, that is not the topic under discussion is it?"

"Give me the book and we will have done with the matter." The point was unconditionally made: there were men who waited and there were men who were waited upon.

"I say again, come and get it. And it is I who is growing impatient. I can not stand here much longer."

"What will you do?"

Christie eased the book toward the fire.

"No!" Bennett thundered.

"Then get out of that bed and come and get it. I will give you to the count of five: one..."

"You wouldn't! I repaired your leg. You'd be a cripple if not for me."

"Two..." The image of Nolan and then of Collin and how many more like them one legged or one armed to come?

"Give me the book and I will forget all of this."

"Three..."

"Hand me the book!"

Tongues of flame danced deep in the reflection of the glossy ebony of the wardrobe. Christie was hypnotized by it. The book was warm to the touch, but not hot. Christie risked all-or-nothing, and eased the diary within inches of the fire. Bennett gasped. The sheen of silk barely rippled, but one foot and then the other set upon the floor. The doctor had been so long in bed that his limbs were weak. He was slow and steadied himself against the bedpost. With his first step his legs buckled.

"Four..." The number was as bold and unforgiving as the

slam of a judge's gavel.

Bennett humbled himself to beseech Christie for mercy; instead the book dropped a fraction toward destruction. Then Bennett damned him. Christie said nothing. Bennett pushed off on one foot then the other; each step came at excruciating cost that told on his face. When he could go no further, he flung himself the rest of the way, pressing Christie against the mantle. Bennett's fingers clasped the diary hungrily. Christie gave up the prize so easily, Bennett almost fell backwards but Christie caught him. When Bennett was convinced it was truly won, he slammed the book hard against Christie's cheek. Even as he absorbed the blow, Christie kept them both from collapsing to the floor. Such benevolence shocked Bennett and softened his rage. The effort astounded Christie—he did not know from what well it came.

"Sir, I grieve for the loss of your son, I am truly sorry for his death, and those of your daughter-in-law and grandchild. But, sir, you have not been left empty-handed—you have another son and a daughter."

"Sir, you are up!" Miles stood in the doorway balancing a tray loaded with a cup and a teapot.

"Yes, man, I am up." Bennett's eyes never left Christie's face. "Mister Brent saw fit that I should be getting some exercise—'Physician heal thyself'." The last flame of his rage flickered out. "Leave it on the table, Miles, thank you."

When the valet had gone again, Bennett turned back. "You are a mystery, Mister Brent, one that I cannot decipher. Right now I wish very much to be done with you. On the other hand, my feelings may be a grievous injustice—could you have been sent by Providence for my own good? Which is it?"

Christie answered nothing, but settled the man into his chair, with his prize firmly in his command. He turned and pulled the big door closed. The latch dropped. He had not hobbled many steps...when he almost turned back. No, tears would do the old man good.

XII
Court of No Appeal

The poison went well with his headache—sage tea, miserable stuff. Collin set the cup back into its saucer. He did not want to believe what he had heard about James Brent. Yet Carolina had evidence and had presented her case most convincingly over breakfast. Rachel agreed with every charge. This was a solid indictment and no mistake—the two had an intuition about such things. They could smell out a Christian or a traitor as soon as he came up wind. Father had come to the same conclusions from an incident that embarrassed him almost too much to tell this morning. Collin had fought down his own suspicions, but last night's episode in the surgery made the charges undeniable.

It was betrayal of the worst kind. Cold dread made for a bad breakfast. There was no time to order his arguments; James's crutch already peg-legged down the central hall. The patient breached the doorway. He stopped, having caught something in the wind, and was turning in retreat when Collin called, "James, join me if you will."

The invalid was haggard and red-eyed and it took him some extra minutes to cross the room. Finally he settled into the next chair.

Collin poured him a cup of the sweet potato tea. He was finding it hard to begin. But the inevitable was to be faced, so he began. "Well, my good friend, my sister is on to your game. She has found you out."

The tea went down in a lump. "What does she know?"

Collin pushed his cup away—nothing good was ever served with sweet potato tea. "You look innocent enough. I think that is what tipped her off. You can't fool a nun—they have divine sight. Believe me, I know. I didn't wish to believe it, but now how can I not, with Rachel adding fuel to the fire? Your words and actions have betrayed you." Collin pushed the bread toward him. Christie picked up the knife. The squire went on, oblivious to the eight-inch blade clenched in Christie's fist. "And I must say, I hold you solely contemptible for what it will portend. I have tried to hold them off until you are better, to spare us both, for God's sake, but I can't any longer. Your fat is in the fire to a fare-thee-well. You had better start praying now, because you will most certainly be doing plenty more tomorrow. We both will be."

"Where will we go tomorrow?"

"Church!" The knife came down through the loaf with such force against the cutting board that the flatware bounced. Collin looked at it absently. "Stale already? Still would you cut me a slice?" Collin continued. "You know Father Kessler has called for a special day of prayer, fasting and humiliation for the Confederacy. Sackcloth and ashes are a specialty of his. I have tried to beg off for both of us—that God would certainly not miss a couple of invalids. As for fasting and humiliation, we have done our share: that is what the army is all about. But Carolina wouldn't budge. We are going to church."

Christie choked, "Church!"

"By a long list of your actions, Carolina and Rachel have found you guilty of not only being a Christian, but a *church-going* Christian. Since you have been spared death and amputation and have been restored to your people, you would wish to thank God personally for His mercy and His goodness. You are most certainly blessed in the sight of the Almighty, the battles and dangers that He set before you notwithstanding. She muttered something about Joshua and animal sacrifice, but I did not get all that. What I got was this—as your comrade in arms and your host, I must accompany you. Secretly, I think she feels you are a good influence on my soul."

"Actually, it is due to my having been spared the ministrations of military doctors that accounts for my miraculous recovery. Sir, upon my honor, I am unjustly accused. I can get a lawyer!"

"I am a lawyer, and I pleaded the freedom of religion or not to. I also pleaded incapacity, even temporary insanity. I threw our case on the mercy of the court. The motion was never entertained, not for a second. Women hold sway in these matters."

Christie's mind was reeling, his father must be laughing in his grave. Never had Christie ever been mistaken for a Christian. This was a nightmare, and Collin had no compassion for his implication. "On *what* evidence?"

"Your language has been restrained, your small acts of charity observed, you were even kind to Aunt Mamie and civil to

Father Kessler in the face of overwhelming cause to be otherwise. Even my father has found your behavior suggestive, that there is a compassionate soul in you. And I must say I too have had chance to experience it. So, you have been condemned, and tomorrow we must mount the steps. Why are you laughing? There will be no beatitudes. We will have to sit back and take two hours of hellfire, without intermission for a flask or a cigar. Right now, Carolina is upstairs talking with Father. Even he may not be pardoned. If you go he will have to, in all courtesy. You may have created a couple of enemies."

Christie struggled to keep his face straight. To escape the hangman's noose, he would endure a nine-day novena raised for the health and happiness of ole Jeff Davis himself. "You know, there has been a fever of religious conversion through the army. I hear General Lee is an Anglican and attends services as regularly as he can. General Jackson is a Presbyterian deacon. Church might be good for us."

"That is treason, James! General Lee and General Jackson are saints and face God eye to eye as equals—they are not cowered in any church. They go only to set an example of humility for the rest of us prodigals, who need it. And they have made no friends with the unsanctified. No man can lose his shine quicker with his fellow men than for him to be held up as a good example. You know that's true, don't you, James? Only people who go to church are those who don't need it."

"That's blasphemy. You will burn for that."

"Only if Carolina heard me." Collin dared, "I bet you were even an acolyte."

"Well, I am not entirely a savage. My mother volunteered me. My father wishing her every whim be pleased, slipped me a silver dollar every time I served. So I volunteered at every opportunity, which did much for my bank account and my standing with my mother, if not with God and Father Gilbert, who can see to the very soul."

"Carolina will be impressed."

"You really don't want to go to church, do you?" There was something deeper than this farce.

"To answer your question—no, I don't want to go."

"Why?"

"Do you want to go?"
"No."
"Why?"
"I asked you first."
"Fair enough. I was never quite comfortable in a business that mixed politics and salvation—that made its capital on blackmailing people with their own damnation. In that way they are like insurance men. My mother, who never committed a sin in her life, used to live in perpetual dread of her soul and those of her husband and children being lost at the last minute. When Carolina was sick, a priest came to pray over her, he beseeched God 'to save the life of this wretched sinner.' I will never forget what he said—she was disgraced in the sight of God for her face to have been so horribly disfigured. It was the sign of God's punishment. Why, Carolina never committed a sin in her life, that's her one fault."

Even on such short acquaintance and with nothing more than intuition, Collin took a leap of faith to entrust Christie with an intimate family secret: "When the pain got more than she could stand, she tried to drown herself in the creek. I saved her barely in time. But the old priest would not give her the last rights for her attempt at suicide! I stopped going to church then. Carolina forgave them, but I don't." Collin knew his fate: "We are both going to hell by the plank road."

Christie shook his head. "No worry, the women who love us won't allow God to send us to perdition. They are all martyrs just for trying to save us, and God promised them eternal happiness long ago. That's where they got Him, they won't be happy without our stained souls right beside them. They will put our salvation in the small print, and God will have to admit us on a technicality."

"You were wrong, James—you would have made a great lawyer. You strike me as a man who knows his theology and his law well enough to hedge his bets even with the Almighty." Collin raised his cup. "To Father Kessler and his guided tour of hell. May we all come back warm but unscathed."

"Yes, even though we walk in the valley of death we fear no evil for our God is truly at our side. His hand is on our shoulders."
His pince-nez were too small and they pinched Father

Kessler's nostrils together giving his face a rabid, hawk-like appearance. While he dragged the hymn in a guttural minor key, two bars behind the choir, his stark black eyes took in the entire congregation, and condemned the clean and unclean together. A thin smile creased his face as the Bennett family took the last pew. The priest polished his lenses to see Collin and his friend more clearly. Black souls they were, and mercy was not on his mind that morning.

His pulpit rose up to his shoulders like trenchworks, and he pulled himself up on his arms to see over the immense Bible butting against his chin. All these souls were his regiment. It was he who had guided them these two years against the satanic Yankees. He labored to keep the fires of rebellion hot as defeat upon defeat brought the enemy closer to their firesides.

"His staff bears His vengeance on the necks of our enemies because they are His enemies. We have entered the time of our testing before God and the just and we will not be found wanting. The enemy is at our gates. Our God anoints us with the chrism of our redemption. It will be better for a man to die covered in the boils of leprosy than to shrink from his duty in this hour of our birth. As Sara and Rebecca screamed in anguish as they brought forth Israel, so can we do no less!"

Today God had delivered up his enemies before him — Collin Bennett and James Brent — he could see their defiant hearts harden against him. They were black angels. And like the hound of heaven, he would not let them loose until they surrendered.

"The light and the way is clearly set in front of us in a pillar of fire and smoke, our faith a beacon set firmly to the far shore where Braham awaits us. The reign of terror will not be played out. God will not let it! The enemy will be crushed under the boots of his angels..."

So many mothers, wives, and sweethearts wore perpetual black now, hanging on the arms of fathers with mourning bands — never taking them off as one son after another died. He should have worn the crimson vestments of martyrs or even the black of requiem rather than the purple of penance. No, purple is as it should be, better to have them look to their faith, look for fault in their own hearts rather than contemplate the mortal price they had paid and doubt God and the Cause. And they understood, for they nodded and answered, *"God's will be done."*

But some did doubt. Doctor Bennett grieved for his son,

his sorrow was unyielding because he had lost his faith. Grief had become his faith, his dead son a false god. Even now, the words washed off him. Abraham had been willing to sacrifice his only son—why were they unready to make the same holy sacrifice? This pain was a blessing, a sign of having been chosen, a testing to be worthy of a greater kingdom. They must see that and rejoice in it. First, they must submit—all of them.

Collin sat ramrod straight, eyes forward, everything a prelate would want—except his mind had gone to some far-off place. Christie watched him. He feared that even though the place where he escaped was not a comfort, someday Collin would not comeback.

Christie bowed his head, and wavered on the threshold of prayer. On behalf of this family that sheltered him, he had resolved to open his mind to Kessler, this priest who so confidently understood the intentions and higher purposes of God. For Christie did not think he could find God on his own. They had spoken only once in a very long time. Christie closed his eyes to wait for God to make the first move—even berate him for his sins—would be a fair beginning.

With Jamie and Quinn dead and Nolan gone home, no other man had breached his inner vaults, but Collin had come close. Last night the lame lieutenant had been so deep in melancholy that Christie could not shake him out of it. Carolina had pleaded a migraine and retired early. It was Christie who had reached for the whiskey first and Collin of course accepted. Old comrades were saluted one by one, then companies, regiments, and they had been working up to brigade, when Collin changed the tempo. He raised one last toast "to an eternal peace." The toast—or his tone—had unsettled the raucous mood and Christie did his best to distract him.

"*...Satan who will send an army to trample the liberties of a just people, to turn a people practiced in our care into chaos!*"

By the time the doctor came down, Collin and he were well on their way to being drunk and scandalizing the birds and squirrels with their ribald limericks. The surgeon stepped up to the table under his own power and stood by his son's chair. Collin waited for the lecture, but Bennett simply put a hand on his son's shoulder and asked, "May I join you?"

Knowing his intolerance of drink, Collin poured his father barely a few sociable drops, but Bennett took the decanter and filled the glass to the brim. Then he made himself comfortable at the table. No one spoke. The two waited. Bennett raised his glass. What he studied was so clear, it could have been spring water. "Will this kill me?"

"No, father, but drink enough of it, and you will wish you were dead."

"Ah yes, at first I did not recognize it. It is some of that lamp oil Eban conjures out of potatoes down by the river. How much of your inheritance did you swap for this?"

"Grandmother's portrait?"

"My mother or your mother's mother?"

"Mother's." Collin was playing a new game here—the doctor had never been the joking kind.

"Well," Bennett said finally, "you got the best of that bargain—even if it makes you deaf, dumb, and blind." He sighed wistfully then saluted. "To the old...hmmm...lady, wherever she is!"

"The Yankees have risen up and move cloven-footed over the earth." Kessler's baritone cannonaded off the rafters. *"But God will strike them down from our midst before they defile our land. The forces of God are all powerful..."*

The three men had passed the next moments in uncomfortable silence. Bennett wanted to talk, but what to say? "Mister Brent, you have been limping badly. Is the leg giving you that much pain?"

"No, sir, I am on my fifth glass—I can't feel my legs."

"That's good, James. I have one leg gone, and I can feel it throbbing all the way down to my toes." Collin cast a sidelong glance—a caution to his father who had just refilled his glass.

After that, all manners be damned. The second drink was more daring—twice as much, drunk twice as fast. Bennett coughed and gasped for sheer life. "Not as good as the stuff we made in Mexico. We used chilies to bring out the bouquet."

He raised his glass to finish it off, but his son pulled his arm down, "Father? You don't have to."

Bennett tried to focus through watery eyes. "Of course not,

and neither should you, but that will not stop either of us."

"God said I am the way, the truth and the life..."

"Well, gentleman, I fear tomorrow, when the righteous Father Kessler sees you, me, and Mister Brent here, like three hens on a fence post, he will shoot at will. So drink up, a good headache will dull the pain of all that retribution."

"And we will defend this cause to the last man!"

Kessler's harangue had upstaged the main event; the changing of bread and wine into divinity was all but anticlimactic. The Mass wound down to a few worthy of Eucharist and the final blessing. After the last hymn, and before freedom, there was the gauntlet of priest and elders to pass. Christie angled his crutch to extend his hand and get by, but Kessler stepped in front of him. "Ah, Mister Brent, I did not take you for a churchgoer!"

"A case of mistaken identity!" Christie turned toward the door.

"But you believe..." Kessler challenged.

"My credo is my own." Christie moved toward the sunlight.

As if the last two hours were not enough, Kessler would have another go at him. "For your immortal soul to be saved, you must surrender to the will of God, who has a plan for you. I will lead your way. Confess your sins, embrace your salvation—it is within your grasp." Christie did not answer, but Kessler grabbed his shoulder, and was about to say more.

Christie's instincts were swift and he jerked free. If he were soiled—and he did not dispute that— he would tend to his own sins in his own way. He bent close to the priest not to draw attention to what he said next. "You have been baiting me ever since I met you, supposedly in the interest of my salvation. Believe me, I know about salvation and how near it can be. On two occasions I have come close enough to see the angel beckoning through the open door. But I am still here. And I think you have other reasons. What they are I have not yet been able to get you to admit, but I have ideas. And I do not like your motives—or your methods—even if you think they are sanctified."

"What are you saying? You have no need of God?"

"Is it conversion or surrender you want?"

"Is there a difference?"

"Oh, yes, for a thousand years the church and the monarchy have been in an alliance to convince my ancestors under the threat of the ax or the stake to give up our free will. 'Let your liege or your bishop do your thinking for you and rejoice in your servitude for it is holy.' We have not repeated that mistake here! Now take your hands off me!"

The clergyman was purple. Christie shuffled down the steps and across the path dividing the garden of tombstones.

But Christie was not done with persecutions. The old carriage wobbled over the plank bridge, and was turning up the drive when the gray column of cavalry intercepted it. "Lieutenant Colonel Clark Barteau, at your service. Whom may I have the honor of addressing?"

"Doctor Graham Bennett, at yours, Colonel. We have been expecting you."

Mister Joshua Christie's student had indeed changed. He was worn, exhausted, thin, and visibly older than his thirty years. Christie would not have recognized him without an introduction. Christie hoped the reverse true, and pushed deeper into shadows of the back seat.

While Barteau paid his respects to the doctor, he tugged and pulled at the reins, but the commander's sleek, high bay was determined toward the rear. The big animal pranced and jerked, its ears swiveled, the nostrils distended, and finally, it had its way. An equine nose poked between the spokes of the canopy's brace. Barteau was nearly decapitated by the buggy lid as the horse all but crawled inside to sniff the pockets where he knew sugar must be secreted.

"Gunshot!" Christie breathed.

Barteau turned the horse away. "I apologize, Doctor Bennett, he fights me. As fractious as any Yankee, the spoils of war, you see. Sir, I have put my men in bivouac on the edge of the field this side of the pine wood to be near good water. I hope it does not present an inconvenience to you and the people of Starkville."

"To the contrary—your presence would be a comfort to us all. There is more sweet water in the lake east, but the new grass perhaps is too young yet for the horses."

Carolina leaned closer to welcome the gallant dragoon. Barteau momentarily forgot what he was about to say. Christie enjoyed the Confederate's confusion. Don't fool yourself, Colonel, she is more than you can handle.

"Colonel, my daughter, Carolina Magdelina. In back, my son Collin, lately serving under General Longstreet, and a guest, Corporal James Brent, also one of our patriots until his untimely confrontation with a Union bullet."

Barteau only momentarily disengaged the attention he held on Carolina's large eyes to accord Collin and Christie the barest acknowledgment that courtesy demanded. Then he returned to more delightful business, accepting a supper invitation from a gracious hostess. "Your servant, madam." He raised Carolina's wrist to his lips. Unused to such knightly flourishes, the damsel returned his gestures with her broadest smile. The eyes of the cavalry officer had been too long restricted to a diet of dog-faced troopers and horses not to be enchanted. Long absences make a plain girl pretty, and a lovely one positively glisten. Jealousy growled in Christie's breast without his knowing exactly why.

"I think we could find something to suit the colonel's tastes in our humble stores. May we expect you and your aide near 'The Angelus?'" Carolina offered.

"Yes, we would be most grateful. Until six." Barteau tapped the brim of his Stetson, then pulled his mount away. The buggy started while the column moved down the eastern road.

The hair on Christie's neck relaxed, but his legs were dead weight in contrast to his heart, which was racing like bloodhounds.

"Why, James, you look like paste." Collin was genuinely alarmed. "I told father that this trip to church was entirely too much for you."

"Agreeing with my brother on any subject sets an uncomfortable precedent, but on this one, I must. I think you should rest this afternoon. Even Colonel Barteau's visit might tax your energies too much. Perhaps you should save your respects for another time."

Doctor Bennett cleared his throat. Christie knew this meeting must be faced. "Although I will agree to your suggestion of an afternoon nap, I most eagerly look forward to this evening's dinner with the colonel. I have been an admirer of his for some time." A balanced statement of falsehood and truth.

If lady luck were with him, the prodigal Buckeye had not smelled her perfume in a long time. He had little beyond promises to seduce her for this one-night dalliance. Barteau just might not recognize him. It had been over ten years; a boy changes a lot in that amount of time. The growth and mustache were growing in nicely but he wished they were darker.

If he could keep his head out of the hangman's noose, some intelligence could be gained. In this family, procuring such military secrets would be nothing more than dinner conversation. But Collin would not prod—he hated war talk. A few agitators to do the work for him: the gargoyles. Aunt Mamie would demand a full report of Pemberton's entire troop displacement, artillery count, ordnance and plans right down to the last cannon. Christie assembled his cast of characters to include one more. He would be ravenous for information and at the same time make such an obtuse jackass of himself, as to distract the commander's attention away from inconvenient recognitions—Kessler. In the august presence of all these guests, Christie would humbly take the last place at table, just one to the outside of the good priest, and his unbounded vanity, casting such a broad shadow as to make Christie all but invisible. And Collin would certainly be hospitable with the bourbon and the wine to sedate Barteau's faculties and loosen his tongue at the same time. Yes, most importantly, we must not forget to place Carolina in Barteau's clear sight. Feminine charm always goes well with port.

Collin was not perplexed at Christie's thoughtfulness—he was outright stunned. However, Carolina was touched that Christie had been so solicitous of her relatives. Yes, a gathering would be more suitable for a man of Barteau's rank. Eban was dispatched to invite them all. And Rachel had made her contribution to the conspiracy: the hero who had stopped the Yankee cavalry deserved as near a feast as her bare larder permitted. By the time Barteau arrived with his adjutant, Lieutenant Samuel Woodward, the chess pieces were in place.

"You have not touched your yams, Mister Brent." The dowager aunt pushed the serving bowl toward Christie. "You need your strength."

"Yes, James, the sweet potato is royalty among vegetables. It was the favorite of Henry VIII." Collin bit into his with mock enthusiasm, knowing his comrade detested them to the point of gagging.

"Yes, and look what happened to Christendom!" Sweet potatoes! Christie was at his limit. For his purposes, the dinner had gone too smoothly. Mamie Powers and her husband had been on their best behavior. Carolina had been an angel. Collin had been attentive, but withdrawn. So far, Kessler had been a lamb. Now they were torturing him with yams.

The hashed mint green peas and the sweet-honey basted ham had been fine. The little wild mushroom pies were quite tasty. He had done justice to it all. Instead of yams, he had taken more than his share of watermelon-rind pickles and turnip greens spiced with ginger and garlic. He had not tasted anything like them before. Now, waiting in the center of the table was the grand finale, a confection Collin called Indian Summer Harvest Cake. But under that frosting, Christie could smell sweet potatoes. These people were positively addicted to the obnoxious tuber. He suspected it was the drug that coaled the fires of secession fever. Yes, he was in a snit! He must light a fire under all this benevolence—and soon, the evening was waning. Perhaps, he could persuade Aunt Mamie to show the colonel the arsenal she carried in her reticule. That might spark something. What happened was almost as good.

"Miss Carolina, you have presented me with an embarrassment of riches to which I cannot possibly do justice. I beg your forgiveness, Missis Powers, not another slice." But Barteau carried no authority here, and another piece of cake was cut for him.

"You will need your strength to catch those savage Yankees, Colonel. Vanilla sauce?" Without waiting for an answer she flooded the cake in syrup, then passed him the plate. He accepted it meekly.

"Have you caught those vile Yankee horsemen, yet?" Nathaniel Powers asked with more impatience than courtesy allowed.

The table went silent. Barteau's face turned grave. "Much

of what we hear is unreliable," he began. "But we know that the Yankee raiders have blown up two trains—one full of ordnance bound for Vicksburg, the other a passenger train!"

Doctor Bennett turned to his convalescent, "You have knowledge of such things, James, do you think there is enough in the west to make up for such a loss?"

Kessler leaned toward Christie. "Do I hear a cock crow, Mister Brent?"

Christie turned to Kessler all wide-eyed innocence. "Then, you do not think that the Confederacy can still hold back the Yankees, Father? I am sure Colonel Barteau does not agree, nor do I." His torpedo having gone off satisfactorily, Christie lit his next fuse. "I hope the Yankees were not so rude as to destroy the train with the passengers still in it, surely!"

Barteau bowed to the ally at the bottom of the table, "No, the passengers were safe—many were refugees from Vicksburg. Odd, the raiders were gallant enough to even unload the passengers' baggage before firing the cars."

"They are still brutes—burning the station, looting the town's people." The seams around Aunt Mamie's comportment were fraying. Christie refilled her wineglass. Fortified, she voiced her displeasure that the horde had gotten away. Even though her words were genteel, she expressed hopes that God would send commanders who could catch these raiders, and have them drawn and quartered— as all barbarians deserved.

"From your mouth to God's ear." Kessler put in.

Christie leaned back satisfied. Yes, events were now progressing nicely.

But Barteau was stunned by the bloodlust of ladies and clerics for Yankees and ineffective Confederate commanders. From there on, he tested his footing with every word. "The riders were bent on destroying war materiel, tearing down telegraph lines, and making us look like bumbling fools. They marched, counter marched, split and split their number again. They covered their tracks by backtracking in every direction. We came and went in every direction until we got it sorted out nearly too late. But their game is about up. It will not last long, Major De Baun is on to them."

"Who is this Major De Baun?" Christie's tone was as

noncommittal as he could manage.

"He is just the best tracker to come out of Louisiana, which is where these Yankees seem to be heading. The Creole knows the territory better than anyone."

So far, Lieutenant Woodward had not cast one verbal stone into the troubled waters. But loyalty to his commander and to his regiment demanded he speak up. "I think these Yankees are a temporary inconvenience. What did our prisoners say his name was—Grierson? Ridiculous waste of men and horses that can do no good for them—no good at all. Galloping too far into our territory without infantry support. His luck cannot possibly hold in a loyal state like Mississippi."

"Not the match of our cavalry in the end!" Carolina soothed her guests' ruffled feathers, as Collin refilled their glasses. "The men of the South are bred to the horse, these Yankees are amateurs!"

Barteau turned a fond eye toward her. "I thank you for that, Miss Bennett, but if truth be told, the Yankees have been doing their homework and have learned our tactics, adding some schemes of their own. The planters who have been raided report that Grierson moves with an advance of Confederate-looking guerrillas to screen his column."

"That's treason!" Christie whistled passed his graveyard.

"The Yankees are camouflaged well—they can affect a reasonable local accent when the need presses, and they hide and strike from the cover of the piney woods, just as arrogant as you please." Barteau nodded at the excellence of Doctor Bennett's port.

"It's that Pemberton—he is a Yankee at heart! You can't trust a transplanted Yankee," Mamie Powers was crimson with rage or drink. "Under the skin, they are all traitors."

Barteau reddened, his jaw tightened visibly. The aide cleared his throat, would have said something to deflect the insult, but his commander gave him no time. The boom came down. "*I was born in the north, ma'am,*" Barteau answered back.

"I did not mean..." Mamie Powers stuttered.

"Really? I had not heard that. Where are you from, Colonel?" Collin intervened quickly.

"Northern Ohio—Cleveland. Can't get further north than that."

Carolina put the best face on it. "Your honor is sterling and my aunt was not hinting otherwise, Colonel. We all know of your writing in the Tennessee *Plaindealer*. Your editorials on states' rights and against the abolitionists have been reprinted down here, and they are very popular." She cast a side long-glance at Christie for help.

Christie would always please a lady, if the advantage was in the end, his. "How did you come south, sir?"

"Like many of us, Mister Brent, opportunity brought me here. Now I have a wife and family back in Tennessee."

"Mister Brent also has people from Ohio, Colonel? Perhaps you have some friends in common, some mutual ties threading back to home still?" Something in Kessler's syrupy tones jolted Barteau. The colonel's icy glare was returned blankly, expectantly, innocently.

Was the priest calling them both spies? Christie respected Barteau, not only for what he was, but for what he had been back in Delaware—an honorable man. Christie would not stand for Barteau to be insulted—have his loyalties questioned. This was not in the game. But to turn on Kessler—that would do no good.

The colonel shifted his focus to the veteran at the bottom of the table. Either out of fatigue or alcohol, he could not see this James Brent distinctly. Kessler leaned back to open a better view. "Mister Brent, by which road did you come to this glorious cause."

"By way of St. Louis, sir." Christie replied. To keep his face in profile, he refilled Mamie Power's glass, which did not yet need filling.

"Really, where?"

"Since I have family under Union colors, I would rather not say."

"I understand, I too had a brother fighting for the other side."

"Had? I hope he came to his senses," Mamie Powers went on oblivious to the glares seething from every member of her family.

"He died at Shiloh, ma'am. No I doubt he ever came to his senses even at the last."

The dowager Powers was blunt to a fault, but she was not cruel. The grief in Barteau's face set her back. She pushed her glass away and said no more.

Now Doctor Bennett blinked as if he had been asleep through it all. As host he had been remiss, his guests had been most carelessly treated. "Now see here, Colonel, I think we have interrogated you enough. Excuse our manners but we hear so little and we cannot get out because of the roads."

"I understand perfectly, Doctor Bennett." Although Barteau clearly did not.

Then Carolina set her guests on a course in which they could do a little boasting. "Now tell me truthfully, Lieutenant Woodward, do those Yankee plowboys really ride as well as our countrymen? Where are they from?"

"Illinois mostly—the ones we chased and nearly had cornered at West Point were from Iowa. Yes, ma'am, they can ride."

"Isn't that where they found you, Mister Brent?" Kessler asked. "Near West Point?"

"I was in that vicinity, but I am not at all sure where I was found."

"Shot by a skittish Yankee," Carolina beheld him compassionately, "and left by the side of the road to die like some animal."

"You were most fortunate, Corporal." Barteau replied.

"Pardon?"

"I meant only that you were rescued in time. Where were you before this?"

It was a natural question from one soldier to another; Christie should have prepared better for it. On the spur of the moment he summoned up a nearly untraceable record of scrap. "Backwater duty in Tennessee, mostly uneventful. And Arkansas Post—before it was captured. I was paroled and exchanged, then joined General Bragg, and was wounded. I thought I might ride with Van Dorn, but decided against it."

"The general, regardless of his successes, is not to the liking of many honorable men." Barteau admitted, then doubled back on the subject, "Deshler commanded Hindman in Arkansas, didn't he?"

"No, sir, Colonel Dunnington, but I wish you were right. Every man would have fallen behind Colonel Deshler—he was ready to fight it out. Right there, with Dunnington's surrender flag flapping in his face, he still refused to hand over his sword. Not tall enough to come to Sherman's shoulder, but cursing the Yankee to perdition—and for Admiral Porter to take the wheel and sail him there."

"I hear General Sherman presses hard when his hair is on fire." Barteau smiled.

"Yes, but it was Admiral Porter's show from where I stood, sir. The fort was right on the river, so Porter brought the decks of the *Black Hawk* right up to the walls, put us nose to nose with the cannon. There was no cover anywhere. He sighted his guns right on our heads and was ready to blow us to eternity. Although I admire Deshler his pepper, I am here because of Dunnington's discretion." Christie prayed that ended it, for he had put period to all he knew. The battle had been one of General Sherman's favorite stories, which no one more than half listened to. Christie hoped he had gotten all his Confederate ducks in the correct order. He could not tell—Barteau's face was opaque.

"Sir, getting back to these Yankee raiders," Kessler prodded, "I cannot for one minute fathom that three regiments of unholy Khans could rampage undetected right down through our best cavalry."

"I thank you for the compliment, sincerely I do." Barteau was ready to let bygones go, "But if truth be told—if we are the best—we are stretched too thin. And the Yankees are not as stupid as you would think. They are excellent horsemen, they are relentless and they are well-led, well-equipped and not above espionage."

"What gentleman could sanction such treachery!" Carolina was appalled.

Christie had heard Carolina's question voiced in other quarters. Did people misunderstand that this was war—men were being slaughtered wholesale? Yet they quibbled over the ethics of spying?

"I hear this Grierson was a music teacher before the war. Hardly bred to horsemanship." Having tortured that yam enough, Christie finally rested his fork on the lip of his plate.

"And I was a newspaper publisher, and you say you were a carpenter. But we learned quickly, Corporal. We took a few

Iowans prisoners at West Point. If you talk to these men, you will soon see what caliber of fighter we were up against. A man who will divide his command while deep in enemy territory...you call it theatrics—and you call it treachery, Miss Bennett, but in war it is a gift of subterfuge. I go over it in my mind—such a blatant risk of such fine cavalry, so I have to think there is some other purpose to it all. What is he covering up?"

The table was quiet. Barteau was a commander whose faith in himself had been shaken. There were answers he should be seeing and could not, and he agonized over them. Christie understood self-doubt; in West Virginia with McClellan, he had a heart full of it. But he was green then. Barteau was not green, he was tested—the best—and that was proving not enough. Blackburn and Surby—Christie wished earnestly that they were well. Grant's lieutenant took up the threads of the conversation quickly to turn them back to his purposes.

But Kessler was not finished yet, "You sound like you admire these plunderers, Colonel."

Barteau had had enough of Kessler's cross-examinations, courtly manners or not. They were insults from a man who intimidated good men but whose own hands were empty. "This may come as a surprise to you, Father, but no, I don't hate the enemy as much as you seem to. I respect him as an equal and pray he is only that. Hate interferes with a man's ability to think and plan."

"No Yankee is the equal of a Confederate gentleman," Carolina hastened to put the best face on what had become a court inquiry on the conduct of the war.

"Miss Bennett, I think future events will render the question of being gentlemen irrelevant. The equation will be made horribly unequal because they have the variable of carbines, ammunition, and equipment in profusion—and do not underestimate their determination. General Martin Smith must rob the rest of the state to supply Vicksburg, although General Bowen is making a fortress of Port Gibson should Grant come that way."

"You talk as if the war is lost already. Certainly..." The strain told in her every word that Mamie Powers had been brought to the unthinkable.

"The colonel is only preparing you for very hard times

ahead, Aunt." Collin patted her hand.

"If…if…for what would it all have been…the death…so many…" Mamie Powers looked at Collin and then Christie — these young men with broken bodies and minds that fought with demons by day and night. She studied them as if for the first time. Then she looked to Barteau who was conversing quietly with Carolina. For a long time Mamie Powers looked at him — through him — passed him and beyond to some world that discomforted her. Pandora's box: visions…despair…questions, all but unsolvable for a woman who wrestled with disappointment. She put a hand on her brother-in-law's. Her touch roused him from his stupor. He looked at her absently, and would have turned back, but her fingers tightened around his palm. What he saw in her eyes startled him at first, but he held them for her sake, and then for his. Finally he nodded a bond — invisible yet they both understood — had passed between them. Tears welled in the creases of her eyes. She patted his hand again, but said nothing.

Christie saw it all. If she had not taken his burden from him, she had accepted a share of it. From something in all this fear and tragedy spoken at the table, she had gathered the strength to carry it. Christie was suddenly cold, alone, here with this family and this Cause that was not his. Their parts were riven and grieving, but it was forged and would not be torn apart by the calamity outside. Having no family, no one to love and be loved, and his cause and comrades so far away, this charade was suddenly intolerable. He wanted to be away — even if it killed him.

Doctor Bennett set his knife on his plate with a clatter. "Gentlemen, let us turn to different subjects. Do you fish, Colonel? That lake near your camp has excellent fishing."

"I have not had time for it, but I used to love it. When I was in school, I used to get away when I could to fish in the Olentangy, back in Ohio. Do you fish, Mister Brent?" Barteau cocked an eyebrow again to the bottom of the table and shifted his position to see James Brent more clearly.

Christie summoned what he could to keep this unholy lie going a little longer. "Only when a show of my manhood requires it, sir. I find it a valid argument against Doctor Darwin's theories that a man with an evolved brain is above lower life forms such as a fish. I have pulled up too many empty hooks to prove otherwise."

"The Olentangy? Where is that?" The priest poised again.

"Delaware, Ohio, I doubt if you have heard of it." Barteau's face was sheer delight thinking on the old times, like a Hebrew thinking on Jerusalem or an Irishman on his Dublin.

"Why, Mister Brent here also has spent time in Delaware, one year at Ohio Wesleyan. Know of it, Colonel?"

"Very well, I studied there. I loved every minute of it. But I doubt Mister Brent and I were there at the same time. However, I would like to engage in a long reunion with him over some brandy and cigars when there is leisure."

"Gentlemen, I think brandy and cigars is a fine suggestion. I have a supply in the library." Bennett signaled the men at the table.

"Thank you, no, Doctor. I must be getting back to my duties." Barteau was again smiling, again the gallant knight, paying court to the ladies and apologizing for indiscretions that were not his own. "As you can see, long months in the saddle makes a soldier a poor guest. I do apologize, sir, for my remarks, and I thank you very much for your hospitality."

"No, Colonel, no apology is necessary. We were graced with your presence tonight. Consider our home a port in the storm. If your surgeon is in need of my help or anything from my stores, he has only to ask for it."

Barteau collected his gauntlets and turned toward the door. "Corporal Brent, would you favor me with a final word in private?"

"Your servant, sir."

Once outside, Barteau dismissed his adjutant, and the two men were alone. The evening was warm, heavily perfumed with the scent of flowering trees. Christie kept his back to the pine torches, and his face in the shadows. Barteau pulled two cigars and passed one to Christie.

The colonel puffed away, lost in his own thoughts for some minutes. Finally he said, "Mister Brent, I can tell you are not yet ready to ride, but when you are I would be pleased if you would join us. We are rather informal now about enlistments, as you have found out. No, that is not true—commanders are shanghaiing good soldiers from each other, and I am not above it."

"I am honored, sir." Christie was more than that. He wanted to throw all pretense away and wrap an arm around the scholar who had been a favorite at his father's table. He wanted to embrace those moments again even if they could not last. Christie wondered if Barteau was remembering them too. The officer made no signs of leaving. He was clearly exhausted and the grilling had unsettled him.

"Sir, you will have another chance at the Yankees."

"Do you think so?" Barteau stared straight at Christie.

"Don't you think there are men in the Confederacy who can beat the Yankees?"

"I did not want to upset the Bennetts, but at this moment, I question whether all of them together can. Grant will be landing three corps south if our intelligence in Louisiana is correct. No telling what he has in reserve. If they gain a foothold on the eastern side of the river and get going, they can stretch all across Mississippi with no slack anywhere. Are they going for Vicksburg or, my guess is, they will come northeast and make a stand some place else, to cut our throats. What do you think, Mister Brent? What is on Grant's mind?"

Barteau waited, but Christie said nothing. Thankfully, the colonel did not seem to expect an answer, he had his own. "President Davis sees bogeymen in every shadow. Pemberton is as bad. And they order us off in every direction. But the enemy has one mind—Grant's—what a luxury, a unified command of generals and troops practically all from his home state—Sherman, McPherson." And what he did not say, these were men from Barteau's home state riding against him. The Confederate commander slapped the dust from his gauntlets but did not yet put them on. "How did we get ourselves into this conflagration?"

"I think the bonfire was lit in Charleston harbor, and each one of us dipped our torches into it. Something about gentlemen's honor."

Barteau worked his cigar down to an ash. "Honor will be the shroud we wrap ourselves in if we can't stop Grant. What did your Father Kessler say? 'We will fight to the last man.' I was unfair to him. He does what he can so the people will not forsake their army. In his way, I guess, he does his good. But there is such a gap between expectations and realities. What will people say when the truth comes at the point of a Yankee boot set right to their doorstep?"

"He is not my Father Kessler and no one could hold you accountable."

"No? You heard it in there—I had barely passed the door before I was accosted about a few Yankee raiders bent upon mischief. Once he gets going, Grant will not be so appeased with a few smokehouses and railroads."

Christie was silent. The glowing tip of the blunt had burned down to Barteau's fingertips, and he smothered it in a pot of sand. He prepared to leave. "Mister Brent, you remind me of my mentor, a man I respected a long time ago when I wove poetry out of elegant ideals. At his dinner table we solved all the crises of the world between soup and brandy. How could we have been so naive?"

"All young men are idealistic, sir."

Barteau studied him intently. Words warred inside him, but at last the colonel said, "Our conscience leads us up many different roads. Some of these make us enemies of our friends—even of our own families. I do understand that. I truly do."

Had Barteau recognized him? Had he judged that Christie had turned against his native state and the politics of his father as Barteau himself had? Did Barteau see the pretense about name and false home as a cover? Or was Barteau only talking abstracts? Was Christie being lured into admitting he was a spy? The hangman's noose swung before his face. One careless word or a flicker of emotion could not be called back. Christie stepped back from the precipice. Barteau took the silence as a response.

"Lilacs, how I miss them." Barteau snapped a blossom from the bush. "When was the last time you were home? One, two years?"

"Seems like it."

"I haven't seen my wife since I went off to Fort Donelson in February of sixty-two. I've got a baby daughter that is probably walking by now. If she's anything like me, she's talking a streak. I hope you get to meet them when this thing is over."

"That is kind of you, sir. I would like that."

Barteau extended a hand, Christie caught it, and their

handshake was firm.

Barteau took his reins from the hitching post. Unrestrained, the horse made straight for Christie, all but knocking him off his crutch. Barteau made no more of it than a high spiritedness. "Corporal, there are times when a man needs to blow off steam...and he can't do it around his own...what we said..."

"...will not be repeated, you can be assured, Colonel." Barteau appreciated that, so Christie took advantage.

"Sir, a favor? When I was shot, I lost my horse. Have you collected any strays?"

"Come by and check the stock. I think we have one or two unaccounted for, but you might have to fight for one. If he is yours, I will do what I can."

Christie stepped back, braced, and saluted. Barteau studied him — there seemed something more he wanted to add. Instead, he returned the salute smartly, and swung into the saddle. Christie slapped the animal's rear, and against his will, Gunshot allowed himself to be turned down the drive.

The Bennetts spilled out the front door. Father Kessler seated himself behind the reins of the little buggy drawn by a bowlegged mule. Feeling the sting of defeat, there was no godliness in his face as he bid Christie good night.

Mamie Powers took her seat behind him, to be shielded from the dust of the Starkville roads. She was still chattering. "I think that officer should be replaced with someone who is less deferential to Yankees. I don't think he is Southern enough to hate them as they need hating in order to win this war...and we must win it, by God!"

"Aunt Mamie, you sleep well tonight and don't let the Yankees worry you." Collin shook his Uncle's hand and motioned him up into the carriage to be rid of them. Kessler slapped the reins and the company left.

Carolina watched them go. "Father should not have abided the priest's insolence and Aunt Mamie's. She was horrid — she should be setting a better example for me. 'Must you be so strident, Carolina? It is fine to have a mind, but must you use it, Carolina? Just sit there and be beautiful and quiet like a vase of flowers, Carolina. Try to be more this, and less that.' And then she treats our guest like a traitor. Good manners are terribly hard for us amateurs when the paragons are so forward."

Collin agreed. "Where she gets it, I don't know. Mother was such a gentle soul. Why Uncle Nathaniel lets her have her head...if father were not so aggrieved... And for Kessler? Whoever it is, I fear for his victim."

Christie did not follow them back into the house, he needed air. Carolina was about to protest, but Collin held her back. Christie had already turned toward the back and was making slow progress down the path in the direction of the family cemetery. He did not know where he was going, it was all new territory just beyond the gate of the cloister gardens. His mind was a flux and he needed to clear the cigar smoke and perfume from his lungs.

The walk detailed into a side path half hidden by a hillock and beyond lay another cemetery—of some curious sort. It was not at all what a cemetery should be, and as quickly he second-guessed himself. Yet, these were not flower or herb beds gone to seed. No, by default they must be grave plots. But there was no respect for the dead here. The bramble and wild rose overflowed the rectangles of white rocks, in total numbering about a dozen. The headboards were rough-hewn planks with no names on them, only a single date and crudely lettered. Only the most recent markings, although blistered and faded, were still readable. One was a year old, two were laid to rest six months ago, two more only a month ago, the last in this row, two weeks ago. This was a queer cemetery, for being remiss of names. All the more mysterious and suspicious for some real purpose in keeping the dead unknown. Didn't they matter to some one?

There were no signs but these mysteries hiding in the seclusion of evening's deepening shadows bid no trespassing. But Christie could not pull himself away. With every step, ivy and wild grape coiled around his ankles, each leg was extracted with difficulty. He was puzzled by these nameless souls. Who were they? The Bennetts had had no slaves for a long time. Indigent patients of the doctor's? Perhaps here was the final rest of unnamed soldiers killed close by. He struck a match and peered closer. As he shifted his weight, his wounded leg buckled. A mound of softly packed earth rolled, and he swayed on a wave of tumbling dirt. It swept him along until he caught the outstretched arm of a magnolia branch and held fast. Just in time, below—the abyss of an open grave.

He swung himself clear and dropped. He cried out as his leg collapsed under his weight. Enough of graveyards, Christie tested his footing. The wound ached but the first stabs were ebbing. So he headed not right but left. Enticed by an ever ripening glow and the beacon of voices, he took the path along the creek until it came to a fork. He could continue along the bank where the stream opened into a lake. Was it here Carolina had gone to find quiet at the dearest price? Now a long peaceful mirror reflected back the campfires of the troopers on the far side. Christie turned that way, and crossed a footbridge into the camp of the enemy.

There was no sweet perfume of coffee boiling up, but otherwise it was a camp like any other, with the pungent sting of burning tobacco, the scent of frying bacon fat, and the sweat of bodies. A banjo twanged accompanied by a mouth organ. Rough laughter rose and fell. A Rebel Yell seared through the pines to celebrate a well-played hand of poker rejoined by a yowl from a dog. Scraps of camp talk among comrades filtered through the low-rolling murmur and Christie caught one and then another as he came on.

"Damned blockade—I'd sell your soul for a cup of real coffee."

"My soul? Why not your own?"

"Why, Jobey, yourn is virgin. Devil already corrupted mine. No new business there."

"Who's there! Give the password and be recognized!" Christie stiffened. The picket stepped out of the scrub to bark the command one last time, "Who goes there and give the password."

"Corporal Brent," he swallowed the last syllable of his name just in time. "I am staying up at the Bennett house. Meant no inconvenience, soldier. Just out stretching my legs. Colonel Barteau invited me to inspect your stock for my mount that run off."

The rough-hewn sergeant appraised the intruder up and down. The visitor was as clean as a hospital specimen. No soldier in the war was that clean. But say this, he was skinny, battered, and spavined. "Send for the lieutenant of the watch," the sergeant barked.

Christie relaxed until an officer arrived to relieve the sentry of him. He too looked Christie up and down as if he were some curiosity. "Who did you say you were?"

"Corporal Brent, a convalescent living up at the house."

The sentry eyed the shillelagh of Collin's, on which Christie leaned. "You can hardly stand, boy. What you doin' down here? Tryin' to get yourself shot?"

"I seem to be able to do that without any practiced effort, sir."

"Well, just couldn't stay away, could you, Mister Brent?" Lieutenant Woodward's handshake was genuine. "It is all right, Sergeant. He's a soul mate and a prodigal trooper from the tribe of Bragg. We are trying to convert him and bring him into the true fold of the Second Tennessee, so let's be kind." The sentry stepped back, so Woodward could lead the way. "Let me show him around our humble camp."

"I lost my horse when I was wounded. Colonel Barteau gave me permission to see if he was among yours."

Woodward nodded, "This way."

Christie followed the officer through a maze of campfires. The evening was warm, and most of the men in this migrant city lazed like farm dogs under the open sky. The spirit was up among them. Spring had infused what a victory over the Yankees could have, what two-months back pay could have, what an issue of new boots could have, even what a bag of mail could have—if it could catch up with them. Balmy breezes and flowering trees—and the promise of fresh fruit and vegetables—had given them faith—so none of the rest really mattered. They had come through another winter and things were not so bad.

As they passed a deck of cards hissed as four bad hands and one good were dealt. Dice clattered into the bottom of a split canteen. Below him billowed the haze of smoke from cigars rolled from scavenged tobacco. Christie tried not to eavesdrop, but when the soul is starved for camp talk the ear becomes practiced in picking up news even if the home is not his own.

"The baby died. Sarah buried it beside Mother. She's alone now to carry on all by herself. I worry about her peace of mind..."

The friend of Sarah's soldier mixed the stew with a calamity of his own: "Michael very nearly burned down the barn. Maggie wrote that he got hold of a couple of Roman candles and set them off—scared the cow and she is constipated as hell. Our mule won't go near his stall and Maggie has to keep it in the shed. The boy has been a trial to her. Since he's not her own, he don't feel he has to mind..."

Somewhere else: "They say turnips are the big crop at the farming expositions—finding all kinds of uses for them I hear."

"That be in Chicago, Caleb. What you worried about turnips in Chicago for?"

"This war will burn itself out someday and, well...there was a girl in Chicago I have tried not to think about, but I do. I plan to forgive her bad judgment on this matter of disunion and marry her. And Chicago might be a good place to start..."

The paddock was just beyond. The horses, many with swayed backs and protruding ribs, were at least well cared for to the limits of the riders' resources.

"Here they are. I am afraid if you try to ride out with one though, you just might get shot, by accident you understand. It would be a shame, but the horse won't get far. Some of the men are riding mules."

"I wanted to come while the invitation was still fresh in his mind."

"It's the family that binds."

"Pardon?"

"The pull of the camp. As filthy and craven as it is, a soldier feels more at home on the ground than in a bed, and among his own rather than at the table of civilians." Woodward's ability to read Christie's mind was unsettling—or were all soldiers of one mind? Woodward motioned over his shoulder, "Over there, that's the officers' corral. Your horse might be there. Look there—why, I think you have a friend here, Corporal."

Grant's two refugees drew to one another—Gunshot uncaring what the Confederate officer made of it, Christie caring very much and trying to hide his feelings behind a show of jealous admiration. Gunshot's long arched head bent and nudged Christie's pocket. Christie's palm stroked the long flat nose, and with the other, pulled the prize the horse expected. Woodward offered his pocketknife, and Christie sliced away at the edge of a winter apple.

"What a beautiful animal!"

"He *is* a beauty. Colonel calls him Napoleon. Compliments of a dead Yankee. There's a U.S. brand on his flanks."

"Dead Yankee?"

"Seemed so—when we found him there was blood all over the saddle. Part of the cavalry that tore through here, I'm guessing." Woodward nodded, "The night of our little set-to over at West Point. He was running wild down the road when we got him."

Lost in a day and time all but irretrievable, Christie's thoughts went to other separations, other comrades gone—all casualties of war. He continued to stroke the chestnut coat, but said nothing—could say nothing at another separation from another comrade.

"Pardon me, Corporal, my wife tells me I patter like rain when I get tired. You see your horse in there anywhere? No? Too bad. How about some coffee? We have our own formula. It was pretty bad two hours ago, and by now it should come when it's called."

Christie had seen what he came for—there was no chance of stealing Gunshot away. It could have been tonight, he wanted very much for it to be tonight. He wanted to breathe free air, to be who he was, to find Grant. Barteau said he was landing below, his army—Christie's army as much—was on the move. Christie stroked Gunshot's long mane one last time then turned back for the creek.

"I will walk you through the lines. Colonel says we will be moving out at first light, thought we might get a day's rest. "

Christie paused at the bridge, "Lieutenant, I do wish you..." What could Christie say—success? No, that was not it. Criscrossed feelings caught in his throat. "...I wish you a safe ride."

Woodward took the stuttering for homesickness and bid the soldier a speedy recovery. Then he extended his hand again.

Shaking hands with the enemy, Christie was losing himself. Jamie MacGowan, Quinn, Nolan, would they understand his accepting protection from the enemy and he returning it with consolation and comfort? How much of it was pretense and how much of it was real? Was Collin the enemy? Was Carolina? Her grieving, broken father? His own father's student? Or was the enemy that force that turned all these people against him? Nothing was clear any more.

The tip of his walking stick was catching between the stones and with every step all but rocking him into the holly bushes and berry briars. Christie's pace was slow accordingly, and when he saw the house, he stopped. He breathed deeply, reaching for enough resolve for yet another performance. Then he reached for the gate.

Who it was must have been waiting in the shrubs. That fatal lapse of concentration—those few seconds wrestling with doubt—just enough for the attacker to strike, phasing no more than a shimmer out of the corner of Christie's eye. He slammed Christie over the wrought iron, the spiny rods tearing him in half. Then a rag was pressed against his mouth and nose. Fumes seared up into his head, and his stomach knotted. His dinner heaved up into his throat. Then all was void.

Heaven or hell? Was he alive or dead? His eyes burned and he wanted to vomit. Oblivion rolled and ebbed in waves. Light turned to shadow, then Doctor Bennett—and the barrel of his LeMat—lowered to Christie's temple.

"Suppose you tell me what you are doing in my daughter's bed? Be careful—I will not be so gullible a second time."

Carolina, pressed against the wall, pulled her wrapper to her naked shoulders. Her face was a contortion of horror and shock. Christie closed his eyes and opened them again. But she was still there, as was the LeMat, stirring his brain to work. Oh yes, this war was going very well, General Grant's lieutenant had everything under perfect control, the general would be so proud.

But easy deaths were not the doctor's way. Bennett pulled Christie out of the bed and slammed him against the bedpost. The physician had made a remarkable recovery. All Christie heard was the crack of the hammer and all he saw was the black maw of the barrel in front of his eyes. The room spun. Carolina, a whirling angel in muslin, begged for his life.

"For God's sakes," Collin pushed into the room. "What is going on here? Carolina, your shouts could bring the cavalry!"

An execution was in progress. Because of his dead leg, Collin was barely in time to deflect the barrel, as his father pulled the trigger. The charge exploded into the wall. Christie's brain was pulsating like a drum, but he was not dead. Yet.

"Father, have you gone completely mad!" Collin wrenched away the gun. "Carolina, what happened? James, you're going to faint!"

Christie fought the dizziness, and reached for anything to steady the rocking, heaving floor. Nothing did and he collapsed.

But Carolina was remarkable. A gun shot only two feet from her face and the near murder of her patient had not sent *her* into a fainting spell. Instead, it crystallized her senses. She awoke as from a dream, gathering up the shreds of what she knew to explain, and she did quickly. She had come upstairs to undress for bed and found James lying there, moaning and groggy. "It startled me, that's all. I did not expect to find him there. I was in no danger. He seemed strange, but by that time I had already screamed."

For Collin the room was a collection of question marks. "James, what are you doing in here?"

"I don't know." Lame, inadequate—but that was all there was to tell so far.

Collin glared at the state of his sister's undress. Carolina flushed, her lips tightened into a thin line. She escaped into the hall and returned with her wrapper around her and tied. Her brother was waiting for an explanation, he got something else. "How could you think such a thing of me...of either of us. I will slap your face if you do not straighten it this minute. I came up to ready for bed, and he was there in the dark. Now, if this misunderstanding is over, help James downstairs and please leave me in peace."

Carolina was impatient, but Collin held his ground the relic at the end of his hand.

"You heard me, Collin, help James downstairs. And take father with you. I think he is beyond his senses."

Christie studied one and then the other and shook his head. He was very dizzy. Then he saw it, *Uncle Tom's Cabin* hanging precariously by the tip of the cover dangling from the frame of the rope bed. That he was the only other to see it was her salvation. This fine Southern lady was not defending his honor, but her own! If the book fell, with all this tension, it would hit the floor like a pistol clap. So it was not him but this that froze her against the wall. Christie saw it, and when she realized that he saw it, her agitation heightened. Their eyes met, his amused and incredulous, hers daring. The ultimatum was not misunderstood by either one: if the book were discovered, she would claim it to be his, brought there and secreted by him. And who would believe otherwise—she a nun and he a brigand who had been trusted too far?

They would lynch me sure, for a book. Christie wanted to laugh. In fact, it was all he could do not to howl. How would the letter to his mother go? "Missis Christie: your son was shot by an enraged Confederate father when he found him in his daughter's bed. He had been summarily found guilty and executed on the spot for spying, compromising a lady's honor, and smuggling into the Confederacy unlawful literature for purposes of inciting treason. Your most obedient servant, Jefferson Davis, President of the Confederate States of America by way of President Abraham Lincoln." Something to console a mother on long winter nights.

"I will avenge your sister, if you will not. You seem to have forgotten your responsibilities as a man in this family." Bennett's words were all but unintelligible with rage.

Collin did not give way. "I see no outrage, father. I don't know what has happened here. At the very most, James took a wrong turn and ended up in the wrong room."

"You don't believe it. All the bedrooms are upstairs—he sleeps in the surgery downstairs. It is not possible, even if he were drunk. But I do not think that is it. Mister Brent, have you been the one into the morphine?"

There was nothing Christie would answer.

When the surgeon got no reply, he ordered, "Lock him in the smoke house!"

"He will suffocate in there." Collin was taking command now. "I will lock him in his room until morning. We will turn him over to Colonel Barteau with no more explanation than James changed his mind—wanted on his way as soon as possible. The way the war is going, you will probably get your wish, father, and he will be dead in a month. He will collapse of infection or the Yankees will shoot him."

"Just get him out of my sight!" Bennett's face was as it was the night he slammed the diary across Christie's cheek.

"James, let me help you up." Collin clasped him under his shoulder and pulled him to his feet. Christie braced himself between Collin and the wall to keep from falling down the stairs. "Where's your cane, James? How could you have gotten up these stairs without it?"

Christie needed time to think. Answers—coherent ones— were illusive just when they were most urgent. Collin was still waiting for them as Christie lay flat on his own bed.

"Can you tell me what this is all about?" Collin asked as he sat down beside him.

"I was coming back from Barteau's camp. I was just coming up the walk—and someone set upon me, slapped a rag in my face, and pulled me down. I remember I couldn't breathe...the smell of chloroform or ether. And then I woke up in your sister's bed. So help me, that's all I know." It was preposterous—Christie could hear how unbelievable it all sounded.

Collin leaned closer. "You do smell like ether. You gonna be sick?"

"Oh yeah." Christie rolled over and Collin pushed his head down into a chamber pot.

It was still dark when Christie jerked awake. He lay in a bundle of sweaty sheets, trying to work his mind, to forge a plan of escape. Collin was gone. How late was it? How much time did he have until dawn? What were his chances? He was on the first story with a story above. The walls were over a foot thick, the sole source of light was a skylight above and a cameo window— smaller than the passage through which he was born. No escape there.

Not through, not over—but how about under? This part of the house had no cellar; it was set on a raised, open sill. If a board could be pulled up, he could drop down between the ground and the floor and crawl away. Christie pondered each step one at a time. The critical factor: How far could a gimpy-legged fugitive travel in a country expert in the science of hunting down runaways? The floor and then what? Rattlesnakes and poisonous spiders making such crawl spaces home? Stop thinking and do.

The twilight effect of the anesthetic still made him queasy. But he went to work in the dark, his fingers tracing along the seams of the floorboards. They fit slick and tight and, thanks to Rachel, filled with dutchmen and cemented with an inch of varnish and wax.

His concentration was total, and he did not hear the turn of the key. The door was already swinging wide when Christie pressed himself behind it.

"James, it's me, Collin. Don't even try. Now let me come in before I am discovered. That would be bad for both of us." Christie moved back letting Collin step inside. "How are you feeling?"

"How am I feeling? How do you expect?"

"Calm down. You are going to need a cool head for what I am going to tell you, and there is work ahead, so settle yourself and listen. My father has given guns to Miles and Pitch, these are men you don't want to deal with. He also gave your scent to the Eldridge hounds, they are only slightly more humane than Miles and Pitch." Collin eased his weight onto the bed. "Now, listen, your only chance of getting out of here alive is with my help, but you are going to have to trust me."

"Why would you help a man who assaulted your sister?"

"I am not a stupid man, so don't treat me like one. You could have defended yourself against the charge of taking the morphine, but you kept quiet—even with a revolver at your head. Such men do not ambush women in their own bedrooms. If I thought you had, I would have killed you myself. And if my father truly believed it, you would be getting married tomorrow instead of being turned over to Barteau. You would have solved one of my father's more pressing problems—a Confederate patriot for his spinster daughter who is growing more spinster by the day. No, this insanity was inspired by a more dangerous enemy, a zealot with no conscience and a hair-trigger temper preying on a grief-stricken man."

"Who?"

"Father Kessler. While you were talking with Colonel Barteau, he took my father in private discussion to the library. I was not invited nor was Uncle Nathaniel—a confidence between a man and his confessor, they said. And I have gathered from my father's ravings that it is Kessler's assumption that you are a Yankee spy." Collin massaged the nub of his stump. Even in the dark, Christie could tell he was suffering, yet had taken no morphine to keep his mind clear. "That makes the whole situation dangerous because they are working on half-truths. You *are* a Yankee all right—a smart one. But you are not a spy, just one who was shot, ended up in a Southern house, and wants to go home very badly."

"How did you come to that conclusion?"

"Oh, I didn't have to come far—you told me of your own accord, but you were delirious at the time. I spelled Rachel and Carolina for an hour or two by your bed while you were raving about Fredericksburg. Not that you had it by name, but any soldier who had been there knew what you were talking about. Except, for a Confederate, you told it from the wrong side of the battle line. It told me who you were—or enough. So it was I, who suggested father summon Barteau. Didn't say why—but he caught the smell of suspicion. In the meantime he had you locked in, but I had laudanum put in your tea. I thought the apples would disguise the taste, it obviously didn't from the ruckus you made. And then you refused to take it. You sure know how to make an impression on my family, they thought you were crazy. Rachel still does." Collin laughed in spite of himself.

"You were a complication and growing more with every day! The hard part was biding my time until Barteau arrived. To keep from crashing in your skull, while you slept, I stayed away as much as I could. But you won over Carolina and my father. Carolina even invited you to our table—ever the saint! With the whiskey I drank, and you sitting there at supper like some gentleman patriot—my anger got the best of me. I wanted to see the look on your face, when I confronted you with the truth, right in front of my family. First, I told my side of Fredericksburg, I wanted to see some rage, some vengeance, something of the enemy I hated. I thought you would betray yourself—at least to me, that would have made exposing you so sweet. But, you were as stricken with all the death and the unfairness as I...everything you said, I could have said...and I didn't plan for that. So I changed my mind. I wanted to study you awhile. Then I didn't plan on the compassion in the dispensary. Everything was confused. And then there was the letter in your pocket. I know Billy's family, and you aren't a part of it. With the blood on your jacket...I..."

"I did not kill Billy, at least...perhaps I did—there was a battle. He gave the letter to me before he died."

Collin seemed to understand. "West Point was a fair fight. I took the letter when I undressed you, and I burned the uniform. When you are gone, I will deliver it to his father and tell him that he died in the arms of a comrade. That's true, isn't it?"

"Yes, that's pretty much it. Who else knows all this?"

"No sane person, but after Grierson lit a fire under everyone, and with Grant landing south there aren't many sane ones left. Kessler sees John Brown behind every tree and is ready to lead the holy war from behind. Oh, we both had our hate and our war—I just don't like Kessler's methods."

"Not that we have time to discuss this at length, but that doesn't make any sense."

"Oh yes, we have a little time yet. And you had better learn this lesson if you want to get out of the war alive: things don't have to make sense, they just are."

"If your father wanted me dead, he could have killed me anytime. Injected me with something."

Collin thought. "No, Carolina knows enough medicine, and would have been suspicious. He needed to do it clean, above board, to cover up his real purpose. If our neighbors found out we gave comfort and aid to the enemy, even innocently, they would burn us out. No reprieve. But if my father shot you, to save Carolina's honor, that is forgivable. Honor over treason, her reputation would have been tainted still. I don't think he thought it all through. Shunned or exiled, chastity or treason—the mission ends badly regardless. As it turned out, I gave him the only way out—to turn you over to Barteau as a recruit instead of a prisoner. No one would be the wiser. If you were smart enough, you could make your own escape later. But father will not have even that. He means for you to be shot and make it look like an accident. He can not see that his lust for your blood can only bring ruin upon himself and his family."

"But how would your neighbors have known?"

"Kessler, our beloved priest, sees you as a bastard of Satan. He would have proclaimed it from the pulpit. Make an example of us. The man must be stopped, but that is my affair."

"You believe me, then?"

"Yes, I believe you. You have already come to the conclusions I have: my father is the only one big and strong enough to have attacked and dragged you up there. Or he could have had Miles do it. I found your cane under the holly bushes."

"That's strange—my first impulse was that you found me out, and had set upon me."

Collin shook his head thoughtfully. "No, James, now my days of fighting are over."

"I wish I felt the same. I don't understand it either. I listened to you talk about Fredericksburg. Oh, I hated you all right—the only thing that kept my blood pumping that night, I lay cold and bleeding out there, was hate. It damned near burned me to a crisp. But a lot has happened since then, things aren't so simple any more. Still and all, I still want a Union of us. Perhaps knowing you, I want it harder."

"Do you mind telling me, just who you are?"

"Brenton Christie, Fourth Ohio, Company C. That long blue line you saw coming at you? You remember? That be us." In the darkness he could not tell the effect his admission had. "Now what?"

"Now you are going to get out of here." Collin rose wearily. "I came to keep you from escaping too soon. Miles and Pitch should be asleep now. My father posted them front and back of the house, in case you tore the floor up and dropped out of here. A couple of hours ago I took them some of my famous apple cider."

"And the dogs?"

"Them too. We need to go before it gets light."

Christie was not so sure of anyone anymore. "Why are you doing this?"

"Allowing them to kill you here and now, the way my father wants, well, that isn't war, that's murder. That's just cold-blooded murder. It has come to matter."

"Your family will know you helped me."

"That is my problem too. Now let's get you going north. I

know a few people who can help you."

Night was fading. The floorboards that were so tight in the bedroom, in the hall ached and groaned with every step. The two invalids scuffled down the back gallery steps and toward the path. Just before the cemetery of the unknowns, Collin sidetracked through the bush until he reached the bank. He motioned Christie to follow as he stepped into the creek. The current made the way clumsy and cold, but they kept to it for about a half-mile. Then abruptly Collin turned up the bank again, and pushed through the reeds. He unsheathed a knife and tapped the hilt three times against a rusty cup hanging from a tree. The branches parted. A man larger and blacker than pitch strode to meet them.

"This is Eban. He is the man who found you. He will take you to Father Lyons, the Catholic priest over in Columbus, about twenty miles from here. He is Southern, but for it, an abolitionist. He will see you back north through the Underground. Here is where our friendship ends."

Collin turned to leave, but Christie reached for his hand to shake in farewell. Instead, Collin pressed the hilt of the skinning knife into his palm. "Bye, Yank."

There was one more account to be settled for Christie. "If it is any comfort to you, we weren't at Sharpsburg when your brother was killed. The Fourth had no part in that."

It did matter to the Confederate, and more to Christie than he would admit. Collin struggled to keep his feelings inside, "If not that battle, then another. It was my fault. My father is right there. I should have saved Lorin, at whatever the cost. Some men should not die — their price is too great for any cause." He thought for a second and then turned back. "I should have brought you a hat." In front of him a hand was extended and Collin now took it. "Since that first day at supper, I have been able to forget that you were an enemy. For a few days I have had a brother more than I ever had before in effect."

"Thank you, Collin, for everything."

"We best be getting on, mister." Eban broke in. "We got only a little while of dark left, and we can't travel once the sun comes up. See you in three days, sir."

"Got your papers, Eban?"

Eban touched his pocket. "Got 'em."

"Take care, Christie. You only got about six lives left, and this war isn't half over." Collin's handshake was firm.

"You do the same. Go easy on Carolina—she is fighting for a place in this Camelot-in-the-clouds you Southerners have created down here. She never found it before, and she knows there isn't any future if the Union wins. It makes her lonely and more afraid than she will admit."

"I will hold the New World off at gun point for her sake."

Pink and yellow clouds feathered out of the eastern horizon, and the house rode against it like some majestic ship lowing at sail. Collin saw it anew, there from his vantage at the cloister gate. It would have been Lorin's had he lived, and it will be Lorin's even though he didn't. Lorin's mausoleum. Collin knew that soon he would have to find some purpose to fill his life.

"Your father is waiting for you in the library, Mister Collin." As soon as his message was given Miles turned his face away.

Collin shortened his steps for his wizened dog to catch up. "Are you sure you want to come with me? There is going to be a hanging."

The house was still and dark except for the translucence waking through the palladium windows. It framed in relief the only two people he loved in this world. His father was fully dressed, his valise and medical bag open by the front door. Carolina had dressed in haste, without hoops, her hair unpinned, her feet still in carpet slippers. Father and daughter parted abruptly as Collin entered. She had been crying, her face was swollen and blotched. Collin would have comforted her, but she pulled away from him.

"He is gone?" was all his father asked.

"Yes."

"You helped the Yankee escape?" Bennett's tone was despair and disbelief, rather than anger. He returned to his packing, arranged some instruments inside, and snapped the valise shut.

"And a certain man came down from Jerusalem to Jericho and fell among thieves..."

"My son, a Southern gentleman and Confederate officer,

rationalizes his treason in the role of good Samaritan to a Yankee spy? I hope that will be a comfort to you. I hope it will be a comfort to your sister if our neighbors find out and she is shunned. I hope your brother can forgive it from the grave."

"Where are you going?"

"A rider from the Committee of Correspondence came through an hour ago. Grant is marching toward Jackson. They need surgeons."

"Who will take care of your patients?"

"Carolina."

His daughter was incredulous. "What? I can't."

"You do not have to operate, just treat their aches and pains. That you can do. You have been at my elbow since you were six. The nuns have taught you the rest. We had no fault with your nursing, child, only your unbending will, now it will be of good use to you. I have left you with some supplies, but I must take the rest."

"Father, I will come with you." Collin reached to stop him.

"No—as soon as I leave I want you to pack everything you own and be gone. Your presence is a sacrilege to this house. I do not wish to see you again. I will not abide your name mentioned in my presence or admit I know you."

Carolina stepped between them. "You cannot leave this way, father."

Bennett kissed her gently. "I must go. I will leave the horse at the station. Look in on your Aunt Mamie and don't let her trouble you too much—she is a tarnished old relic, but she loves you."

Then he reached for his luggage. With his hand on the door latch, he stopped and turned to his son. Neither could find a word. Bennett stepped outside and closed the door behind him.

XIII
Jubilee Marching by the Back Door
Early May, 1863

"You really one of Mister Linkun's soldiers?" That this puny specimen could be among the legions of archangels flying down to free the black race took a leap of faith. Certainly more than Eban could muster just now, when this only example he had ever seen sagged on spiny legs and the next deep exhale would throw him backwards.

"You were expecting thoroughbreds?" The blue soldier had long ago lost his bearings—north-south-east-west or anything in between. And he didn't trust him, Eban could tell—never took his eyes off him. All the time they walked, Eban could feel the cold green eyes boring through him, waiting for a wrong move or even a move that seemed wrong. Patience was a keg at the end of a short fuse for this Yankee—and he had the big knife.

"Thoroughbred? Not so much, but even an old plow mule got more kick than you."

"Just keep walking. I'll be behind you."

This exchange was as testy as the others. In the three days since Mister Collin had left them on the banks of the creek, there had been few words, none of them cordial. The gentleman had ordered him to take this rag doll of a soldier to Father Lyons in Columbus. But they had not set off a hundred feet when this uppity runaway said they weren't going to Columbus at all, they were going to the bottom of the Big Black River, which was the opposite direction entirely. He didn't care about passes either. Eban had been of a mind to just leave him there to find his own way, but then what would he report to Mister Collin? That was a puzzle with no happy answer.

Mister Collin's friendship with this Yankee was an insult. White men made friends on short acquaintance, on skin not blood. To top it off, he had given the soldier the knife that had been the present of Mister Lorin to Mister Collin. If he gave the knife to anyone, it should have been Eban, his old friend. As boys, Eban and Mister Collin had prowled these fields, fishing, hunting, and scaring up mischief like young foxes. Then was a good time, until Mister Collin had gone off to school. Eban had wanted to go along, have Mister Bennett buy him from Miss Tallie to be Mister Collin's man—carry his bags, perhaps learn a little readin' and cipherin' 'way from the plantation. Mister Collin had promised to take him. Even taught him to talk proper so he would fit in with the Memphis' and Natchez's best boys. But Mister Collin had been sent to Harvard, where Eban could not go. Still the morning he left, Mister Collin had met Eban behind the big magnolia to swear their trust forever. Then the doctor's son had gone, forever it seemed like. How Eban had missed him—the house and the fields missed him.

The first Christmas Mister Collin got down off the Starkville train; he was changed toward Eban, toward Doctor Bennett and Miss Carolina, toward everyone and everything. Quiet to himself most times, his mind was full of puzzlement. There was a far-way look; when he did talk, he talked about funny things that made no sense. It got worse every time Mister Collin went off and come back. It was like he wasn't all there no more, even when he was at home, like he didn't bring his soul back with him. At first Eban thought he left it with a Yankee woman, he supposed that was the cause of the fights in the house. But no woman came and Mister Collin never talked of one to Eban at any rate. He just left it back at that uppity school, in his room, or in a book on the shelf.

Then there was that big fight between him and his father about not going back the last time, could hear it clear out in the garden. Instead Mister Collin wanted to read law in Starkville or Vicksburg. But his father sent him back anyhow, said it would be good for him to know how Yankees think. Eban didn't know how the Yankees thought, or if they thought at all, and could not see what good it did to know down here.

And this war business just made him all the worse 'cause Mister Collin had no fire for it—for or ag'in. But he went. They all went, and he didn't take Eban then either. This time there were no sworn friendships behind the magnolia bush. He just packed up and rode off a couple of weeks after Mister Lorin—went into a different regiment though. There was good talk about Manassas and Richmond and bad talk about Sharpsburg where Mister Lorin died. Eban suffered that Mister Collin might have died too. So many from the county died. So many killed by the same army that brought this Yank here.

Mister Collin was so far in the clouds now to forget all his bearings, to make the blue soldier a friend and forget grudges, to lose friends and forget covenants! Eban didn't forget grudges so fast. Likely as much this Christie—and he would not call him by name ever—had been among them that killed Mister Lorin, yet Mister Collin turned against his own family to help this one escape. The Yank and him had shook hands.

Puny, no-starch, blue soldier! But Eban would help him for old-time sake and no farther. The Big Black was two more days, as slow as this soldier was limping. It flowed north to south along the railroad—too near the Natchez Trace with too many soldiers and too much traffic for a black man to feel comfortable traveling. But the soldier said that he was meeting Grant by the Big Black. Eban knew a lot of people in that direction, but no one by the name of Grant. The cripple would probably be so rude as to die on the way, and then Eban would be caught alone by the plantation patrols with a dead pass. With every man was a rifle and a hound seeing runaways—he might have to become one just to keep from hanging. Eban stopped. It wasn't the first time he had thought about running away as principle, but it was the first time he thought about it as fact. The sensation made him giddy, nearly lifted him off the ground. Freedom! Gave him purpose to stay out awhile and give the option some thought.

Momma Wise had a cabin at the headwaters of the Big Black and between here and there Eban had time to think on that. No friend to the Northerns, but she was a friend to Eban and to Mister Collin, and she was a Choctaw doctor. This human package would need a doctor or an undertaker—by the time he got there. Momma Wise could do both, so there Eban in good conscience could rid himself of this huckleberry.

"When did we cross the border into hell? I didn't see a sign, but I think it was five miles back." The Yankee wiped sweat on his sleeve. He looked red and foamy like a fried salmon.

Eban snorted. This Christie had never been to hell, but he had been to Mississippi in the near summer—guess that was close enough. Eban pulled the lank soldier up and braced him with an arm around his ribs. His legs buckled with the next step, but Eban caught him and half dragged him a ways before the soldier tried to shove him away and try again on his own. But Eban kept a tight hold, and the two walked on three legs. Eban shook his head. Pain mad, but the soldier didn't really complain about it. Give him that.

"It ain't so hot. Ain't near as bad as last summer—that was worse than I ever saw. You hear about Moses in the desert? You just payin' for your sins is all."

"And yours too." The soldier's mouth was too dry to spit.

"What you mean? No, I think I got it—you wouldn't be here if it wasn't for eman-ce-pation. Yes, I hear of the word. Well, I got several words on that subject, which I could tell with my fists. But our first job is not mine eman-ce-pation, it's yours."

That should set fire to his gumption and get a few more miles out of him 'fore breakfast. Best to say no more. Even a near-dead dog could rise up and chew a man to pieces, only to lay down and die with satisfaction. No, Eban would let him be for a short spell. It was maybe four, five miles to the upper creek, depending upon how far the rain had swollen up the backwater. Maybe there would be a flat boat and he could pole a ways, get the soldier off his feet. Or they would have to track through the backcountry. That was the hard route. Death shadowed a man here. He could die from a snakebite in four minutes, in three he could drown in an eddy, in a second he could be shot—never found and never missed.

Eban bent Christie in two, one arm held him tight in a knot, while the other drew Mister Collin's nine-inch steel blade out of the boot. Might made for right. He dropped the near-lifeless body into the rushes. With the prize once in his hand, Eban did not attack, did not smile, but just stood there with his legs spread. "You stay here." He laughed at his own joke. "Yeah, as if you would be runnin' off."

The blue soldier slumped over to massage the bad leg. There was blood on the pantaloon, fresh with the stain getting wider. "You going to leave me here? I can't say as I blame you. You saved my life once—no man can be made to do it twice, especially at risk of his own."

Eban ripped open the trouser leg and packed the wound with knotweed grappled from where it grew wild along the deer path. Even the lightest touch made the soldier wince, blood overflowed his lip from where he bit through, but he did not cry out. Eban finished it off with a dirty bandanna.

The soldier was sweating even harder now. "Thanks again."

Some ledgers needed correcting even right there. "You got it wrong. I never saved your life, not on purpose anyhow."

"You're the one who pulled me out of the reeds and brought me to Doctor Bennett, that right?"

Eban licked the salt from his lips and nodded. "I did that. Like I said, not on purpose. You was so near dead, I picked you up for a body for Doctor Bennett, and I expected you to be dead when I got there. That way you not stink and blow up so much afore we got to the house, like a dead one would. I didn't think you would live. The doctor collects dead men to cut open and see how the live ones work, I guess. Pays me five dollar for every one if it ain't too black."

"You mean you collect cadavers for Doctor Bennett to autopsy?"

Eban deciphered the words a syllable at a time. "I heard him use words to that effect. Sounded evil, but he said it wasn't 'cause the soul was gone out of the body, and it was of no more use to him or anyone no more. It's a good payin' business, with more bodies now than I can collect with dead soldiers, runaways, no-accounts—nobodies to be missed. Not as if I shot 'em afore any one of 'em was ready to die."

"The graves dug behind the Bennett gardens in the back woods? That's where you bury them when he's done. The empty, you dug that one for *me*, isn't that right?"

"Don't be gettin' insulted. You ain't so precious." Eban tested the knife against a broad leaf. It cut clean to the vein; then he threw the tattered leaf into Christie's face. "You just one soldier Linkun had already crossed off the rolls as a dead certainty. There be many more soldiers comin' to take you place. Not like you would be missed."

Not begging any insult! Eban was the one short changed. "It made no difference to Doctor Bennett. Either you make it, Doctor Bennett fix you up, and learned by it—or you didn't, and he had another to skin. But to me, I was out five dollar. I don't get paid for living carcasses, only dead. You gonna pay me, soldier boy? I guess Doctor Bennett out too, about ten dollar, 'cause I don't think you paid for his services, bed, or all that food you et. Now that I think on it, you are an expense all around—and still costin'."

The humor of it all brought the blue soldier to life. "By rights I owe you five dollars for my good fortune and your bad. Since my body and soul is owned by the Secretary of War, you can send him a bill if you want. I don't know about the tab at Doctor

Bennett's—had too much breeding to collect—but he was ready to shoot me a couple of times for lesser offenses. Though he can write Stanton too—that exchange should be lively. Then there are the people of Mississippi who want paid for the damage the cavalry did. Pound for pound, I don't think I have enough flesh to cover that bill either, and Stanton won't want too. And there is the matter of General Grant's horse I lost, so my tab is pretty high. I guess I am just lucky I am not in that empty trench you dug."

"Maybe you alive 'cause of the other dead men Doctor Bennett opened. Think on it."

In another half-hour the sun would be up and boiling to burn away the rolling fog from the fields. They had traveled all night, most of it with the blue soldier straddled on his back. He gave out about midnight. He would need tendin' soon or he was going to die. Eban saw the signs. Momma Wise was still a day away, so must now do something Eban and the Yank did not want to do—travel by the day light. That travel would be ginger. The guide and the fugitive Yank had come to one mind: not to be caught like a stag in the open. Eban disconnected himself from the suffering and from the cramping hunger that made his mind foggy. The soldier's head bobbed and he set him down against a tree and slapped him awake.

"That field there, we got to get across it. It's wider than it looks, make no mistake—we are going to be seeable a long way. I hoped we could get it afore light, but you too slow and gettin' slower. You walk?"

Christie took one painful step and then another. They were not steady or sure, but they were promising. "I can walk," the soldier answered defensively.

Eban surveyed the far horizon. "Set your sights on the tree line yonder. Don't take your eyes off it. Keep goin' for it all the time."

Christie waded down into the first rows of knee-high corn and was ready to bolt. Instead, Eban slammed him backwards.

"Just where are you lighten' off to? I didn't say go yet! You think you some damned angel, just goin' to fly over them fields with that dead leg? You are a fool!"

Eban didn't wait to be answered back. The field hand

disappeared into the high cane, and soon he was back with a pole. He hacked about six inches off the bottom, then fastened the top with a stub, and padded it with his hat. He slammed the crutch under the soldier's arm. "Lean down on that! How it feel?" Christie teetered. Eban pulled it out and shaved two inches more. He fitted it more gently this time as the rough treatment made the boy flinch. Christie laid his full weight on it. Pleased, Eban steadied him upright.

"Now you are a three-legged soldier, Mister Lunkun'll pay you extra. Even still, you not as valuable as me. Now, in that soft ground, that crutch gonna sink a bit, so be ready for it. Don't go fallin' on you face."

The blue soldier said he would be careful.

"This fog not gonna last long. We need to make it over while it still hides us. Not going to stop till we reach the scrub. There's water in the glen beyond. You can make it, sure?"

Eban had given the soldier something to aim for, and Christie stiffened in resolution. "For water I'll run barefooted across a field of burning briars. And the next time you want the knife, just ask. Now give it back."

Eban turned the hilt over in his hand. Too good for this Yankee, but he surrendered it and Christie sheathed it in his boot. Who had it didn't matter—Eban could get it anytime he wanted.

"We'll not stop. If you fall, I will not wait till you git up. You caught, that's one dead spy. But *you and me caught,* that's slave revolt. You ain't just runnin' for you life, you runnin' for mine." Eban poked a finger into the Yank's chest to re-emphasize the point.

"All right." Christie was converted to humility. "You're the sergeant, you set the pace. I'll keep up."

Eban smirked. "Sergeant—I like it." He turned his rank over in his head. "What you?" In military affairs there is no emergency that can't be postponed until the matters of rank and command are fully made clear.

"Pardon?"

"In the army, what you?"

"Lieutenant."

"Sergeant beats lieutenant?"

"Sergeants think so."

Eban smiled triumphantly. His mind and his starch—which only got him in trouble on the plantations—were actually worth something in the white man's army. Men got rank for it. Something to color his thoughts on freedom. "Till we get to Momma Wise, I'm sergeant, you just lieutenant."

Christie had no choice but to agree, "Yeah, but you can't leave your lieutenant."

Having jumped to the rosy conclusion that sergeants could do what they wanted, this last condition made Eban seek a clarification. "What happens when a sergeant loses his lieutenant?"

"He's court martialed for dereliction of duty."

"What's all that mean?"

"If he's lucky he's just shot, if not he spends the rest of his life filling out papers for every cubby hole of every bureaucrat in the U.S. Government who thinks he should have a record of the matter. Lieutenants are very important to the army—more important than the Secretary of War, congressmen, newspaper reporters, or even generals—and less important than a crate of good rifles, a good mule, or a barrel of hardtack. But he costs money and time to replace. A hell of a lot of explaining and paperwork for the sergeant who does the losing."

A plantation bell rattled—a signal that they might have waited too long. Eban slapped the blue soldier on the back, the fugitives exploded into the field. In one stride they were kicking up red talcum, in two they were in the open, in three they were beyond the point of return. Eban pulled the Yank by the arm, forcing Christie's legs to turn over faster than he could make them, so they knotted into each other. The soft earth swayed under his feet, the Yank jerked and slipped, but Eban only held tighter.

The soldier's heart would explode in ten more paces. But Eban would not let him go. Tender shoots of corn—row upon row—like a rugby field, passed under. Ahead the far "shore" shimmered in waves of heat.

The soldier swayed like wheat, but fear won out over pain. Again he pushed ahead, placing one foot ahead then another, one and another, his crutch tilling the earth under him. Eban had never seen a face so fiendish. One foot forward and then the other. Up and down, over and over. Pulling and pushing until the Yank could go no more. He staggered and dropped into the ground. Eban wavered between the far goal and the beaten soldier — the mist was burning sheer. A lot was being asked of old promises.

A pair of black eyes deep-set within crevices of wild brows and ridges of ebony cheekbones marked the two men just as they broke from the rim of trees. He studied what course they headed. The work column closed up behind him, grateful but not sure why the line had stopped. But they were uncaring how long until it started again. The bell rang, but the field boss did not take them out.

"What yo see out there, Polk?" His brother nudged him ahead — the overseer would not like this.

"Soldier patrol or a jackrabbit? He see sumptin," a cousin whispered.

Another replied, "Maybe it's Yankees and we free! Hope so, rather be free afore we work all day than afta."

The overseer jerked the nose of his swayback mule to angle around the field hands suddenly drawing up. On their own, the crew closed on either side of their field boss to hold the overseer back. Only Polk could see beyond the gap in the long wall of boxwood that buffered the plantation grounds from the heat and dust of the open field. On the horizon two men — one black and one white — tore through the corn like flying scarecrows. An escape in broad daylight. Bad.

The overseer reached over the head of his mount and swatted the big black with his riding crop. The slave's tattered willow-reed hat toppled to the ground, but Polk gave no sign he felt the slap at all.

"You see a snake? What got you spooked? Fractious as mules!" Alcohol and sleepiness made the overseer's voice slushy, an omen to mind if a bare back did not want to feel the whip.

Polk saw it all. The black had already reached safety, but the white boy went dry about twenty feet from the tree line. Then he stumbled, lurched, and straightened to try again. Too confused and dizzy with sun blindness to see his salvation within his reach, he collapsed again.

"Run! Run! Save yourself. " Polk hissed. For the brother who now wavered between safety and his crippled companion, the field hand was fast losing patience. Cross-purpose warred inside him. "Let the white boy die where he lay...No, no, damned ya—don't come back for him. Shit, yo a fool. Leave the boy, save yo ownself."

The mule's breath blew vile and hot on Polk's neck; the overseer would be on him soon. Those men needed time. Polk gauged he could give them a minute, that was all. But the cost would not be pleasant.

"Damned! Polk! You ain't got brains to be boss! Get the hell amovin' afore I make you move!" The overseer's crop snapped across Polk's neck.

The big slave bristled. It was too hot to be mad this early. With one jerk he could pull the overseer off the mule and make sure he never got up again. He wanted to do it on two accounts, for his own soul and for the black man who just made a bad choice. But there would be no revenge today. The word was out; Mister Linkun's soldiers were comin' but not this minute. Polk would not be hangin' from a tree when they did.

Out there, the white boy was being dragged by his guardian angel to the far tree line. Soon now, maybe a half-minute more till they got clear. Polk pressed his lips together and raised from deep in his throat one long guttural growl. On cue, twenty field hands took it up. They groaned and hummed like the howl of the wind. With faces as blank as masks, they split away from the line and circled the mule in a swoon-like trance, until it danced and honked in a frenzy. The big overseer cocked the shotgun, but the warning went to no effect. The barrel exploded just above their heads. Men froze. With no more word, they hoisted their spades on their shoulders and settled back into line—all except Polk. The overseer lifted the smoking, black, barrel and set it to the back of Polk's head. The heat burned against his scalp. Polk turned over his shoulder. The field was empty; the two men were gone.

Panic blistered the overseer's face. His finger was still hooked around the trigger, "Polk, you lazy, drunken, bastardized son of Satan! I will whip you hard if you aren't moving in two seconds. Lead them out—it's going to be a furnace in an hour."

Polk set his mask of humility in place, and hung his head in earnest contrition for having aggrieved the overseer. "Must be the sun, sir. I gettin' old and don't have my wits any more! I feel it more ever day. I beg ya pardon. I surely do! But I thought I saw

Mister Colton ridin' over the field on Big Caesar, just like he used ta in the morning."

The overseer reared. "The Mister's son is dead two years. You saw nothing. Don't be spookin' us with ghosts. You stupid drunk is all."

Polk thought the overseer right—he was getting too old and was losing his wits, but the old man would have to live with it. Work must be done, with what he had to do it with—the plantations were leakin' men. Polk swung his hoe onto his shoulder and led the procession out into the vast field, away from the broken trail the runaways had turned.

Eban cut through the hedgerows and melted into the trees like an apparition. With the Yank still on his back, the big "sergeant" pounded over a spiny carpet of nettles and trampled the marsh grass in his headlong pursuit over the bank. Eban bucked his load into the reservoir; the explosion rustled a commotion of crows and squirrels. Eban dove deep. The waves closed over him caressing every aching muscle and quenching the burning dust, salt, and sweat from his body.

When Eban broke the surface, the soldier was floating on his back—as still as death. Eban pushed him down, but the soldier just bobbed up. The Yank sighed in clear ecstasy, "Now I know what bliss is, it's right here and right now. From now on, I will judge anything that comes close to it by what I feel right now." The blue soldier actually laughed. It was infectious so Eban did too.

Even under torture Eban would never have admitted to the Yank that he too had been nearly emptied out at the last. All the while he had the sense that somewhere there had been eyes watching them, but they had come through it. Eban pushed the Yank down under for another dousing, while he let his own body buoy up and the water trickle down through his thick knotted hair and onto his steaming scalp. They both would have floated there until moss covered them over if Eban had not broken the spell.

"You hurry up and get cleaned off. Clean that leg good. Drink up your fill here—you can't drink the water when we get to the river. It give you the disease—turn your insides out." Eban took out the bottle they had shared as a canteen, uncorked it, and angled it up stream to fill. "Now fix yourself." Eban threw him a shirt he had had tied around his waist.

"You want me to wrap my leg up in this? I'll get gangrene!" The soldier held the rancid rag by its tip, well away from his skin, as if its very shadow was infectious.

"That be my good shirt. It better than you got?"

The Yank muttered something Eban took for insubordination. He put one immense hand against the pink, sunburned forehead, shoved it under the water, and held it there until all the fevers of rebellion had bubbled up. Then he let go. "Remember, *I am sergeant.*"

The Yank gasped and coughed up a lung full, yes he would remember. "I didn't think you would take it so damned seriously."

Eban finished filling the bottle, dropped in a sprig of peppermint from the bank, and tied it to his belt. The Yank did as he was told. He rinsed the russet clay and blood from his body and then tended his leg. The scab floated off, blood and fluid spread out in the water. The brown sutures strained against the swelling. Already a couple had torn.

It was the first time Christie had ever examined the wound closely. "I wonder what the good sisters would think about this? I thought stitches were supposed to be white."

Eban winced, "Doctor Bennett don't have good thread no more, 'cause the war. He used horse tail."

"He used what?"

A case of Yankee squeamishness was more than Eban wanted to tackle. "Doctor Bennett took a hair from his horse's tail—damned nag almost bald by now. He boiled it and sewed you up with it. Don't worry, you won't neigh, but you'll get a hunger for hard corn and oats for breakfast."

Eban made a sling for the crutch out of river vine and pulled it over his shoulder. He scooped up his burden and stretched an arm around Christie's waist for the last miles of their journey. "We'll walk awhile, breakfast later, and you can soak that leg. It'll come along if we keep it wet."

In and out among the ribs of the mandrake roots, cypress, and willow reeds they went, Eban sometimes supporting, sometimes carrying, sometimes pulling Christie along the current and over the mossy stones. It was cool under the canopy of trees, and they were grateful for the road of water that left no scent for the hounds to track. When they had gone some distance, Eban pulled two sweet potatoes from deep pockets and handed one to his charge. The Yank slapped it away; Eban jabbed it back.

"You eat. Except for river crab and cat fish, this the only thing you get until we get to Momma Wise but that's a long way off. You puny. Can't see where Linkun's going to win the war with the likes of you, even if he gets you back." Eban slammed the turnip down into the white palm. "You eat, or I make you eat."

The Yank studied it. "I used to call it 'devil shit' and my mother slapped my face and sent me from the table."

"Close you eyes and eat it."

The Yank bit off a nugget, but it caught in the back of his throat and lodged there. He rolled his tongue up and swallowed hard, but gagged it back up, then spit it out into the creek. Eban was disgusted with him, but said nothing.

The Yank swore, "No more sweet potatoes—not mashed, boiled, parched, baked, or fried. The next man to force one of those obnoxious turnips on me will need a heavenly miracle to put him back together."

Eban clucked, "For all your grit, you just a white bread boy."

"I'd be just fine with a little jerky and hardtack."

"Got none of you fancy white army food." Eban shook his head. "Suit youself. When you get hungry enough it taste good." Eban pocketed the Yank's share, trudged passed the uppity little spindle in borrowed clothes, and lumbered down stream until he disappeared around the bend.

But the Yank could not sit here and wait for a ride from Saint Christopher. With what seemed like boulders tied to his ankles, Christie pushed down stream. He had not gone far, when he heard them, just beyond a growth of reeds.

"Well, whose boy be you?" a stranger asked.

"I ain't nobody's boy." It was Eban and he stuttered fitfully.

"Uh huh, you a runaway!" the voice drawled.

"I got a pass! I show you."

"Well, it just don't matter, cause I can't read. So I will have to just guess what the papih says, and I says that it ain't no pass. So I says you is a runaway! Makes sense to me, you bein' out here by youself!"

A sod-busting brat feeling himself a man had cornered Eban, and to keep him cornered, Christie guessed he must be armed.

"Yep, that's how I reads it—a runaway, with a bounty I expect. How much you worth, Sambo? One hundred fifty dollar? Yeah, I bet ever bit that." From the whine of the gun being primed, Christie guessed it to be of a large gauge, decrepit and unreliable—go off by accident as fast as by intent. "What you worth dead, boy? Fifty?"

"You a might small for a bounty hunter." Eban was playing the stalling game too. Ripples of creek water coiled around the pile of drift on which the boy sat. The Yank must be coming on, but he better hurry, the boy was getting impatient. " M a uncle is the bounty man. Me, I just fish and trap ta put food on the table. But today is ma lucky day. I catch a big fish. Money is money, no matta how smull the fisherman. It's the fish that count. You a big 'un, a good catch fur the day. Now why dun't you jus muv ahead and we'll go up ta the shack und meet ma uncle. Then he cun do his business with you, the sooner the better fa all uf us."

Eban cursed. The ripples had stopped. The soldier would be holdin' back, playin' possum, countin' chances, even thinking better to save his own skin. Eban wished he had treated the Yank with more patience, be of a mind to come on the quick.

"What you growlin' about, boy?"

"Don't matter much no more!"

"No, I guess it dun't at that."

Christie slid to the right, his telltale tracks disappeared into the eddies slicing around the sand bar on which the boy roosted. Christie could see the outline of him now through the brill of reeds, his fishing line was drifting out in the channel.

"You ain't goin' to shoot me are you, farmer boy?"

"I'd hate ta du that—git only half what ya worth. But a smart sum still again," the boy spit.

"I ain't no runaway. I got papers, like I said." Eban reached inside his shirt.

"Naw, I wouldn't do that. You just stand up there straight,

face around and make fa the bank. You stay ahead uf me, but not too fa." The boy let the gun cradle in his lap until he could pull himself up. With his finger now off the trigger, Christie lunged through the reeds, catching the boy's neck between his hands, pushing him into the eddy. The soldier came after, skidding over the rocks and under the submerged tangle of drift.

The boy's wits were sharp. By reflex he smashed the Yank's face into a rock. But Christie jerked, and with his good leg kicked the boy away. He caught a strand of the swirling fishing line and wrapped a length around each palm. The boy pulled his skinning knife and sliced through the murky silt, but Christie slithered out of reach. They grappled as the suction of the vortex pulled them deeper. Eban lost them in the mushrooming mud and sand. The guide broke off a stump and held it high, ready for the sodbuster to break through the surface and put an end to his dreams of bounty.

A blond head bobbed, spewing mud, sand, and invectives in equal profusion. Eban's club dropped away. Only a Yankee soldier could swear like that. Immense black hands grabbed the soldier by the shoulders and sent him flying onto the bank.

"Stupid! That what you are." He examined Christie's leg; the stitches had broken through. "I can't believe no government in its right mind would give you a gun. You ain't got the brains God gave goats." Eban pressed a rag to the wound. "You are a fool. You nearly scared me to death. What were you doin' down there? You let him sucker you down into that hole." Then he tied the bandanna tight. "This creek full of holes." The incision still drained bloody water, and he cinched the knot tighter. "There could have been a gator down in that hole!"

"Get your hands off me!" Blood ran from his mouth and nose, which Christie wiped on his shirttail. "Were you going to just stand by and watch that boy drown me? Did he come up anywhere?"

The surface was foam and floating drift. Eban reached for the cane pole still hung up in the reeds. Together they pulled and jerked and finally, the boy came up by the neck. He was dead. They bore out a grave under the mandrake roots and stuffed the body inside. Christie wanted to get away, but the fight had taken all he had. His muscles were lead, his stitches were on fire, and he was still hungry. The Yank was beyond sermons, beyond apologies, and well beyond the reeds, agile for an invalid where food was concerned. The boy's lunch, but the entire inventory was a share of cornmeal and sweet potatoes tied off in a towel.

Eban grabbed them. "We eat them later!"

"Like hell..."

"Now, I got something you like. You wait. I was bringin' it when I was interfered with." Eban tore across the creek, up the bank, and through the cane. The Yank was not in suspense long. When Eban returned, his face was as bright and shiny as a torch. In a grand gesture, Eban thrust a fist into the Yank's face and slowly uncoiled his fingers.

"All this for sand? Sand?" Christie looked closer, "I save your life and you want me to eat sand... and pebbles?" Christie thought Eban unbalanced from the sun. The big black hand snapped back to square under Christie's nose. Frosted amber beads bespectacled in the sunlight vibrated in Eban's palm. Christie shook his head emphatically, "I don't know what that little specimen is, but I am not going to eat it!"

Eban nodded, "Uh huh."

Christie flushed, "You people down here have strange habits — miracle you survived so long."

Eban wet the tips of his thumb and finger, pinched a nugget between them, and brought it to his lips. He bit away something and spit it out. The rest he sucked back, swallowed lazily, and rolled his eyes euphorically. He wiped juice oozing down his jaw with his hands. "Sugar ants! Try!" Eban left no misunderstanding that now he had had enough of the Yank's fussing.

"You're crazy if...those aren't gum drops in your hand. Probably droppings of an unholy sort."

"You eat or I will stuff them down your mouth!"

"Ah, the sweet voice of command." Christie mocked, but Eban's face was inviolate.

The Yank closed his eyes with dread, holding the nugget only inches from his tongue. Eban grabbed the frozen digit and slammed toward the soldier's lips. Christie took it in a lump sum.

"Damned white-bread soldier. Don't eat the ant! Spit the ant out." Eban whacked the back of Christie's neck with a force that nearly toppled him over. Christie tried to cough it up, but it was too late, the ant went down."

"Try another. Bite off the ant and spit it out, then swallow back the rest."

Christie obeyed only because he knew his whole future depended on passing this test here and now. If he refused, he would never see Grant, never see the end of the war, never see home.

"Die in the land of plenty 'cause of fool stubbornness. Just stupid. Be you Moses, you would refuse manna for bird droppings. No wonder Yankees got no slaves—got not enough brains for their own self. Stiff-necked people."

Christie selected a small one. This time he was careful to bite off the ant and spit it out, before slipping the rest into his mouth. But he did not swallow, not right away. Instead, he let it ride on his tongue to test it. It turned to syrup. "Honey!" The soldier reached for a second helping. "You are a gourmet, Eban!"

"Gourmet" was not in Eban's vocabulary, but he liked its tone and took it as a compliment. "Sugar ants—like I said. Down around the bend, lots of 'em. They gorge themselves on the sweet milk from the flowers and blossoms, and take it back to the hive down in the ground. As good as bees, but not so cantankerous."

"You are a marvel of enterprise." The Yank saluted. All grudges forgotten, Eban accepted the recognition as overdue.

That was not all. From his pocket Eban pulled out a hand full of berries. They were slightly bruised, but mendicants aren't choosers. The two picnicked from the bounty as they trudged on their way down stream—the sweet potatoes happily forgotten.

As they passed Eban pointed to a space of parched earth. "That's what sugar ant hive look like. You know it for next time."

"I hope there will not be a next time. I plan to get my old job back on Grant's staff, play solitaire with the general's papers, and be the best military bureaucrat that ever was. I want never so much as to get my boots dirty."

"Life of a planter boy."

"I think I have been insulted...yeah, I know I have."

Theirs was a truce—not a friendship by any means, but an understanding that Eban was in charge for the time being. There was a respect for what the black man could teach him, and in return a respect for the Yank's mission.

The creek was ever changing with every mile. By turns it was serene and frenzied. Here, it was wide and lazy where coots and mallards paddled in tea-colored pools held back by dams of rock and debris. Yards further the channel could narrow, fed to overflowing by springs and runoff. The current surged well up to their hips nearly sweeping them over. Coiling eddies like the one that had nearly drowned Christie bid caution every bit as much as the stagnant water, its crest foamy with moss and grit. Then Eban led a safer track overland through razor-sharp brush, the domain of savage insects. When the going was too thick even to hack a narrow path, they would splash back into the current to half-swim and half-trudge over foot-slashing rocks and logjams of debris. Just as their resolve had all but run out, the water would turn velvet and serene around the next bend. This lasted never very long and the two fugitives would be again fighting for every yard.

Vines of ivy coiled up massive trunks and spiraled over limbs to secret every species of bird—and would have gone undetected—except for their bleating and cawing. The jungle hid cottonmouths, rattlesnakes and alligators that Eban scouted for. And then there was the pug-sized boar with the manners of a drunken overseer that challenged their right of way to a land bridge. Later a flush of quail and then two squirrels scooted just ahead of a panther not yet hungry enough to conceal her movements. Coming at a safe distance, a red wolf and two tiny cubs bobbed their heads above the tangle, and then disappeared in the reeds again.

Near evening they supped on hard berries. The Yank said they tasted like bitter coffee, but the juice put electricity through his slack muscles. When they stopped again, Christie was covered in rashes. The beans still made him too jumpy to rest and he itched to distraction, so they kept on. Eban would not say how far it was to Momma Wise, but he gave signs that they were coming close. The leg looked bad. Although Eban had tied it off tight at the groin, the stain on the Yank's trousers ran red in the water.

Toward evening, the breezes flushed the woods, raising the scent of the runaways in the direction of a kennel of plantation hounds. They barked furiously. Eban froze, but the Yank put a steadying hand on his shoulder. "About feeding time. Meat of a different sort will get them to stop in a minute."

"If they don't..." Eban stood ready to carry the soldier back into the untraceable wilds. But the Yank was right. The rhythmic croak of bullfrogs and the orchestra of locusts and crows soothed Eban's alarm, and they started again. "Momma Wise is close now."

"You have said that before—about thirty miles back, and ten miles ever after."

"True enough—and I was right, she was closer every time I said it."

The Yank admitted that indeed he was right.

All afternoon the clouds had been luminescent as pearls, now they were dull gray thunderheads, pulsating with lightning. The scent of ozone, tainted with dust and sweat, buffeted his face. Eban's reaction was intuitive rather than educated. His forehead furrowed, he could not see for the tall grass, only hear. On his own, the Yank was heading out into the road, but the guide heaved him back behind cover. "Wait!"

With Eban pressing him against the tree, there was nothing for Christie to do but wait. By reflex he cursed, but Eban slapped a hand over his mouth. Through gaps in the sword grass they saw them come on. A line of dust-covered skeletal horses trotted around the bend two at a time, to a count of ten. They were ridden by a squad of mismatched men, loaded down with shotguns and sabers, and hypnotized to senselessness by the rhythmic pounding and rocking of their mounts.

After they had passed, Eban dropped his hand from the soldier's mouth. "You damned lucky to have me. I just wish I had a me to save my butt on the way back." The Yank answered nothing in defense. Still braced against the oak, Christie had fallen asleep. Eban wrestled a better grip. A low whine and a flutter of eyelashes were all that told of the agony the soldier was in.

"Why don't you save youself a mess of misery and die? You can't have any sins not cleaned three times over, no matter what you done." Eban buffeted Christie's sunburned cheek; the eyes did not even flutter. "All right. You sleep, white boy. I get you there soon now."

XIV
Sanctuary Road

They were roadway signs to a cold harbor. A towel whipped at its cinch around the fence post. In the hollow, a rag doll, nothing more than a twist of muslin around an old sock, jerked at the end of a rope tethered to a bough in a sycamore. The scrap of towel gave the all-clear for the pilgrims to come on. The doll, however, was no talisman of her culture or her religion, which had been Mennonite. But it conjured up a superstitious foreboding to encroachers and by rule they took the long way around the land measured between the red stakes. They were wise to be tactful. Momma Wise had demonstrated a steadfastness to hold these last few acres of what once was her family's cotton plantation. Now what she lived on, what she wore, what she squeezed out of the ground, and what she prayed for — were all scraps, like the towel and the doll. She mourned what was dead every day.

The good land had gone to Andrew Jackson's land-hungry white planters according to the conditions of the Treaty of Dancing Rabbit Creek. In 1833, three years after the treaty was signed, her husband left her to move with the last of the Choctaw to Oklahoma. Jackson would have moved her with him if she had not been stubborn and sly; she had outmaneuvered the drunken land agents and held on. Here she would stay, no matter what now came. She looked up and down, but there was no sign of comers, and she went inside out of the rain.

There was no one, man or woman, white or black, that Eban admired more than Momma Wise — or feared. Under the expansive live oak that made midnight out of the evening dusk, the cypress cottage with its daub and river-biscuit chimney huddled in dark relief. The glow from its windows was the only beacon. Eban banged a spoon against the hanging tub to announce himself. With no more warning, he kicked back the door, and with the soldier bouncing on his back like a peddler's pack, strode inside as if he were expected. He was, for the lone woman stirring the caldron did not even look his way. Eban eased his burden on the floor where the fire could warm him — the spring storm had made the last miles wet and chilly. The white man favored his battered leg, but otherwise lay as he had fallen, as lifeless as a corpse. The woman, nonplused about this invasion, brushed back the cascade of charcoal-colored hair from her flat bronze forehead to examine the gift her former slave had presented her.

"I ain't goin' be able to take him no further. I should be back two nights already, so be late four days when I do." Eban, without invitation, took the ladle from her hand, patted her long tattooed arm, and then filled a bowl from the caldron simmering over the iron spider.

She had been warned that two fugitives were tending her way, one was Eban and the other a white but that was all. "You walked him nearly to death. Where does he come from?"

"Mister Collin bid me bring him to Father Lyons, but the blue soldier, this 'Christie' he calls himself, wanted to come this way. No talkin' him out of it and I couldn't just leave him there to die—might be caught and give me away. And even at that Mister Collin never trust me again. Now he your problem."

"Blue soldier?"

Eban let the spoon stop its hungry business, but for only a second. "Yankee."

With armies on the move, forage patrols on the prowl, bushwhackers, raiders, scavengers, and deserters roaming the countryside, she did not want to be found giving protection to a Yankee. She made that known with a scowl that said volumes—all of which Eban ignored. He knew that Mister Collin had power over her as they both had power over him. He pointed to the project that brought them together, the Yank. If Mister Collin had found something in this man worth saving, she had better be about doing it. Life was fading out of him; his breath would not shoo a feather.

"Fetch some spring water from the creek." Eban was slow to comply, and she ordered again. "The bucket is by the door, if you did not shatter it with your clumsiness." Then she went to her shelves. The cabin was an apothecary of nostrums—herbs and blossoms drying from the beams. She gathered up a few ingredients and turned to the fire with her mortar and pestle.

"You gonna take him out to the sick house?"

"No, better he stay here." As a last warning for Eban to get to, she pointed to the door.

Her authority held sway. Eban found the path between the goat pen and the chicken house. He brushed away the vines, red root, and morning glories snaking up the shed and along the fence enclosing Momma Wise's herb garden. White and orange poppies swayed in company with the other precious plants she grew by the deep clear spring of sweet water. The ripples coiled beyond the cove to blend with the syrupy headwaters that became the Big Black River.

The blue soldier was her problem now. He had told the Yank that Momma Wise was an "alikchi," which was true enough, just about the best—man or woman. But the less he knew of the reputation of Choctaw doctors, the better. If old legends were to be believed, a patient had to be wary. These were not medicine men who dealt in spells or prophecies but medicinal healers. Many healers were good, better than white doctors. But the less honorable treated their patients only as long as the family could pay, or the doctor thought his medicine good. Some families used to go crazy when a relative died and they killed the doctor because his medicine was bad. If the outcome was iffy the Choctaw doctor hedged his bets. If an invalid did not seem to revive, took a turn for the worse, or was slow to pay, the Choctaw doctor warned the family that the patient had seen the "shilup" in a dream. A fox or an owl had come for his spirit and nothing could save him. True or not, that could be the end of it. The family would confer with the sick one—if he could speak for himself. If not and the family came to the same conclusion as the doctor, they would spare the patient unnecessary suffering and strangle him to death. Eban thought his discretion wise, no need for the Yank to worry about Momma Wise's medicine—or worry that he would wake up in the middle of the night with her fingers around his throat.

Eban bent to wash his face. Then he drunk his fill, and filled the bucket. Not to raise her wrath this time, he pressed the door open quietly. The tiger cat scampered between his legs, as slick as a thief, content from its feast. Eban cursed himself for having left his bowl on the floor. The woman was fully absorbed in the needs of her patient, so without a word Eban set the pail beside her. She wet a towel in the clear water, and more tenderly than could have been imagined for arms so muscled and a face so stern, patted away the dust and grime from the soldier's face.

"Who is he?"

"He's the archangel Gabriel goin' to take us to the Promised Land. Archangels just comin' a little smaller these days." Eban called from the hearth where he was refilling his bowl with gumbo.

"Don't sass me. Why is this boy so important to Mister Collin?"

At times such as these Eban remembered she was Charity Dunross before she was Momma Wise, a mixed blood as much Irish and Scot as she was Choctaw—and not at any time given to humility or patience. Eban shook his head. "Don't sell him short. He may be puny, but he badger-mean and sly. You be careful. He be one of them cavalry raiders that scared the daylights out of Starkville when they came flyin' through few weeks back. Got himself shot. Doctor Bennett and Miss Carolina saved him and gave him the will to live."

Momma Wise nodded. "Sight of Miss Carolina even still do more good than anything in that doctor's shelf to make a boy rethink dying. Why she let him off before he healed?"

"He was goin' to be shot, I hear tell. Doctor Bennett found him in Miss Carolina's bed, but without Miss Carolina. So I don't know what that means—not that he could be any match for Miss Carolina even on a good day. Curious business, but Mister Collin thought him worth saving and got him away before Doctor Bennett could lynch him."

If the word "skeptical" were in Eban's power, he would have used it to describe the look Momma Wise now fixed on him. But that was all he knew, and then he wasn't sure he had even that right. "He was pinker when we set out. The walk wore him down to nothin' but nerve. That leg look bad. You goin' to cut it off? I ain't stayin' around to hold him for you. Too late. And I think it too late for him too. Expected him to give up and die anytime, but didn't. Wouldn't. Just kept mumblin' somethin' about meetin' Sherman and Grant. I don't know yet what that means. I brung him this far. Got to go back."

"And where was he supposed to meet these men?"

Eban shrugged his shoulders. "Somewhere on the Big Black, he said."

"Where? That stretches from out back all the way to

Bruinsburg." So far Momma Wise had not heard anything she liked. "A Yankee, you say? Mighty little David he is, the Union going to need a lot of these shepherds to beat the planters' army." She pulled off the bandanna. The leg was swollen, red-streaked, and foaming with puss and mud. If he had been bleeding for four days, the boy couldn't have much blood left, so she would not cup and bleed him more. He wheezed like a steam kettle and he was hot all over. She shook her head and grumbled under her breath, "If not for the leg, I would put him in the sweat box. Strip him down."

Eban did as he was told. Momma Wise pulled clean rags from a basket then gathered more bowls and jars of salves and herbs. She washed away the layers of blood and dirt, then washed him down again. He lay beneath her ministrations compliant and quiet—except for a sigh or gasp when even her gentle touch was too much. She covered his legs in blankets, then cooled his face again. He licked the water from his lips hungrily. She blotted away the salt welts and soothed the blisters. She continued to bathe his face long after it was clean.

"You are nothing more than a bag of bones."

Eban shrugged his shoulders. "These folks called Grant and Sherman—he'd better find them or the folks is gonna string him up if they find him first. You got to get 'em well and get 'em to his own people for the good of all of us." Eban rolled his eyes to the direction of the rafters. "He got plenty of ideas and he's a lieutenant—thinks we all got to do what he says."

Momma Wise stifled a smile. "Well, I am in no army but my own. He won't be giving no orders around here."

Eban was now satisfied that the woman would adopt this sorry lame pup, even if he would be a test of her powers to the fullest. She would do what she could to make him well, just to show him who was boss. Eban counted himself blessed to have seen the daughter of his old master again. Old days were good, new days were confused. He crossed the pitted wooden floor, then paused with his hand on the latch to look back, as if she and this place would all extinguish like a candle flame as soon as he was gone.

He opened the door. The electrified winds of the by-gone storm blew full in his face. The scent of freedom! The soldier shivered on the floor. The want of it brought him here, even if it nearly killed him. The blue soldier was running for it—why not himself? Eban had helped others of the same mind. Never thought his life was that bad...to escape himself. But how bad was that? Yet, Rachel was waiting for him. But she was free—could come or go at will. Meet him somewhere north, if she was of a mind. This was his chance. Except for his promise to Mister Collin, but Mister Collin had no chains.

Momma Wise did not hear the door close. She was berating her old neighbor, who had more heart than sense. Debts long unpaid now lay before her on the floor. Mister Collin picked a bad time to collect. It was over ten years ago when the floods had washed out the white poppies and she had no opium to give her daughter when she had her baby. When she needed morphine and chincona bark, or what the white doctors called "quinine," Momma Wise could do nothing but humble herself and call at the house of her cousin Anne, the wife of the doctor. Times past she would have come in the afternoon light and been admitted through the front door as an esteemed neighbor and relation. But with her land and position gone, she had put her pride in her apron pocket by her own decision rather than her cousin's preference. So Momma Wise had come at night to the back door. Rachel would understand, speak for her.

But young Mister Collin had answered instead. He stood there open faced, small and delicate even for thirteen. His mother was resting and could not be disturbed. "But I am your servant, madam, how can I help?" He bowed gallantly. She related that her business was earnest, her daughter and granddaughter suffered with fever. She needed these two medicines, so would he please fetch his mother? Soon he himself came back with the precious quinine and morphine. He offered no explanation, only asked she not mention it to anyone. The baby had lived but her daughter had not.

Not again would she depend on any white man for medicines. She grew her own and bargained her family ring for the cinchona bark from a Peruvian sailor in New Orleans. Out of respect to the young master, she had come back that winter to bring foxglove tea when Missis Bennett was heartsick. But the tea did not help, her heart exploded anyhow.

Momma Wise had not seen the son again until the summer trees were mellowing into autumn—a young man struggling with a grieving son's tears. He was standing over his mother's grave and would not be consoled. She had reached across their two worlds, with an old tradition. "Once a relative dies, a Choctaw never mentions the name again. When I see you suffer, I feel there is hard wisdom in that...in shutting the door on the past. You must do the same. If you need me ever, for any reason, you send word."

All these things Momma Wise told the sleeping soldier, keeping up a gentle stream of talk to get him to hear, to open his eyes, to come back to the living. She smoothed more salve of river fish over the festering sores. The soldier did not need the cinchona, for he did not shake from the ague, but he was hot and his chest was heaving like the bellows. She boiled willow bark tea with desiccated radishes and made him drink. If it didn't cool him, the ivy tea might, she would brew that later. He sputtered, choked, and turned away. Doctor and patient struggled with the virulent stuff; he pushing it away and she making him take it. He splashed more of it on her than she got down him, but in the end she won.

She scolded him for scratching the salves away from the bites. She ground more from the crushed sage, dried potatoes, and peanut oil, lathering it thickly over his legs and hands and wrapping them in clean spun cotton. Before he left she would give him a poultice of wormwood and apple cider to keep the mosquitoes off—it was better than the vinegar the soldiers used. With tender, expert hands, she wrapped him in a white blanket cooled in peppermint-scented water. Then she let him sleep.

The Choctaw doctor then tended to business outside. At the tree, she replaced the calico kerchief with a solid red one, and on the clothesline hung a muslin shirt. The message: the cargo has arrived, one man, and now a conductor was requested.

She went to the compost pile to scoop out the fattest maggots and set them into her pail. Inside, she cleaned them delicately, and set them gently in the festering bullet wound. The larvae nestled in the folds to feed on the dead skin and drainage. She covered him again and the soldier slept fitfully. Momma Wise toweled away the perspiration from his cheeks. Later, she pressed the bowl of tea to his mouth. Again, he fought it, but surrendered sooner this time.

"Momma Wise is sergeant now, Yankee boy," she smiled knowingly.

Then the healer let him drift in the arms of the lady whom he called within his fever. Momma Wise leaned back against the cabin wall, closed her eyes, and hummed a prayer.

The soldier slept, but not alone. He escaped to a twilight world far removed from the cabin where Julie and those he called Jamie, Quinn, and Nolan came to him. As the medicines took hold, he sunk deeper and stayed with them until past sun down the next day.

The shutters were already closed against the cool evening drafts when he awoke, naked under his blanket. He asked no questions of the exotic woman and she gave him no answers. He was well beyond explanations. She could have poisoned him twice over, but didn't. Eban could have left him stranded, but didn't. Collin could have let his father shoot him, or the neighbors hang him, but didn't.

"I feel the South is a series of stops on Sanctuary Road," he said by way of thank you for the bowl of peppery gumbo that made his eyes steam.

"You don't make sense." She looked up from her own dinner, suspicious of anyone speaking in riddles.

The Yank found that very funny. "Ma'am, someone only lately warned me about sense. So I found it cumbersome with everything else I had to carry, and no one else was carrying any. I found sense of no use in translating purposes and deeds in this war. But if you insist, I'll come back and get it before I go home."

"Where you going, Lieutenant?" She knew but wondered if he did.

The answer startled her even though. "South—and as soon as I'm able." He would travel wherever the creek took him, around or through the Rebel army and anything else that got in his way, till he found Grant.

It wasn't that the soldier had no sense—he was insane. "Mister Collin said to take you north on the Underground," she corrected severely. "Finding your little army in the middle of so many other armies all scraping at each other is like finding a pet alligator in a creek of them. How will you tell before it's too late?"

The soldier would not be put off. "I mean to meet up with

him and General Tecumseh Sherman somewhere comin' or going. They are riding with a big army."

"Mister Collin said I was to help you go north. That I mean to do."

"Then I will go by my own means!" He pushed the empty bowl away. The long sleeves of the unbleached muslin shirt she had given him fell over his wrists, and he pushed them back self-consciously. He looked very small and weak for such a long mission.

Eban had warned he bore watching. "How you going to find this General Grant and what's-his-name Sherman?"

"I'll find them."

It was a revelation. A general named for the warrior Tecumseh leading an army right toward her back yard. "Jubilee!" she breathed. "Your General Grant be Eban's Moses?"

"No!" the soldier snapped.

"He is not here to lead the dark people out of bondage?"

"No, he is here to defeat the Rebels. I hear that your people are soldiers fighting under the Cross of St. Andrew."

She nodded. "Mounted scouts fight with General Maury now. Some lost at New Orleans and were taken to prison in New York. Many Oklahoma Choctaw fight with Stand Watie in Arkansas. My sons are just down the river with the Mississippi First Choctaw—they hold against your General Grant. You, my young Lieutenant, are my sons' enemy. So what should I do with you?"

He parried with a challenge of his own. "My father used to say that the Choctaw was like a man who took refuge in a burning house to get out of the rain."

Momma Wise realized that the lieutenant must understand her history very well—a paradox balanced precariously on the apex of a pyramid. The Choctaw nation had never raised an angry hand against Americans, but it had always found itself on the wrong side of their prevailing interests. At first they had sided with the Spanish against the French, and the Spanish left. They had cast their lot then with the French against the British, and the French were driven out. Then the Spanish came back briefly, but were of no help. Then again the British, by now against the Americans in their war for independence, and the

British lost. Even when they had chosen right in 1814, a Choctaw chief commanding his own at Old Hickory's side at New Orleans—they lost in the long run. Andrew Jackson soon forgot their alliance in the clamor of land seekers and forced most of the Civilized Tribes to resettle beyond the Mississippi.

In 1861, President Jefferson Davis had signed a treaty to ally the Choctaw with the birth of this new Confederacy. He promised once the war was won they would gain representation in their Congress and win back much of what they had lost under the presidents in Washington. She was not sure she believed it. How much vote could they carry in any white Congress? These same planters had taken away her plantation in the first place, and they fought for the Confederacy. If they won, would they allow their lands be taken away by their government? Why would they fight if not for their land and more land for their children? Where would that land come from? How could both sides be appeased? Why would Richmond take from them to give to the Indians? It did not add up.

None of the omens were good. When the end came, and with the Union Army riding at will through Mississippi, it seemed inevitable now—Washington would free Eban's people. But Washington would not be kind to her people, who had taken up arms against it.

"I am squeezed between two mountains," Momma Wise said.

"President Lincoln is a kind man. Do not underestimate him."

The doctor pulled down a rag doll from the rough-hewn mantle. It was well embroidered, even if sewn from a sock and dressed in a yellow and green dress of faded silk. Momma Wise caressed its braided cotton pigtails. "I have no faith left in Washington or Richmond."

She broke off, and what she said now broke all barriers and taboos, but she doubted he would live long enough for it to matter. "My daughter ran off and lay with an African at the Bovey plantation. She did not know him to be so—he was nearly white and looked like the master and the master had so many sons. Times were very bad and he said he would marry her and move her into the big house. She knew no different, which sons were spawned in the big house and which in the slave cabins. But he said he was the favorite of his father. That might be so, but he was Negro all the same. The seed gave her a daughter. She named for me but we called her Sunflower. My daughter brought her to life right where you are now and not in the birthing house out back. My daughter was so tiny and the baby took too long. By the time it came, it was too much. For two weeks, she lay with her child in her arms, stroking its big round face, forcing smiles right away. She warmed it with her own milk and sang it songs until she bled away. She was not seventeen."

Momma Wise nestled the doll in her arms and hummed a lullaby that Christie found odd to his ear.

"All I had was this little baby. I bought the goats for milk and made out all right. The baby was mine for three...almost four years. As soon as she could talk she asked so many questions: 'Where does lightning go in such a hurry?' 'Why do ducks float?'

"I said lightning sleeps in the clouds until noisy children wake it up and thunder was its rage. Ducks are full of soap bubbles to keep from sinking. She laughed at my answers, called me 'Momma Wise.' That is the name I have kept for it was the greatest compliment I ever received."

She mastered her grief only with great effort, and would not even admit to the tears that gathered in the corners of her eyes. Christie lowered his head not to see, but he did see.

"Then Master Bovey come. He said my child is spawn of his slave and the baby was his by law. By Choctaw law, the child belongs with her mother's family. But he had men with guns and dogs, so he could take my grandchild...my little flower. He wrapped her in his arms and put her up on his horse. Said that I should move to Oklahoma and forget about the child. I could do nothing while they rode away, she crying my name all the while. She would be almost fifteen now, and what would she remember of me and her ways?"

"I am sorry."

"Sorry? How much is that worth? Will President Lincoln help me find her and give her back to me? Is she Negra or is she Choctaw? My people will not accept her as theirs. But she is mine and I am theirs. As Choctaw, I can lose the last scrap of land I fought for, if the Confederacy dies. But if it wins I could lose it anyhow. If my sons come home defeated, what will they own? As Sunflower's grandmother my hope is with the Union that will free all slaves, but will it enslave my sons? What do I pray for?"

The soldier had no answers. For him the war had been so clear—it was a battlefield with an army at either end; the enemy was the man aiming his gun at you. There were no other considerations. You kill him before he could kill you. Only lately had Christie come to see that there were too many wars wrapped up in this one to ever see mending them all. He said nothing. Momma Wise sat with her back to him. He closed his eyes and dreamed himself to another place.

Momma Wise shook her head. Maybe the guide would not come or perhaps would not take him. The thought made her queasy—very dangerous now, with the war boiling. And he said he would not go north. The soldier could not go alone anywhere, that was clear. Wandering around out there to be captured and made to talk, then the whole thing would be up. She did not like this business, had not gotten into it until she had no choice. A runaway slave could be crazy if he were not helped and moved on—a soldier was something worse. Their own soldiers who were all fought out, were giving up at the line, and going to Mexico. Now Yankees. No, the Yank would not go alone, and he could not stay here any longer than necessary. She estimated it would take nearly a week to just get him on his feet.

As soon as his fever broke Christie became as impatient as his host. He tried to piece together the days and weeks since the battle at West Point and estimated two weeks had passed. This should be about the first week of May. Grierson would have been up at the mouth of the Big Black to meet Grant. The army should be marching across the state by now. He was itching to be up and gone. He watched the door every time the cat pushed it opened. He listened to the birdcalls, expecting each song to be a signal. But no one came, and Momma Wise kept pouring her potions and teas down his throat. He slept and ate—and waited.

"You leave when it is safe and not before. You rest while you can—not all your harbors will be as kind as mine." She would give him something else to think about. "You mark my word, they don't like whites down here of any kind. Planters are suspicious;

field hands are wary. A strange face has no history and no conscience to count on. You just better than the rest if Mister Collin and I say so. So no lip from you at any time, you hear me, Lieutenant? Soon a conductor will come. She will be skittish—you are going the wrong way. So don't make her curious. I will tell her all she needs to know. You go when she says go, stay when she says stay, and stay as long and where she says stay. You hear? Little Shepherd Boy? Don't think President Lincoln is staying up nights waiting for you. So if you don't come home, it will be of no disappointment to anyone but you and your mother. There's a lot more where you come from."

Christie opened one eye. "As you said, Momma Wise, the Hebrews were led by the likes of a little David. Size doesn't matter when you got faith."

"You got faith, David?"

"I guess I do."

"In the Lord?"

"Yes, some there, some in President Lincoln, some in General Grant—a lot in General Grant—and General Sherman, my old regiment, the rest in myself—that amounts to enough for present purposes."

"What about this Julie? You got faith in her?" She watched his reaction slyly.

"How do you know about her?" Christie pushed the subject away without seeming to care, which did not fool her.

"You call her to be at your side in your sleep, that's how. No offense in conjuring her name—she's good medicine. Is she your wife?"

"No!"

"Going be your wife?"

"No. God must have not thought me worthy. He was probably listening to my mother's advice." Christie pulled his blankets to his chin, for suddenly he was cold. "He just gave her to me long enough to inspire me to be a good man for her sake, to want her for the rest of my life—then He took her away and gave her to another man. Why should you care?"

"Then it seems you have little faith in this God of yours." Momma took the empty platter from him. "You want more rabbit? Fatten those bones."

He shook his head. More would give her time to ask questions to which he had no answers. With impatience churning inside him, and the fury of lightning and thunder crashing over his head, he found little sleep and nothing to dream on. Julie did not come and Christie held Momma Wise accountable.

The storm had worn itself out to a fine drizzle when the guide knocked on the door. She was wet, weary, and edgy as a doe. She stood off in a corner with Momma Wise, listening to instructions she clearly did not like.

"South? Not south! North! By the polar star!"

Momma Wise shook her head vehemently and repeated her instructions more forcefully this time. The young woman held back and put her hand on the latch to leave. The Choctaw woman pushed the door closed.

"He has no sense! We will be caught! If we are hanged, what good would that do the rest that follow?" she hissed. "I will not take him!"

When her patience was exhausted—Christie estimated that there was never a great reserve of it at the best of times—her luminous blue eyes narrowed to slits. Her face and body hardened, and down deep she growled, "You will do what I tell you." The young woman backed away. She still did not agree but she came to terms with it.

When she was sure that the guide would not fail her, Momma Wise motioned she wait outside, and then went to the sideboard. She pushed a loaf of fresh bread, a knot of jerky, and a jar of preserves into his sack. "Eat the squirrel first, save the cold rabbit and venison. I do not have a map, but you will not need one—Sarah knows the way and is reliable. I will not forgive you if you let anything happen to her or any of the others who will help you." The woman turned, her face suddenly soft. Christie thought she would embrace him, and he would have been warmed by some tenderness now. Instead, she held out the gunnysack and he took it. "I fear for you, little David, I do not think you will make it. Your visions and dreams—for it all you are a lone fox shot in the night. It tells me much." Her authority was so strong he believed for the first time that this might be true. "If you see that you do not, I want you to send Sarah or the others away before it is too late. Your fate is of your own making, not theirs. Do you understand?"

He did. Then she went on, "I hear your General Grant has landed in the bottomlands below the river. You do not know where that is but that does not matter because he will not lay there like some lazy hound on the doorstep. Which way he will march I do not know." She caught his surprise. "Yes, I know of him. I am not so alone as you think."

Remembering the map and the sweep of blue lines he saw so long ago, "I know where!" Too late he bit his tongue—the absolute stupidity to admit such intelligence. Momma Wise would be paid well by General Pemberton for such information or, even better, providing the man who knew.

It was an eternity before she continued, "Sarah will take you to the next station. She knows what to do. Be patient. A child born in the fields does not always come out right. Her mind dances sometimes, but she is strong. You'll see." She walked him out the door and passed a lantern to the girl.

Christie reached out to take her hand, and Momma Wise carefully closed his firmly in her fingers. "Little David, you must be humble and find this faith you have lost. Find it in something that will last—you will need it before this war is over." Then she pulled a handkerchief to blindfold him. "Sarah will take this off when you are far enough not to find your way back. Do not try to come back here. If we see each other—and I do not think we will—do not admit we were ever acquainted." She tightened the knot behind his head. Before Sarah took charge of him, Momma Wise bent close to his ear. "You're wrong, Christie." It was the first time she had ever spoken his name, "Jubilee will come with your General Grant, we each will have to make of it what we can—you, Eban and I."

"We leave now." His guide clasped his arm. Momma Wise let him go and his journey began. Sarah pulled him along, at times telling him to raise his feet over a branch, at others to step wider over a channel of runoff, to turn to the left or the right. She was not only his eyes and ears, but also his brain. It could not have been very long when she stopped to unbind his eyes. It made no difference, by now it was night. She tethered him around the waist. "We'll not lose each other in the darkness."

With the North Star at her back, the tiny woman moved

along the edge of the pastures and cotton fields as deftly as a mountain cat, sure of her way for having traveled the inner weavings of these paths all her life. The drizzle warmed to steam. When it grew too dark for her to see at all, she lit the lamp and shrouded it. This pale glow at her feet was her only guide, but she never lost the trail. It was near dawn when the mist turned to rain. The steam kept the day a dull gray fog. If at all, she quickened her pace. When she walked she tilted her frame to the left to compensate for one leg being slightly shorter than the other.

The whole mission of escape was like becoming a soldier all over again. Back in West Virginia all of his training had made him a soldier of the line. Now he was a soldier alone, a skirmisher, a scout without a regiment. He fought alone against the enemy and the people...and the place. He lived only as long as his wits and his courage stayed sharp and he would surrender his fate entirely to no one, not even his guide.

"What is it?" Christie saw nothing remarkable in the tree she studied. Only when she swept her hands over the "X" crossed by two trails of ivy did he understand that it was the signal.

"Not safe to stop here." She curled a lock of her hair around her fingers as she thought. "I was to go only this far."

"I can go on alone! Just tell me where the creek is. Will you be able to get back?"

"Yes, I can get back. Of course I can get back."

"I never thought to insult you," Christie retorted.

"But you, I cannot leave you—where will you go?"

"I'll find my way, I am not helpless. You have done enough, for it I am obliged." Even without the old doctor's warning, he would not push this delicate girl beyond what she bargained for. "The army snakes out for miles. I'll slam into it sooner or later."

She did not seem to be listening, "If I go more south, the Dunbury place is somewheres around there. Calley told me once." She was talking to some inner voice, completely forgetting him until she had made up her mind. Then, emphatically she pointed to the path leading back into the bayou. "We go now."

"All right. You lead the way."

She made no pretense about liking him, but she would see him to another conductor. Christie no longer cared whether she liked him or not, or whether she respected the cause that sent him here or not. "We fight our own wars," he whispered to himself. It was enough to give him pride, even though he felt like some dead weight—like some parcel being handed off on a long line of freight carriers.

The trail broke and swerved through cane and scrub, the path nothing more than a figure of her imagination because he certainly could not have found it on his own. But she followed her inner compass farther from the river, which he estimated to his right somewhere, but he had not seen it in several hours. The morning must have turned to day—his stomach said so—but the sky was still opaque.

It was mile upon mile of walking on faith towed by Sarah, his back rubbing against the tether as she pulled him this way and that. His brain wanted to sleep, and his legs wanted to follow his brain but he shook it awake. The constant dreariness gave it nothing to study, nothing to keep it focused. The dull wet curtain churned and billowed out of the bottomless shadows and gullies. He could see the next step, but the one beyond that was a guess.

There was a turn and then another, and out of the mist suddenly bolted a human form. Christie's hand went for the knife in his boot as the attacker scooped up the girl. Christie set the blade to the back of the attacker's ear. But Sarah giggled, bussed each cheek and encircled her arms around his neck. "You scared me nigh to death, What you doin' here?"

"What *you* doin' here? Heard of comers, not knowin' it be you. Who is *he*?" The man regarded Christie as a skunk found in his trap.

"Calley, the Parker place off limits. We did not stop."

The man knew why, "Patrol closed in. They are keeping an eye on all the Quaker places for runaways. But this here Yankee soldier should bring a prize bounty. Good thing you were not ambushed. You crazy, girl? Out here this far by yourself!"

"She is not by herself." Christie stepped up.

"You're a lion to strike terror and that's for sure." The big man spit.

As it was only this puny invader, Calley signaled his reinforcements out of cover—only one in fact called Zeke. He too had a knife in open sight—Christie had seen smaller blades in sword scabbards. Zeke was a man who would haunt Christie's dreams into old age. It was the eyes and not a mind that ordered the massive body, reacting instinctively to danger with ruthless force. Cornered, he would strike, rather than escape, and strike to kill. From the first, he had not liked this Christie.

Sarah stepped between them and faced the brute. "You stupid, Christie, he could kill you! Calley, you stupid too, but Zeke, you more stupid for blaming this man. I walked him here on my own. I am not sorry to help, and don't make me sorry I come to you. We are hungry and tired, and if patrols prowl the woods, we need to be out of here now."

The big man glared at Christie then back at Sarah. She was right. The three spoke a few words coming to some conclusions among them, and motioned Christie to follow through the forest.

There was no harbor at the next station—pinecones stuffed into a knothole of a tree warned them away. They took refuge deeper into the bayou, exciting a population of bullfrogs to croaking as loud as a locomotive. The crickets and locusts sing-songed in a mind wracking din. Zeke led them into knee-deep black water and through acres of marsh thick with reeds, only to come up to another no vacancy signal. The party again turned to the deep swamps.

"We try the Bovey place. We have no choice, can you make it?" Sarah said she could, and on that, Calley turned left, entering a path over grapevine bridges, reeds and sandbars.

"I can make it too, thanks for your concern." Christie thought better of saying more, but he thought plenty. He would have paid a year's salary plus his pension to speak his mind just then. Why there was such a blame fuss to keep this miserable land in the Union was beyond his comprehension. Cantankerous—people, animals, bears, leeches, and mosquitoes—everything wanted a bite out of you. He squeezed another leech out of his calf, then snapped the rope from his gunny sack and tied his pants' legs snug around his ankles.

Christie's private war was with himself. By absolute necessity he had to all but trust others. He had to do something to keep fatigue away. Even if they did not want his talents, he would give them anyway. He looked to their rear and watched the flanks. The translucent mist was more suspicious than the black night. He second-guessed his eyes with every shadow to keep from humiliating himself by raising false alarms. But with the last fifty yards, he was sure something was moving apace by his left. He motioned to Sarah but she shook him away. Then he must slow them down. Christie said that nature called. That the Yank would think that the entire party would stop was all conceit. Zeke spit and Calley warned they would not wait.

Christie broke through the shallow fen, dropped back and turned parallel with them. He felt like a fool. He wasn't positive he had seen anything more than the shadow of a heron, the satin finish of a big broadleaf, or the glare off a puddle. Good news—he was not addle-brained; bad news—they *were* being stalked. Only one ahead and he waited against a sycamore, watching Calley and Sarah coming on. Calley passed and Sarah was nearly dead even when the attacker struck. But Christie pounced first and slammed the ruffian against the hulk of the tree, Collin's knife in hand.

"Settle down, friend." Christie called just loud enough for the others to hear.

"Friend is it?" The man twisted, but Christie jerked the arm up hard enough to make him curse. "All right—you win. Calley, get the hell over here before this jackass takes off my good ear with his toothpick!"

The leader broke through the bush, his own knife drawn. Sarah coming behind him was also armed, a condition Christie had not considered. In the end it was much about nothing,

"Let him go—that's Bovey," Sarah stifled a giggle but not very successfully. "You are ugly enough to scare a man to death but that's about all. He's the conductor on this line. The Yankee caught you this time, you swamp rat."

Bovey growled, "Get that sticker out of my ear."

Christie lowered his blade and Bovey took the advantage. He swung around, jerked the soldier by his crotch, and lifted him off his feet—all in one slick motion. "You say no word about catching me off guard, or you are a dead blue soldier, you hear?"

"Anything you say. In case you are interested, the patrols are coming. Can't you hear?"

Bovey did not waste time looking, but motioned everyone to follow Christie already pushing deep into the swamp. The blue soldier did not know where he was going, so Bovey pointed beyond the morass of sandbanks and tangle. They hid among the moss-velveted ribs of blighted trees—well down wind of the dogs should some be trailing the riders. Christie doused the lantern.

Five horsemen reined up just yards from the cane break where the small party had been. The horses danced as the riders gaped and squinted into the thickening soup. Men who enjoy the safety of numbers bark loud.

"I saw something, sir, a glow or something. Right about here. I am sure of it."

"Do you see it now?" a tired baritone countered.

"No," the voice stuttered, "but it don't mean I didn't see it and it wasn't here. Could be beyond that cane there."

"Are you suggesting, Sergeant, that we take our horses down into that jungle in this pea soup to find some light you thought you saw?"

The sergeant did not answer.

"Yea, Johnny, you could be seeing ghosts," and voices jeered in agreement.

"Or alligators. You know them eyes glow like hot coals in the night. It should be an interesting expedition. We'll follow, Johnny, if you lead the way."

"I said I saw something. If it be a runaway, that's a hundred dollars by the last reports—that amount of food and whiskey could wash down a lot of road mud."

"And if it's not, we can break a horse's leg and have nothing to show for it." The impatient baritone was growing more so.

Nerves were running raw in the den as well. Warm mud seeped over Christie's instep, inching up his ankles, and by the second, up his calves. The leeches came with it. He was sinking slowly, but sinking just the same. A rider was pushing the face of his mount toward the wall of sword grass, nosing into the hollow the best he could without really committing himself. A breeze blew from Christie's back, giving the animal his scent. It shied.

"What's the matter, Johnny? Your horse got more sense than you? You still want to risk it? Well, call us if you need any help, but yell loud. Watch out for the Indians, rattlesnakes, and panthers. We don't have a treaty with panthers and rattlesnakes."

But the baritone put a finish to this game. "Even God

won't be able to find you at judgment. Now git up here and let's git movin'."

The scout was not ready to give up; he fired three rapid shots into the fog. The first snapped the leaves by Sarah's arm, and the second skimmed so close that chips of bark nicked Zeke's face. By the grace of God and the nature of the gentle properties of quicksand, Christie had sunk those two precious inches to keep this last bullet from creasing his skull.

"Them slaves are sending word up and down the river to the Yankees. Some are hiding in there somewhere, I just know it. Even dead they will be worth quarter bounty," Johnny demanded.

"Cease fire, John. I think you killed yourself a log. Now, if the rest of you haven't conjured any more phantoms, banshees, or werewolves dressed in contraband fleece, let's be joining the rest." A popular suggestion all around. With the crack of reins and a strain of leather the horse hobbled backed to the road and the patrol moved on.

Only then did Christie allow himself the luxury of a deep breath of muggy, mosquito-infested air. It tasted wonderful! He shifted his weight in the ooze, reached over head for a branch, pulled himself up, and swung himself onto firmer ground. Then turned to help Sarah—the others could go to hell. Bovey had found solid ground on his own. But Zeke extended a hand, Christie pretended not to notice. Zeke growled; the slime was rising faster up his legs. Christie thought again, and with Bovey and Calley, he pulled the man free.

"Now, Bovey, what you doin' here?" Sarah asked. The reunion had changed her—the skittish doe was gone, the voice was alert and sensible.

"I heard you were coming on the line. The stations are shunning all migrants—too many runners isolated and crazy with fear. You come up to the house and we'll put you up."

"Bovey," remembering her purpose, she turned to her companion, "this is Lieutenant Christie! He came through with that Grierson, you heard of. He needs our help. Momma Wise said so."

Christie was not prepared for the effect this intelligence had. The big man, who had moments before been at the other end of Christie's blade, reached for his palm and shook it so hard that he nearly detached it from Christie's shoulder. "You boys raised a terrific fuss. You would think you were nine choirs of angels the way the militia was buzzin'. We heard Grierson was nearly bagged at Wall's Bridge at the Tickfaw River."

"When?"

"On or about the first of May. The word on the line is that De Baun was ready for him, hit the scouts pretty hard. You know a Colonel Blackburn?"

Christie nodded that he did.

"Well, if he isn't dead, he soon will be. And they got the sergeant. I don't know his name."

"Surby?"

Bovey thought that might be the name but wouldn't swear to it—the grapevine news was not always precise. "But the rest of the column made a good break for it and should be in Baton Rouge by now. But they took care of Newton Station. All the hardware going west to Vicksburg to help Pemberton is rubble. Your men were thorough. How many were you anyhow?"

"Not quite nine choirs—more like three." The news could have been better. Christie had come to respect these men even if he did not feel them to be brothers. But Grierson had made it. Had Hatch made it home? Bovey did not know.

Sarah took over. "He got shot up around West Point. We tryin' to get this lost lamb back to the flock."

"She's right, I had no part in the best of it." Christie admitted.

"Doesn't matter—the praise still goes." Bovey countered.

"Have you heard anything about Grant?"

Bovey nodded. "Heading toward the capital with three corps and making good time. Had a bad go at the landing, but finally broke free. But when he reaches Jackson, he is going to get slammed hard. General Joe Johnston is waiting there with about thirty thousand troops he's been hoarding like miser's gold. Going to be sparks for sure when they clash. Pemberton's army got Tennesseeans, Georgians, Alabamians, Mississippians, and Louisiana boys, men from fighting states that have felt the Yankee boot kicked in their vitals. They are going to be furious to keep the wolves from the door. Stevenson is up with four brigades, General Stephen Lee among 'em. Forney and Martin Luther Smith got divisions of their own, and of course there is Bowen. Twenty thousand I expect, maybe a few more."

"What about Forrest?"

"Forrest...well, for some reason Pemberton sent him to Tennessee to help Bragg. Forrest and Bragg—flint and steel. Forrest has threatened to kill Bragg more than once—so I guess it makes sense to Pemberton to send him there. Don't that beat all! Still, we keep our ears open, got eyes in Vicksburg, Jackson, and abouts, but that's our last count. Vicksburg isn't going to fall with one shot—like a dead calf, it's going to put up a hell of a fight."

Christie asked the forbidden question: "Why do you care so much about Grant?"

Bovey regarded it fair. "I am a distant cousin to the family. They brought me down from Cincinnati as a teacher back before the war. Ever hear of Levi Coffin?" Christie admitted he had back at Camp Dennison. "Coffin and his Society of Friends out of Cincinnati organized the freedom railroad, getting Negroes over the Ohio River and up to Canada. We were—how can I put it—associates? Listen here, we don't abduct slaves or put them in revolt, we just help them out with no violence once they make up their own minds to go. I am a pacifist, but it doesn't mean I am not involved in this war. We put our little house on the line, right here under the nose of my big brother-in-law. We do a thriving but careful business, which now includes escaped Union prisoners. Not to the liking of Momma Wise. It's a small world. Her grandchild worked up at the house, and my wife and I kept an eye on her as best we could, in return for her cooperation. The child has good ears and can read enough to let us know what comes and goes. Her daddy died last summer—not that he ever claimed the child at all. But being his, at least he stayed away from her, and made others do the same. Not kind, speaking about my own relatives that way. Been thinking of...I don't know...how that will lay with Momma Wise. The oceans widen in this business...if she will feel the need to help us after knowing her grandchild has let off."

"She's a might small to be up to work like this." Christie motioned in Sarah's direction.

"Sarah is one of our scouts further back. You gave her cause to come this far and visit her swain, Calley. She pretends not to be too bright, lopes along in a fog, and can appear quite addled. Did she roll her eyes back in her head? That really sets people off. But she is smart and she's sturdy. This is the first time she worked down instead of up. Anybody tell you, you're going the wrong way?"

"Yes, I have been told."

They arrived at the back door of the neat little cottage secluded in elms and live oaks. "Come in and rest a bit. We'll put you up until nightfall. Then Possum will take you on."

"And who might Possum be?"

But Possum remained a mystery. Instead, Bovey introduced him to Emily, who stood at the door, balancing a baby on her hip. She was tethered by small hands and arms to one peaking around her legs, and there were three more, of various ages roosting in the loft like chickens. Sarah lifted the youngest from Emily Bovey's arms, and with a bowl of stew and two spoons, she went out on the front porch. Then Emily pointed to a place at the table and bid Christie sit. While the men talked, she saw to the comfort of her guest personally. Christie watched as she worked at the stove. She was tall—regal rather than servile—her manner straight, efficient, benevolent, rather than bent, stooped and beaten by her lower condition.

Bovey's eyes followed his wife with more love than seemly for a married man. He was clearly humbled by his good fortune, and not embarrassed that other men thought he was unworthy. "We don't have servants. Not that we believe in it, but gossip is deadly in our business. Emily could have had silks and diamonds, servants for every bidding, a big house and a husband to give her a secure future. So she married a third cousin who could not even give her his name—she had that already. So I gave her calico, work, and sleepless nights—and she counts herself blessed. Some men are lucky beyond their dreams." Christie thought the man's estimation of himself short by half.

When everyone had been served, Emily took the other baby and went out to sit with Sarah—two women absorbed in the business of infants and hearthfires. But it was a knowing eye that kept watch on the path up to the big place—where the politics were less tolerant of Yankee fugitives and runaway human farm machinery.

Emily had served up bountiful helpings with the largest in front of Christie and with a big spit fork he dug in. With his eyes on his food but his ears on Bovey, he digested both at the same time. The conductor was not at all optimistic as to what awaited them down the road.

"...and the backcountry is mean, slaves running away from the plantations robbing anything on two or four legs. They are scavenging as bad as the quartermaster patrols. Between the two, the supplies are cleaned right down to the bare ground. Pretty soon howling stomachs are going to get the better of caution, and things are going to get nasty even amongst our own."

"But with summer coming on—and the corn crop looking like it's going to be good..." Christie had just passed field upon field portending abundant harvests and kitchen gardens promising full stomachs.

"And who's to say the people are going to get it? Pemberton? Richmond? The planters? Or Grant? After what happened at Holly Springs, Grant has been pushed into a corner, and will not think twice—his army will come first and take what he wants—Pemberton and the devil taking the hind most. What scares me is that nobody will get it—Pemberton or the planters will fire it to keep it out of the hands of the enemy and we'll all starve. Or Grant will destroy it with the same result. People are just short of lunatic."

Christie absorbed it all: the numbers and movements of the Confederate troops seen by the scouts and the desperation of the people with uncertainty and starvation staring them in the face.

From the porch, Emily was shaking the baby's rattle. A signal: somebody's coming.

Bovey pushed Christie back. "I hate to put you down there, but people as skittish as they are, they come breaking through a man's castle without knocking. You understand."

No, Christie did not understand. Down where? There was no down. The cabin was supported above two feet of thin air, enclosed by a stockade of lattice. Where was this "down there?" Bovey and Calley pulled the table back and raised a plug in the floor. Calley wrapped the fugitive in a blanket and pushed him toward "down there." Christie dropped to the bare ground and spread as flat as he could. The door slammed him into the spongy soil. The space was so tight he could not even breathe. Dampness passed up through the blanket—along with it the rankest stench. "Down there" was foul and putrid. Through the lattice he saw men dismount and come on.

"Emily, is your husband at home? We got urgent business!"

"And hello to you, brother dear. Yes, the babies are all fine." She cut off the visitors just as they set a boot on the lower step. "Except the youngest boy has the mumps and Maggie has the chicken pox."

"Brother dear" drew up short. "Uh, well, we don't want to bother the babies any. Would you fetch him? These men want to talk to him? We'll just wait out here, not to disturb anyone."

From his vantage Christie counted boots enough for three men, one pair recently blackened and shiny, the other two worn and caked in creek mud. They stamped only yards from his face.

Emily's excellent stew congealed to acid. He locked his jaws together and held his breath to keep from vomiting. "Control, Christie, they can hear you blink at this range." He willed his mind to anywhere but there. But his state of affairs only inspired visions of a slop pile, a sink, a sewer—no happy distractions to save him in the here and now. He searched for Julie back in his mind. But even in visions she would not come to such a mire as this.

That was inside him, out was faring no better. Some infernal nuisance was poking holes through his pantaloons, and something with teeth like ten-penny nails needled up and down his legs. Christie jerked and kicked, accomplishing nothing but bumping his head on a low rafter. He pulled his arms around his face and braced himself.

"What was that under there?" One of the visitors in filthy boots went down on a knee. "I heard a yelp. Something in there is being butchered." He was bending closer to the lattice, just as Bovey stepped in front.

"My wife's chickens—once in awhile snakes come up from the swamp and spook them. You want a closer look, Henry? I don't think you could get down there even with a crow bar, but you, Sergeant, you are welcome to try. Got your gun loaded? If it's a rattler, I will let you keep him for supper."

When Calley finally pulled him up, Christie was just one breath away from raving lunacy. "Was that the only hell hole you could have dropped me in? Why not the outhouse? A slop barrel? How about a hill of red ants?"

"What you carrying on about, you only been down there ten minutes!"

Christie beat off the spiders and slugs, shook out his pant legs and emptied his shoes, all in one feverish contortion. But he was brought to by the explosion of a shotgun. Christie slammed down flat on the pinewood floor.

The children were ecstatic; they clapped their hands and cheered from the safety of their perch in the loft. "Mom got 'em, Uncle Calley, look!"

True enough, from out of the crawl space, Calley pulled out a rattler by the tail and swung him close to Christie's face. "He was just about a foot from where you lay."

Bovey regarded it of no consequence. "He's just a baby."

Christie fixed them all with a homicidal glare. Bovey backed up a step. "You sure are skittish for a battle soldier. Okay, okay—you don't have to stay down there. I guess you can sleep by the stove till night. But if we get any more visitors..."

"I'll crawl in and bake with the biscuits!" Christie shoved the filthy quilt into Bovey's stomach.

"Now, stop fussing and go down by the creek and wash up. All of you." Emily handed Christie clean clothes, a cake of lye soap and a towel.

The men obeyed. As they went, Christie took a closer look at the barnyard fowl strutting and pecking from the captivity of the underside of the cottage. One eyed him with particular vile. "Why are your chickens under there?"

"Gave up the luxury of a real hen house some months ago, because it just invites everything from the swamp from weasels to the quartermaster foxes and runaways to clean it out."

The breakfast had been filling, the accommodations, if not private or luxurious, were comfortable, and the company, disallowing Zeke, benevolent. But there was little sleep to be had—and the inconvenience came from a shortage of hands. Christie had only two, and his arms were raw with poison ivy, oak, and the effects of other poisonous fauna he could not name.

Under his tender skin, chiggers and bugs bore tunnels from his neck to his ankles, and everything craved scratching at the same time. He had run out of Momma Wise's salve. When the Yankee was nearly berserk Bovey poured off a healthy measure from a jug that also had come out of "down there." "For what ails you. Soak yourself in it and drink the rest."

"Obliged." With one gulp, Christie had no voice for ten minutes and saw double. With one more, he quite literally fell unconscious for the rest of the day.

"Boy is a cranky sort! Little inconvenience was all, and carried on like a cat dropped in the rain barrel." Zeke watched the soldier sleep where he had dropped. "He left his sweet potatoes." Zeke slid them onto his plate. "No sense in wastin' good food."

"This be Possum." The night was late in coming, but when it came it fell black, Christie could not make out the little slip Bovey introduced.

"I be taking you to the next stop."

Bovey raised the lantern, and Christie was convinced he was going to die. "He's barely taller than a stump."

But it was the boy who was of the opinion he was getting less on the deal. "I eight! That enough for the job! How old are you?"

"Twenty-one!"

"If you so smart at twenty-one, how come you down here runnin' around the countryside at night, and not home sleepin' in your own bed?"

Christie felt better. The boy may be little, but he was sensible.

The next stop came at the end of a two-night trek through pounding rain, but Possum was a bat through the dark. They took refuge in a barn. For all the stalls, the only tenant was a skeletal cow that lowed beside a hound. When they entered it barked and strained to the length of its hitch. Possum and Christie collapsed in a pile of straw just beyond the tether of the mastiff with the large teeth.

"Move over, sweetheart, make room for company!" Christie patted the rump and Bossie backed away. "You wouldn't have any coffee to go with that milk, would you?" Christie pulled off his wet boots and settled back pretending more tired than hungry. All that was left were two biscuits rain-soaked to paste and some jerky oozing through his pocket. Such as it was Possum was hungry for it. Christie was just closing one eye…

"You took your time getting here! Expected you afore this. You be a Union man, I hear."

"Yes ma'am," Christie was most eager to give the right answers because of the shotgun hanging lank from the woman's arms.

"I be Missis Meade—of far relation to the Pennsylvania people, you might heard of." Christie did not know of any Pennsylvania people by that name except General Meade. He said as much, and that must have said it all, for she settled the gun against the beam and unhitched the dog. Christie and Possum scooted deeper into the stall. Instead of going for their throats, the mastiff made for the woman's feet in one bound. She patted it and it whined. "You big baby! They aren't going to hurt you." The dog was not convinced and moved to a safer vantage behind her skirts.

Then she took up her pitchfork and jabbed at the dry clover, settling a mountain of it into the manger. "I just be beddin' down the cow and I'll see to some supper for you. Must have had a frightful run, can't see how you found the place in the storm. You still hungry, I expect. They always come hungry."

"*I found* it fine!" Possum asserted.

"Well, my meals ain't much—just some sweet potatoes and salted fish caught yesterday. All I have."

"We are very obliged for your kindness" Christie took the pitchfork and finished feeding her stock. She walked to the door, carefully settling her balance on one foot and then the next, her back was bent and one arm hooked against her hip. She was as cadaverous as the cow, Christie didn't see how either had much to share, and was humbled that she would. Missis Meade motioned to the door with a forward nod. "Cabin is yonder. Well, are you comin'?"

Possum was already gathering up his shoes. "Yes'um. We most definitely comin'."

Her haven spread into two rooms, but she seemed to have consolidated her life entirely around the hearth. A cot, her churn, a spinning wheel and a cabinet was in the space of only a few feet.

"I'll feed you presently, and then you can bed down by the fire. But you hear any sound at all, you crawl into the wood box over there." Christie could not see how or where, since the woodbin was filled to overflowing—no room for a beetle let alone two small runaways. Seeing their confusion, Missis Meade pressed against a side, and it swung away to reveal a false floor. "It leads down into the cellar. It might be flooded a little, but that's all."

As for supper, the woman was better than her word. The Lord's multiplication of loaves and fishes ranked second to the miracle she blessed them with that night—ambrosia out of bottom-feeding crab and catfish with a side dish of pulpy carrots and apples bronzed in molasses and ladled over biscuits. She served something called hush puppies, which Christie had never tasted before. There were also sweet potatoes—his share, he gave to Possum. When they were satisfied, they settled by the fire, respite for awhile against the rain, wind, and war outside.

"You run this farm by yourself?" Christie asked. The giant head of the mastiff was resting in his lap and Christie massaged its ears. The animal cuddled closer like a kitten seeking warmth.

Missis Meade rolled a tuft of cotton between her fingers and caught it onto the yarn that wove around the big spinning wheel. She systematically kept it fed from the basket by her feet, working and talking with equal agility. "Not much to run now. Quartermaster with his ten-percent option for the army kept coming back, till he took off the horses and emptied the silo, chicken house, and hog bin. I live as I can off the river and what I can snare and shoot."

"Where's your family?"

"My husband died at Perryville fightin' along side your General Thomas. My other two boys they were there too, but on the other side with Bragg. They dead too. I pray, but I don't have to worry about them no more."

"You talk as if you're from..."

"Indiana! Came down here as a bride when my husband inherited the farm from his grandfather. When the war flared, we was still too northern to go Confederate, and my boys were too Southern to fight Union."

As the big spokes turned before the crackling flame, flecks of red and yellow danced in his face. A full stomach, warmth, the drumming rain—all were as soothing as an after-dinner brandy. He shook it off, "What do you hear of Grant?"

The woman motioned him closer. "He nigh on to Jackson. The piney bottom full of your boys comin' up from Port Gibson—three long columns skinning the farms and plantations of everything they can eat, wear, or ride. Even so, Grant's soldiers march hungry, footbare, sick and sore. Pemberton is going to fret 'em every step of the way though, so when Grant gets to Jackson his army will be played out. There, Johnston and Pemberton will swallow them up whole. I hear tell that's the plan. Nobody makin' a secret of it anymore. This rain has got to slow him down even more. Cannon will be hard to move in the sandy bottom. Sink clean down to the axle, if they stop at all." Her tone was detached and matter of fact, as if the subject was of no more than the temperature of the weather or the price of eggs in good times.

"Grant never let rain or Confederates stop him before."

"I hope you're right. Jeff Davis says that Vicksburg must be held at all costs—if orders were cannon they could hold till judgment. Bein' they're not...well...they are in for a bad time if this summer's as hot as last. Vicksburg wells run shaller."

Christie settled back. Grant had broken away from the river. Those pencil sketches across the map were now wagon ruts and infantry tracks flooded with rainwater. He was moving with an enemy at his back and one at his front. Christie tried to think of an eastern general to match Grant for sheer audacity. He could think of only one—Stonewall Jackson. If Grant did not win outright victory, he would be crushed between Joe Johnston and John Pemberton. The fate of the war would turn on a card. It was winner-take-all and Christie wanted to be with his general when it was played.

"Grant can do it!"

Missis Meade thought so too. "Joe is old, sick, and heartsick of this war, does nothing and waits. So it has not improved him any in the estimation of Davis or Pemberton—they still hold Joe to account for Grant being on them in the first place. Said he should have been at Port Gibson to keep Grant from getting ashore. General Bowen was screaming for anybody who would listen—thank goodness, nobody did until it was too late. No, the tiger is loose in the Confederacy. Joe has to win at

Jackson."

"How you know so much about Grant and all?" Christie asked coolly.

Missis Meade chose her words carefully. "That I cannot tell you, Lieutenant, but I know. And if you see your Grant, tell him this: Johnston will not fight him anywheres else if he loses at Jackson. The Confederate soldiers are withering on the vine, so he's going to hoard what he's got left—for a time nobody but he knows. And you tell Grant one more thing. This is important."

With her ready intelligence of division movements, she sounded like General Sherman briefing the war council. "Go on," Christie said.

"Pemberton has no cavalry. He is marching blind. Horse soldiers running helter-skelter chasing ghosts. That Grierson stirred 'em up plenty. All 'cept Forrest. He must keep his eye on Forrest should he come back. But for now Forrest is in Tennessee, so far as I know."

"What about Van Dorn? He is going to be very concerned about Union invasion in his home state."

Her lips spread in a thin smile. "He dead last week. Shot by a jealous husband he cuckolded."

"Well, well, I don't know whether Grant will be relieved or disappointed that he didn't get to do the honors himself. A jealous husband is worth a division, I guess."

After Possum came a succession of guides, each in turn kept Christie moving. Nights were shortening and days lengthening as spring matured to summer—the rule became twice the pace in half the time. He slept, but seldom more than an hour or two, and never stayed more than two nights in the same place. And so he remembered them in later years with greater or less vividness as dreams and visions. Even now, in his exhausted state he could not remember how they came and went through the country except that the smell and rush of the river always came along the right. More than once his bed was at the bottom of a canoe or there was no bed at all, just a nest of reeds, branches and pine cones.

There had been an Indian by the name of Beale, so ancient he could look into a mirror to see his own corpse staring back.

There was a naturalist, his cabin walls a museum of stuffed butterflies and birds; their eyes boring down all night like stone saints in a cathedral. And there was Pike, a mixed blood, trapper by half and preacher by the other half. He watered down his gospel with home-brewed lightning: "I got some mash in the barrel. You want some of that instead? You got to have somethin' 'man does not live by bread alone.' You can sleep in the loft. I think I poisoned all the snakes, but can never tell."

Pike was wrong, he still had snake trouble. A tempest blew up and with it a squad of profane troopers and panicked horses. They barged through the doors and took possession just as Christie and his guide were nodding off up in the loft. But none below had the least curiosity or energy to examine anything except the six-by-three-feet of dirt floor needed to lay a bedroll. Instead of bedtime prayers they pacified themselves with curses heaped on Jeff Davis, Grant, the rain, and the war with such equal vigor that it took Christie some minutes to figure them Confederate or Union. Finally they served up John Pemberton's head on a plate for putting militia at the vanguard of the Confederate defense. All this intelligence rose up like sweet incense.

The profanity mellowed to growls, then one by one, even those lowed into a chorus of snores. As they slept below, Christie and his guide slept above. When he awoke the barn was empty. The Confederate patrol had awakened, mounted, and left without disturbing them.

A storm kept him a virtual prisoner in an abolitionist's cellar for two days of fire and brimstone scripture and prayer in heavy doses. Christie was more than ready when Job came. He was a slave long crossed off his master's inventory as dead when his shanty burned to the ground, his family in it. For five years he had lived deep in the Big Black bayous, traveling primeval country, conducting human cargo along the Underground. No words good or bad came from him—he could not hear or talk, nor did he seem to miss these senses at all. Only sight as passive and non-judgmental as a breeze came from the deep, black eyes all but enveloped in over-hanging scars.

Angel had explained it—and many other mysteries— when she took charge of Christie at the last. "Like the Savior, he rose up in three days from the dead and took up the work of

Moses to empty the South one black soul at a time until all are gone or the bounty hunters and the dogs chase him down. Got no purpose to go north and stay there on his own. That would be giving up. Vengeance is not the sole claim of the Lord, so far as Job is concerned."

The river ran wide now, too deep and treacherous to wade. When the current was sluggish they poled miles of it on rafts and Red River boats. When it ran fast they let the freshet carry them along until it slacked. The rest they walked—always keeping close to the wild banks, with the billowing willows and reeds to cover them. Angel was barely a woman, but her abdomen swelled with a child of her own. When she was worried or impatient her cheekbones narrowed to a wedge around a thin, long nose. Her jaw was chiseled and blunt just below generous heart-shaped lips. Angel was not rough-hewn with callused hands and leathered skin. Her words were well spoken, for one so young, she had taken every advantage of her time working in the big house. Angel did not reveal anymore about herself than she let off the night, she heard the Union soldiers were coming up from the South.

"Frederick Douglass would approve: He stole from his Mister '...this head and body which he took off to freedom.'" Christie said. Angel said that she liked this Mister Douglass sight unseen.

Grant's juggernaut rolled across Mississippi and wrote new chapters in tactics. Each sanctuary that sheltered Christie and Angel relayed some news of that progress: a battle at Raymond on the twelfth, Clinton, just west of the capital on the thirteenth, and Jackson on the fourteenth. Their last stop gave Angel something precious even if it would not accord them safety there. "My baby's father sent word along the line that he is a freeman now and enlisted with the army. So I will find him where you are going. Holy words or not, I am a wife—and of a Yankee soldier. Our child will be proud. The miles are shorter now between us."

"You can't even walk," Christie protested. The gulf winds had been gathering dampness through the evening, and now they were blinded with rain. But Angel would not relent. Christie feared for her and the baby. He feared for himself. If the child came with only him to deliver it in the middle of this nowhere—that fate terrified him more than any battle. He wished with all his heart he had studied more biology than philosophy—a lot of good philosophy had been in this war.

"I walk, you see," Angel said, as they turned into another path—one more strand in a large spider web of backcountry paths. This one reached beyond the scent of a Confederate regiment marching not twenty yards to the left. They could hear the sergeants barking orders, and the clang and jangle of the cooking pans and canteens. The storm would keep their flankers from wandering too far.

Rain-saturated clay was grease under their feet; Angel slipped, recovered her balance, and then stumbled. Christie caught her just before she collapsed in the mud. "Yeah, I see. What I see is we've got to get out of this storm."

A fluorescence of lightning, and like a zombie it lunged out of the darkness. No more than a gutted hulk with a few flailing branches, still the Pirogue cypress looked deep enough to hold the two of them. Christie pushed Angel inside, and the three—Christie, Angel, and the baby—huddled together with Christie plugging his back into the breach. They were pressed so tightly that he could feel the roll and kick of Angel's child against his ribs. She massaged her abdomen. "Go to sleep, little Sunflower. You will be born free. It will be well on the morrow, I promise." Angel sighed and released herself into the care of the Yankee.

"Angel—a lovely name."

"It is the name my master give me."

"Not your mother?"

Angel was nearly asleep. "I don't remember her at all, only my grandmother and not very much—just a little cabin in the woods." Her head nuzzled against his chest, and her breathing became shallow and regular.

"Sunflower!" Christie whispered.

From deep within her dreams Angel stirred. She patted her tummy again and hummed a lullaby that he had heard not long ago.

XV
Into the Lion's Den
Friday twilight, May 17, 1863

Morning had passed with no hopes for breakfast, noon with no lunch, and now it was nearly dark and Angel was faint. This wayside farm was as far as she could go. From the tree line, it looked abandoned and overgrown. Christie bedded Angel against the well, and drew her some water. Then he went searching for supper.

He had barely gone ten paces, "Get over on the step! Leave the woman alone!" Christie could not see from where the command came but a big hound did as he was bid, pressing himself flat as an old rumpled carpet on the top step of the house. "Is she all right? Is she set to come?" the yeoman stepped out of the barn with a long-handled ax leveled on his shoulder. He was big, spare, and from the ease and length of his stride, agile. Christie stepped in front of Angel but that was all he could do.

"I'll be right in a few minutes. Then we will go," Angel sighed.

But the farmer did not believe it. He looked from her to Christie and then to the woods from where they had come. By way of some conclusion he swung the ax over his head and it wedged into a stump. "Name is Tyne," he stretched out a hand, "and I'm afraid that water's all that's good around here. But I will pep up some cold biscuits and gravy for her if you want." Christie thanked him.

Tyne led Christie into the summer kitchen, there he gathered up a pan and went to work without a wasted motion. He did not do twice the work for having only one arm, but from practice had cut a two-handed job down to one. ("Soon there won't be a whole man in all of the South.")

"You runnin' from Grant's army or our own?"

Christie did not answer, which did not seem to matter to Tyne.

He wet his hand in a bucket and kneaded his biscuits with course flour. "Don't have salt, hope you got good teeth." When the hog grease bubbled in the frying pan, he added jerky, stirred, then dropped the biscuits over. Like eating candles, Christie thought.

"Heard cannon over by the Champion Place all day yesterday—the armies are tearing at each other like the hounds of hell. When the storms came, I couldn't tell what was thunder and what wasn't. Fightin' in all that rain—terrible hard battle. Terrible. Your boys up there?"

"Yeah, my boys are up there." Christie answered evenly.

"You goin' up?"

"I am. Should have been already. But I was wounded a while back and was slow to mend."

"Have some milk for her, coolin' down in the well, should be still good."

"We are very appreciative."

"You limp some, I hope you are in the cavalry?"

"Mister Tyne, I have done it all!"

The farmer's gaze was so long and penetrating that Christie was sure he could read the truth etched in his mind. "That your wife?"

"No, she's not my wife."

The farmer winced. "Well, what's done is done. I don't judge. But listen to me—go home and have your baby, put your crops in while there is still some spring left. Forget about the war—it's over."

"What?"

"You heard me!" Tyne repeated with some remorse but no shame. "This war is a humbug! Bragg...Johnston...arguin' with themselves and arguin' with Richmond. One suspicious of the other, holding back, fighting piecemeal—men killed for no good. Bragg shoots his own men just for meanness, I know—my cousin... Listen, men are dyin' for nothing! Nothing! Soon there will be no men left. I saw them mowed down like ripe wheat at Perryville and Murfreesboro. Nothin's changed since then—nothin' is going to get better. All we got for it all is one cemetery after another."

Christie did not answer. When Tyne spoke again, he was a man giving a graveside eulogy. "Here and now ain't no better. I hear the Yanks slammed through our line like a bolt. Joe Johnston didn't stick around to make a repulse. High-tailed it up toward Canton, leaving Pemberton fighting for every foot on his own. They couldn't hold—nobody blames 'em for falling back...no, that ain't fair...*pushed* back they were. And if nothin' stops Grant, they'll be hammered, hammered, and hammered some more, until they have the Mississippi at their backs and the whole Yankee army in their front."

"Where are they now?"

"About two hours, maybe three, to the south. Hard to tell, things change so quickly. But far enough to be out of my hair. I have managed to get some turnips, apples, and some hay scavenged, and some corn planted from old seed. And I found a cow adrift down in the bottoms. A beginning…a tomorrow. This farm has been in my family four generations—I am not going to let it die with everything else."

Tyne ladled the slapjack on two chipped plates, and Christie took them outside. He settled down beside Angel. Gently, he woke her, and pressed a plate in her hands, urging her to eat. He was gentle and careful with the little mulatto girl.

Tyne watched with some envy and something else—that he could not abide—and it told on his face. These two would have it hard. Their mix would not settle with those around here. But they had tomorrows ahead to work out this ugliness—if it could be worked out. He looked around at his blighted farm. He had yesterdays, but tomorrows? He wanted to believe he had time to think things anew, but wasn't so sure.

"Stay the night—your woman is done in. Not room enough in the house, and the roof leaks like a sieve, not even fit for that hound. He prefers the barn—dry—in the center at any rate. Make your bed there. Him and the cow live better than I do. Worth more, I guess, " he laughed.

"I thank you. We will." Angel protested, but Christie was firm, "We stay."

"You got people hereabouts to take her in when you go back to the army?"

Christie nodded, "Yeah, not too far off now."

Tyne was right, the straw was clean, and the barn was as good as barns went, except around the edges where the wood rot made it sour. The cow didn't snore, but the old hound did. The lantern was put out and the dark blanketed them over. This was the last night of their sojourn. Tomorrow Christie would find the army and arrange quarters and rations entitled to Angel as a wife of a soldier. As it was, the army found him.

"We don't need authorization! We take what we want and what is left will stay only if you get out of the way, you old traitor!" Men were coming on. Tyne was protesting, but the thudding of boots was resolute and the voices mean. The hound set himself at the barn door and snarled. Angel wrestled Christie awake.

"Hide! Over there—the corn barrels. Hide in there."

Christie did not like it and said so; "We will hide together. In the loft! Up the ladder!"

"You crazy? I can't go up that ladder!" She rubbed her ample stomach.

He stood his ground. "Then we face it together!"

She saw this as a time for sense, not gallantry, and pushed him toward the kegs. "No! You are in more danger than me! I can put them off. You get in those barrels and hurry!"

His mind was too befuddled with exhaustion to disagree especially when he had no good plan of his own. He hoisted himself over the rim of a huge grain cask set under the eaves. Angel pushed his head down and slid the lid snugly over. He sank down into the darkness. But the barrel had not been empty! Mush flooded up his chest to his chin. He tilted his head back and dammed up his ears with his palms. In seconds, his tired, scarred body went from ice to fire—he was pickling in one-hundred-proof grain alcohol. Two years of catching rain, and by the turn of seasons freezing and heating, the waste corn had fermented into skin-peeling acid. The fumes ignited Chinese rockets in his brain. He set the blade of his knife between his teeth and bit down to keep from screaming.

Outside, Angel composed herself to deal with the invasion as it burst through the door.

"Merciful God! What is this?" a sergeant sighed. His men poured around him with weapons drawn to face down every threat posed by this tiny woman and her cow.

"Stand off! You makin' Cotton skittish," Angel ordered, and went back to her work at the cow's utters. Milk squirted into the pail.

A sergeant stepped into the dull crescent of the lantern. "Who might you be?"

"I be owned by Mister Tyne. And who might you be?"

"Never you mind!" The quartermaster had already lost interest in her but not in the milk she was harvesting. Assisted by a few slovenly privates, he looked to what else there was to be had. They knocked over barrels, turned over mangers, and kicked up bins, but they were all empty. The milk would bring a pretty price at the officer's mess, but that was about all they would get. "Mace, check to see if the old man is hiding any food up in the loft. Banner, you go see what's in those barrels over there."

An officer had been holding himself in reserve of the little detail, but seeing that the area was under control, he took charge. Contrary to his sergeant he was not interested in food or forage, but in Angel. Her sable skin was luminescent in the lantern light. Slowly he ran his hand over the cascade of black hair and let it slip around her waist. He pulled her against him. "Well, girl, you alone in here?"

"You keep your distance now. Get your hands off me!"

"Well, for a beginning, show the good private where the oats are. And then for a second..."

"Got no oats, ain't got no horses—nobody got much of nothing no more even for their ownself." Angel affected the role of cabin slave so well the lieutenant took her as cheap goods—his for the wanting with no restraint. While his men searched the barn, he pushed her toward a pile of dried clover.

"Leave her alone, Canfield, she's just a babe."

"Old enough to have a babe of her own. Now, sweetie, tell the truth. Is that little biscuit you're baking here," he pulled her close and rubbed her stomach, "belong to the big master here?"

A private pressed the big farmer back and shook his head. However rude the officer, interference would be unwise. They will be gone in a few minutes with nothing molested, if he just bid his time. The rage simmered, honor was small change here.

"I told you, Canfield, leave the girl alone. Help me haul these barrels open, they weigh a ton."

"And I told you, Brady, cavalry don't do the heavy lifting, that's you boys' department. We just provide protection, and from the looks of this little thing here, you need protection pretty bad. So I'm just going to take her over here and..."

"I'm tellin' you to leave the girl alone," Brady barked. "Get you hanged, Grant's orders."

"Grant's not here. And who are you to be giving orders, Sergeant? Now, sweetheart, how about we get acquainted. If you are good to me I might even save you from the evil master here."

As soon as he touched her, Angel slapped his face. She would have again, but he caught her hand and twisted it behind her back so hard she screamed.

Canfield did not see what came flying at him over the rail. He was pressing Angel down into the stall, calico ripping apart in his fists. Canfield was nearly decapitated as Christie yanked him back by the collar. Angel rolled away and reached for the pitchfork, but the private seized it and would have slapped her if Tyne had not pulled her into his arms. Christie rolled Canfield onto his back and hammered his head into the floor. When the officer was nearly senseless, Christie brought the tip of Collin's knife against the lieutenant's jaw.

Canfield blinked. "You're dead!"

"Just why would you think that?" Christie growled.

"Because..."

"Because?" Christie pressed the blade tighter, the jaw dimpling under the tip. "Because you pulled the trigger?" Canfield jerked to break the vise, and the steel nicked the skin. Blood beaded down Canfield's throat. Long into old age, there would be a scar just above the knot of his tie, to remind him of this night. Waving back any rescue from the men standing by, Brady let the lieutenant cower.

Canfield shouted to his sergeant, "Get him off me! Do you hear? I'll have your stripes!"

Canfield waited for what came next. Christie pressed the knife deeper. In the presence of these men, the terror and humiliation on Canfield's face was some satisfaction. In fact there was satisfaction to go around.

Reluctantly, Brady broke it up. "Kill him, and you won't get out of here alive. And we kill the girl and the farmer as well. It all depends on you, Reb."

Christie relented and the two were pulled to their feet. A private whipped Christie's hands behind his back and bound them. With the odds now to his liking Canfield set his right fist into Christie's jaw, and his left into his midsection. The explosion of Brady's revolver brought Canfield under control.

"Just hold it right there, Lieutenant. You can have your Rebel scalp after the provost gets done with him." The sergeant turned Christie about roughly. "That's real smart, Reb. Just stand there and breathe in easy. Don't need to be having anything we'll regret later if we just keep our heads."

It should have taken only one burly private to handle Christie; instead it took two. No man was allowing more than one hand for the purpose, with the other they pressed bandannas over their faces. The Rebel reeked.

Canfield held back. "I say let's hang him right here and now."

"I say let's not," Brady pushed the lieutenant out of the way. "You hold the shoulderstraps, but I hold the vote—these men work for me. Besides, dead men don't talk much, and I've a feeling that he might just have plenty to say about who and what is on Joe Johnston's mind. General Sherman would be mighty interested."

This capture should be no more than business as usual, but Canfield was set on immediate execution. The privates were exchanging glances—something about the Rebel had melted Canfield's iron and made him rickety all of a sudden. To press his case, the lieutenant brought the lantern to Christie's face. "That's no Reb. No, Sergeant, what we have here is a real live Union deserter and a damned murderer to boot. This is the coward who tried to shoot me in the dark and left me for the Rebs back in West Point."

This news hit a responsive chord in the group. Treason was no small matter. "You say this man is National?" The sergeant examined the prisoner with renewed interest.

Behind him Mace expressed the sentiments of the entire party. "I'd forgive him secession, but I don't take kindly to cowards. Maybe the lieutenant's got something there. A little regimental justice—what's one Reb or one traitor one way or the other? Who has to know?"

The sergeant turned on Christie. "We'll take him back to the provost, they can sort this out."

"Yes, let's do that. This is a very small universe—planets are colliding all over the place. I should be able to find somebody to vouch for me." Christie spit each word into Canfield's face.

Canfield pushed Christie into Brady and raised a fist to threaten other reprisals. But Brady motioned two privates to take control of the lieutenant and then steered Christie to the door. "We'll do it my way."

"There's no time for that." Canfield was as shrill as a whistle. "He don't deserve the rights of a soldier. He's a coward and a murderer, I tell you!"

Christie smiled over his shoulder, "Keep talking, Canfield, you've got until we get back to headquarters to state your case. Just who do you think they are going to believe when I state mine?"

Canfield pulled his revolver and pressed the barrel into Christie's abdomen. The time had long passed when Christie would have flinched, and he held Canfield's gaze with his own.

"You're not going anywhere," Canfield spit. "We are going to finish this right here. I don't have to listen to a bull-faced sergeant—I'm senior here."

Mace grabbed Canfield's wrist and snapped it, he screamed as the Colt flipped into the dirt. Banner picked it up and set it in his belt.

"Let's go, Lieutenant," Brady ordered.

Canfield surveyed them all. "Mutiny, that is what this is. Sergeant, you will see a firing squad if I have my way."

By now Brady was out of patience, not a virtue he had by the quart in Canfield's case. "If your charge of mutiny is anything like your case of treason against the Reb here, well, Lieutenant, you are going to need a lawyer. Now I am tired and hungry—what about the girl here?"

Christie looked back at Angel and hoped his face expressed all the thanks he felt. "Just as she said. She didn't even know I was here."

The sergeant wanted to believe it. There were enough plantation refugees clogging up the arteries of the army. He turned to Tyne. "She yours?"

Tyne nodded.

Brady continued, "You know by President Lincoln's order she is free?"

He nodded again.

Brady turned to the girl. "You're smart if you stay here.

Don't go running off. No jubilee out there just yet."

Angel said she understood.

The sergeant reached into his blouse pocket for one of the cigars that he had liberated from a planter's library that afternoon. He struck a match.

Christie recoiled, "Sergeant, keep that away from me, or I will go up like a Roman candle!"

Brady stepped back, lit his cheroot, and snuffed out the match between his fingers. Then he ordered the privates to load the prisoner into the quartermaster wagon and not forget the milk.

"Gag him!" Canfield ordered. A filthy handkerchief was cinched around Christie's jaw and they stuffed him between a crate of potatoes and another of smokehouse meats. In spite of his circumstances, the captive was regarding himself on the leeward side of lucky. *Old boy, you did the impossible—you found Grant's army. Now let's hope Grant finds you before they string you up.*

Christie was bruised, raw, and exhausted; the alcohol chilled him through. But for the first night in many, he was not walking. He dimmed his brain to beckon forbidden but soothing images of Julie. The chime of her laughter: "Brent, you never could handle the least little pain—you're such a baby. It's the soft life you live, too much privilege makes a man squeamish." Within the seclusion of his mind, he pulled her close and made love to her even as the wagon tossed and pounded him over every mile.

The night was still black when they passed the pickets. Christie was fast asleep when the big sergeant with his bullhorn bark shook him, "Out!"

"Easy there with that prisoner!" The provost captain caught Christie as he nearly tumbled out of the wagon. He took a closer look, then backed off. "He is a mess! Where did you find him at the bottom of a still?"

"Skulking in a barn! He's a deserter and a murderer." Canfield stepped up to press his case nose to nose with the superior who was paying not the slightest attention.

The captain snapped. "Take that filthy rag off his mouth. How did he get this way? Any of you responsible for this?"

Sergeant Brady pulled off his gauntlets. "That's just about the way we found him, sir, less the bloody nose. That was Lieutenant Canfield's contribution." Brady motioned the captain aside. "I'm giving you a horrible puzzle, Captain McCoy. I think there is a lot more here than just a Reb or deserter. Canfield was awful upset when we found him—wanted to string him up right away!"

The captain regarded the prisoner with some respect.

"Tried to shoot him right there," Brady emphasized.

"That so?" was all the captain would say.

"I think the prisoner might give us a way to get rid of Canfield, sir."

McCoy smiled. "A man who can do that deserves some patient handling."

"My thoughts exactly."

Brady went back to his work. However, the captain was not too distracted by this puzzle to forget his original purpose for the rendezvous at this ungodly hour. "You got something for me, Sergeant Brady?"

The sergeant smiled sheepishly. He reached under the seat for the mahogany humidor. "Spoils of war, sir, minus one...to ward off the night chill, you understand."

The officer checked the quality of the brandy and the cigars then slammed the lid shut, "Yes, Sergeant, very good. I see no reason why we can't overlook that recent unpleasantness with the teamster. With only one week to go, it was a regrettable loss of temper—should hardly keep you from graduating out of the service. You will think of us fondly when you get home?"

The sergeant saluted. "I will bless your name every day, Captain."

The officer returned to the business of the prisoner. "You are in sorry shape, man! You stink to hell! Even for the army you are an abomination."

The private interrupted the provost with a private joke. "He said he wants to see General Grant. Said he has information. But Lieutenant Canfield said he is a murderer and a deserter, sir."

"What's your name, Soldier!"

"Second Lieutenant Brenton J. Christie of General Grant's headquarters staff!"

The admission hit the captain as so ludicrous that he nearly slugged the prisoner for insubordination. But all he said in those pre-dawn hours in the middle of the war was, "That so?"

"That's so! And I think he would want to know that I am back safe and fairly sound."

The captain thought the revelation over briefly and decided that things would unfold to every advantage if taken by the numbers. He turned to an aide. "Something in the articles of war has got to say a man can't stink this bad and be such a nuisance. After he has had a bath and properly dressed, bring him to me."

The guard took Christie away, but the captain had an addendum. "And Corporal, you are not to talk to the prisoner and I don't want any one else talking to him either! You hear? And keep him away from Canfield."

"Yes, sir."

Christie's alcohol-saturated clothes were dropped into the nearest campfire, setting the coals to flare and nearby companies and horses to stampeding. Then a wagon axle was slipped under the hanger and a caldron of boiling water was hauled off the fire. Christie, wearing nothing in the firelight but a suit of temper, did not like the direction the steaming pot was coming. "Where are you going with that!"

"We're going to boil you up like a Christian." The corporal was not in a forgiving mood. "A lot of soldiers were fightin' and dyin' while you were rolling in the loft with that dolly. I saw the way you looked at each other."

The guards upended their prisoner into a horse trough and very nearly drowned him in the rigorous pursuit of cleanliness. Christie shrieked in high C as layers of precious hide were peeled away. He endured by turns scalding baptisms, freezing deluges, and lye soap applied with a stiff horse brush. For good measure, they dunked him and cleaned him over a second time.

Finally Brady entered the little circle with a uniform under his arm. "Put this on, and be quick about it. You will be disappointed but we're out of shoulderstraps, but I doubt you will be in need of such formalities—just weigh you down when they hang you tomorrow."

As Christie was going to die anyhow, he turned and asked as if the noncom were nothing more than a steward at a seedy wayside tavern, "Could use a cup of coffee, Sergeant!"

"You want what?" Brady growled.

"Coffee—haven't had any in weeks."

The sergeant glared and then he smirked. "Can't see any harm. Private, get this man a cup of coffee." And to Christie, "Is black all right, your lordship? Or do you want coddled cream and white sugar?"

"No, black is fine. No sugar."

So precious was this uniform! Christie pulled it over his body reverently. The shirt was roomy enough to fit a fat teamster, and the blue four-button sack had only two and its blue had faded to green. The pantaloons had bleached to slate gray and he gathered the waist in inch-wide tucks under his belt. The brogans were cracked and missing nails vital to attaching the soles to the gaping uppers, but he was lucky, only one sock had a hole.

In uniform Christie was a dead man restored with his soul. He surveyed the camp; he longed for sight of the candy-striped colors more desperately than he wanted food or a priest. Instead, he got a half measure of the last two. A quart-sized private, who could have been no more than fifteen, was holding a steaming cup and something in a towel. Christie reached for the coffee but the private held back, fixing a hateful reproach on him.

"Were we ever so young?" Christie asked himself. And then to his Samaritan, "I didn't betray my country, Private. You will see that soon enough." Christie let him think on that a moment and again slowly reached for the cup.

"You really know General Grant?" The private was clearly overawed by the name.

"I really know General Grant."

"They say his staff ain't worth spit!"

"There have been rumors to that effect, I admit some true, but I'd like to think I am an exception."

"What makes you think so?"

What to say but the obvious. "I couldn't end up in this kind of mess lounging around headquarters."

To a green soldier with the halo of idealism weighing on his brow, such preposterous claims could be true. Christie reached for the cup again, this time the private let go.

Boiled from tainted river water and hot enough to sear tar off a gunboat, but it was coffee. "How I missed it!"

"Left over from breakfast!"

"And what year might that have been?" Christie blew away the wisps of steam and took another swallow.

The private had a second course: two-day biscuits and a scrap of green pork—very green pork— the lard had already soaked through the towel. "All I could get. Nobody wants to give a traitor nothing."

"As I said, I am not a traitor. Ever hear of guilty until proven innocent?"

"Not in the army."

"Can't argue with that. Therefore, I appreciate your gifts mightily."

"It's nothing! You still a child of the Lamb." The boy blushed, having been caught in a trap of his own sentiment. Christie pitied what the war would make of him before it was over.

"You ready?" Brady strode up flanked by two sentries with bayonets affixed to their rifles.

"For what?"

"Trip to the guardhouse, an interrogation, and probably a firing squad—all by afternoon mess tomorrow. If the O.D. isn't a stickler for paperwork, you can be in hell in time for supper. This way."

The door of a sulfur-tainted smokehouse slammed shut and the precious air with it. In the dark, Christie slipped on a pile of vomit and slid backwards.

"Get off me!" A brogan slammed into his shins and Christie careened against the wall. He slid down onto the fieldstone and coiled up into a knot. For this he got a bath.

The call of the first bugle rolled over a glacier of tents. The last note had barely flickered out when the next regimental Gabriel picked up its two/four time to ring it again, and then another, and then another, again then again. Carried on the wind, it sang its litany, but each time fainter and fainter as the call reached the very edges of camp.

The guard kicked in the smokehouse door. "You—Christie? The provost wants you!"

The prisoner was jerked to his feet and dragged to

headquarters. There was a plate of sauerkraut and raw beef on the chair beside a clerk. The private looked up from his papers only to encourage the newcomer to dig in. What benevolence was responsible for this no one said, but Christie obeyed.

Before the clerk left on his rounds, he handed the prisoner a letter — frayed, wrinkled, and well traveled. Christie's first piece of mail of the war, it was addressed in a woman's hand to the care of Major General U.S. Grant, Army of the Tennessee. Christie took the page to the window to read:

Friday, April 24, 1863

My Darling Brent,

Your mother brought your letters to me this evening They arrived with a letter of condolence from a Colonel Hatch. Her grief was total, and my shock upon seeing her and her purposes was so great that I was not much comfort to her. She is determined that you are dead, but she is undone in the conviction that we have been in correspondence all this time — her son in open adultery. Her grief was at war with her fears for your soul. But I can only bless her, for she brought your letters to me instead of shredding them into the fire. I do not — cannot — believe you are dead. I do not feel the emptiness that would haunt my days if you were truly gone from this earth. And so, my Love, I have been so audacious as to write in the hopes that this small missive will find its way to you somehow. Your letters came as a revelation. They washed away the anger and remorse hardening my heart against hoping and even praying for you. That you could still love me after all this time, and have forgiven me for marrying another even though I pledged my eternal faith to you. I must testify my unworthiness for the devotion of such a gallant soldier. I have been such a failure to you, to my family, to my faith, and to my husband. At least he has taken some measure for release. He could not bear my barren prospects and divorced me last year to marry another with the full blessings of his Church. He testified that I married in full knowledge that I could not give him a living child. My father holds the responsibility with me and shuns me even though I live in his house and eat at his table. The days pass one after another in silent punishment. But your letters have given me life again and I read them one after another over and over.

We are now two castoffs, my darling, but life has given us a blessing with all that. You see we are now fit only for each other. You, who has lost your station and fortune through no fault of your own, and me, a divorced woman through no fault of my own. We are unfit for anyone, so we are finally a match. What a twist of fate! I laugh to think on it. We can at last be united in our unsuitability if you can tolerate the scandal. I await your answer, my love. But if you see this is impossible, I will understand.

I have sent this scapular to mark you as God's own and my own. You will remember it to be the one you gave me so long ago. I pray that He will raise you up and keep you safe from your enemies until we can be together if you see fit.
Julie

The weight of the words drove him to his knees. Could this trial have been to some divine purpose? Momma Wise, in what she said about faith, could she have foreseen? Christie clasped the silver medal until its duplicate was impressed into his palm. He reread the letter to make sure it was all true. Until now Christie had played carelessly with his life, living on rations of hate and revenge. His future, the length of days were as trivial as so many pebbles. Now that he desperately wanted to live free, he faced a hangman's rope or prison.

All morning Sherman had blistered the brass off every officer so misguided as to breach his presence. General McClernand had come at dawn and put him in a terrible mood. Down wind from Grant's headquarters, profanity exploded in every direction like canister. Battle-wise staff had been staying out in the open air, enjoying this morning's sunrise as if it were as miraculous as an eclipse. Inside, the general now was in discussion with Generals McPherson and Logan, fomenting a united stand to take to Grant: If McClernand could not be shot, he should be fired, the sooner, the better. Grant had the authority, he had the cause, and now was past time. Logan, who had the eruptive predacity and almost Sherman's vocabulary of invectives, was ready to sign anything that would rid him of the pompous commander of the XIII Corps. Logan's casualties were heavy due to McClernand's incompetence. In spite of McPherson's youth, he was the only voice to counsel patience. Sherman brushed him off and fired another salvo, first at McClernand and then at the devils and lemmings that kept such incompetence in command—congressional cronies and the press.

"Well!" Sherman growled. "Did you read this?" He slammed the newspaper onto the field desk.

They had.

"Can you believe the reporters have turned that barnyard chicken into an eagle?"

They couldn't.

"Can we tolerate this humiliation that purports that we are all cowards and incompetents?"

They must...as long as Grant said they must.

"Would they sign a letter to General Grant urging that General McClernand be sacked?"

They would most heartily sign, but only under the stipulation that it would not be presented to the commander until such time as they all agreed. Sherman shoved the statement under McPherson's pen. Now it was only paper, but at first opportunity, it would be a guillotine.

Outside, Major Taylor, chief of artillery, dismounted and half-saluted to Colonel Hammond, Sherman's long-suffering chief of staff. Major Taylor motioned toward the general's tent, but Hammond shook his head and raised his eyes heavenward. He took the officer's dispatches for presentation at some more tolerable moment. Major Taylor, a man whose business was explosives, understood and would wait for an answer at the general's convenience.

But Provost Captain McCoy, coming hard on the heels of Taylor, refused all good counsel about getting while the getting was good and was bound to see Hammond and then Sherman. He had urgent business that he wished to discuss. McCoy had smelled something raw about his new prisoner, who wasn't of the stuff that made most deserters. If he were of Grant's staff, as far-fetched as that might be, there would be a court martial—or worse—for the officer who mishandled it. The captain dearly wanted the matter out of his in-basket and into someone else's. But Hammond had motioned the captain to cool his heels.

As the line in front of Sherman's tent grew longer, a poppycock lieutenant rode up. He demanded to see the general— that he be fetched into Sherman's presence with all possible speed. The general's aide Lieutenant Dayton stared at him as if the officer was babbling in Prussian.

"You want to see General Sherman at his first convenience you say, Lieutenant."

"Yes, that is what I said. Do you know who I am, Lieutenant?"

"Your reputation is infamous, Lieutenant Canfield." Dayton knew it was an incautious position to be in Canfield's front—something unfortunate always happened to those careers.

McCoy ignored the exchange of the two juniors, concentrating on his own case, which did not tally into any coherent mission to be taken to a corps commander—let alone Sherman. The curses and thunder coming from inside the tent made the provost weigh his mission seriously. McCoy would change his mind and walk back to his mount, then think again and come back. Go-leave—he was sunk either way. The spiffy, half-sized Canfield planted himself a yard away from the tent flap and waited. He gleamed like a new buckle, and he had no misgivings as to his importance. Dayton did not dispute him the honor—to the contrary—the staff needed a sacrificial lamb about now.

What transpired inside was heard by the lieutenants, the staff, and several nearby regiments. McCoy heard McPherson's voice, sharp, hearty, and tainted with venom, unusual for the tall Buckeye who even in the most difficult circumstance remained amiable, controlled, and deliberate. Sherman was all of these as well, except when he wasn't. A man could tell the weather of his moods immediately. Right now he wasn't. And that morning God's name was being solicited frequently and with a fury. Finally, the two commanders left, each clenching a cigar so tightly in his teeth that no minion stepped in his way.

Dayton turned to the provost. "Are you sure you want to go in there, Captain? He may blow like a double boiler at any time!"

But Canfield brazenly stepped in the way. "My business is most urgent, if you don't mind!"

His manner was next to insubordinate, but McCoy let himself be bypassed. He still had not come up with a satisfactory narrative. Canfield disappeared inside as Dayton braced and saluted. The rest of the staff rose and did likewise. "May God have mercy on your soul!" Then the flap dropped like a coffin lid.

Sherman was unshaven, rumpled, rheumy-eyed, his officer's coat lying adrift over a trunk. A pyramid of ash and cigar butts towered in a dish, "Sherman's old soldiers" the men called them. Several cups of coffee weighed down a travel desk full of papers. And McClernand's stench still suffocated the air. Protocol would have had Canfield announced, but Dayton had not done that. The grizzled general was unaware that he had a guest, and concentrated on a dispatch not liking its contents. On second reading he liked it even less and cursed, but bad news never goes away on its own. Both the report and Canfield remained. Sherman bit down on his cigar, the trooper thought he heard a growl but would not testify to it.

Finally, Sherman looked up and glared. The visitor was not one to sweeten his disposition: Congressman Canfield's pup — a tadpole in the Canfield gene pool, and the one weak link in Sherman's staff. The man had been shifted from pillar to post down Grant's chain of command, from McPherson's XVII to Hurlbut's XVI corps. He had been assigned to Grierson only to bottom out with Hatch, and he would not die, but only started all over again with Sherman's XV.

There had been few options left. Captain Pitzman, Sherman's chief engineer, had been nearly insubordinate when approached to take his turn as Canfield's superior. Likewise, Taylor of artillery. Grant had his McClernand, Sherman his Canfield. The objective was to find some employment for the blueblood so he could earn advancement, keep his uniform clean, and, in sufficient time, go home to run for office.

With stutters, humms, and ahhs, Canfield reminded the general he was there. "If the general doesn't mind, a matter of much urgency if it were convenient..."

It wasn't. Sherman's asthma was making him wheeze, and he drew even deeper on his cigar, blowing gray smoke in Canfield's direction. "Has Easter come early, Lieutenant? Or did you get all dressed up just for me?"

"Sir? I wish to register a grievance."

"A grievance?" Sherman choked. "A grievance! Why not! A lot of that going around."

Canfield was staked into the ground in front of the commander's table. Lieutenant Dayton entered with a fistful of telegraph dispatches, saw his commander had gone from red to purple, and thought better of it. He exited with all speed the dispatches still in his possession. As he escaped the tent he grabbed the arm of a fellow officer en route to the general, held him back, and shook his head. Dyer was a good man but sometimes ventured without testing the winds, he did not always understand that he needed to be protected from himself.

Dyer could not believe he was being detained. "These dispatches are for General Sherman from General Grant!"

"They'll keep." Dayton said and inclined his head toward the tent; "It's only a war. In there—*that's* going to be a massacre."

Dyer stepped back from the brink.

Canfield had not yet recovered from Sherman's unenthusiastic reception. He had thought he would be warmly received since he and the war chief—they being practically Washington family. Sherman's father-in-law was Senator Ewing, and Sherman's younger brother John sat behind his father in the senate chamber.

"Sir, a prisoner has been taken into custody as a Rebel—he is actually a deserter. Sir! He is getting rights he does not deserve." Canfield's tongue was shoe leather and the words tripped with an embarrassing lisp. He was still braced with eyes forward, in that there had been no "at ease" let alone the offer of one of Sherman's excellent cigars.

"What about it?"

"Sir, he is the man who tried to shoot me in the back at West Point."

"West Point?" Sherman was unsure where he heard of the place before. But he was of a mind that the defendant should be court martialed for bad marksmanship.

"Yes, sir, when we were both with Colonel Hatch, detached from Colonel Grierson."

"Detached! Yes, you have a history of such detachments, don't you, Lieutenant? Why is this one so significant?"

The general was not getting the point. "Sir! Both Colonel Grierson and Colonel Hatch have my reports on the incident."

"And they would be with General Hurlbut, not here. Perhaps you should take the matter up with him—you will find him in Tennessee." However, shadows were taking shape in

Sherman's mind now. Grierson's ride had been brilliant. Sherman himself had praised it in dispatches and reports to the highest levels as the most brilliant expedition in the course of the war — rare praise from infantry for cavalry. Had Canfield actually performed well? Had he contributed to the expedition's success? Had Sherman misjudged him? The general leaned back to give the swallowtail a second chance. "And you are going to give me an abbreviated version, I suppose."

So encouraged by a softening in Sherman's voice, Canfield launched into his story outlining events as he saw them. "The battle had been fiercely contested, sir. We had held — I myself was in the thick of it. That night this other lieutenant and I were sent to scout the front — first him, and me later when he didn't come back. It was dark and things were a mess from the day's fighting. Then I found him — the deserter was giving aid and comfort to the enemy. Talking to him gently — like he was a brother. I think they were friends or maybe contacts, the Rebel just pretending to be wounded so they could exchange information. The deserter saw me. While I was making my escape, he shouted for me to stop, and when I didn't stop he just shot at me and made off — his cover blown."

"He saw you at midnight! With such eyesight, the man could split atoms with a penknife. And how were all these contacts established, Lieutenant, this being a first for the army into this territory?"

Canfield missed the warning. "Sir, we had not been getting on and he had been damned insubordinate. I ranked him by a couple of weeks and was about to bring him up on it later. But he made off. We caught him yesterday hiding out with a half-breed in a Secesh barn."

"Get to the point! Who shot you?" To himself, the general pledged that soldier, whoever it was, the best lawyer in the army. Sherman smiled — that might just be myself. All of a sudden the general was warming to the mystery man. "Who shot you?" Sherman asked again evenly.

"Lieutenant Christie!"

Sherman snapped up like a whip, "Lieutenant Christie you say? Where is he?" Sherman's fist slammed down on his desk and both it and Lieutenant Canfield bounced three inches.

"Colonel Hammond! Now!" Then Sherman leaned into Canfield until the smoke of his cigar was swirling into the lieutenant's face. "Where is he?"

"Brought in last night. I guess he's in the guard house."

The war-weary chief of staff materialized to be accosted with rapid-fire instructions: "Check with the provost for a Lieutenant Christie. Have him brought here immediately." Hammond just as instantly evaporated.

The whole exchange had not been missed by those outside. Captain McCoy, seeing his mission accomplished without any loss of his own hide, turned to Dayton. "I don't think I'll be needing that audience with the archbishop anymore. I will have the lieutenant here in fifteen minutes."

"A wise man will live to be old bones!" Dayton nodded.

Inside Canfield still hung at attention, but the starch was out of him now. Sherman-the-lawyer had taken over the body of Sherman-the-general. "Now tell me about this attempted murder charge, Lieutenant. You say Lieutenant Christie shot at you, and you want me to punish him for that? Haven't you been shot at before this? I seem to remember a case in Raymond — the father of a farm maid. Then there was the wife of a vicar in Jackson. Even one of Miss Dix's nurses, she can't recruit them too ugly for you!"

"I have made out a full report, sir."

"Yes, a report. What I need is another report to add to my collection! For intrigue reports are better than French novels."

"Sir, it is within my rights as an officer and the son of..."

That was enough. "Listen to me, Lieutenant, I have an army on the gallop, the enemy on the run, and you want me to read your report and organize a court martial?"

"Sir, if the general finds it inconvenient, I can take it up to other venues."

"Are you threatening to go over my head, *Lieutenant*? And just how much higher did you plan to go? General Grant? Perhaps, your daddy in Washington? Or were you going to have your momma take it all the way to Missis Lincoln at the White House?"

"Sir! I am within my rights."

Sherman did not let him finish. "Leave your report on the desk and get out."

Canfield dropped the pages and saluted obstinately.

However, Sherman had his own methods, he called for Hammond again. "Colonel, don't let that man anywhere near a telegraph key, a pen, or a newspaper reporter. I want you to find a place for him, Colonel, so he won't be a menace. How are things in...shall we say...Texas or New Mexico, fighting Cherokee Confederates, *Federales*, Apaches, and rattlesnakes! You get my drift, Colonel? "

Sherman did not know Christie well, but remembered their meeting on the Steele Bayou expedition and knew of Grant's and Porter's high estimation of his abilities. Sam had been apprehensive even grumpy around the edges, when Christie was reported missing along with one of his best mounts. An officer who earns his pay on that staff deserves salvaging. Wheels turned in high gear with Sherman's name greasing the axles. In minutes Christie was mustered into Sherman's presence.

"Good, heavens, Lieutenant, it's like putting a uniform on a dead body." War was hell, and Christie was walking proof of it. He stood lopsided. His face was raw, scaly, sunburned and puffy and he saluted with a hand wrapped in bandages. And that rag—the quartermaster must have taken the uniform off a scarecrow. Sherman returned the salute, motioned to a campstool, and Christie slumped into it.

"Well, Lieutenant, it's been a long time since our little soiree on the *Cincinnati*. You've lost some of your starch since then."

"Yes, sir."

"I hear you have been asking to see me."

"Yes, sir, I have some information for you and General Grant."

In preparation for a long briefing, Sherman cleared the table of reports, manifests, and a few pen-and-ink sketches. Then he found a couple of cloudy glasses, and immediately the tone was set as he poured two fingers of whiskey in each. "A little anesthetic for your discomfort and loosen your collar before you choke. Now, let's hear it."

"I've been behind the lines for about a month, have seen more than I ever wanted to see of Mississippi, and have learned a little that might be of some use." Sherman nodded for him to go on. Christie's mind began to turn like the pages of a ledger. "The visions are very interesting not only from the military, but also from the civilian standpoint." Christie raised his glass to his lips. Good Secesh bourbon to wash down the sauerkraut would be just the ticket. He caught the scent, "What witch's pot did this come out of?"

"Vintage!" Sherman nodded. "Compliments of the Forty-Third Buckeye. Have some more!" Sherman "refreshed" Christie's drink. "Now, what are we up against? Dodge has been sketchy with his scouting reports. Where in the blast is Johnston?"

"From what I heard in the back country, Johnston is the least of your problems."

Sherman's eyebrows arched with surprise and skepticism. "With Grierson at the front door and Grant at the back, the danger should have put Johnston in high agitation. There was something of him at Jackson, then he evaporated. I heard from some of his cavalry that he's hightailing north around Canton — just waiting to see which way the winds blow. Old Joe isn't Joshua or Aaron, but he has got to factor in this some how."

Christie continued. "Perhaps not. Except for the main force at your front, what they have is mostly disorganized. There's several wolf packs prowling up and down the road, but in the main, the best of cavalry are De Baun, Wirt Adams on a good day, and Clark Barteau who's got half a regiment that fights like a brigade. But they are ordered one direction and then another chasing down phantoms. Pemberton's intelligence is no better than smoke signals, so pretty soon they are going to be worn out and useless."

"What else?"

"So far as infantry? Besides what Pemberton has to defend Vicksburg, there is some support coming up from Grand Gulf under Bowen — might even be attached by now. The rest of the reinforcements are local militia, determined only to keep us out of their own backyard mostly. Joe Johnston would make it an even fight, but the Freedom Line says that he doesn't have the craving anymore. Brigands and scavengers are on the loose everywhere. Escaped Negroes are prowling through the backways and swamps, gathering their own from the plantations. The planter's patrols are hired to track them down and deal a rough-and-ready justice, but they don't want anything to do with real battle. No less troublesome are the deserters on both sides, bushwhacking and stealing spavined horses and mules, raiding gardens, and poisoning wells. General, hell is in session. No one is safe. Things are so bad, the home guard won't leave the neighborhood to fight with the army, afraid for their farms and families. And the men are as tired and lame as the stock."

"Sounds encouraging," Sherman hummed.

"You were right."

"Stop buttering me up, Lieutenant, you already got my vote."

"No, sir, I mean what you said about the people...in the papers."

"You read the papers?" Sherman looked over the brim of his glass.

"Only when they are highly complimentary, sir."

"Then you can't be reading much. When was I right, and about what?" Sherman drained his drink and poured himself another. He was reputed to drink a lot but was never drunk—just enough to keep his hair red.

"The people—you couldn't exaggerate enough to do them justice. They hate us with a brimstone passion. They will hate us if they win—and more if they don't. If we make them surrender, they will bite us in the rump as soon as we turn around. This thing will never be over as far as they are concerned. It goes too deep. But they have reached the limits of what they can do about it. The wounded are beyond use even to themselves and are going home to stay. With Kentucky, Louisiana, and Mississippi nearly out of it, some in the ranks aren't about to risk their lives fighting for Georgia and Carolina. This is where state's rights is on our side. Many veterans see that it is only a matter of time and want peace while there is something left to save. But too many of the civilians believe in miracles. Manassas, Fredericksburg, and I hear, Chancellorsville in the east are giving them false hopes. They think Lee, Pemberton, or Bragg will save them at the eleventh hour. English men-of-war will blast into their harbors with divisions."

Sherman had been listening quietly. His breathing came in low whistles; he took another drink to loosen the tightness in his chest. "You know, it was one thing for the armies to go up against each other and for one side to take a licking. But the war has come to the doorstep of the citizenry, and when their high ideals and bluster become the conscience of the army fighting in their front yards, something bad takes over. What did these people think would happen?"

"You sound almost sad, sir."

Sherman awoke suddenly. "I am, Lieutenant, I truly am. Some of those men we fight are friends and officers I trained back at Louisiana State before the war. That school was one of the best things I've ever accomplished in this life—proud of fewer things than that." He lapsed there again, and then, "God forgive me, but I truly am sorry. Who do they trust?"

"Not Pemberton—nobody trusts him. They're putting their faith in Stephen Lee, Martin Luther Smith, Stevenson, and John Bowen. Bowen is well regarded, I hear."

"I remember Stevenson at the Academy. Didn't graduate at the bottom of the class, but he made a damned good fight for it. Bowen graduated with McPherson, and Jimmy respects him highly—I think they were drinking buddies at Benny Havens. Smith too—he graduated the year between Grant and me. I think he was from New York; like some of us, fell in love with the South and just couldn't break away. Old home week on any battlefield they choose."

Sherman refilled Christie's glass. The lieutenant's eyes were watering, and the pages in his mind were going fuzzy. One more drink and he would be inebriated.

"Let's go back to Joe Johnston," Sherman challenged, "will he join Pemberton if we press him hard?"

"Not from what I hear! Johnston has ordered Pemberton to try and cut loose join up with him somewhere else—how and where he wasn't specific."

"Davis has ordered Pemberton to hold Vicksburg at all cost; we intercepted the message."

"Pemberton has gotten lots of orders, but Richmond isn't sending him anything to hold with and neither is Johnston. What I can judge, sir, if you attack Vicksburg from the east, I don't think you have to worry about Johnston at your back. I think he will be going to Tennessee to help Bragg."

"Now there will be a triumvirate—Forrest, Bragg and old Joe." Sherman smiled. "A challenge, but nothing Old Rosy can't handle, could clear out Tennessee by the summer, if he decides to move a little faster. Ohio is making a fine name for itself. Won't that be a story for the reporters? I'll buy them all new pencils if they write that one and spell the names correctly. It would get their mind off the oysters-and-champagne picnics with the Army of the Potomac and talk about some real fighting. No offense, Lieutenant."

"None taken, sir. And by the way, Missis Meade sends her regards."

Sherman smiled at something he remembered from long ago. "Bless her soul." Then the general picked up a couple of cigars and handed one to Christie. "I think we should go see General Grant. He will be glad to see you."

Christie shook his head. "No, sir, I don't think he will. He lent me a horse and I didn't bring it back. I just got the general's hat paid off. I've had nightmares of being in the army for an eternity paying off that animal."

An army career for this lieutenant didn't sound half-bad to Sherman. He could arrange that. But instead he asked, "You know where it is?"

"Yes, sir, right under Clark Barteau's rump—the spoils of war. I'm assuming when some civilian or his pickets shot at Canfield, after Canfield shot me while I was helping a dying Reb..." Christie remembered it clearly now, two shots—different calibers. He concentrated harder. Canfield was standing over him, and there was a Rebel swinging into Gunshot's saddle and raising his pistol. Christie slammed a boot into Canfield's shin and he fell over just as the blast went off.

"Yes, that unpleasantness about treason—must tend to that." Casually the general took Canfield's report, rolled it into a taper, and held it over the lantern until it caught. Then he brought the flame to the tip of a fresh cigar. "He charges you with giving care and assistance to the enemy."

"I was sent out to the front of the lines by Colonel Hatch. Saw a wounded boy the enemy left behind. He was on the doorstep to eternity. No man's an enemy that close to God."

"I'll put that with Canfield's report and we will tend to it if it doesn't get lost. More pressing is this intelligence for General Grant."

At the council Christie was ranked by every officer by several grades, but Grant had greeted him with one of those smiles that his staff saw rarely these days. Christie was roundly slammed on the back by McPherson, given a cigar by General Logan, and met by Colonel Rawlins with a few blue invectives of warm greeting. But McClernand stood grim and apart, insulted that such good will should be wasted on a lowly lieutenant. Grant pulled Christie into the circle gathering around a map so thoroughly obscured by cigar smoke that Christie felt like a god looking down through the clouds from Olympus.

Grant began, "While we have been tramping from one battle to another, Mister Christie here has been enjoying the hospitality of the enemy. Lieutenant, what can you say for yourself? Can we break through to the Mississippi before June?" Grant did not stand on pretense. If the best information came from a lieutenant, a sergeant, or a buck private, it didn't change its truth and value. And he needed good information — metaphysical as well as physical.

Christie slowly shook his head, not liking the question or the spotlight. He relayed basically what he had reported to Sherman. Then he turned to the intangibles, the X-factors that were immeasurable, unseeable, unfathomable, yet were the deciding conditions in wins and losses. These he struggled to explain. "Sir, the Rebels will hold Vicksburg not because Davis says so, and not because Pemberton says so, but because the people say so. It's their home, and what I hear they mean to hold to the last man... woman, and child. You are fighting not just the army but the army *and the people*. I think eventually their goals will be at odds with each other. And when the army does surrender, they will have to face the bad feelings of the citizens. In the churches the men of God rant like zealots, working the congregation up to a fever pitch. This is a holy war and nothing would suit them better than to go down in history as the American Masada. So they won't let Pemberton surrender, not this side of starvation."

"Not a pleasant picture you're painting for us, Lieutenant." Grant's face was sullen. He was translating all this into strategy necessitated beyond the here and now. "The people! You sound like General Sherman here."

McPherson slapped Christie's shoulder, "And you don't want to do that!"

Sherman blushed the color of his stubble. "What have you heard about this holy war?" Sherman well knew, but the rest needed to hear it.

Christie did not think he could to it justice. "Strictly Old Testament and the main course of *civilized* dinner conversation — even from ladies, their talk would freeze your blood to ice. They are the match oath for oath of any of our fire-eating abolitionists when it comes to Armageddon. The ministers have the people stirred up and keep them stirred up twice a week with exhortations that Satan is at the gate, ready to trample their faces into the mud, rape their women and children, burn their city to ashes, make masters of their slaves, desecrate the graves of their ancestors, and sew salt in their fields. I seem to remember a parson shout 'We will fight with our backs at the altars of our worship and the graves of our dead. Choose the dungeon and scaffold a thousand times rather than transmit the taint of this leprosy to your offspring.' One fired-up clergyman like that is worth a brigade."

Grant worked the equations in his mind. How these variables translated into opposition against cannon and shell he could not calculate specifically, but that it was the deciding factor in the long view, he understood. They were not fighting army against army on an open field. Those days were probably over for good. The war had come to the hearthfires when a city was the strategic objective because of its railroads, ports, warehouses and factories — the enemy had decided that not him. This war was more than to vanquish an army, but vanquish industry as well. If Pemberton did not take his army outside to attack in the open, Grant would have no other choice but to invest, ring his army and the city with his troops and gunboats and strangle Vicksburg to death.

Grant asked in one final attempt to find an alternative, "Cump, you lived down here. Do you think they understand the grief of a siege? The women and children, once it starts, no one escapes for as long as it takes!"

Sherman's silence said it all. Around the table it was total.

What would the country say? But there was no other

strategy for Grant. He had made up his mind in the winter of sixty-two to commit whatever it took to win unconditionally. He too would fight to the last man—but he had more men, cannon, and ammunition than the Confederates.

"Very well, gentlemen. We will stay the course. I see no change in orders. Tomorrow we will be across the Big Black. We will try to run the enemy over or push them aside and save the people from themselves, but if we can't, we will seal Vicksburg off."

The commanders turned for a few parting comments to each other, a final welcome home to the young lieutenant, and then they filed out.

"Lieutenant Christie, a moment?" Grant's measured tone slammed the door of escape.

The lieutenant nudged Rawlins, "I think I am in need of a good lawyer?"

"The Constitution isn't going to help you here, Lieutenant." He left Christie to face his commander.

Grant unbuttoned his coat. His face was tired, but the eyes were still sharp. He got down to cases. "I am in your debt, Lieutenant. Your news was not what I wanted to hear, but it was definitely what I needed to hear and what I knew I would hear. As you can see, General Sherman does not think we will succeed here. But we are out of alternatives. As for you, I hear they were even going to shoot you!"

"I think a few still plan to, sir, on both sides."

"Well, I think I can prevent that. What are your plans, Lieutenant?"

"To find out how much leave I have, go home and get married. Then I'll join General Hooker on the Rappahannock?"

Grant brightened! "Married? Congratulations, Lieutenant, you *have* been busy. I heartily recommend the honorable institution of marriage—have tried it myself and found it most agreeable. But not on company time."

"Sir?"

"There is the matter of a mount, Lieutenant. General Sherman says that my horse now is back in the service of the Confederacy, from where he was liberated with much trouble. I want very much to have that mount back—I have suffered the loss of too many already, and this one was a particular favorite. I wish you to find it for me, and it will not be in Ohio or in Virginia. The horse, quite simply, is somewhere in Mississippi, and since the Army of the Tennessee is in that territory, wouldn't you say that your best chances of finding him are by staying with this army, Lieutenant?"

Christie blushed. Grant was offering him again a permanent position in his military family—to be at his side, among Sherman, McPherson, Logan, and regiments from his home state. Christie remembered the long, sweeping arcs Grant had drawn on the map only weeks ago. He doubted very much if General Hooker drew such goals on war maps, or ever thought so intricately. It would be these western men that would press the war to Richmond by way of the back door, while Hooker spent the summer playing chess with Lee in Virginia. His heart leaped to be apart of it. "That would seem so, sir, but a transfer would take some time..."

"The transfer was effected several weeks ago, Lieutenant. Mister Rawlins has your name among his AAG's, and your pay has been post dated since your arrival here. Hire yourself an aide, buy your lady a dandy ring on a lieutenant's pay, and the cavalry probably has some old nag for you to ride. Nobody around here is going to lend you a horse." Grant fumbled in his drawer. "Oh, Colonel Grierson sent this for you, should you turn up."

"Sir?" Christie accepted the sack.

"I have no idea—generals are not all provident. Open it!"

Christie pulled the string. Several of his carved chess pieces fell out on the table, but the sack was not yet empty. From the bottom he extracted a handful of sun-faded wool. The bill was gray and cracked, but the crown glistened with the brass of the precious 4 and C. Christie caressed it.

"You aren't thinking of wearing that around here?" Grant challenged.

"With your permission, sir."

Grant stuffed his cigar into his mouth. "I hope you are good with your fists—there are some Buckeyes around here who might take exception."

XVI
The Waiting Game
Late May 1863

Sherman had foretold it well. The Army of the Tennessee had come to the very gates of Vicksburg and hammered hard, but the Confederates held fast. Two swift battles, one at the northern redoubt along the Graveyard Road on May nineteenth tested Sherman's mettle at a point called the Stockade Redan near Chickasaw Bluffs where he had been defeated the December before. His forces went against the best the Confederacy had— Hebert's Louisianans, fighting shoulder to shoulder with Francis Marion Cockrell's Mississippians, men defending their own homes and families. Bowen's elite First Missouri Brigade, Grant's neighbors from pre-war days, was beside the home staters, and their repulse was no less desperate. Coming at them were other neighbors, the Union Sixth and Eighth Missouri, with no little help from the Buckeyes and the Ilini troops. They gave as good as they got, and when it was over, Graveyard Road was aptly named.

Three days later, with Porter's gunboats booming in the Confederate's rear, Grant tried again with an all-out attack. A four-hour bombardment hammered away all morning. One hundred and fifty volunteers from Sherman's best Buckeye regiments leading two more divisions—marched by column of fours down that same Graveyard Road and again into the guns of the Confederates. At the same time, McPherson sent two brigades into his front and they fought to a bloody stalemate. From his point further south in the line, McClernand committed his troops against the Alabamaian riflepits at the Railroad Redoubt with some small success. And at the bottom, the big Prussian General Peter Osterhaus pushed his Union division just as hard at Square Fort against General Stephen Lee. General McArthur, with support from Admiral Porter's gunboat booming from the river, also charged South Fort, closing a circle of almost constant firing.

But the gray line rolled the Union wave back on itself. Generals McPherson and Sherman, seeing that nothing useful was coming of it, called off the attack early, before more good men were killed. But McClernand had dispatched a courier to Grant protesting he could carry the day with reinforcements. He had taken two of the forts in front of him—or so he reported. Then Grant ordered his two Ohio corps commanders to renew their attacks. Sherman and McPherson did so, even if the credit for the victory went to McClernand.

But McClernand's brag had been over-ambitious. The forts had not been taken as he had boasted, and what had been a judicious order to retire from Sherman and McPherson, had been reversed—because McClernand wanted headlines. Instead, he got wholesale slaughter. Sherman was in high rage and went to Grant with the signed declaration. McClernand stormed that he had been betrayed—that the troops had not committed themselves—in other words—they had not fought hard enough from his vantage point back in the rear.

The Illinois Congressman and presidential hopeful was still smarting from the insult when Colonel James Wilson rode up with an order from Grant. When he read it, McClernand went over the edge, cursing everything and everyone down through the ranks, skipping generalities, and focusing on those particulars who had graduated from West Point past, present, and future.

Colonel Wilson, a touchy man when indelicately handled, slid down from his horse to confront the general—fists raised. "Grant, Sherman, McPherson all graduated from West Point, sir, and so did I!" Wilson was ready to fight it out for the honor of the Academy right there.

The aides stepped back. General Whiskey Smith turned to his captain. "Fifty bucks says the engineer can take him in two swipes."

The aide's head wigwagged—no takers.

McClernand backed off, suddenly mellowing his tone. "I was simply expressing my intense vehemence on the subject matter, sir, and I beg your pardon."

When enough salve had been lathered on Wilson's bruised pride, he rode back to report the incident to Grant and his entire staff. Thereafter, when an officer or soldier combusted into rage, Grant would explain to the uninitiated, "He's not swearing, gentlemen, he's just expressing his intense vehemence on the subject matter."

On the twenty-fourth, two days after the last battle, the putrefying smell of bodies blackening in the hot sun had become too much for civilized men to tolerate. Many wounded who could not make it back to their lines had also died for want of aid. The Confederates demanded a truce to bury the dead and it was arranged. Warriors from both sides stacked their muskets and crawled out of their gun pits to tend to the grim work.
As Christie walked the lines he came upon two men—one Yank and one Rebel—their shovels by their sides and their attentions intently on each other. They were brothers from Missouri. The crest of these rifle works was their first meeting since leaving home to fight against each other at Shiloh.

And so it went down the line—neighbors, brothers, cousins—exchanging letters and news of births and deaths, as their spades worked up the clay. A Confederate asked if the Yank had a copy of *The Chicago Tribune*, the best Sesech paper printed above or below the Mason-Dixon Line. Opposing regiments exchanged greetings as if they had known each other for years. Indeed they had—they had fought each other at one place or another since sixty-one. It might as well have been Christmas—except for the acres of dead around them.

Christie pretended not to notice this outright fraternization and kept on his rounds—until he saw a Confederate officer in a powder-blackened linen coat. He stood on the crest of his earth works supervising a detail of diggers. Courtesy demanded Christie pay his respects as he passed. As he came abreast, the officer bid him an embarrassed good afternoon and went on puffing his cigar.

"Hot!" was all that Christie could think to say.

"That it is—we are just into the sickly months and it is inclined to get hotter." Then thinking nothing of giving orders to a work party of both his own and the enemy, he said, "You there! Bury that man deeper. The next rain will float him up." Thinking that the order was in no way improper, both Yank and Reb kicked their spades down into the Mississippi clay.

If the Yankee lieutenant was not going away, well, the Confederate officer dug into his pocket. "Cigar, Lieutenant?"

"Thank you, Captain."

By stints and halts, Christie and the Confederate warmed to some pretense of a civilized exchange and then into an earnest conversation to find they had much in common. Both were men recently betrothed and in a hurry to get home. A motion of compromise was passed that each was marrying the most beautiful woman in the Union and the Confederacy respectively. They toasted to each other's happiness with an exchange of flasks, bourbon for whiskey. It was as to the day of the nuptials that put the new friendship into the fire. They were divided as to when these blessed events would be. The Confederate captain maintained it would transpire sometime after the Yanks had given up and left Vicksburg. However, Christie assumed the dates would be scheduled after Vicksburg surrendered.

The captain bristled and in a Louisiana drawl, "It was *you* who invaded *us*, sir!"

"After you fired on Fort Sumter, sir!" Christie countered.

"It was in our harbor!"

"It was where it has always been—on federal land, sir."

It was more than heat that turned their faces red. Christie did not want bad manners to mire the cease-fire, yet he could not call back the words in front of his men. "I do not wish to inconvenience our first meeting with talk of war. That would be ungentlemanly."

The Confederate accepted the olive branch. "You are quite right. A million men and two years of fighting have not answered the question to anyone's satisfaction, nor will we two in ten minutes. There is the bugle—our time is ended. I wish you and your lady a long life and a blessing of children."

"My sentiments to you and yours, Captain."

The two officers parted.

By early June, two Union lines of entrenchment formed back to back to seal off Vicksburg from top to bottom. One line of Union soldiers trained their guns west on the Vicksburg citadel; the other line turned their guns east toward Jackson and Canton. Grant still had not counted out Joe Johnston. His thirty-two thousand added to Pemberton's twenty thousand would outnumber the Union's forty-five thousand. If he came, he would come that way, squeezing Grant in the middle.

Sherman commanded the northern third, McPherson held the center, and McClernand the southern tip west to the river — sealing off Vicksburg from the landside. On the river Porter's gunboats cruised. Sherman and McPherson dug their trenches deep and as wide as a country road — plenty of room to drive cannon through without disturbing the riflemen leaning against the firing side. On the leeward side the men gouged out caves, there they slept and cooked their rations out of the sun. McClernand's trenches were not so neat and accommodating, and his men suffered more.

Nor were the lines static. Every night the Federals went to work with their spades and picks and every morning the Confederates awoke to find the enemy's earthworks a little closer than the night before. The closer they got, the more cautious their digging. To protect themselves from troublesome sharpshooters, the Union boys tore apart empty quartermaster barrels to lay over roofs, with a layer of dirt on top — making their trenches veritable tunnels. In a short time the lines became so close the aroma of Union commissary turkey and yams wafted into the Rebel rifle pits, where its occupants were eating mule meat and rice. Hungry Confederates hurled shells and upturned kegs filled with powder, nails, and scrap iron on the Union encroachers.

The Union soldier was not without his own methods to answer the assault. As Grant's courier, Christie often traveled the length and breadth of these trenches, and got to know many of the regiments very well — and to admire their sense of enterprise.

"Friend, that is some contraption!" Christie had been watching several of Manning Force's Twentieth Ohio chiseling the marrow out of a robust tree trunk. "It's too small for a bathtub and too large for a cooking pot."

A private straightened up. "Yes sir, we are quite proud of it. Designed it myself!"

"What exactly is it?"

"That, sir, is a mortar."

"The hell you say!"

"I hope that will be the effect exactly, sir." Christie wanted to know more, and the private was not too modest to explain. "You remember the Quaker Cannon? You know the logs Joe Johnston's Virginians cut down and trained on Washington way back in sixty-one when Lincoln believed Johnston met business? They didn't shoot or nothing—just scared the bejesus out of Congress."

"I remember."

"Well this is pretty much the same thing. Only this is not just a pretty face—ours shoot. We'll just finish hollowing this out and round out the bottom. When that's done, we'll reinforce it with a couple of iron bans around the outside, and she will shoot good enough to put a shell right down Johnny's throat—no extra price to the army. We can make a whole siege battery as long as the war and the forests hold out."

Christie was impressed. "You have my compliments, mister..."

"Friend, at your service, Lieutenant."

"And your friends?"

"Precisely. They are all named Friend too, sir. It's better to work with family—no arguments about pecking order."

The "Friendly" cannons were given their respectful places among Grant's nearly one hundred thirty that bombarded Vicksburg day and night from the east. From the river, Admiral Porter's gunboats lounged like black terrapins in the summer sun, but their big guns told that there was constant activity under the shells as well. At night the trailing fuses streamed like shooting stars through the skies raining shrapnel and shell into the city on the hill. As lethal were the incendiaries that exploded like blue and amber stars. There was no respite for over forty days and forty nights.

But the Union did not have it all its own way. On May twenty-seventh, the *Cincinnati's* luck ran out. The Confederates sunk the ironclad with a shell through her boiler, just as Hall had feared. Twenty were killed and wounded. Even at that Lieutenant Bache would not give up the fight. Still, the ship sank, drowning fifteen more. Christie wondered of the fate of Hall, Pearce, and Booby.

June 1863

"Prairie Dog Town" the soldiers called it. Whatever the Union cannoneer set his focus on became wreckage, except for the brand new Vicksburg courthouse. The tower was pocked and riddled as cheese, but the Italian clock still kept perfect time. And on the steeple, the blue flag with the white cross still rippled. It taunted the artillerists, but was never hit. What safety the citizens could find now was in the caves they burrowed into the hillsides. In time some of these were made quite comfortable, furnished with carpets and furniture brought from home. As the siege continued, residents took to living in them day round. But even at that, they were not always safe—especially from a direct hit from the big guns. Twenty- and thirty-pound shells furrowed deep channels gouging out the roads and shaking the hillsides. Caves collapsed and buried their dwellers.

The people endured. Their spirit lived on hope and faith, their bodies on stews fortified by pet animals, mules, rats and squirrels. Flour cost two hundred dollars a barrel, thirty for sugar, corn a hundred for a light bushel, and ten dollars for a pound of mule meat. They charged their neighbors living on the Big Black with hoarding their produce and selling it to the Yankees. These civilians saw it differently—those caught outside the city, lived with enemy camped in their lawns, officers in their parlors, and their wells and larders confiscated.

On the thirteenth the ax fell on McClernand and he was replaced by General E.O.C. Ord, a friend of Sherman's since their days at the Academy. General Logan thought the promotion should have been his, and the slight was not mended until he and the redheaded general were both old gray veterans.

The full blast of summer came, but Old Joe did not. And so the Confederates dug in to fight it out alone. The life of the soldiers Blue and Gray were mirror images of each other. Each among his own, hunkered down to a primal existence in the hot Mississippi sun. The heat was unrelenting and set the lice, mosquitoes, and chiggers as big and hungry as crows, into a frenzy. The men cinched the cuffs of their trousers tight around their ankles with twine to keep the dust and vermin out. They bathed only when they were blessed with tropical showers, ate commissary rations, and breathed the dusty steam tainted with sulfur nitrate.

Their lives passed a moment at a time, cramped in their tiny nooks along miles of rifle pits. All a soldier saw was the small piece of enemy ground just in front of him, and all he talked to were the fellows of his regiment. As the numbing boredom pressed down, he sang songs, exchanged novels, two-bit police gazettes, and old newspapers, brittle with use. The chaplains moved among the redeemed and gave comfort and a Testament. The unsanctified played cards, hummed their mouth organs, sang ribald songs, practiced their cursing, and waited.

To blow off steam or just hungry for a different voice, a man would yell over the top: "Johnny, I hear Lee surrendered why don't you give up!" And the comeback, "Hey, Yank, I hear Lincoln put in another outhouse, made it Stanton's office!" "Johnny, we're eating General Pemberton's horse for dinner!" "Yank, let me know when you're eating General Pemberton! I'll send over cigars."

As the weeks past, these exchanges extended into something more familiar than catcalls and insults, and in the process, they got to know each other well enough. Still, no measure was given over to carelessness. A casual moment to stretch a cramp or check the horizon for rain—a head bobbing above the earthworks for a split second—was entitled to no mercy even from an enemy who had wished him happy birthday not a minute before.

Now, soldiers did not die in hundreds as they had in battles, but in ones and twos, targets of sharpshooters, or in handfuls from sickness and thirst, or in squads from a hand grenade or a shell. But still the men of the South held on, and their Union adversaries kept digging westward—his works coming closer every day, until in some places he was not ten feet away. The Union soldier fought on full stomachs, receiving rations and coffee. His Confederate brothers, however, did the same work on half rations, then quarter, then whatever fraction his quartermaster scavenged. The wells and springs within the Rebel works went dry, just as Missis Meade prophesied.

Grant's commanders studied their maps and tactical manuals. If they could not take the enemy from over the top, they thought they would try from beneath. A mine was planned. Details of diggers and sappers, working by shifts, hollowed out three long channels under the Confederate redoubt at Fort Hill on the Jackson Road. Then they packed the recesses with twenty-two hundred pounds of gunpowder. But the Confederates would not be taken by surprise. They heard the enemy tunneling below, and dug counter mines so that the explosives would blow out instead of up. On June twenty-fifth the fuse was lit, and the tunnel blew. It was a signal, for every Union cannon and every musket to fire into the redan. Union troops charged through the flying dirt and rocks, dropping down into the basin hallowed by the explosion. The men of Louisiana aimed their barrels straight down, and from their parapets, shot at point-blank range at a desperate enemy groveling in the abyss. Union regiments from Illinois and Indiana could only take it. As they clawed the cavernous sides, the walls gave under their fingers, and the dirt collapsed under their shoes, burying them in drifts. As shot and shell rained down on them, desperate men tore at the sides with bayonets, and pressed themselves flat into bare inches of cover to wait for night.

A second mine was planned near the same site. The temperatures were over one hundred degrees on that July first. Men under arms cooked in the broiling sun and waited. When the powder was finally detonated, they charged with all they had. But the results were much the same. In the end nothing was gained and the slaughter was dreadful.

Compiling the grim casualty reports had been Christie's responsibility, and they had made him sick. Dead upon dead for no ground at all. What would the country say if mothers and fathers could see the blood of their sons poured out across these fields? That night fatigue and horror had dulled his reflexes when they should have been alert. In the dark, among the meandering earthworks, Christie had put ginger in his step as shells snapped at his ankles. He lost his way again, then found it—he thought. He hoped these were friendly trenches he scaled in the sulfur fog—the smell of boiling coffee wafted from somewhere and that made him think so. He was congratulating himself for cheating the Rebel sharpshooters when he was grabbed and jerked backwards.

"Don't struggle and don't say a word...not a word!" There was no danger of that with the man's hand clasped over Christie's face. "Here me, Yank. Say nothing, or you're dead!"

Christie nodded and the filthy hand was loosened slightly. "This is the bare bones of it: now, you can be our prisoner or you can have one of us as a prisoner—it's all up to you. When I take my hand down, you are going to just listen and I am going to explain. Got it? Listen, that's all, Yank."

Three Confederates, as cadaverous and filthy as scarecrows, raised muskets to their cheeks to reinforce the point. Christie nodded.

The voice continued, "Now this is the game, Yank. You're going to take Tom here prisoner. He's sick and we can't do nothin' for him. He's gonna die afore this is over. Thing is, Tom...well... that's all his mother will have left of five boys. So Tom's gotta go home—and not in a box. The only way is for him to get to a doctor, get better, and get paroled. Which is what's goin' to happen eventually anyhow, but Tom can't wait that long. You can do that, can't you, Yank!"

"How do you know that you all are going to be paroled?"

The leader was insulted for being taken as a fool. "Hell we broke your code. Been readin' it from the gunboats for two days. Porter said he don't want to waste his boats takin' all us up the river to the prison camps. So parole we will all be, only Tom's sooner than the rest."

He motioned behind him and three men came out of the trench. Tom sagged between his two mates who were barely strong enough themselves to keep on their feet. They moved him closer in evidence. As fragile as he was, he still held to his mission.

"No, Charlie. I ain't goin'. I told ya, we stick together."

"You be quiet, Tom. We have decided here." Charlie turned on Christie. They had risked caution too long already. "You do that or we'll take you prisoner, and believe me, your chances will not be so good as Tom's."

Christie feared that the three had waited too long—the man was barely alive as it was. "Is he wounded?"

"Yeah," Charlie whispered softly, "twice. Nothing much... in the leg and hand, but they're infected. The fingers are near purple. And he's had nothing to eat but mule meat and pea bread for a month. No decent water neither. You take him?"

Christie nodded, "Yeah, I'll take him."

The two hoisted their comrade on Christie's back. Christie shifted his burden from side to side, until the man settled evenly, and then he straightened. The enemy was no burden at all.

"I ain't goin'. You hear me? Put me down."

Charlie slapped his friend on the back as Christie moved

away. "Too late—you're already on your way. Kiss the girls when you get home, Tom, but stay away from Sandra, she's mine."

Christie turned toward headquarters and the Confederates melted back into the darkness. Only a few paces separated the lines. Even with the load squirming and pulling at his neck like a noose, Christie made it easily.

"Stop and be recognized!" the picket ordered and rifle hammers cocked.

Christie reported his name and position, but even with Grant's name attached, the picket was not impressed.

"The password, Lieutenant!"

"The last one I got was 'Geronimo,' before that 'Red horse' or something like that!"

"That was this afternoon! Try again."

"Infernal! I don't know what the password is then. That was the last I got!" Christie dealt the whole system of passwords to be the work of men deprived of any other military talents. As soon as you got one, and went on your way, the provost changed it—sometimes five times in a single day. The one or the other never got to the man who needed it. The Rebel fainted and slacked down his back. Christie shimmied him back up. Christie made up a few passwords that might apply, all of them defamatory.

The pickets finally gave in. "Close enough." A corporal stepped out of the darkness. "You are cantankerous, Lieutenant. You sure you don't work for General Sherman?" Then the corporal looked closer. "What's that you got there? For God's sake, the lieutenant's got a prisoner. Private, get the surgeon. You did him in pretty hard, Lieutenant. Resist?"

"No, tripped over him in the darkness, already done out, pretty near. He needs some of Missis Wittenmyer's tender ministrations. Get him to her hospital, Corporal."

"Supposed to take him to the provost, Lieutenant! For questioning."

"And if you can get him alive enough to talk, what is he going to tell us that we don't already know? Where the Confederate army is? I think we can let this one slip by the books for now, eh Corporal?"

The picket accepted the reasoning, and motioned for two burly privates to unload Tom from Christie's shoulders. The prisoner was hoisted on the back of the biggest, and the party moved toward the rear almost tender in their duties. "What's your name, Reb? Tollman? Where you from? Missouri? Us too! Got Tollmans around St. Louie—them maybe yours by any account?" The voices drifted fainter. "You come to the right place. You want some turkey, Reb? We had turkey for dinner. Got plenty left. Taste like horse plop, but it'll fit you right up."

Vicksburg, Mississippi
June 23/63

My dear Julie,
Write me again of the sunsets and picnics by the river. Are mallards and geese roosting there yet? We sit here by the Miss. like cats at the mouse hole, waiting for the Rebs to twitch. If it is not too late in the spring, walk to my old house and pick a dogwood blossom to send by the next post. Father planted the tree for mother to mark their tenth anniversary together. When we marry, I will get a start of it for our front garden. Did Gary Delancy marry Susan Ross? He was afraid she wouldn't on account he lost his arm. I bet him $5.00 she would. You must write and tell me all. Are you going to the courthouse for Independence? Will there be a concert? Will you have ice cream? Will there be raisin pudding and apple pie? Were the strawberries full? Will there be short cake and cream? We have plums, raspberries, and peaches here by the ton. The pickets get to them first, cleaning the briars and trees like a blight of locusts before we officers get a share. Of course they will sell us a cup full for the price of diamonds. We have more than we can eat of turkey. Where the quartermaster gets such a booty, there must not be a turkey left in all the Union. It is dry and tough as twine and sits in our stomachs like rope. Yesterday, Grant was inspecting the lines and a picket without a salute or a "How are you, General!" shouted to his lordship "Tack!" Then his pard took it up, and another, until the whole line was chanting like a drumbeat. Not tobacco, or coffee – but hardtack! I was riding right behind the general when it happened! He took it in stride and said now that the boats can get to us we should be getting rations. I was embarrassed, but Grant thought nothing of it.
I look to our wedding with impatience. But it cannot be until after Vicksburg falls. General Grant has promised a short leave for me to come to St. Louis. I will send you fare. Can you come? My Aunt Cordelia

has agreed to chaperone you on your voyage, then you can stay with her there until I can come up. She has already written your father, as have I. She would walk barefoot to China to see me corseted in marriage strings. And she would be the match of your father and General Forrest if they stood in the way. General Grant is for it. He said that there is nothing like a good woman to save a man from the devil and give him religion. The staff is in agreement and sends best wishes except for General Sherman, who is not for any baptized faith. Missis Sherman is as devout a Catholic as my mother and fears for the general's soul. (So does General Grant on occasion.) But so far General Sherman keeps command of his own soul. He reminds me very much of my old messmate, Nolan.

Please do not trouble yourself with worries of your father and the neighbors. They can accept us or not. Save my pay for a house in St. Louis — fewer eyes to know of our past and fewer tongues to wag. St. Louis is the town of the future. With the new country coming there will be plenty of work for a carpenter. I am set on having my own business. Working for another man is just renting a livelihood. After taking orders for two years, I will be my own master.

May God bless and keep you, my love.
Brent

XVII
A Rabbit for Dinner

It had not been the subject of surrender, abolition, emancipation, or the Union that set the boyhood friends from Delaware County at each other. But the competition for the best shortbread and ice cream had brought Christie and Tom Evans, a second Lieutenant of the Ninety-Sixth, nearly to blows. In two days, Independence would be celebrated at home, to include a baking contest. The two friends had been mentally savoring every entry in absentia, each casting his ballot in several different categories. With memories of apple pie and homemade ice cream on their minds, and hardtack and salt pork in their bellies, the pleasant respite turned ugly when allegiances became involved.

There had been some lack of respect shown on Tom's part for Missis Terry's cherry pies. Missis Terry had cooked for the Christie family for fifteen years. She had a reputation for her pastries that Tom, in the fires of heretical dispute, had boasted to be only second to those of his mother. Christie would have none of it and denounced him soundly, reminding him of the pies that the two had stolen from the window of his own kitchen and then had savored down by the creek.

Tom had owned up that they were indeed tasty, but that they were ill gotten gains had sweetened their taste. However, his mother baked a raspberry cake, that would put Missis Terry's in second place and he would risk his promotion to stand up for it. Christie footnoted his opposition with the accusation that Missis Evans boosted her recipe with enough brandy to inebriate the judges, which accounted to a bribe and a blue ribbon under false pretenses.

Others with not much to do but study mounds of barren trench works and buzzing mosquitoes cast their votes for their own candidates, and the referendum traveled down the line. Home boys volunteered Missis Bunn's apple pies as favorites, and Missis Vance's Shaker custard was also a contender. That it was brought to their consideration by Joseph Vance, her husband and colonel of the regiment, did not carry it by acclamation. The visions of such fantasies had driven the friends and comrades to forget their brotherhood. They were about to roll up their sleeves and fight it out over the honor of their ladies when the war interrupted.

"What's that?" A corporal pulled himself up out of the earthworks to see what was coming from the Confederate trenches. "White flag, Colonel! Over there!" a private pointed. Christie slid the bishop he had been whittling into his pocket.

A small retinue of gray-clad men had already cleared their own rifle pits and was making slow, solemn progress to Union lines. The officers advanced to the picket, stated their business, and were passed. A Federal brigadier greeted the party, was saluted, which he returned in kind. General Bowen and Lieutenant Colonel Montgomery, they said, with a letter from General Pemberton for General Grant. While the dispatch was taken to Grant, Christie and several senior officers motioned the Confederates to a fly-tent, and some hospitality was mustered for them. Christie was eager to see General Bowen—having heard so much about him. Christie was not disappointed. Bowen had a fine face, was of medium height but walked with great difficulty. He was thin and ashen, it was obvious to all present, Bowen was deathly ill.

"A cup of coffee, sir?" Christie apologized that it had been over the fire for several hours. But General Bowen beamed, grateful at the taste of the first real coffee in several months. Christie wished he had fresh.

A close circle of officers dismissed the momentous consequences that just now hung in the balance in order to enjoy these moments of fellowship with men they respected. When Grant's reply was brought, Bowen and Montgomery left, but their good impression remained after them. If the decision to war had been weighed by such men as Grant and Bowen, instead of Greeley and Ruffin, Christie thought so many soldiers would now be alive. He cared very much what became of Collin and Carolina, the Missourians he met that night in the trenches, and General Bowen.

Bowen's dispatch had been the beginning of the end. The next day Pemberton and Grant met to hammer out terms for surrender. From the first Pemberton was agitated, disagreeable and insulting. He was arbitrary and complaining of everything including Grant's estimation of the weather, which was not hot but tolerable. Getting nowhere and not wanting this opportunity to be lost, Grant suggested that the two move off and let their lieutenants work out terms mutually agreeable to their commanders. General Bowen and General Andrew Jackson Smith—equals in long service to their respective causes—and with grace and respect did come to an agreement far from the terms of unconditional surrender so famous with Grant. In the end, unlike the Gettysburg cataclysm erupting on the other side of the country, an entire army and a city would surrender quietly. The Missourians had been right—the Confederate soldiers would be paroled and not waste to death in military prisons. Instead they would go home to their families until exchanged. In fact, they would get a respite from the war, an advantage the Union soldiers would not have.

Grant had stared into the eyes of the Confederacy and made it blink. The citizens of Vicksburg were forced to accept what was arranged for their army. On July fourth, with the Union flags flying and every musician playing, General McPherson and his XVII Corps took occupation with the rest of the army close behind.

J.M. Sword's newspaper was among the first prizes to be confiscated—but soldiers did not get much. At the end, with no newsprint to be had, the *Daily Citizen* had resorted to printing its last editions on wallpaper. But it was what Sword said, rather than what he said it on, that made the newspaper a high priority for the Federals. Sword boasted that Grant had promised his army he would eat rabbit in Vicksburg on the Fourth of July. Sword chastised, "The way to cook a rabbit is first catch the rabbit."

The first order of business for the Federals was to shake out the type tray, set their reply, and run off the last edition: "'Gen. Grant has caught the rabbit;' he has dined in Vicksburg, and he did bring his dinner with him."

Close by, the provost set up another printing press and began printing up paroles, keeping a division of army clerks busy throughout the night. Tired Confederate cannoneers and footsore soldiers lay down rifles and lined up to sign. According to the terms of surrender they would not take up arms again until notified of exchange. Each Rebel took his copy, slipped it into his pocket, or pressed it behind the rope holding up his pantaloons, and headed for home. If he marched east over the honeycomb of earthworks and the caves that pockmarked the hills, he met wave upon wave of well-fed Union soldiers and full commissary and ordnance wagons—stretching to the horizon. If he trailed west, he saw the big Mississippi, clogged with Union gunboats, transports, hospital boats, and commissary barges. He thought again, if he had been among them who had damned Pemberton for a hasty surrender.

And if the vanquished expected catcalls and insults as he passed the long blue columns, he got something else. Billy Yank reached into his haversack and pressed on him hardtack, salt pork, and coffee: "Say hi to the missis, take some extra for her from Grant's boys. Tell 'em Cump said there are no hard feelings."

From the men of the regiment that had faced him every day for weeks without relenting: "Kiss your lady once for me, and take care, Johnny, don't get lost. Hug that baby for me too. Sarah? Wasn't that her name? See you another time and another place."

And they added a caution to the Rebels going south: "Port Hudson's about to fall to General Banks and he's not as friendly as us. Massachusetts man, you know. Better not go that way."

But many of the Johnny Rebs from Kentucky, Missouri, Tennessee, and Louisiana, their home states now occupied by Union forces and the matter of secession forever settled there, would not be back. The war was over as far as they were concerned. Virginia, Georgia, Alabama and the Carolinas could fight for their own purposes, but they were going home to plant corn, fix the roof, and see to their families.

Fri/July 10,'63 Vicksburg

My darling Julie,

Vicksburg is ours, although I do not know what we will do with it. It is a hovel of burned-out craters and desolated people. We ease their suffering where we can, but get no thanks for it. Pack your bags and come. Aunt Cordelia will be arriving on your doorstep any day with the tickets. Do not fear, Julie, she is a whirlwind but has a good heart – she was the only one in mother's family who approved of my father. You worry that we will not have children together. We will lighten the load by a half dozen from the foundling homes – and more if you want. The good Sisters say the war harvests orphans by the battlefield acre. With your loving care I will be blessed with better children than my mother had...

A long shadow fell over his writing paper. It was Sergeant Brady. "Sir, Missis Wittenmyer asks that you come up to the hospital. Things are an awful mess."

"I guess I am ordered! Lead on, Sergeant!" Christie pressed his letter into his dispatch case and pulled himself up to follow.

But the hospital wasn't a hospital at all, just the shell of a mansion. Men overflowed the rooms, the porches, and lay over every bit of ground. Under small swatches of shade Sanitation Committee volunteers spooned soup into the mouths of Confederates with no hands and some with no arms. Other men rolled and tossed – delirious with pain and hunger. A casualty pleaded with his surgeon for the reprieve of his leg. Would the surgeon understand: how could he go home a one-legged farmer?

Still others excused gaping wounds to be nothing at all; they would be of no trouble if someone would just assist them down to the docks.

Doctors and surgical cadets were working against great odds. For the most part the cadets were students rounded up from medical schools and laboratories, and shipped wholesale to these battlefield surgical factories. Most had already surrendered military discipline for the heat, and had hung their coats on the branches of the magnolia. Instead of leaves the battered old tree sprouted boughs of blue jackets with the emerald slash marks of the medical service. But one had not, and he looked as if he would faint.

Christie bent over him, "That coat will absorb the heat like a clay brick. No one will think the less of you if you take it off. Save it for the parades when you get home."

The words went unheeded. The cadet was bent over a dead man cradled tight in his arms. It was then, Christie saw that it was not so much sweat but tears streaming down the man's cheeks and Christie let him be.

"Sending us babies, they are!" Christie swore.

The sergeant restrained an impulse to correct his lieutenant. The significant point was that the lieutenant was the "baby" here. He was certainly junior by at least two years to any of the green-faced cadets around, but the noncom said nothing. Christie told Brady to wait while he met with Missis Wittenmyer, and Brady was all too glad to comply.

Lieutenant Christie had been on a short fuse for the last two days, living on air and no sleep, to be everywhere at once. Grant had made him liaison between his commissary headquarters and the Sanitary Commission as well as liaison to the medical department—that was two departments under one very junior officer. In those weeks Christie was as close to Frankenstein as he could get. Then Christie shanghaied Brady, the same quartermaster sergeant who had kept Canfield from shooting him in the barn the night he was captured. Brady had been an accounting clerk in a Cleveland dry goods store before the war, a needle and thread counter with a very good reputation for his sums. He had been on his way home to take up his old profession—in fact, he had one foot on the gangplank when

Christie sought a word: "Go home, if you have to, but don't expect anyone to understand what you've seen and what you've heard. They don't want to listen, they've got their own ideas—all fashioned from the newspapers—that war is very different from this one. I give you two weeks with the cracker-barrel generals and dry-goods strategists before you commit murder. The ones who understand are all here."

The seed planted, Christie countered with an offer of second in command in his department—reserving until after Brady had signed on the dotted line, that he was the junior partner in a department of two. (Some things take their time in revealing themselves.) Brady bore up well and set about to straighten out the lieutenant. But this lieutenant was a marvel. The blue cap with 4-C covered a head that digested reports on the first reading and kept perfect records of every manifest, inventory, or accounts that would bonker a whole department of clerks. Grant had appointed him precisely for these talents—and because the lieutenant, even though he could be quick with his temper at times—was also honest to a fault. Honesty, accuracy, and distemper were valuable assets when millions of dollars of medical supplies and rations were being purloined off the wharves into black market warehouses.

And so a hundred times every day the transports slammed into the docks to unload supplies, food, and ice from the North. Christie was adamant that not one yard of bandage, ounce of lint, pound of ice, or jar of jam would be misappropriated—especially with the Sanitation Committee ladies peering over his shoulder. The lieutenant would add the new manifests to the inventories already in his head and never look at them again. He could recall every case of every conceivable item on every ship and warehouse, deduct what he had allocated, and keep the remainders like an abacus. Once or twice the lieutenant's figures did not tally with his own accounts which Brady carried for ready reference in a leather satchel. But after some licking of his pencil tip and scratching of numbers, the "insubordinate" found the lieutenant's estimation had been correct in the first place. Brady was insulted.

Day to day, such perfection is hard on sergeants who value their indispensability, and it begs to be brought down. In an imperfect world, even the lieutenant would make a mistake; the only question was when. The day and hour Brady did not know, but it would happen. To bored soldiers, such predictions are temptations for a side enterprise. Brady had sold bets, and in an army whose soldiers will gamble on the speed of a cockroach or the number of invectives General Logan could squeeze into a single sentence, the prospects went through the ranks like fever. Some ticket holder in the Vicksburg occupation force would be a rich man when the lieutenant finally got his comeuppance. When it came to pass it would be a financial victory as well as a moral one. Brady himself had taken out fifteen chances with his last pay, and he would help it along by befuddling the lieutenant if he saw the chance. General McPherson had given his blessing by taking twenty-five chances and General Sherman twenty, with orders that his staff also contribute. If either commander won or if one of their staff won, the proceeds would go to the Sisters of Mercy hospitals.

So far, the subject of all this speculation went on, unaware he was a walking gold strike. However, he was growing increasingly conscious that men regarded him curiously. Christie was receiving some of these stares now as one foot tottered in front of another over the narrow beam that replaced the broken stairs to the high porch.

Christie stepped into a parlor, the walls braced from collapse by beams elbowed outside and in, like Gothic buttresses. The roof and upper story had been shelled away but the ceiling was intact. The windows were agape and the walls molted wallpaper. It was a field hospital made if not livable at least serviceable, first by the ladies of Vicksburg, and after the surrender, by the Sanitation Commission, one of their esteemed number now flew at him in high agitation.

"Lieutenant, we are in desperate need of food here...water...soap...and bandages. The surgeons have been operating without them—tearing up curtains and everything else. I have come nearly to the end of my supplies and have contacted Doctor Irwin, but things are slow...dreadfully slow! The filth—it is incomprehensible! The sick are covered in lice and roaches. How can we help them if they are so filthy?" Christie called to Brady and he came on the run. "Sergeant, order up some anesthetic and clothes for these men."

"Sir, they are Rebels—they won't wear them."

With motivation, Christie thought they would. "I don't intend on asking their permission. We'll strip them completely naked and see what they decide then."

"Yes, sir. Right away!" Brady hustled away, muttering to himself that officers used "we" when they actually meant "you."

But the lieutenant was not yet finished. "And detail some men up here to help—make sure every one of them is hauling two buckets of water for drinking and bathing—and soap." It was the little things that were overlooked. If an order wasn't given, no matter how obvious the need, the deed went undone—a catastrophe of inefficiency amid human want. "And a cook pot full of soup with some biscuits, that means baked since Lincoln was elected!"

Missis Wittenmyer led him to the next emergency. Christie followed respectfully. Anne Wittenmyer had been deputized by the Iowa legislature as its agent for the Christian Sanitary Commission, and she could teach the army something of organization, command, and accounting. She was the sister of Doctor Turner, a surgeon on the *Nashville*, a permanent hospital boat at the Vicksburg wharves. But her domain was the land, and Missis Wittenmyer had visited every barn, farmhouse, shed, chicken coop, and hospital tent she could—all dense and overcrowded. In the past weeks she had doled out a king's ransom in supplies raised in her home state—but had seen the need triple for every one she helped.

Grant would complement these with rations and medical supplies from his own commissaries, as Christie saw fit. As Grant's lieutenant, Christie was to be efficient, untiring, and charming at all times to make sure only complimentary reports of the army and its commanders were sent home. Christie did his best to make order out of chaos, cut the red tape and set fires under men—most of whom outranked him—to keep up. It was his job to keep this "angel," and the women like her, from his boss's door. And they were legion.

If the South had had their own angels of mercy before the surrender such as Missis Breckinridge and the Sisters of Mercy, the Union ladies would not be seen slacking after. Missis Beele Reynolds of Illinois had gone to war with her husband, ministering to the troops from the first battle the army fought back in Tennessee. Missis Hogue, who represented the Sanitation Commission of Chicago, could turn rocks into onions and boil up a soup rivaling the best restaurants in the Windy City. Missis George of the Indianapolis Sanitation Commission was indefatigable. But pre-eminent in the heart of the Buckeyes was Mother Bickerdyke, an herbal healer from Cincinnati. She adopted every soldier — blue or gray — as a son. She was their champion and to the contrary, a terror to the commanders who did not heave to when she set forth demands in her soldiers' behalf. Even Sherman authorized she is given anything she wanted: "She ranks me."

As Christie followed his guide from one crisis to the next, a Rebel sergeant set himself weakly on an elbow: "Water, Lieutenant, some water!"

"I have only a little left," Christie pulled his canteen around and uncorked the lid. The Confederate inhaled it greedily, much of it overflowing his lips and washing down his cheeks. Christie ripped a piece of curtain and wiped his face. The mask of black sulfur smeared away.

"I'll see to him, Lieutenant." A chaplain set a bucket down and began to bathe the man's face.

But the Confederate did not take his eyes off the canteen. Christie raised it again. The Rebel drank more slowly this time, letting the contents wash out his mouth, and then flow down his throat as if it were something more precious, more rare, than just dank well water. When the canteen was empty, he clasped Christie's hand in gratitude. "Obliged," he rasped. From it, he seemed to gain clarity and strength. He gazed around the room, confused at what he saw or where he was. Then his focus settled back on Christie's face, searching for an explanation — some reason for all the misery. His palm closed tight around Christie's. He coughed, fought to hold on, then his grip softened. His eyes fluttered, and his head rolled away. Christie had seen it so often. Men seeming to be holding on, getting better, then just dying off in a second. While others next door to death, pulled through minute by minute, day to day, by a miracle.

As the needs of the living pressed harder than the needs of the dead, the chaplain made a Sign of the Cross and pressed a hand to the man's heart as he repeated the Lord's prayer. Then he motioned the litter carriers to take him, and a new man was quickly set in his place. The chaplain rose, but his balance was unsteady. Christie caught him, just as he would have fallen back. "Watch it there, good fellow..." Christie went dumb, the other man gasped.

It was the chaplain who found his voice first. "James! I see you found General Grant...and he has found us. What would have God and the South done with you if you hadn't?"

Christie could not restrain his joy. "Collin! How can you be here?"

"I have been here since the beginning, doing what I could. Our cause—how do you like it? What I wouldn't give for just one chance to call it all back." He surveyed the horror of just this one room, "To raise them up and restore them to their mothers, wives, and sweethearts. To have the power to wipe it all away."

"Come, you are about dead yourself." Christie gave his friend his arm.

Collin pulled back, "No, I must stay here. They need me. My work is here."

"Your work?"

"Even the most unworthy spirit aspires to a special mission. It is the best work I am suited for—to hold the hands of sinners—I know all about sinning. I can help them pray for forgiveness, lighten their souls; for most of them, it's a short journey home from here."

"Collin, you are exhausted. You are talking nonsense."

"My friend, have you seen my father?"

"No, is he in Vicksburg?"

"Yes, somewhere. I saw him a couple of weeks ago. We were side by side, pulling away the rubble; a family was buried in a collapsed cave. I looked right into his face and he would not even say my name." Collin set his crutch under his arm.

A Rebel steward interrupted, wanting Christie to follow him, "Sir, you are needed."

"Yes, coming." Christie turned to Collin, "Eban—did he make it home?"

Collin smiled. "He made a run for it, I haven't heard more, so that might be good news."

"It is my fault. I should have gone by myself."

"No, I knew he would run soon anyway." Collin appraised Christie up and down. "I see you are an important man. A lieutenant? Your regiment is close by?"

"No, I am of General Grant's staff."

Collin laughed, "Oh, would Carolina hemorrhage. Grant's own man in our house—and she missed the chance to poke out your eyes with hot coals. Yes, to be a fly on the wall when my next letter reaches home!"

There were no words to thank him for saving his life, and in this confusion that pulled them in different directions, all he could do was extend a hand. Collin was aware of the Confederates around them—one had spit in disgust at the warmth of their exchange. Collin shifted his weight onto the crutch and took the hand and held it tight.

"If I can be of any assistance..." The words were inadequate and Christie broke them off.

Collin shook his head, released the hand, and hobbled away.

Later that night, Christie returned to the hospital to take Collin back to his tent. But the nurses said he was gone—where they did not know. Missis Wittenmyer did not look up from her work as she spoke. "Collin Bennett comes and goes during the greatest need. He works among the ones who have lost all hope and reason. I do not know what we would do without him. Some of these men are insane with fear, pain, and despair. He is the only one who can reach them. I saw that you know him. Is he a minister?"

"No, just a soldier. Learned the Word the hard way, as did Saint Paul. Bless him!" Christie did not see Collin in the other hospitals he visited. Missis Wittenmyer and Missis Bickerdyke had promised to look for him and send him along should they find him. Days passed and Christie's inquiries were answered with shakes of the head and confused indifference that one Rebel could be so important.

"Sir, you will come to the courthouse. There is going to be trouble!" Brady was at his sleeve now. Christie shrugged it off, but Brady did not get the signal and go away. He just stood planted, waiting for Christie to follow.

So Christie followed. His legs had barely enough spring to

pull him over the rolling hills, but he went. He had seen the courthouse glisten in the sunlight from Young's Landing last March, but now it was dirt-faced and chipped. But the clock on the steeple still timed the day perfectly, and it had just begun to mark the noon hour.

Below it had gathered a tiny congregation of Negroes — mostly men and women smudged from their morning's work — intermixed with a few blue uniforms from the Union colored regiments. Oblivious to the taunts and the jeers coming from the toughs on the curb, they bowed their heads and the minister began the Twenty-Third Psalm. He spoke in a sure, rich bass that carried like a bell, and should have soothed instead of heated the resentment growing around them. Other freedmen came running to join their fellows, but were blocked at the curb. With the arrival of more freedmen and more toughs, the scene was growing ugly with shoving and threats.

"Get the provost!" Christie growled.

Brady did as he was told, even though the lieutenant himself might need a seasoned fighting man by his side, before reinforcements could arrive. The blacks turned their backs and ignored the danger. In the center, their leader began a prayer. But he could hardly be heard, even by his own, for the jeers and shouts coming from the street.

"What you prayin' for? You got a black-faced god up there! You think we licked? You think you free? Think again!"

Christie cut through the mob looking for the leader. He was careful not to push or threaten, but his tone was firm. "Break it up! Did you hear me? I said go home!"

On the edge locals gathered to see what course the encounter would take. But they kept well back from these drunks and rabble that swelled up from the river wharves to stalk their town.

"We ain't got homes! You Yanks saw to that! You want to give me back my home?" A thug sneered, through a gap of vacant gums breathed stale whiskey and decayed teeth in Christie's face. The pack shouted their agreement, and knuckles curled around rocks. The unholy brethren jostled and pushed Christie into a swarthy giant of a man. He too was foul with whiskey, dirt, and sweat, and he brought it to bear — to intimidate the little officer, too clean and well turned out to amount to any real threat.

Christie had met such a man back in Cincinnati in the beginning of the war—a Copperhead bent on killing him. But Christie had crushed the man's skull with a rock. That same rage boiled up in him again, and his fingers rolled into a fist. "Go home to whatever hole in the ground you call home. Go home now, or so help me, they will be burying you in one after I am finished!"

The brute had found this funny and was about to vent his humor with ham-like fists wrapped with leather straps around his knuckles, but the thunder of hoof beat carried the point. The mob turned mute under the glare of provost swinging down from their saddles with carbines cocked. All except the thug ignoring the good sense of his friend pulling him away. "It's no good, Jess. Let it go!"

"Let it go! This ain't our town no more! Desecrated with Yanks and niggers walking around free!"

Captain McCoy pulled his revolver and laid it against the agitator's neck. "Arrest this man!"

Two troopers pulled Jess back, but not before he spit in Christie's direction. "Yank ain't going to fight his own battle? Yellow!"

"Come on, you're under arrest." And the troopers jerked him away.

McCoy then reined his horse into the pack. "Any of you want to join him?" Men backed away. Having lost the advantage, the toughs were already losing their taste for a fight. To keep it that way the rest of the provost formed a shield wall against the townies milling at the curb.

"Sons of whores!" a woman sputtered, "that's all you Yanks are—Sons of whores!"

"Go home, madam!" A corporal ordered in thickly accented Prussian.

She sneered, "Foreigners! Vicksburg is a bedlam of stinkin' foreigners and cut-throats!"

She turned on Christie and found hatred for hatred in his eyes, then backed off. Jess was put into a wagon and taken away. Christie thanked McCoy, the provost just shook his head still incredulous that the shavetail was one of Grant's. "Saving your hide is getting to be a habit, Lieutenant."

The freedmen had commenced their prayer meeting in spite or because of the near riot. For half an hour more they prayed—for Lincoln, Grant, and holy inspiration in their new life. With the last amen, they shook hands with each other and melted away—all except their leader. He turned back, surprised to see Christie still there.

"Thank you, brother!"

"I am not your brother!" Christie answered coldly.

"I thank you anyhow!"

"What are you doing here? Do you think it wise to taunt these people? They are on edge as it is."

"All through the siege, we came here to pray every day about this time. The cannons did not stop us! Why not now?"

"What for? You got what you prayed for. Isn't there somewhere else for you to pray?"

The man's face had no compromise in it. "I had a church, but the people burned it down. Then we met at my house. They thought we were praying for freedom and the enemy, so they burned it down. So we come here. If we can't pray in private, we will pray in public so the people can hear our prayers—join us if they have the heart. We meet every day at noon—under the clock. The gunboat shells didn't hurt the clock for it was protected by the hand of God. God saved this place for us, and we come, and we will keep on coming. Just to pray, that's all we want."

The moon face of the steeple clock showed its hands toward one. Christie had duties and they were impatient to be done. "Well, I can't keep you from coming. I will make General McPherson's provost aware of your ritual, and he can post a guard to keep your little gathering from becoming a funeral."

"I appreciate your kindness." The pastor nodded and passed by him.

"Sir?" Christie called and the minister stopped. Christie thought of Eban who had been as obstinate as this man here—but not so reckless. Christie wondered what his old guide was doing now in the first flush of freedom—oh so precious, too precious to lose over dares that can't possibly be backed up in the end. The pastor turned and Christie continued, "The future now has promise with a new country, it would be a tragedy to lose everything before you even have time to taste it. Like I said, it might be wise not to push these people too hard."

"You're wrong, Lieutenant, it is not the people of Vicksburg we need fear. It is more what they fear in us. They have to see it is nothing." He resumed his descent down the hill toward the river. Christie still held an audience of one.

"And now you understand the mess we are in?" The heat of the midday sun had set the brush of his red hair afire, his face glistened in sweat, but the cold steel in the eyes had watched it all without a single drop of compassion. General "Cump" Sherman pulled his short-brimmed hat lower over his eyes. With the new year President Lincoln had commissioned the organization of African troops under white officers to be incorporated into the armies. But Sherman had steadfastly refused to have them fight under his command. He had said at the time, "If the Africans revolt to wage war on their own against their white masters or on us, or this country, there will be a guerrilla war with no resolution."

Sherman waited for Christie to join him, and they walked toward McPherson's Crawford Street headquarters. Sherman's family had joined him and he had set up camp on the Big Black where the water was purer and the air cooler. He came to the city rarely—Christie estimated the general could not bear to see the devastation of the old Southern jewel.

The heat made them both feel dull and unwell. "This place is as hot as hell." Sherman was given to little talking unless he was crossed, then he had much to say and with great vigor. "I have heard that Rosecrans has broken through Tennessee and pushed Bragg into Georgia. And Mead held Gettysburg. Funny, I almost wish he hadn't."

"Sir?" It was asides like these that had given fuel to claims that Sherman was still mad.

But the lieutenant's tone was one of curiosity and so the general continued without offense. "Well, think on it, Lieutenant, where would Lee have gone if he had won at Gettysburg?"

"To Washington or Harrisburg, I suspect."

"Okay, so just for argument's sake, let's assume the worst—Washington. It's closer and it's Southern. What's there?"

Christie played what he knew of Lee's campaign through in his head. "When word got through to Washington that Lee was on his way, they would have put the president on a train for Ohio, and congress with him—that was the plan I hear."

Sherman nodded. "The British took our capital how many times in two wars? But every time we just moved it. So Lee would have taken Washington and gotten what?"

"Mountains of paper and maybe two tons of low-level clerks and bureaucrats."

"And he was welcome to them. I hate the blasted city anyhow. Eastern commissaries are in Alexandria, anyhow, well guarded and damned impregnable."

"Papers estimate that the war would have been over though."

"Reporters are idiots. The lot should be hanged! But in this case they were right, just not the way they think. We would have the fox in the bag—Lee would be moving through enemy territory without much in the way of ammunition or supplies and with a tired army hauling prisoners. General Crook would move his troops out of West Virginia to intercept. Then there's the home guard in Pennsylvania that John Reynolds trained before he died. There are troops in Alexandria and Georgetown—in fact Washington is one large barracks—not to mention what amounts to two divisions just guarding every damn door to every damn office to every damn bureaucrat in the city. If we are desperate there is John Wool's Department of the East. Add them up: men at nineteen posts along the coast ready to be put on a train. And if push came to shove we could use General Sigel in the Shenandoah, although I wouldn't want to depend on him. And let's not forget the two crack brigades from the Army of the Potomac sent to New York to quell the riots—your Fourth Ohio among them, I remember. They were never scared of Lee. Every one of these detachments marches with full supply wagons, bright shiny rifles, full cartridge boxes, and are followed by cannon and artillery wagons with full caissons. The fox would have been in the bag, as I said. Yes, with Rosecrans holding the railroads in Chattanooga and us here in Vicksburg—the war in the East wouldn't have lasted another month. But Meade won at Gettysburg and saved Lee from himself, and let Lee get away into Virginia. I hear Lincoln wants a piece of Meade about as much as he wants Lee."

At the house, Sherman opened the gate and turned for a

last word with the junior officer still standing on the walk. "The next year is going to be the toughest. Only friend we got is the man in the big white house. I didn't like him the first time I met him, and he didn't like me much in return. But we have revised our opinions of each other since. We got to win to keep him there. We got to wind up this war by the next election."

As they stepped to the gate, a boy rocketed through the front door, down the porch steps, and at break-neck speed plowed into the general, nearly sending them both sprawling into the street. Willy Sherman, the general's oldest son, clasped his father in a vise. "Uncle Charles brought me a present—a new pony! And he brought a goat for John! Come see them, they are in the back. The goat ate all General Pemberton's azaleas. Mother is quite at odds, says Uncle Charles should keep to his army and she will keep to hers. Do you know what she means, Father?"

Sherman brushed his son's hair through his fingers and the ice in him melted. "I hear you're getting married, Lieutenant?"

"Yes, sir, leave in ten days."

"I wish you the happiness of children, it gives reason to all the hell." Then Willy's father let himself be pulled to the door. Christie watched them go, envious of the general, his wife and family waiting for him inside. He ached for his own. But there could be no honeymoon; Grant was already bent over his maps, drawing more blue lines toward Alabama and Georgia.

"Sir, amended manifests." Brady was at his elbow with a sheaf of papers.

"And Missis Bickerdyke needs your help, sir."

"Now, I find it hard to believe there are any waters she can't part, Brady."

"Missis Bickerdyke is at the big house. A Confederate surgeon is operating without anesthetic. His men are suffering something awful and..."

"You brief me on what's in those papers while we go play knight errant for the fair lady."

"Sir?"

"Figure of speech."

"Yes, sir."

They passed the school that had been the pride of the Sisters of Mercy before the war. Christie thought it to be the one in which Carolina had taught before being drummed out of the convent for insubordination. Carolina had courage—not even General Sherman had the rank to speak up to Sister Sumner. It was only a half-mile more to Missis Bickerdyke's hospital. Christie braced himself at the doorstep, the stench of rotting flesh and dried blood made him lightheaded.

"It wouldn't be fittin' if the ladies and the Confederates see you plummet, sir."

"I will not embarrass you, Sergeant." Christie drew himself up, and allowed Brady lead him to the surgery. It was in what was once the billiard room. On the table a Confederate was spread, stripped to the waist, his arms and legs tied down to the carved oak legs. He heaved and jerked, screaming for the God of Mercy to let him die before the surgeon could cut into him. A man in filthy linen bent over, his scalpel poised and ready to strike the first incision as soon as the nurses got control of the casualty. Instead the soldier screamed and bucked against his restraints.

"Stand back from that man!" Christie shouted. Instead the doctor set the knife closer to the skin. "Hold that man!" Christie ordered anyone who would obey.

The nurses leaned to but the surgeon snapped back slashing the air in wide arcs. The blade danced in the face of one aide and then the other. Both men stepped well clear. The doctor eyed one face then another face, daring any man in the room—ally or enemy—to interfere. "Just go away and leave us. I told you, we want none of your heathen medicine!"

Christie turned to Brady. "If he starts to cut that soldier, shoot him."

"Yes, sir," Brady let the pistol rest in its holster for now, and clasped his hands behind his back while the lieutenant did his work.

"Doctor, can you hear me? I am over here. Look at me, Doctor!" Christie called.

To gain full light, the doctor had the operating table set in an alcove recessed by a huge bay window. Shafts of sun glared over the patient and turned the rest of the room to dusk. The surgeon covered his eyes to see who called him.

"Doctor, I am here."

Something in what the Southerner heard shocked him, and

he peered deeper. Finally, he found what he was looking for—a Union officer ever so casually coming toward him. He squinted to make him out. Then Christie stepped into the twilight. Every muscle in the surgeon's face went to stone. He stuttered something, and swallowed it all back. He held the knife up and motioned for Christie to stop. He did. The crimson sun flickered off the steel hypnotizing him as it lulled back and forth. The surgeon studied it as if he did not recognize it, and did not recognize the hand that held it. One of the attendants moved. The doctor snapped awake and jerked the blade back. With deliberate speed he set it just behind the patient's left ear.

Brady set his hand to his holster. Christie motioned him to wait. In a reedy, mocking tone, Christie coaxed, "You want to throw it, Doctor? I am right here." Christie took two steps out of the way of the last patients and pressed against the wall. "Throw it, right here." Christie pointed to the center row of brass buttons down his blouse.

Brady set an arm on his lieutenant—to hold him back. Christie shook it away, and closed the distance to the operating table slowly. "Right here, can you see me better?" The doctor trembled, Christie thought he was having a seizure. The surgeon steadied himself against the table, watching the officer come—and kept his advantage—the knife set against the boy's ear.

"Get out of here!"

Leather hissed as a Colt was eased from its holster. Christie called again. "He is one of your sons—isn't that what you called them, 'Sons of the Cause'? Your sons!"

The soldier on the table lay rigid under his restraints. His chest rose and dropped. He turned to see the knife—and kept every sense on it—every undulation, every ripple as the surgeon brought it within inches of his bleeding shoulder, circling the wound for a place to dig. The Rebel flinched, got control, then tensed again, gagging back every urge to scream.

"It will be all over in a minute. You'll faint, it will be dark—all will be easy then." The surgeon hummed.

"No!" The Rebel heaved against his restraints, and they slammed him back.

Instead of shouting, Christie's voice was barely a whisper. "Don't make this man suffer anymore, doctor, he has suffered enough. There is no need, not when the drugs he needs are right here. Who cares where they came from? Consider it paybacks." The surgeon did not look up. Christie eased closer his voice lulled into a sing-song rhythm. "Let our surgeons help you. You are exhausted. You need rest. You have done all you can for your men. Let us help you, Doctor Bennett, just as you helped..."

"Don't say it. I did not do it knowingly. That would have been treason!" Bennett's eyes turned full on Christie—vacant—he was a ghost—nothing else.

"Are you Doctor Bennett of Starkville?" A Rebel called from a corner. Bennett did not answer. So the man called louder. "Are you Doctor Bennett from Starkville?"

"Yes, yes, I am Doctor Bennett."

"I served with your son, sir. We fought together at Sharpsburg. Brave officer—he saved my life there. You must be proud of him."

"Who said that?" Bennett came around the table. "Who served with my son?" Bennett went from one to another of those sprawled over the floor to find this precious man.

An amputee raised his stump and Bennett knelt beside him. "You served with Lorin?"

The soldier clouded for an instant, and then nodded slowly, "Yes, sir!"

Bennett tenderly stroked the man's cheeks. "His hair was blonde—about your color but his eyes were green, not like yours. But I saw their like not long ago in another man. I saved him, but I couldn't save my son. God had me save an enemy's son but would not give me back my own. I loved my son. Did you love him?"

"Yes, sir, we all thought very highly of him." With his only hand, the Rebel reached up and took the scalpel away. Bennett let him have it in order to caress the face in both of his. Bennett pulled him close and rocked him back and forth. Two cadets then gently lifted the surgeon up and led him away. The business at the table could now go on. A gauze mask was pressed over the wounded man's face, and a doctor began to drop the precious anesthetic over it. The pulsating body finally relaxed. A Union and a Confederate surgeon, one on either side of the table, bent over their work.

Christie steadied himself against the pillar. The

Confederate who had saved the crisis beckoned him down. "Is that Doctor Bennett like he said?" Christie nodded that it was. The soldier swallowed back a bolt of pain, then said, "I wasn't meaning Mister Lorin Bennett. Hell, Captain Lorin was nothing but a drunk—couldn't abide real fighting. Fell offin' his horse and broke his neck is how he died."

"But you said..."

"I meant Lieutenant Collin. He was the bravest man I know. Saved a bunch of us when the line broke at the Sunken Lane. I was wounded and he pulled me out and one other before the Federals could crawl over us. Came back to get the colonel. If he didn't, the South would have lost a good one for sure that day. Wasn't even his regiment neither. That old man got it all wrong. You tell him, will ya?" The soldier pulled Christie nearly on top of him. "A man has got to know which of his sons is blessed. You tell 'em, Lieutenant!"

Christie promised, "I'll tell him."

The soldier lay back satisfied. Christie stumbled out the door and could scarcely balance himself without falling head over. Brady never saw him so done in and said so. He was even limping on that bad leg. Christie made bad time down the hill in the blistering heat. At the bottom he said, "Make sure these doctors have enough of everything, Sergeant. What do we have...half a case of chloroform on the supply wagon?"

"A little more like a case, sir. No ether though, can't take the sun or the ride over these blasted hills."

Christie nodded. "Well, we can get more. No one should have to suffer. That will be all for now, Sergeant. Do what I said, then go get some dinner."

Christie turned to the left and the sergeant to the right. Perhaps a quarter mile past, Brady deep into his own thoughts about this strange officer he had been shackled with—bad history, untamed mind—when it hit him. And he stopped in his tracks. The lieutenant had made a mistake! The lieutenant had miscalculated his inventory. To be honest, it was a long shot calling the lieutenant's half-case estimate a mistake in the face of what he had just been through. But it was going to have to do. The war might be long over waiting for something better. The men were already accusing Brady of holding out on them.

The sergeant finished his duties with energy. No qualms of conscience changed his mind. After rations, he alerted the troops that all bets would be soon settled. Deep in his haversack was a long white, cotton sock with the all-important ticket among the rest. He posted a sentry and began the long task of opening them up, smoothing them out, and sorting down through the numbers and dates to find the winner.

Throughout the evening, Christie had gone from one hospital to the other, inquiring of surgeons, nurses, and the soldiers if Collin had been by. A turn of the head, blank stares, and shrugs were all he got. It was after some hours of futile searching Christie learned that Collin was known rarely by his given name, as if he was not entitled to use it. Instead he was called "the Comforter." And the Buckeye retraced his steps with the alias, asking everyone again but with no better result.

Christie understood why Vicksburg was called "the city of a hundred hills. " By suppertime he had climbed most of them. He searched the Confederate trench works, all but abandoned except for those soldiers who waited on the fate of brothers and comrades agonizing in the hospitals. Then he trudged through prairie dog town and the maize of caves of the city people. He searched churches, schools, hotels, and warehouses—any place where the desolate took refuge. As he crossed and re-crossed the town, the children backed away from the Yankee. Except one—a boy not more than four or five, who knelt tearfully beside a burrow. The officer came on, and still he stayed.

"What's the matter? There's curfew—what you all doing out?" Christie demanded. "It's not safe."

"My rabbit got away, and if I don't get him, somebody will make stew of him by morning. He's just a baby."

His mother flew up to retrieve him. But the child tore away, his love for his pet more desperate than his dread of the Yankee. Christie stared her back, then turned to the child, "The rabbit in there?"

The child nodded. Christie broke off a twig from a half-dead bush, and with his knife shaved its shoots into spikes. He inserted the full length of the twig into the hole.

The boy pushed him away. "You'll hurt him. No!"

"I promise I won't. Here—put your hand on mine. We will do it together." The boy thought it a good compromise and the two hands twisted the stick a three-quarter turn. It caught, then they felt a tug.

"We got him." Christie whispered. Slowly they pulled the stick out of the hole. With it came the bunny, the spikes caught in the down of its fur. The child scooped it up into his arms. His mother shooed him inside her cave with no thanks and no answer to Christie's inquiries about Collin.

The western sky was fading when the pastor whom Christie had befriended beneath the Warren County courthouse passed. He did not recognize the young officer—they all looked the same in their blue uniforms and officious manner. But he stopped when his name was called. He quizzed the young Yankee for some assurance that the information would not betray a friend. Then he pointed to the landing and the warehouses by the river—the Comforter might be found there.

The river was strangling in boats. At all hours the wharves and docks were teaming with war materiel, soldiers and stevedores, teamsters, commissary and quartermaster clerks, and especially delinquent bluejackets by the swarm. There were also prostitutes, slicks, and the brutes that came out when the army turned over rocks.

On rubber legs, Christie descended the bluffs to the flats and worked his way through the jams and blinds asking questions. Begging the word "street" the path wedged him between tents and shacks. A man set a pair of moldy, cracked cavalry boots into his face, "Want to buy—five dollars." A woman reeking in sour perfume pulled him toward a shed. "You look tired, soldier. Come in and forget the war for awhile. Julia can make you happy for five dollars script!" Christie pushed her into the arms of another whore, their bracelets and necklaces jangling like mule chains. "No need to be nasty, soldier. Ain't you got manners? Julia only..." again she clasped long sweaty arms around his neck and he pushed her back again.

"Stay away from me!" Christie hissed.

"No need to be cruel, James! They mean no harm." Christie turned. "Who..."

Collin stepped out of the shadows, and motioned toward a

tin-faced shed. "Come in, I have no good whiskey to offer you this time, but I've got some black-market coffee." Collin held the door open. Inside he tipped a blackened pot into two cups and motioned to a three-legged stool. "It's cold—no cream or sugar I'm afraid." Collin rested back against a bench covered over with a piece of shredded quilt. Christie was outraged.

"What are you doing in this maggot heap? Come back to my tent. You can stay there."

"No, I am quite comfortable here."

"How can you be? You aren't used to..."

"Oh, my friend, it's quite a miracle what the body and soul can adjust to. We both have lived worse on any battlefield you can name. And I am more at peace in my little box than..." He did not finish.

The call of prostitutes and the profanity of the docks rode on the sultry dawn, all songs of the night birds serenaded by the whistles on the river. "I saw your father." Christie said finally.

"Where?"

"At a hospital. He's broken."

"He's...?"

Christie lied. "Just tired. Overworked."

"Work is good for grief. And he has the memory of his son to sustain him!"

"Which one?"

Collin shook his head. Christie tried to be delicate. "I met someone today who knew you—was with you back at Antietam... Sharpsburg. He tells a different story. He made me promise I would tell your father the truth about you and Lorin."

"Tell him what?" Collin asked, "Lorin was human. Who of us isn't? War is not gallant, and it's not noble. It is mud, sickness, loneliness, boredom, grief and blood, until you gag on it and you hope it kills you. Just when your wish is coming true, and there are muskets pointed in your face, you want to live twice as hard."

"Somebody said that very same thing only lately."

"Well, heaven help the truth seers! They will be burned at the stake. So this two-bit truth will have to be our secret." Collin took another sip of coffee. "You look shocked. What did you expect even if I told him? Tearful reunions? No, he is Southern to his very heart and the South is about to lose everything—don't expect them to accept the truth on top of it. They have their own truth. The survivors will embellish it with silver and burnish it with gems, write poems and eulogies until it is totally unrecognizable, just like the lover that got away. Then they will pass the legacy down to their children to take out on holidays and polish like a ceremonial sword. You will take away their colors, their ribbons, and their buttons. And they will hate you for it, even if you save them from starving. They will teach their children to hate you. And you want me to confront my father with what?"

"The truth. It's a beginning. He has not lost everything— he has Carolina and you. That's more than most men have."

"Wrong son. I was not groomed for the hero's mantle. And he will not confer it on me, even if Robert E. Lee, James Longstreet, and Jeff Davis give testimony to my worthiness."

"And the lies will go into the family Bible, you will be shunned, and Carolina's children, should she have them, will never know the truth of their uncle to tell *their* children. What about your family, if you are so lucky? What will you tell them?"

"If I marry, it will be a new tradition—it will not be of my father's. I will not tell them anything but, 'love thy neighbor.'"

The injustice was more than Christie could bear. "You will let it go?"

Collin was resolute. "Yes," he said finally, "I will let it go."

"And you will let the lie live?"

"Yes, it will have plenty of company." Collin whispered, "It is the only way they will be able to go on in the brutal new world."

"Brutal new world? What about the old? Lincoln will do what he can. And so will Grant."

Collin put the cup on the bench. "We'll see! I hope you are right. I do hope that you are right! I wish I had more to offer you, this is bitter."

"What will you do?"

"Me? Hold their hands, help them die, help the rest live. Then go back to law, and help recover what we can. Things are going to be a legal mess down here for a very long time. Don't forget, I studied in the North. When push comes to shove, I can speak your language. I can shove back. And you, what are you going to do?"

"I'm getting married soon. I leave in a few days."

The news broke the spell. Collin was genuinely delighted. "You never spoke of her."

Christie pulled a daguerreotype from his blouse, opened it, and passed it to Collin. He moved it to the candle and smiled. "She's too good for you!"

"I know that, but I don't plan to give her time to come to her senses."

Collin handed it back. "I wish you long life and happiness."

"It will be happier if you come to visit."

"I wish that could be."

"There will be a long time for things to change. Consider yourself invited for as long as it takes." Then Christie pulled himself up and turned to leave. Suddenly he remembered it. He reached into his belt for the knife and handed it over.

Collin caressed it in his palms, then gently ran his fingers down the blade. He turned it over, the intertwined monogram "L" and "C" glistened in the silver butt of the handle. Christie had never noticed the monogram before. "Thank you," Collin whispered.

Christie suddenly understood it all. A future for the entire South built on grief. The thought made him angry. He pulled himself up. "Is there nothing..."

Collin stretched out his hand. "I have everything." He clasped Christie's hand firmly.

The sun was coming up but Vicksburg had not slept. The army was the blood that pumped through its arteries now, and it showed no signs of fatigue. But Christie needed sleep, a month of it. He was bent toward headquarters and his cot. Brady was waiting for him, dozing outside his tent.

Christie would let him be, but Brady wrestled himself up as the lieutenant came by. "Any further instructions, sir?"

"Did you give Sister Sumner her money?" Christie was already unbuttoning his shirt. He slumped down and began to pull off his boots.

A queasiness passed over the sergeant's face. "Sir?"

"Her winnings—seventy-five dollars or abouts ought to go

pretty far in her outfit."

Brady's eyes boggled. "You knew about it, sir? The lottery?"

"Knew about it? I bought the winning chance myself, even though General McPherson is its trustee. I guess you could say the thing was rigged, but you won't, the way General Grant feels about gambling and all. Sure hate to see you transferred to General Ord's unlucky XIII."

"Me too, sir."

"Since we are in agreement, you will see that sister gets the money and your commissions, and any bribes that you collected?"

"Yes, sir." But Brady hesitated, "Sir, if the pot's yours, I thought you might want to give it to General Grant, for the horse you owe."

Christie shook his head. "Do no good. One thing about General Grant. If he wants to keep you, he will invent a way. At least I know where I stand. If I paid it off, I would have to worry how he was going to bushwhack me before I got on the boat. No, I am in this for the duration."

"I guess I am too, sir."

"Good. Then there is nothing else, Sergeant!"

Christie settled inside, and picked up his pad:

Your letter is a consolation, but I am concerned that you want to nurse there in St. Louis. By all accounts Miss Dix does not allow beautiful women to nurse the men, and you are Catholic, so that disqualifies you twice. But you seemed intent. I am concerned because soldiers carry every vermin and you are not strong. That's the end of the discussion. I can see now that this vow of obedience you will take at our wedding will be a crossed-fingers promise. Obedience does not seem to come naturally to women of strong will and good purpose.

Bravo on your cooking. I look forward with unbridled anticipation to sitting down to your sweet potato pie. Sweet potatoes are quite my favorite dish — a favorite of Henry VIII, I am led to understand. And yours will be a presentation that will keep me in anticipation until I see you....

Your husband to be.
Brent

ORDER OF CHARACTERS

Designations in regular print are real; those printed in italics are fictional.

FREDERICKSBURG CAMPAIGN
NOVEMBER – DECEMBER 1862

UNION

ARMY OF THE POTOMAC

Major General Ambrose Burnside, commanding Nov. 7, 1862 - January 26, 1863
Colonel John G. Parke, Chief of Staff
Major General Joseph Hooker, commanding January 26, 1863 - June 28, 1863
Major General George Gordon Meade, commanding June 28, 1863 - duration of war
Artillery-Brigadier General Henry Hunt

Right Grand Division

Major General Edwin V. Sumner, Commanding
II Corps – Major General Darius Couch
First Division – Major General Winfield S. Hancock
First Brigade - Brigadier General John C. Caldwell
Second Brigade - Brigadier General Thomas Francis Meagher
    Twenty-Eighth Massachusetts
    Sixty-Third New York
    Sixty-Ninth New York
    Eighty-Eighth New York
    One Hundred Sixteenth Pennsylvania
Third Brigade - Colonel Samuel K. Zook
Second Division – Brigadier General Oliver O. Howard
Third Division – Brigadier General William H. French
First Brigade – Brigadier General Nathan Kimball (wounded)
    command assumed by Colonel John S. Mason
    Fourteenth Indiana
    Twenty-Fourth New Jersey
    Twenty-Eighth New Jersey

Eighth Ohio
> *Private Davey Mahoney*

Seventh West Virginia
Fourth Ohio - Colonel John S. Mason, commanding
> Surgeons H.M. McAbee & F.W. Morrison
> Corporal George Torrence, Color Guard (member of Co. C. killed)
> *Sergeant Major S.M. Chase*

Company C — Delaware Guards — Captain Byron Dolbear
> Thomas Warner - killed
> *Corporal Nolan Giles - wounded*
> *Corporal Brenton J. Christie - wounded*
> *Private Brian Quinn - killed*
> *Private James MacGowan-died at Harrison's Landing*

Company I - Olentangy Guards - Captain James Ferguson (would die of wounds)
Company E - Given Guards - Captain Daniel Timmons
> Private Archibald Dice - wounded, wounded again at Chancellorsville

CENTRAL GRAND DIVISION

Major General Joseph Hooker, commanding

LEFT GRAND DIVISION

Major General William B. Franklin, commanding
I Corps – Major General John F. Reynolds, commanding
> Chatham Hospital
> Surgeon H.M. McAbee, Surgeon, Fourth Ohio
> Surgeon F.W. Morrison, Surgeon, Fourth Ohio
> Dr. Reynolds, Surgeon stationed at Chatham Hospital
> Walt Whitman - Aide
> Sister Louise - Sister of Charity
> Clara Barton - nurse
> *Doctor Bellows - contract surgeon*
> *Gus - convalescent nurse*

THE CONFEDERACY

THE ARMY OF NORTHERN VIRGINIA

Lieutenant General Robert E. Lee, commanding
I Corps – Lieutenant General James Longstreet
McLaw's Division – Major General Lafayette McLaws
Barksdale's Brigade – Brigadier General William Barksdale
    Seventeenth Mississippi - *Lorin Bennett, officer at Antietam*
    Cobb's Brigade – Brigadier General Thomas R.R. Cobb
        Sergeant Michael Sullivan
Anderson's Division – Major General Richard Anderson
    (Transferred to new Third Corps under Major-General Powell Hill)
Featherston's Brigade – Brigadier General W. Featherston
Oktibbeha Rescue - *Lieutenant Collin Bennett - wounded*
Pickett's Division – Major General George E. Pickett
Hood's Division – Major General John B. Hood
Ransom's Division – Brigadier General Robert Ransom, Jr.
II Corps – Lieutenant General Thomas J. (Stonewall) Jackson
Cavalry – Major General James E.B. Stuart

VICKSBURG CAMPAIGN

UNION

ARMY OF THE TENNESSEE

Major General Ulysses S Grant, commanding
Colonel John A. Rawlins - Chief of Staff
Major T.S. Bowers - Judge Advocate
Colonel John H. Wilson, Engineer
Sylvanus Cadwallader, war correspondent, *Chicago Times* and *New York Herald*
Charles A. Dana, Undersecretary of War (Stanton's snoop)
Second Lieutenant Brenton J. Christie, aide,
Sergeant Brady, Christie's aide
Second Lieutenant Brighton Canfield, aide
IX Corps – Major General John G. Parke (joined June 14-17)
XIII Corps – Major General John A. McClernand (replaced by Major-General Edward O.C. Ord)
Ninth Division – Brigadier General Peter J. Osterhaus

Tenth Division — Brigadier General Andrew Jackson ("Whiskey") Smith
First Brigade to include the Ninety-Sixth Ohio Colonel Joseph W. Vance
Twelfth Division – Brigadier General Alvin P. Hovey
Fourteenth Division – Brigadier General Eugene A. Carr
XV Corps - Major General William Tecumseh ("Cump") Sherman
    Lieutenant Colonel J.H. Hammond, Chief of Staff
    Captain Pitzman - Engineer
    Lieutenant L. Dayton and Lieutenant Hill - aides
    Captain McCoy - Provost
    Major Ezra Taylor - Chief of Artillery
First Division – Major General Fred Steele
    First Brigade - Colonel Francis H. Manter
    Second Brigade - Colonel Charles R. Wood
    Third Brigade – Brigadier General John M. Thayer
Second Division – Major General Frank P. Blair, Jr.
    First Brigade - Colonel Giles A. Smith
    Eighth Missouri - Lieutenant-Colonel David C. Coleman
    Thirteenth U.S. - Captain Charles Ewing (Sherman's step-brother)
    Second Brigade - Colonel Thomas Kilby Smith
    Third Brigade – Brigadier General George Washington Morgan Replaced by Colonel Hugh Ewing (Sherman's step-brother)
Third Division – Brigadier General James M. Tuttle
    First Brigade – Brigadier General Ralph Buckland
    Second Brigade - Brigadier General Joseph A. Mower
    Third Brigade - Brigadier General Charles A. Matthies
XVI Corps – Major General Stephen A. Hurlbut (Department of the Tennessee - Major General Ulysses S. Grant, commanding)
First Division – Brigadier General William Sooy Smith
Cavalry - Colonel Benjamin Grierson
Colonel Reuben Loomis - Sixth Illinois
Colonel Edward Prince - Seventh Illinois

Company B - Captain Henry. B. Forbes
    Sergeant Stephen Forbes
    Colonel Edward Hatch - Second Iowa
    Artillery: Captain B. Smith - Battery K.

Sergeant Richard Surby - Quartermaster and organizer of the Butternut Guerrillas
Lieutenant Colonel William Blackburn - leader of the Butternut Guerrillas
Provisional – Brigadier General Nathan Kimball
XVII Corps – Major General James R. McPherson
Third Division – Major General James A. Logan
Second Brigade – Brigadier General Mortimer D. Leggett
Twentieth Ohio - Colonel Manning F. Force in which the Friend family served
Sixth Division - Brigadier General - John McArthur
First Brigade – Brigadier General Hugh T. Reed
Third Brigade - 15th Iowa in which First Sergeant Cyrus F. Boyd served.

MISSISSIPPI SQUADRON
STEELE BAYOU EXPEDITION

Rear Admiral David D. Porter, commanding
Black Hawk - Flagship (Third Rate)
Porter's command ship
Cincinnati - Flagship - Ironclad Steamer (Fourth Rate)
Lieutenant George M. Bache, commanding; Acting Assistant Surgeon Richard R. Hall; Acting Assistant Paymaster S. R. Hinsdale; Acting Masters J. Pearce; Mate Henry Booby; Acting Gunner J.F. Ribbit; Acting Carpenter G.H. Stevens, *Henri - Ship's boy*
Louisville - Ironclad Steamer - (Fourth Rate)
Lieutenant Commander E.K. Owen, commanding
Carondelet - Ironclad Steamer - (Fourth Rate)
Lieutenant J. McLeod Murphy, commanding
Pittsburg - Ironclad Steamer - (Fourth Rate)
Acting Volunteer Lieutenants William R. Hoel and J.C. Bently, commanding
Mound City - Ironclad Steamer - (Fourth Rate)
Lieutenant Byron Wilson, commanding
Ivy - Tug
Acting Ensign E.C. Boss, commanding
The flotilla included three other tugs and two mortar boats

SANITATION COMMISSION AND NURSES
Confederate - Sister Ignatius Sumner, Sisters of Mercy at Crawford School Hospital
Miss Pauline Cushman
Missis Annie Wittenmyer - Iowa Sanitation Commission
Missis George - Indianapolis Sanitation Commission
Missis Hogue - Chicago Sanitation Commission
Missis Reynolds - Illinois Sanitation Commission
Mother Bikerdyke - Cincinnati Sanitation Commission

VICKSBURG DEFENSES
CONFEDERATE STATES

Lieutenant General John C. Pemberton, commanding
First Division – Major General W.W. Loring
Brigadier-General Winfield Featherston's Mississippi Brigade
Stevenson's Division – Major General Carter L. Stevenson
       To include Brigadier General Stephen D. Lee's Brigade - later to assume command of the division
Provisional Division – Major General Dabney Maury
       To include First and Second Choctaw
Forney's Division – Major General John H. Forney
       To include Hebert's Brigade
Smith's Division – Major General Martin Luther Smith
Bowen's Division – Major General John S. Bowen
       Includes First Missouri Brigade
            Tom Tollman

MISCELLANEOUS TROOPS

Colonel Wirt Adams - Mississippi Cavalry
Lieutenant Colonel Clark Barteau - Second Tennessee Cavalry
Colonel J.F. Smith - First Mississippi Regiment of State Troops
    Billy, private
Major James De Baun's Ninth Louisiana Partisan Rangers
Major M.S. Ward - Mississippi Partisan Rangers
Department Commander Lieutenant - General Joseph E. Johnston
Brigadier General John Gregg's Brigade, Gist's Brigade under Colonel Payton H. Colquitt, and Brigadier General W.H.T. Walker's Brigade
Loring's Division

General Daniel Ruggles - Confederate commander based in Columbus, Mississippi
Brigadier General Winfield S. Featherston – Third Mississippi
Captain F. Ingate Quartermaster at Okolona
Colonel Samuel Ferguson - commanded the Twenty-eighth Mississippi cavalry

GRIERSON'S RAID
See order of battle for placement. However, plantation ownership depicted in Grierson's Raid are true to records.

THE UNDERGROUND

Father Lyons - Columbus, Mississippi, conductor
> *Doctor Bennett*
> *Carolina Bennett*
> *Collin Bennett*
> *Lorin Bennett*
> *Rachel*
> *Miles*
> *Father Kessler*
> *Members and friends of the household*
> Members depicted in Christie's cross-country escape to join Grant

UNION

DEPARTMENT OF THE GULF
NINETEENTH CORPS

Major General Nathaniel P. Banks, commanding

About the Author

Jeane Heimberger Candido attended the University of Dayton where she earned both a Bachelor and Master's Degree. Her career has been in marketing and advertising, freelance writing, and newspaper reporting. She has written for *Blue & Gray Magazine*. This is her second novel.

Candido's first novel, *The Redemption of Corporal Nolan Giles: A Novel of the Civil War*, is available from Windstorm Creative. *Levi: The Smartest Boy in the World*, her children's book about giving new things a try — including step-parents! — is available from Blue Works Ltd., Windstorm's children's division.

The author lives in Columbus, Ohio, with her husband of more than twenty years.

About Windstorm Creative and our Readers' Club

Windstorm Creative was founded in 1989 to create a publishing house with author-centric ethics and cutting-edge, risk-taking innovation. WSC is now a company of more than ten divisions with international distribution channels that allow us to sell our books — paperback and hardcover — games, music and films both inside the traditional systems and outside these paradigms, capitalizing on more direct delivery and non-traditional markets. As a result, our books can be found in grocery superstores as well as your favorite neighborhood bookstore, and dozens of other outlets on and off the Internet.

WSC is an independent press with the synergy and branding of a corporate publisher and an author royalty that's easily twice their best offer. We have continued to minimize returns without decreasing sales by publishing books that are timeless, as opposed to timely, and never back-listing our books. We stand adamantly against the heinous act of "stripping."

WSC is constantly changing, improving, and growing. We are driven by the needs of our authors – hailing from ten different countries – and the vision of our critically-acclaimed staff. All of our books are created with the strictest of environmental protections in mind. Our approach to no-waste, no-hazard, in-house production, and stringent out-source scrutiny, assures that our goals are met whether books are printed at our own facility or an outside press.

Because of these precautions, our books cost more. And though we know that our readers support our efforts, we also understand that a few dollars can add up. This is why we began our Readers' Club. Visit our webstore and take 25% off every title, every day, by typing in the code found at the bottom of the page. No strings. No fine print.

While you're at our site, feel free to preview the first chapter of any of our titles, completely free of charge.

Thank you for supporting an independent press.

Readers' Club code #83596JHC
http://www.windstormcreative.com
and click on Shop

See next page for title recommendations.

The Redemption of Corporal Nolan Giles
(Jeane Heimberger Candido)
A haunting tale of war and redemption
set during America's Civil War.

Nottingham Lace
(Evelyn Swift)
The life of a young lace worker in
working-class WWI England.

Widdicombe Fair
(Evelyn Swift)
A historical novel set in post-WWI England.

The Sitka Incident: Exxon Valdez Retold
(Walt Larson)
A tugboat captain struggles to bring
the damaged supertanker into port.

Breed of a Different Kind: Clell Rainey Trilogy, Book One
(Walt Larson)
Sea captain Rainey battles incompetent crew and bad weather.

Storm on the Docks: Clell Rainey Trilogy, Book Two
(Walt Larson)
Rainey is caught in a dockside war between
labor and management.

Strong Medicine: Clell Rainey Trilogy, Book Three
(Walt Larson)
Rainey heads up a new overseas operation.

Gottscheers
(Rudy Kikel)
A beautiful chronicle, told in poems,
of one family's journey to America.